Never The Bride
Dilbury Village #1

By

Copy Editing by Karen J & Jasmine Z

Proofreading by Tracy G

Cover Art by Kellie Dennis at www.bookcoverbydesign.co.uk

Illustrated Map of Dilbury Village by Holly Francesca at www.hollyfrancesca.co.uk

Book content pictures purchased from Adobe Stock, iStock and Shutterstock

Foreword

Never The Bride is book one in the Dilbury Village series, which will comprise of a number of standalone novels set in the quaint English village.

Never The Bride is the second romantic comedy novel by Charlotte Fallowfield.

www.charlottefallowfield.co.uk

Until We Collide

Dilbury Village Series
Never The Bride

I also write humorous erotic romance novels, under the pen name C.J. Fallowfield

www.cjfallowfield.co.uk

Dedication

Never The Bride is dedicated to all the women who have yet to meet their soul mate, their very own Prince Charming.

Never stop searching, never stop believing, and never settle for anyone who treats you as anything less than you are.

For those of you who have already found the perfect man for you, never take him for granted, never forget to tell him what he means to you, and never let him go. You've hit the relationship jackpot, you lucky devils!

As for the rest of us, we will continue, like my heroines, to live in hope.

Charlotte

Table of Contents

Dilbury Village Map

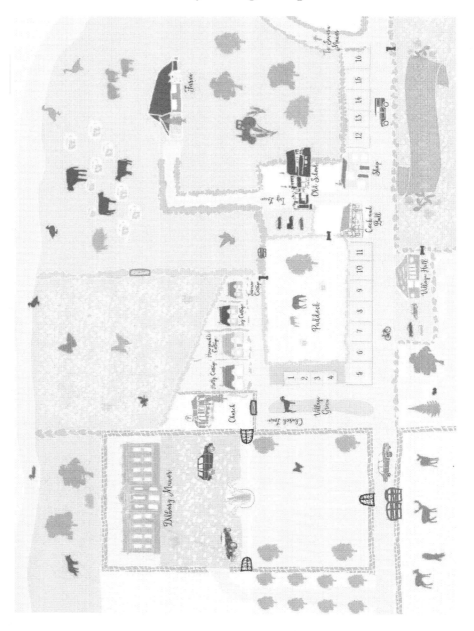

Holly Cottage – Abbie – Accountant
Honeysuckle Cottage – Daphne – Retired
Jasmine Cottage – Georgie – Dog Groomer
Ivy Cottage – Charlie – Author

Chapter One

Abbie Carter

July

'FOR THE LOVE OF God, Georgie, please pick up the phone,' I begged, as I stood in front of the long mirror in the dressing room of the quite frankly offensively named *Bridezilla Wedding Boutique* in Shrewsbury. I just wanted the ground to open up and swallow me whole.

'Ok, what's wrong with this one?' she laughed, as her freckled face appeared on my screen.

'Sssshhhh, keep it down,' I warned, sticking my head out of the changing room curtain to see if anyone else was here with me, or if I could speak freely.

'Abbie, this is bridesmaid dress number nine. The fact that you've hated each and every single one of its predecessors means your reputation precedes you. You're the nightmare bridesmaid, the one who always hates the dress. Everyone already knows you're going to hate this one as well.'

'A nightmare bridesmaid?' I huffed, then blinked at her, not sure if she was being serious. Was I a nightmare? It was true, I hated each and every one of those eight dresses, all shoved up in my attic, never to see the light of day again. But as far as my many, many duties as one of the most frequent bridesmaids in Shropshire, I thought I was exemplary. Which was quite a feat given the messes I normally got myself into. I'd even had a bridal magazine want to do a feature on me, I was that proficient at it. Of course, I'd declined. How was I supposed to attract a man if I was the talk of the county, the one that never got to wear the coveted white dress?

'Ok, maybe I've exaggerated a little,' she giggled. 'But you do have a face like a smacked arse each time you walk up the aisle in one of those monstrosities. How bad this time, on a scale of 1 to 10, 1 being the dress you could see yourself getting married in, it's that perfect, and 10 being "not even for my closed casket funeral" awful?'

'I'd have to go with an eleven,' I sighed, glancing down at my vivid fuchsia froufrou dress, with layers and layers of lime green underskirt and a neon yellow sash that tied in the most enormous bow at the back. To round off the seriously crappy look, as if it wasn't blinding enough, I'd been given a bright purple clutch bag. The shoes were the only great thing about the ensemble. A pair of multi-coloured, high-heeled suede sandals that were seriously cute and summery. 'I wouldn't even want someone to have to try and dress my stiff body in this hideous creation. Seeing my naked corpse would be torture enough for the undertaker, let alone in this … this … I have no words, Georgie, that's how bad it is. It's a first. Abbie Carter is speechless. I look like some kind of 80's throwback, which wouldn't be so bad if I'd been around in the 80's, but I wasn't even a twinkle in anyone's eye!'

'Come on, it seriously can't be that bad,' she suggested as she craned her neck, like that was going to help her see the colour-vomit tableau any better.

'I look like I just threw up a family-sized bag of Skittles all over myself. Trust me, even you'd look bad in it, and you look good in anything.' My best friend was a stunning redhead, with deep burnished copper locks that came straight out of a shampoo or hairspray commercial, gorgeous piercing light blue eyes, and a face and figure to die for. She should be a famous catwalk model, not a dog groomer, up to her elbows in soap suds, trimmed hair, and overexcited pooches who either tried to hump her or left her little brown surprise gifts that she often ended up stepping in by accident. 'And what do you mean, "a face like a smacked arse?" This is my face. I always look like this, thank you very much!'

'You're beautiful, Abbie, but lately your mouth has been in a permanent resting trout pout.'

'You cheeky–'

'No,' she interrupted, holding up her palm to the screen. 'As best friend, my chief duty is not to lie, unless it involves raiding your freezer for ice cream and snacks, or your cookie jar for those delicious home-baked ones you know I love, then denying all knowledge. You have the most radiant smile, Abbie, and it's been too long since I last saw it. But that discussion can wait for our next one-to-one, and trust me when I say I won't be pulling any punches, as enough is enough. Now, let's see this puke-inducing creation.'

'Ok, brace yourself,' I warned, angling my phone and scanning my body.

'Good God!' she exclaimed with a shocked gasp. 'And I really thought I'd prepared myself. Seriously, that would scare someone in the SAS. I think I've just been blinded for life. Surely this Rachel's having a laugh? This is a joke for the hen night, right?'

'Sadly, no. We were measured months ago, but she left the first fitting to the last moment as she wanted it to be a surprise for us all.'

'Hello! Mission accomplished, I'd say.'

'So how do I back out gracefully? It's bad enough that I already have eight dresses I hate in my attic, I can't put this up there too. It makes the others look like gorgeous Vera Wang creations!'

'It's not like you're *that* good friends. I mean, other than this wedding, I've never once heard you talk about her. Honestly, how you keep getting asked to be a bridesmaid for all these women in the first place is baffling. You haven't seen them for years.'

'It's a whole *stupid* boarding school pact.' I plopped myself down on the padded stool in my changing room with a heavy sigh of resignation. I'd given my word to my thirteen classmates, as they had to me, that we'd all be each other's bridesmaid when the big day came. We'd been sixteen years old, it was a lifetime ago. Ok, twelve years ago, but all the same, we'd moved on, grown up, and pretty much lost touch.

Sometimes I hated social media. People said it was great for finding long-lost friends, but this was what became of it. A sad, single, and lonely twenty-eight-year-old spinster, forced to wear a disgusting dress, yet again, for a woman she barely even knew. As if the humiliation of still being single, of never having had a relationship that lasted longer than a month, wasn't bad enough. Well, unless you counted Mr. Sumo. My overweight British bulldog had been with me for seven years now, a graduation present from my dad. Most people got something useful. A house deposit, a car maybe. Hell, I'd have been happy with a new saucepan set or a month's supply of sanitary products. But I got a bulldog puppy. And not just any bulldog puppy. Oh no, that would have made life far too easy. I got the most miserable-looking, overweight, stubborn, gaseous, drooling little mutt ever born. And he hated me!

'Well, as you barely see her anymore, it makes it even easier to let her down then, doesn't it?' Georgie suggested.

'I can't,' I sighed, resigned to my fate, but feeling slightly reassured that my horror at this God-awful dress wasn't misplaced. 'I promised, and I don't like to go back on my word.' My major flaw was hating to let people down. And not speaking my mind, intentionally anyway. And being too nice. And worrying too much about what people thought of me. And … *my God*, I had a *multitude* of flaws. No wonder I was single.

'You're too nice for your own good, Abbie Carter,' scolded Georgie. 'What say we drown your sorrows in a nice bottle of wine with a takeaway later?'

'You're on,' I nodded, cheering up for the first time since I'd pulled this over-starched and stiff kaleidoscope of a dress on. 'Yours or mine?'

'Mine. I spend my days with dogs, I don't need "Eau de Sumo" assaulting my nostrils as I'm trying to savour a lovely Pinot and some delicious lemon chicken, thanks very much.'

'For someone who works with dogs all day, you're not exactly loving towards him out of dog grooming hours,' I objected. Sumo might be a royal pain in the arse, but he was my pain in the arse. I'd never have chosen to be saddled with him for the last seven years, but he was the closest thing I had to a long-term relationship, or family, and I did love him. I'd be devastated if anything happened to him.

'Abbie, *darling*, how are you doing in there? Do you need any help?' called Rachel in an incredibly posh voice. Darling wasn't just *darling* in her world, it was dragged out into a *daaaaarling*.

'Ermmm, no. I'm great, thanks,' I called, grimacing at Georgie. 'Just had a bit of trouble doing up the zip, but I'll be out any minute.'

'Don't be long, you're missing all of the champers and canapés. I just can't wait to see all of you together. I'm beyond excited, it will be a riot of colour!'

'I can believe that,' I called back, and Georgie covered her mouth with her palm as her shoulders started shaking.

'Personally I really love the theme, but I swear, if anyone says anything negative about it, I'll cry. Mummy's been quite vocal that she thinks it's too much, and I don't want her getting any validation of that or I'll never hear the end of it. You must let me know what you think when you see us all together. I always valued your opinion at school, Abbie, you were always the sensible one of us.'

'Sure, will do.' Oh Jesus, now I was going to have to lie through my back teeth.

'See you in a moment, darling,' Rachel called.

'Mmmm-hmmm.' I waited until I heard the door close, then burst out laughing along with Georgie.

'Oh my God, you're so screwed,' she screeched, reaching up to wipe some tears of laughter from her cheeks. 'You can't break the poor girl's heart now. Please tell me that I can come to this shindig as your plus-one? This I have to see.'

'Well, I did have Liam Hemsworth and Theo James on standby,' I mused, tapping my finger on my lips before breaking into a smile. 'Of course you can come. I was dreading being the only single one there.'

'You're not worried they'll think you're a lesbian, turning up with me in tow?'

'Ermmm, I wasn't until you just suggested it. But surely it's better to be a lesbian with a seriously hot date than a pathetic loser on her own wearing a puke-inducing rainbow.'

'You speak such wise words,' she mocked.

'Thanks for making me feel better. I'd better go and put on a brave face. See you later, sweetie.'

'Seven o'clock, don't be late.'

'I'm never late,' I protested.

'Huh, right! Honestly, you live two cottages down and you've never made it to me on time. Go, I'll have the wine chilling and will be dialling the Chinese the minute you step through the door.'

'Thanks, Georgie.' I blew her a kiss, which she returned, then tapped the red "end call" button and stood up. I grimaced as I faced myself in the mirror, then blew out a deep breath and pushed my shoulders back, lifting my head high. It was just a dress. I could do this, piece of cake.

Don't laugh, Abbie. Do. Not. Laugh. Or let your wildly inappropriate subconscious thoughts spew out as normal, I warned myself as I headed up the corridor towards the sound of excited chatter in the main bride's lounge. It was a lovely private area, with a raised podium for the bride to twirl on and be admired, surrounded by a comfortable horseshoe-shaped seating arrangement for her close circle of family and friends who got to see the dress and offer their opinions. *One day you'll be on that podium, Abbie Carter, don't give up hope.* It was a silly pep talk to give myself, as hope was fading with each bridesmaid dress I put on. I was convinced that if I made it to dress thirteen, that would be it.

Game over.

Spinster for life.

I turned the corner into the private lounge, and my eyes widened in horror at the sight of all the other bridesmaids in one place.

'Jesus Christ, it looks like a unicorn farted a neon rainbow in here!' I exclaimed. Crap. *Subconscious restraint fail, Abbie.* I felt my cheeks blaze, quite possibly matching the colour of my dress, as a deathly silence descended upon the room. All eyes turned to give me a warning glare, and Rachel dropped to the floor, a dramatic hand to her brow as she started bawling.

'Sumo, Mummy's home,' I called as I stepped through my front door and shoved it shut behind me, putting my hip and shoulder into it to help me force it into place. This was why I needed a man. Not just for the romance and hot sex, which would be a serious bonus, or a welcome greeting as I walked in the door, but for his ability to fix things. I needed a man who loved to do odd jobs, as my house had lots of little ones that required tending. Like this front door that could use some excess wood shaved from it so I wouldn't have to slam it shut.

I'd lived in a smart, modern, one-bedroomed terraced house with a small garden in the historic town of Shrewsbury until four years ago. I'd worked for an accountancy firm in the more commercial town of Telford, about half an hour commute by car, where I'd been ever since I'd graduated as a Chartered Accountant. Life had been routine and normal, or in other words, dull and predictable.

I'd come to terms with being a motherless child at a young age, my mum having died in childbirth. That only made me respect and love my dad even more. Instead of quitting or trying to find a replacement mother figure for me, he'd brought me up single-handedly. All of his focus had been on our relationship, and my development and future, until I left home to go to university. We'd had such a close bond. My world had been turned upside down when a sudden heart attack had taken him from me nearly five years ago. It was almost as if he'd seen it coming, as only the week before, he'd told me that he was worried about me, that he wanted to see me happy again. He'd warned me that I was in a rut and needed to make some changes in my life, starting with my job. He'd suggested I quit and set up my own practice working from home.

Of course, the practicalities of that when you lived in a tiny, already cramped house, with a portly trumping pooch who hated company, made it a non-viable option. But when Dad left his country cottage to me, along with a considerable inheritance, I'd decided to do as he'd suggested by quitting my job and putting my house on the market. I had enough money that I didn't have to worry about taking my time setting up my business, and slowly made the move into my childhood home first.

It was out in the small country village of Dilbury, about a fifteen-minute drive from Shrewsbury. We were surrounded by rolling green fields, not to mention the prestige of a wooded deer park that formed part of a stately home, where Lord Kirkland, an actual real-life Baron, lived. We had a magnificent church, a village pub called The Cock & Bull, a village hall, and a small post office, which doubled as the village shop and sold local produce as well as staple cupboard and household supplies. It was the kind of village that murder mysteries like Miss Marple were written about, where a neighbour might stab someone to death with a set of pruning shears for winning the coveted first place rosette for their floral display at the village show.

So now I lived here, in a quaint, typically British detached country cottage, set in its own large grounds. White-painted pebble rendering, a thatched roof, sage green painted windows, and stable front door, which sat under a small thatched canopy, gave it that chocolate-box effect that had the Americans going wild. It had been a typical "two up, two down" kind of cottage, with old beams on the ceilings, which I'd painted white. I'd done some renovation work on it, or I should say a team of builders had, as my DIY skills were non-existent. I'd had a modern, white shaker kitchen with oak block worktops put in, and a small island unit that I'd had my heart set on, even if it was only for Georgie to sit at as she drank wine while I cooked and we gossiped. Luckily the room was big enough to be a kitchen diner, so I had a nice chunky oak table and soft padded leather chairs to seat up to six people, and there was a set of French doors out onto the back patio. I had lovely views out over my huge rear garden and down towards the River Severn that meandered across the plain below me.

I'd had a green oak extension put on that side of the house, which gave me a large open bay garage, and at the back of it a decent utility room, with a door that had been knocked through the thick cottage wall to link it to the kitchen. Above the garage and utility room, accessed by an external oak staircase, was the office for my new business. Admittedly, I did most of my work on my MacBook from my favourite position on the sofa in the lounge, but the office was there for when I had client paperwork to sort or meetings to hold.

The front door of the house opened into a large hallway, from which an oak staircase rose to the first floor. I'd managed to have some much needed internal storage space built under the stairs, but I was scared to open the door in case everything fell out and I couldn't shove it back in. I actually no longer had any idea what was even in there. To the right of the hall was my cosy lounge, complete with a log burner set into the inglenook fireplace. A summery colour palette of pink and green, along with more French doors out to the back garden, kept it light and airy, and feeling more spacious than it actually was.

Upstairs I only had two bedrooms and a bathroom set into the eaves. But the equally sized bedrooms were pretty spacious, with enough room for two decent-sized wardrobes, a dressing table, and a king-sized bed each. Then there was the petite, but perfectly formed, bathroom. With some clever planning on the bathroom fitter's side, I'd managed to squeeze in a gorgeous mini clawfoot roll top bath under the window that overlooked the porch at the front of the house. There was obviously a toilet too, as well as a modern, made-to-look-old Victorian sink, a built-in chrome towel rail, and finally a walk-in shower. It was all set off with crisp white metro tiles, with a thin strip of luminescent glittering silver and gold tiles around the middle of the room. I loved the house. Being in my childhood bedroom and still having memories of Dad everywhere I looked was the icing on the cake. I'd adjusted to country life quite quickly, loving the tranquillity. This was home.

I'd met Georgie, who lived in Ivy Cottage, two cottages down the lane, when I'd booked Mr. Sumo in for his first bi-monthly grooming session with her. She had a custom-built log cabin built in the bottom of her garden for her business. It wasn't like my boy had a long coat that needed shaving or trimming, but I'd discovered when he was a puppy that he adored bath time, especially having a massage and rub down, then his claws being manicured. For some reason, he'd only ever allowed my dad to do it, never me. He'd sulked terribly when Dad had died, rebuffing my attempts to pamper him, so when I'd discovered Georgie's handily located business, I'd given it a shot. The traitorous pooch had no problem with her laying her hands on him. Talk about biting the hand that feeds you!

'Where are you, Chubbers?' I called as I shrugged off my coat and hung it up on the hook by the front door. He went by many nicknames, many of them fatist. His official name was Mr. Sumo, but I often used just Sumo, Mr. Su, Chubs, Chubberson, Chubberooney, and if I was feeling in an extra loving mood, Chubbalicious.

I grabbed my phone and put my handbag in one of the cubbyholes of the hall shelving unit, then headed straight for the lounge. Why I spoke to him, I had no idea. I suspected all pet owners did it, though I was sure many would deny it. And as to where he was, well that was a stupid question anyway. He'd be where he always was, curled up on his favourite armchair by the fire. It was the best seat in the house, whether the log burner was going or not. I smiled as I headed in and found him exactly where I'd expected. Most dog owners got greeted at the door with wagging tails, excited barks, and licks of enthusiasm. I had to go find him, only to receive a single raised eyebrow and a disapproving "where the hell have you been" look that made his already miserable face look even worse. Oh, and a few measly grunts and snuffles.

'Hello, Chubbalicious, how's your day been?' I asked as I scratched his head, making him close his eyes and grunt loudly. That was the closest I got to any kind of appreciation from him. But despite all of his failings, and his seriously rank breath and gassiness, I kind of loved the ugly gold and white mutt.

I sat on the arm of the chair and continued to scratch behind his ears while I filled him in on my afternoon from hell. Pandemonium had broken out when Rachel had started crying, with Julia, the bestower of soon-to-be bridesmaid dress number ten, berating me for my lack of tact. The other bridesmaids had all obviously been lying as they tried to convince Rachel that her colour scheme was gorgeous and … unique. There was no discounting the second part of that statement, that was for sure. With only two weeks to go before the wedding, it was too late to have the custom-made dresses changed now, and no amount of dye was going to dull the garish colours. So, with no other option, everyone had convinced her it was a marvellous theme and she soon perked up, though she shot me the odd daggered look as I kept myself out of everyone's way before sneaking out early.

'Sumo!' I groaned, quickly reaching up to cover my nose as I screwed my eyes shut. My God, his farts could melt your eyeballs. I coughed, then started to gag, choking on the foul-smelling odour as I quickly stood up and scuttled away to minimum safe distance, which in this case was right out here in the hall. 'Jesus, what do they put in that dog food of yours?'

He responded with a grumble, then there was a thud and the sound of him shuffling across the plush cream carpet. Mention food and it was the fastest you ever saw him move, if you could call his pace fast, that was. He waddled past me in the hall, panting like he'd just run a marathon or had some aggressive doggie-style action, and headed straight through the kitchen and out to the utility room to plonk himself down by his empty bowls. I followed him in and he nudged my hand out of the way, as he always did, before I'd had time to empty the can of chunks, smothered in doggy gravy, into his bowl, resulting in a load of it landing on his head. Completely nonplussed at his gravy hat, he devoured his meal with noisy gulps, belches, and grumbles of what I could only assume was pleasure. Chunks of meat went flying over the side of the bowl onto the wisely placed wipeable mat underneath, protecting my floorboards from his messy eating. After chasing the errant morsels around with his tongue, he sat back with a loud belch that rumbled up from his tummy as he lifted his back paw to scratch behind his ears, then leaned down to lick his doggie bits a little too enthusiastically.

'See, this is why you're single,' I reminded him with a shudder as I headed into the kitchen to make myself a much needed coffee. 'What fancy lady pooch is ever going to want to date you when you have those sort of table manners, not to mention the amount of gas you expel?'

As if on cue, he let out a rare bark and rose a few inches in the air, startling himself and me in the process, as he let rip another odious fart.

'Jesus,' I groaned, pulling my top up to cover my mouth and nose.

How the hell a fart that long and bubblingly loud could take the culprit by surprise was beyond me. I looked down as I heard the pitter-patter of his claws on the oak floor, and he wobbled his way past, heading back to his armchair for an after-dinner nap. Not even so much as a glance up at me to say thank you.

'You're welcome!' I yelled in a muffled tone as I tried to escape the blast zone by darting back into the hall. Dogs, they were as bad as men!

Chapter Two

'COME ON, SUMO, WALKIES,' I called from the lounge door, waving his lead. He lifted his head and eyed me over the arm of his chair, as if suspicious my motives for rousing him from his sleep were genuine. When he saw the lead, he yawned and had a gentle stretch before making a meal out of getting up, then trying to ease himself off the chair. He put out a paw, then retracted it, and repeated the move again and again as he stared at the floor, performing some kind of doggie hokey cokey. 'Come on, it's hardly an abseil over the edge of a canyon. You have no trouble when it's time for dinner.'

I giggled as I was rewarded with an immediate response to his favourite word and he threw himself down, landed with a thud and ambled over. As I was going to be out for the rest of the day and was paranoid about leaving the dog flap unlocked when I was out, he needed some fresh air, as well as a tinkle and poo.

'Oh no you don't,' I warned, crouching to grab him as he tried to shuffle past to the kitchen. 'Walkies.'

He sulked as I clipped his lead to his studded brown leather collar. I shoved my front door keys in the back pocket of my jeans, grabbed the invoices I needed to mail and a poop bag, then yanked open the stiff front door to a gorgeously sunny summer's day, even at nine-thirty in the morning. After much coaxing, I got him to walk the few paces out onto the stone doorstep before he promptly sat down and looked up at me expectantly as I wrestled the front door shut.

'I know, I know, it's not like we haven't been doing this for years,' I sighed, as I grabbed the long metal handle attached to a skateboard parked at the side of the porch and pulled it around to line up with the raised flagstone. Sumo immediately stepped onto it, then plonked his arse back down, his fat pink tongue hanging from the side of his mouth as his eyes shot back and forth, surveying his domain. 'Ready?' I asked, and he gave me his "I was born ready" look.

I hooked his lead over the handle, on the off chance he decided to make a run for it, then started walking up the path, pulling the skateboard along behind me. I knew we were the joke of the village. The twenty-something spinster with the dog that went for a walk without actually walking. But I'd tried everything, he just wouldn't walk unless he had to. I'd never met anyone as stubborn as this dog. And being stuck indoors all of the time wasn't healthy for him. So "walkies" consisted of him sitting on his arse as I tugged him along on this contraption Dad had made for me, which had required me adding an "extension" to the sides of the skateboard for Sumo's ever expanding overhang to rest on. Granted, pulling him around the nicely tarmacked pavements of the town centre route I used to take him on had been far easier than the rough country lane I lived on now, but I'd had someone adapt it with shock-absorbing suspension and all-terrain wheels. It was like a gym workout for me, without the extortionate fees. I cursed out loud as I caught my arm on the holly tree, which was overhanging my front path. I assumed it had been here longer than the cottage, and was what had inspired the name "Holly Cottage." I glanced down to see a white mark where one of the vicious leaves had marred my skin. Luckily it wasn't bleeding, that wouldn't have been a good look in my sleeveless dress. We headed out through the ornate black metal gate and onto the lane, and I turned to pull it shut.

'Morning, Abbie, and a fine one it is at that,' came my neighbour David Jones's voice. I was really fond of the elderly couple next door. They were like surrogate parents to me, but they could both talk the hind legs off a donkey about nothing. Today I really didn't have time to waste. I had a taxi booked to take me to the bride's parents' house so I could get ready there.

'Morning, David.'

'Taking Sumo for his walk?' he chuckled, as he leaned over his gate and angled his head around his hedge to look at us both, as if he'd been expecting us. Nothing happened in this village without everyone finding out. And his wife, Daphne, was the most ardent collector of all the news.

'Just popping to the post office. Do you need anything?'

'We're fine, thanks. Georgie did our shopping in Welshpool yesterday, isn't it,' he replied. I was Shropshire born and bred, and proud of it, but I still hadn't worked out this bizarre colloquialism of adding a random "isn't it" to the end of sentences. It didn't make sense, and there was no pattern to when you did, or didn't, add it.

'Is Daphne still ok to come and check on Sumo tonight?'

'That she is. Where is it you're off to again?'

'A wedding.'

'Not yours, still single then?'

'Yes,' I sighed with a quick and discreet roll of my eyes, as he reached up to pull his tweed cap a bit lower to shield his eyes from the sun. Being reminded by the villagers on a daily basis was getting really old. 'I'm sorry, David, but I'm going to have to hurry to make it to the post office and back, as I need to fit in a quick pamper session before I leave. I can't be late.'

17

'You'll be wanting to trim that bush of yours, it's getting out of hand.'

'I beg your pardon?' I looked at him wide-eyed, wondering if I'd just heard him correctly. I knew I hadn't had a wax in a while, but how did *he* know that?! I tried to remember when I'd last worn a bikini to sunbathe in the garden, where there was a remote possibility that he might have noticed some stray hairs if he'd been hanging out of his bedroom window using a pair of binoculars with a telescopic lens, with the sole purpose of muff spotting. But with our usual wet summer weather, I was drawing a blank.

'Your bush, it's looking a bit of a mess. Might take someone's eye out if it's not tended to soon. Too much for me to handle, I'm not much good unless it's already neatly trimmed and has some sort of shape for me to follow. I know a fella who won't mind getting right in there, head first, isn't it. He's even got a qualification in it.'

'In … bush trimming?' I squeaked. What bizarre world had I woken up in this morning, where my "been drawing a pension for over two decades" neighbour was openly discussing the state of my fanny hair and factoring me out to local muff-diving stud?

'Hmmm,' he confirmed with a nod. 'My big purple plums were hanging too low, Daphne swung around too fast the other day and got smacked in the face by them, ended up at casualty with a black eye, isn't it. He soon came round and sorted them out for me as well. By God, he's multi-talented, and easy on the eye, too,' he winked.

'He swings both ways?' That was all I needed, a blind date with a bisexual romancer of the elderly. This guy was sounding like a real catch. Not.

'Swings? No, he doesn't do swings. Just carpentry, bushes and trees, mowing and the like, isn't it. He'll even do your overgrown hedge while he's at it, as I know how busy your job keeps you. I'll tell him to pop by one day this week for you.'

'Oooh, you were talking about my *holly* bush, about sending a gardener around.' I breathed a sigh of relief, cursing my overactive imagination.

'What other bush needs trimming? He'll do them all. Very reasonably priced. *And* he's single,' David added, giving me a poignant look.

'Awesome,' I replied with a sinking feeling of dread. I'd stopped accepting recommendations from some of the well-meaning busybodies in the area. All of the blind dates they'd fixed me up on had been disasters. 'I really must go, David. Nice to see you. Don't forget to remind Daphne about Sumo tonight, she knows where the spare key is. And I'll see you for Sunday lunch at mine tomorrow.'

He gave me a salute and disappeared back behind his hedge as I yanked on the handle and got Sumo's ride moving. Jesus, and people thought life in the country was dull.

'Bisexual romancer of the elderly,' Georgie chuckled, after I'd recounted my morning during the taxi ride to Rachel's family home, situated in Kingsland, the posh part of Shrewsbury, of course.

'Honestly, I swore we were having an entirely different conversation. And as for the "he's single, easy on the eye," comment, I'll believe that when I see it. Do you know any single, good-looking gardeners in our parts? If so, I'd have thought you'd have been all over that action already.'

'No, I don't,' she replied with a shake of the head, then pulled a slight face.

'Sorry,' I whispered, reaching over to grab her hand and give it a gentle squeeze. Georgie was all talk, but took after me with no action. She'd been engaged only five months ago, before she found out he was cheating on her with one of The Cock & Bull barmaids. Quite apt really, turned out Greg was a cock, and totally full of bullshit. One minute she'd been talking about her own wedding, which would have taken me one step closer to the dreaded thirteenth dress, the next she was in puddles of tears, having broken it off and kicked him out. 'Still hurts, huh?'

'Like you wouldn't believe,' she replied with a forced, but brave, smile. Never having been in love, I couldn't even begin to imagine putting myself in her shoes, but I'd seen how devastated she'd been. I'd been the one to try and help her pick up the pieces and get through it. And the well-meaning Joneses too. They really were a sweet old couple, as long as you didn't spill your deep, dark secrets to them. Daphne never meant to be malicious, but always forgot what she'd been told to keep quiet. Not that I had any secrets in my closet, my life so far really had been dull.

'I'm so sorry, Georgie,' I repeated sincerely, squeezing her hand again and wishing I could do more, then letting it go.

'It's not your fault. I have good and bad days, but I'll get there. Each morning I wake up and it doesn't hurt quite so badly. I hope that one day, I'll fall in love again, be able to trust a guy completely and get that "happy ever after" that I'd been sure was so close, but I'm not ready yet. So if this gardener turns out to be a Hemsworth or James look-alike, he's all yours.'

'Why thank you, kind lady,' I grinned. Georgie wasn't one for wallowing in the woe-is-me pity party. She got stuff off her chest and moved on, and liked me to treat her without a pair of kid gloves.

'Besides, who says you won't meet someone tonight, or at any of the other weddings you're going to this year? Bridesmaid and best man or usher, it's a classic get together. Everyone's feeling emotional and needy, seeing their friends all googly-eyed as they exchange their vows. I've had some super-hot wedding encounters in my time.'

'Are you serious?' I scoffed. 'For one, I'll be in *that* dress, and for two, they'll all think I'm a lesbian with the most stunning date,' I reminded her. 'You look gorgeous, Georgie, as ever.'

It was the truth. Her long red hair was pulled back into an elegant but sexy chignon, tucked under one of those huge-brimmed cream and navy hats. They always looked so classy on everyone else, I just wasn't a hat person. Some navy eyeliner enhanced her baby blue eyes and her navy and cream patterned shirt-dress, with a pair of navy suede shoe-boots to round off her ensemble. Casually elegant, that was Georgie's style all over. I was so envious. I was more of a t-shirt, jeans, and trainers kind of girl.

'And so do you, and will continue to do if you smile, regardless of what you're wearing.'

'Humph,' I trumpeted, rolling my eyes.

'Don't make me pin you down with the dog clippers and give your bush an obviously overdue trim,' she warned with a giggle. 'Last week during a long and much needed arse kicking, you promised me smiles and making an effort to get out there. If Prince Charming doesn't come knocking, the modern-day woman goes out looking for him.'

'Then I'll do as I'm told, as long as you promise to do the same when the time's right, that you won't close your heart to love forever.' I held out my little finger and she wrapped hers around it with a solemn face.

'Deal.'

I kissed her cheek as I was dropped off at Rachel's parents' Georgian house in the leafy, posh part of town.

'Will you be ok on your own until the service?' I asked. She had a good two-hour wait before it was time to head to The Abbey, where the service was taking place.

'Please! One of The Peach Tree's famous brunches, with the odd mimosa or twelve, I'll be fine,' she laughed, shooing me out of the taxi. 'Remember, whatever your head is thinking, don't say it.'

'If only it were that easy,' I groaned. I shut the door and waved her off, then hurried to pull the heavy black wrought iron handle of the bell.

'You look so lovely and radiant,' I told Rachel as she stepped out of her limo with her dad, then went to adjust her askew veil, as her maid of honour was too busy chatting to the other bridesmaids to notice.

I wasn't lying, she did. It was us thirteen bridesmaids, and her maid of honour and flower girl, that looked ridiculous. I mean seriously, colour tone aside, who needed fifteen people walking up the aisle with you? I knew it wasn't like she couldn't afford it, but it seemed a total waste of money to me. Rachel was in a gorgeous, obviously expensive designer dress, with a thin, hot pink belt as homage to her "riot of colour" scheme, and was carrying a bouquet of brightly coloured gerberas. They were the focal point for the wedding flowers. Quite how Sarah at *Rosie Posie* had found so many gerberas to adorn all of the women, button holes for the men, pew and floral arrangements in the church, not to mention a floral arch, more arrangements, and table centrepieces at the after-wedding venue, was beyond me. Thousands of fields of gerberas must have been slaughtered to put these gorgeous displays together.

'Thank you,' she smiled.

'I'm really sorry, again, about the comment I made about the unicorn farting.'

'It's ok, I was just super stressed and I forgot that you were just being you. In school, you always had a way of blurting out whatever you were thinking, however appropriate or not it was.'

'I do try, honestly I do,' I added, desperately trying to redeem myself as the rest of the girls finally noticed she'd arrived and swarmed around us.

'Just make a conscious effort to rein it in around Dean. He only moved here a few months ago, he's not accustomed to such … forthrightness,' she replied, squeezing my upper arm. That surprised me. He was American, and I was under the impression that Americans were quite vocal and far less reserved than us stiff-upper-lip, polite-at-all-times British.

'He's so dreamy,' sighed Julia.

'He's a keeper alright, but what I wouldn't give to be single so I could get me some of that Miller action,' groaned Rebecca, maid of honour. 'That guy is so smouldering, I swear he could melt my underwear just by staring at it.' There was a murmur of agreement and vigorous nodding of heads all around me, along with some girly giggling.

'Miller action?' I enquired, my curiosity peaked. Who was this supposed Adonis they were all getting worked up over?

'Dean's best man,' Rachel confirmed. 'He wasn't at the rehearsal dinner last night as he lives in New York. He had a business meeting and was getting an overnight flight.'

'Is he still single?' piped up the easily recognisable, high-pitched squeaky voice of Fi-Fi.

'Very much so, but you aren't,' Rachel laughed. Fi-Fi had got married to Dave last year. A looker he wasn't, but he was loaded and she'd always been money obsessed.

'For the love of God, someone tell me why a man that hot hasn't been snapped up,' sighed Julia with a shake of her head.

'He's just not the settling-down type. He's young, rich, and gorgeous. What guy wouldn't want to play the field when women throw themselves at his feet? Not that he does, but he's not exactly made it work long term with anyone either,' suggested Rebecca. 'Right. Much as I'd love to keep talking all things Miller, I'll just have to settle for gazing at him lustfully all day. We have a bride to get up the aisle.'

Hmmm, hot and single. If only I wasn't in this damn dress, and I wasn't me, apparently undesirable and undateable Abbie Carter, spewer of inappropriate thoughts, and he wasn't an obvious commitment-phobe, I might have been exploring the whole "bridesmaid and best man" cliché tonight.

I exhaled heavily as Rebecca started herding us all into our positions outside The Abbey door, with me taking the last spot behind the other bridesmaids, Rachel and her father bringing up the rear. Georgie was right. I needed to go out and look for my soul mate. Sitting back and waiting for him to find me was never going to happen. And I seriously didn't want that unlucky thirteenth bridesmaid dress making it up into my attic before I'd got married.

One by one, they all started filtering in as the organist played some tune I'd never heard before. The Abbey was packed, not surprising as Rachel came from a large family, Dean too, and this was *the* wedding event of the season for this town, in fact the county. I squared my shoulders, positioned my bouquet, and put on my best bridesmaid, "I'm really loving this" smile as I started walking. Crikey, any casual passerby who stuck their head in here would think they were attending a gerbera convention, not a wedding. They were gorgeous, but personally I preferred subtlety rather than a slap across the face. Now for my wedding, I'd have … *My wedding, yeah right*, I silently scoffed. Like that was ever going to happen. I heard murmurs of approval from the crowd who were all facing the back of the church, and deduced that Rachel must have entered and be following me up the aisle, as there was no way they'd be cooing over my dress.

I spotted Georgie out of the corner of my eye and she threw me a double thumbs up and a wink, making me give her a quick scowl. She was trying to make me embarrass myself by giggling uncontrollably, but it was not going to happen. I was going to keep myself in check and for once, not embarrass myself in public. I approached the top of the pews, where the bridesmaids were all lined up on the left, facing me, with Dean and his entourage on the other side, facing the altar.

Nice tight arse, I thought to myself as I studied the blond-haired guy to his right. Very tasty indeed. As if I'd said the words out loud, he turned his head. The air was sucked from my lungs as his rich brown eyes met mine. Holy hell, my ovaries spontaneously combusted as this Greek God smiled at me. All soft, full, kissable lips, movie-star teeth, dimpled chin, and square jawline. My heart started racing and I was suddenly finding it hard to breathe. He was gorgeous. He was staring at me. Why was he staring at me? Did I have something on my face? A bat in the cave? His lips curved up into a sinfully sexy smile. Oh God, my legs had turned to jelly and I felt lightheaded and dizzy. I only had to make it a few more steps and I could just stand and stare at him to my heart's content.

I tried to put one foot in front of the other as he continued to watch me, but he threw me when he gave me a cheeky wink. *What was that all about?* Oh crap, I felt myself wobbling. I couldn't feel my feet on the ground. It was like one of those moments when you stood up too fast and your foot was numb because of pins and needles, and you weren't sure if it was actually on the floor or six inches higher. I tried to find my centre of gravity but started swaying alarmingly, unable to right myself. Cue emergency *Titanic* move. My arms shot out in a "King of the World" moment, causing my bouquet to be flung right at Rachel's mother in the front pew, smacking her firmly in the face as I stumbled forwards on my slender high heels. I tried to right myself and went backwards, then forwards again. My arms were windmilling furiously as I heard chuckles and gasps doing a Mexican wave down The Abbey. No! I was doing the hokey cokey front and centre at someone else's wedding, and I'd quite possibly knocked out the bride's mother's front teeth, split her lip, or given her a black eye. My legs decided to join in on the embarrassing dance party and turned to spaghetti as I teetered like a newborn fawn testing out his sea legs on ice.

'Man down, man down,' I shrieked as I felt myself falling, the ground rushing up to greet me at an alarming pace while the organ abruptly stopped playing mid-tune. I shut my eyes, screwed up my face, and braced for impact.

Nothing.

Instead of the cold hard floor, I felt myself fall into something warm and hard, something that smelled like freshly baked hot cinnamon buns. Hmmm, delicious!

'Are you ok, miss?'

'Huh?' I moaned, trying to bring myself around after being hit with an adrenaline rush from the excitement of seeing a hot man, assaulting someone with a lethal gerbera bouquet, and almost falling. Man, that smooth and sexy American accent, combined with that lickable scent, wasn't doing anything to help slow my fast-beating heart. My eyes fluttered open as I felt myself being levered upright, with a pair of strong arms circling my waist and a firm, muscular chest pressed up against mine. 'Wow,' I murmured.

'Are you ok?' he repeated.

'Super sexy lips. I wonder what they'd feel like on mine, *all of them*,' I wondered.

'Is that an offer?' he chuckled. I blinked a few times as I lifted my head up from the lips of sin to meet the amused brown-eyed gaze of my rescuer, the gorgeous blond. Crap, had I just said something about kissing him out loud? And … and about … that?! *Nice job, Abbie*, I thought. My untainted bridesmaid record was over. I hadn't even made it five minutes through the event of the year without embarrassing myself.

'Sorry,' I grimaced, my fingers curling around his strong and bulging biceps. 'I'm Abbie, frequent-putter-of-foot-in-mouth and apparently says-what-she's-thinking-out-loud, Carter. I seem to have lost my brain filter today.'

'Hey, Abbie Carter,' he smiled, a set of cheek dimples joining that oh-so-sexy one on his chin. 'I'm Miller, best man and rescuer-of-damsel-in-distress, Davis. Pleased to meet you. Are you ok?'

'Just great,' I squeaked, wondering if I was going to embarrass myself any more when he let me go, which he didn't seem to be in any rush to do. 'Ermmm, thanks for saving me.'

'Anytime,' he replied, his voice like warm melted chocolate, sending a delicious shiver down my spine.

'Ermmm, hello?! It's supposed to be *me* standing in front of the altar, the *actual* bride,' came Rachel's stressed voice.

'Sorry, sorry,' I muttered, quickly letting go of Miller's arms. He slid his hands from behind my back to support my hips as he slowly backed away, as if making sure I wasn't going to fall again. Wow, hot, sexy, and chivalrous. I felt like I was in Vegas at the slot machines, and the jackpot had just sounded the alarm. I somehow found my feet and hurried over to take my place at the end of one of the rows of bridesmaids, sans bouquet. Miller took his place, and the organ started again to let Rachel make it the last few steps towards her future husband. I looked over the sea of heads, some still sniggering, to meet Georgie's amused gaze. She shook her head with a smile as I grimaced at her. *Epic fail, Abbie. Epic fail.*

I barely took in any of the service, I was too distracted with avoiding the furious looks Rachel's mum kept shooting my way and trying not to look at Miller. I'd caught his amused gaze once or twice and must be having one of my overactive imagination days, as I was sure I'd seen something else in his eyes. A spark of interest, a heated look as he'd scanned my body up and down. I was just plain old Abbie, nothing special, not drop-dead gorgeous like Georgie. My long, mousy brown hair was poker straight, I had a full mouth, pouty lips that looked like a trout's apparently, a small straight nose, green eyes with hazel flecks, and petite ears. I'd say I was pretty, not stunning. Certainly nowhere near his league. I had a curvy size ten figure. Ok, maybe that was wishful thinking, as my jeans were getting harder and harder to pull on. Not even lying on the floor and breathing in hard as I tugged the zip was easy. So, my size twelve figure had some shape. I had a well-rounded backside, decent waist, and my boobs were a good handful. I'd had no complaints from previous boyfriends, but none of them had looked like Miller. I decided I must be imagining his interest and instead focused on a spot on the wall behind him.

I joined in the applause as Rachel and Dean were pronounced man and wife and kissed. I couldn't help looking at Miller's lips again as they did, and felt my cheeks flame to see him wink at me again. Great, that wink was what had got me into trouble in the first place. I grimaced as Rachel gave me a look right before she started her walk down the aisle and Rebecca, as chief bridesmaid, stepped forwards to join Miller. There was a brief moment of confusion as he stepped forwards, then turned around and muttered something to the long line of ushers, and one of them approached her instead, holding out his arm to take. *Ok, what was that all about?* I tapped my foot as I waited for my turn, perfected wedding smile plastered on my face, and breathed in a shocked gasp as I realised that Miller had waited back until the end to escort me down the aisle. I swallowed hard as I slipped my arm through his, someone from the pews shoving my slightly battered, rescued bouquet back in my hand.

'So, Abbie Carter, is that how you usually make an entrance?' he drawled as we followed the slow moving procession.

'It's a great way of attracting attention. I mean, it's kind of hard to get noticed when you're not the one in white,' I replied, keeping my focus ahead of me, not on him. I didn't need any more incidents to add to my catalogue of failures for this damn wedding.

'You think no one would notice you in that damn dress? What the hell was Rachel thinking?' he chuckled. I giggled. Thank God I wasn't the only one who thought it was awful.

'I may have told her it looked like a unicorn farted a neon rainbow, but seriously, it's all about the bride today, or at least it should be. I'm supposed to shrink into the background, not make a spectacle of myself. Everyone's focus should be on her.'

25

'Mine wasn't, and it wasn't just that awful dress of yours I was looking at all through the service.'

'What?' I exclaimed, my eyes shooting to his involuntarily as we approached the arched exit. What was he trying to say, that he found me attractive? Him? No, no way could someone with male model potential be interested in me, especially not after my embarrassing display of body and verbal inability.

'I think you're gorgeous, Abbie.'

'Yeah, right,' I scoffed. Miller frowned at me as we ground to a halt on the crowded gravel forecourt outside the main door. None of my boyfriends had ever said I was gorgeous.

'I'm serious. Are you here with anyone?' he asked.

'My ... my friend ... Georgie,' I stuttered. 'Who's a girl ... a friend ... a girlfriend. In a totally non-lesbian way,' I quickly added.

'Good to know,' he replied, angling his beautiful glossy chocolate eyes down to mine. 'So if I come to ask for a dance later, you won't say no?'

I opened my mouth, then closed it again. Was this really happening? This gorgeous man was implying he found me attractive and wanted to spend the evening in my company? After I'd embarrassed myself earlier?

'I'll take that as a non-refusal then.'

'I'm not exactly Taylor Swift on the dance floor,' I replied.

'I won't be looking at your feet, Abbie. I'll be looking at those utterly kissable lips of yours. And if you really behave, I may even let you sample these "super sexy lips" of mine,' he added with another wink as he let go of my arm. *'Everywhere.'*

With that parting comment, he disappeared into the crowd as I stood there, stunned.

'Amazing wedding entrance, Abbie, and holy hell, who was that guy who grabbed you and walked you down the aisle? Smokin' hot,' came Georgie's voice as she sidled up next to me.

'Best man, Miller Davis,' I replied, still in a stunned daze. 'Pinch me.'

'What?'

'Pinch me, please pinch me. I'm really not sure if I'm awake. I mean, I caused a scene and took the focus off the bride, not to mention attacking her mother inadvertently. That sounds like me, right? But then I got rescued by some kind of handsome knight on a white steed, who told me he thinks I'm gorgeous and he wants to put his sexy lips on mine. Both sets! Things like that don't happen to Abbie Carter, stuffy and boring accountant. Owww, what the hell was that?' I demanded as I rubbed the top of my arm, which suddenly stung.

'The pinch! You're definitely not dreaming. You're an intelligent, beautiful, sexy single woman who, granted, doesn't live a wild life, but is far from stuffy and boring. But forget all of that. Let's focus on the fact that you appear to have struck gold. You're telling me that hunk of a man made a play for you?'

'He was teasing, he must have been teasing,' I stated, feeling my stomach sink, especially when I saw the excited look on Georgie's face. 'Men like that aren't into girls like me.'

'There are no girls like you, Abbie. You're unique. I honestly don't know who gave you this complex that you're not desirable, you so are, but you give out the not-interested vibe more often than not, which probably scares men off. And why would he tease? He looks like the sort of guy who can get any woman he wants. He wouldn't make a pass at you if he wasn't interested.'

'Humph. We'll see,' I retorted, my eyes desperately searching the excited, chattering crowds, hoping to get another glimpse of him.

'Rachel and bridesmaids, follow me please,' called James the photographer, holding his camera up in the air so we could see where he was going over the sea of heads.

'Go and be captured in your favourite bridesmaid dress for all posterity,' giggled Georgie.

'I really hate you sometimes, Georgie Basset,' I scowled, then gave her a wink before squeezing my way through the crowd.

'Abbie, how are you?'

'Oh hey, Caroline, fancy seeing you here,' I teased. I saw her at most weddings I was a part of, bridesmaid or not. As the other half of *JOL Wedding Photography*, wife of James the photographer, we were on first name terms. 'Please tell me James didn't get any pictures of my humiliation?'

'Actually,' she chuckled, 'a great one of the bouquet hitting the mother of the bride.'

'No, seriously?' I groaned. Was I ever going to live this morning down?

'If they pick it for the album, it will at least be a talking point.'

'Very true,' I confirmed, sure my cheeks had gone pink again with mortification.

'He also got one I think you might want a copy of, the moment you fell into the best man's arms.'

'He did?' That piqued my interest.

'What's the story there?'

'No story at all. I just met him today,' I confirmed as we approached James, who already had the bride in position and was directing the sea of colour where to gather around.

'Watch this space then,' Caroline replied with a suggestive waggle of her eyebrows. I shooed her away with my hand and a laugh, but couldn't help but notice when Miller came to watch us, which made me stand a little taller, suck my stomach in, and push my breasts out. A girl had to work it sometimes.

I was surprised to find myself disappointed that I didn't get a chance to talk to Miller again. It was a blur of photographs at The Abbey, where he had to be positioned close to the happy couple, then it was the same as we headed to Severn Manor, where the wedding reception was being held. It was such a lovely venue, set in beautiful grounds only a few miles from Dilbury, which the river meandered through. It was a timber-framed, 16th century Tudor building, tastefully extended to keep up with the demand for functions. Violins were playing as we gathered on the lawn, while waiters in penguin suits carried around silver platters of champagne and canapés as the pictures were being taken. Every time I tried to grab a glass of bubbly, I was called away for yet more pictures.

The "riot of colour" theme continued indoors. Poor Sarah of *Rosie Posie* must have slaved away for days with the amount of gorgeous floral work she'd done in the room. I had to admit, much as I disliked my dress, not finding it at all wedding appropriate, the stunning bright flowers and sweeping layers of coloured voile that created a canopy above us did look lovely and summery, and definitely unique.

Much to our mortification, Georgie and I were seated at a round table with some of the old fuddy-duddies, and worse, my back was to the top table, so I didn't have line of sight of the gorgeousness of Miller Davis. With the old cronies being family, it wasn't like I could ask them to swap either. I was sure I was going to get a neck spasm from casting longing looks over my shoulder throughout the meal.

Adding to the lesbian rumour that had already started circling the event, I reached out to hold Georgie's hand as the wedding speeches started. I'd told her I was worried it would be too much for her too soon, but she'd insisted she was going to be fine. Funnily enough, it was me that found myself suddenly choking up, not her, especially during the father-of-the-bride speech. Even if I ever got lucky enough to get married, I was never going to have that. I had no one to give me away, no parents to smile proudly at me, to tell me how beautiful I looked, or how ecstatic they'd be to see me looking so happy. If I had children, I'd have no mum to give me well-meaning advice or be a shoulder to lean on. And my babies would have no grandparents, on my side anyway.

I was suddenly overcome with emotion and felt the sting of tears at the back of my eyes. I could not cry. I'd already hogged the limelight this morning, I was not going to do it again.

'Are you ok?' whispered Georgie as I started dabbing my eyes with the white linen napkin.

'I … I think I need a moment, some fresh air.'

'Do you want me to come with you?' she offered, a look of concern on her face when she saw how close I was to tears.

'I'd just like a few minutes alone if you don't mind. I'm so sorry.' I shot to my feet, grabbed my purple clutch bag, and quickly weaved my way through the tables. I shot out of one of the open patio doors and took off my shoes, holding them in my hand as I ran across the lawn towards the river, where some ducks and swans were happily gliding along. There was a bench situated near the old stone bridge that crossed the river, so I plonked myself down on it and gave in to a rare pity party as I shed a few tears. I was sniffing and snuffling so loudly, I sounded like Sumo, which made me giggle as I tried to blot my eyes and not streak my make-up. Crossing my ankles, I swung my legs back and forth as I closed my eyes, raised my face to the heat of the sun, and let out a slow, calming breath. I frowned when I thought I heard someone calling my name.

'Abbie … Abbie … *Abbie*!' It was repeated again and again, the tone of the speaker getting louder and more insistent. I opened my eyes and looked around to see Miller racing across the lawn like his life depended on it, the tails of his morning suit flying behind him. Oh hello! If only he was wearing a little less, it would be like watching some reruns of *Baywatch*. 'Move, get under the bridge!' he yelled.

'What?'

'Get under the bridge, quickly,' he urged as he approached. I stood up, baffled. Was this some fancy American chat-up line? What the hell did he mean? 'The sprinklers, they're about to–'

I shrieked as I was suddenly blasted in the face by a jet of freezing cold water, as the lawn came alive and looked like some kind of second-rate English version of the Bellagio Fountains in Vegas. All we needed were the violinists to come out to add some musical atmosphere. Miller burst out laughing as he reached me, then grabbed my hand and started to run again, water spraying us from every direction.

'What the hell?' I cried, as we scurried down some crude steps on the riverbank and he pulled me along the towpath to shelter under the bridge.

I didn't have a chance to worry about how drenched I must look, or how badly my make-up would have run, or how the water would have affected my very carefully done wedding up-do. All I could think about was that he was holding my hand, and how lovely it felt. Like they were born to fit together. He let go to sweep his wet hair back from his chiselled face as I shook my hands, trying to get rid of some of the water pouring down them, then tried to push my own hair out of my eyes. I was soaked, and so was he. Damn that jacket and waistcoat he was wearing. I could be having a total wet white shirt, *Pride and Prejudice,* Mr. Darcy moment right now. We finally looked at each other, and both burst out laughing.

'What the hell?' I repeated when we finally stopped and caught our breath.

'I saw you slip out. You looked upset, so I thought I'd follow you and make sure that you were ok, but someone stopped me and told me that the sprinklers were timed to go off while everyone was inside.'

'So you chased me out here to save me?' I looked up at him, touched.

'Well, I told them to turn them off first, but the guy didn't know how to shut down the automated system, so I tried to warn you, but you were too far away to hear me yelling. I had no choice, damsel in distress and all, *again,*' he added with a grin, then his shoulders started shaking and he roared with laughter. I watched him, perplexed. It had been funny for a moment, but not *that* funny, especially now that I was cold, dishevelled, and shivering without the hot sun beating down on me.

'Well thank you, but I fail to see the funny side. We're both soaked, and I probably look like a drowned rat, with make-up running all down my face. I'm not staying here at the hotel, so I have no change of clothes, no make-up, nothing.'

'I wouldn't worry about your make-up,' he chortled, struggling to get his laughter under control. I scowled at him and crossed my arms over my chest. His unexpected and very sweet chivalry points were rapidly declining. 'You look like a ... what was it that farted a neon rainbow?'

'A unicorn, but it's not like I got changed, you saw me in this damn dress all day.'

'Not when the dye from it was running all over your chest, arms, and legs,' he guffawed, bending over to clutch his sides as he started to hyperventilate.

'Are you freakin' kidding me?' I groaned as I looked down to see he was right. I was a human rainbow now. 'Oh my God, can this day get any worse? What if it doesn't come off?'

'I'm sure it will, you just need a hot shower and a good scrub. Come on, you're shivering, we need to get you changed and warm.'

He reached for my hand, taking it without asking permission, and pulled me along behind him as we headed out into the sunshine on the other side of the bridge and made our way carefully up the bank to find a fence bordering a large field, full of grazing sheep. There was no sprinkler in sight, not that I could get any wetter. And what was I going to do for clothes? I was going to have to call a taxi to take me home to get changed and come back. But what taxi driver would want me in his cab, risking his seats getting soaked and stained with bright dye? Miller gestured for me to climb the fence first, so I offered him my shoes and bag to hold and turned around to grab the metal wire, hoping to lift the top section and shimmy between the gap in the three parallel sections.

'Jesus Christ!' I screamed, my whole body juddering and the fine hairs on my arms and back of my neck standing on end as a forceful current zapped me and ran through my body. It was only an electric damn fence. I let go of it quickly, still shaking from the shock as I stepped back, with Miller laughing again behind me.

'I'm so sorry, I shouldn't find it funny, but your face was priceless. Are you ok?'

'I just don't believe this,' I moaned, lifting my hands to cover my mortified face. The first guy I'd been attracted to in forever and he seemed to have liked me too. I had no chance with him after these disasters.

'Come on, we're not risking going over that, and I think you need a bourbon. You can come and shower in my suite. I'll find you something to wear before I take a shower too.'

'I'm not swimming across the river to try the bridge from that side, not the way this day is going.'

'I wouldn't risk it either,' he confirmed. 'We're already wet, so we may as well just walk back across the lawn and get a bit wetter. Safer than an electrical current and possible flesh-eating sheep.'

'Flesh-eating sheep?' I giggled, finally seeing the funny side. I dropped my hands to give him a look and he shrugged with a grin.

'I have a vivid imagination. I design video games.'

'So much cooler than my job,' I stated. I accepted his free hand as he offered it, still holding my clutch and shoes in his other, and we started to make our way down the bank to retrace our steps.

'Don't even ask,' I warned, one palm firmly in the air, as we squelched past an astonished Georgie and group of onlookers standing out on the patio.

'Never a dull moment with you, Abbie Carter,' she laughed, trying to keep up with our determined march towards the main hotel entrance, where the reception desk was situated. Miller immediately asked for more towels to be sent to his room, suggesting dark ones if they didn't want a rainbow of dye all over their pristine white ones, and asked if they could dry out our shoes while we took a shower. Georgie raised her eyebrows as she mouthed, 'Move fast much?' at me.

'Separate showers,' I advised her. 'Could you go and see Rebecca, the head bridesmaid, and find out if she's staying over? Maybe she could lend me some mascara and eye shadow, so I don't look completely awful bare-faced.'

'You look beautiful bare-faced, but sure,' she agreed. 'Don't do anything I wouldn't do,' she warned with a cheeky grin as she spun on her heels and disappeared.

'Who was that?' Miller asked as we headed barefoot up the stairs.

'My best friend, Georgie,' I replied, casting a glance his way to try and gauge what he was thinking. Most men fancied Georgie, and that was without her looking so glamorous next to me in my current state.

'Ah, the non-lesbian girlfriend,' he nodded.

'Hmmm, though if I was a lesbian, I'd be totally into her. She's gorgeous, isn't she?' I tested.

'If you like that kind of look,' he agreed. 'She's attractive, but she's not my type.' I suppressed a smile. He actually seemed sincere. Wow, a man who wasn't panting after her was a rarity indeed. 'Aren't you going to ask what is my type?'

'No,' I replied as he led the way along the corridor of bedrooms. 'You've already implied that you're interested in me, and I like to think I'm a trusting kind of girl. So you're either being sincere, in which case I'm extremely flattered, or you're pulling my leg and pretending you like me for a bet or something, and if that's the–'

'I'm being sincere,' he replied forcefully as he ground to a halt at bedroom number fourteen and turned to face me, a serious look on his face. Jesus, it was as hot as his smiling face. I think I'd find any of his faces hot. 'I've never led a woman on, Abbie. I'm known for being direct. There's just something about you I can't explain, something that makes me want to get to know you better, something I find incredibly attractive. Come on, you're still shaking. Let's get you out of those wet clothes,' he suggested as he turned to open his suite door.

I followed him in, giving him a quick smile as he shut the door. I couldn't believe what I'd just heard, or that I was here, in his room, and he seemed genuinely interested in me. Even if he was only after a fling, which was likely seeing how he was only here for the wedding, I was seriously flattered. It had been a long time since I'd been flung. But I knew what he was saying, as my attraction to him wasn't all about his face or potentially hot body either. I hardly knew him, but it was like I'd known him for years.

'I think you'd better go for a shower first, or all of that dye is going to leech into the carpet,' he advised. 'I promise to wait out here, and when they deliver the extra towels, I'll knock, close my eyes, and hand them to you.'

I just nodded, speechless for once, and trotted after him like an eager puppy as he headed to the bathroom and showed me inside, then went and opened the glass shower door and adjusted some dials.

'I like a cold shower in the morning, it wakes me up. I don't want you to be hit by that when you're already freezing. There, that should be nice and warm.' He stepped out and flashed me one of those amazing smiles that nearly made me swoon. 'I have a spare black dress shirt, it should fit you and come down low enough to look like a dress. I can lend you a belt as well if you want?'

'Thanks, that would be great.' I smiled at him shyly and he lifted a hand, gently palming my cheek. My chest started heaving as we stared at each other, my heart soaring. My God, was he going to kiss me? I barely knew him, but all I could think about was how his lips would feel on mine. It took a concerted effort not to speak my thoughts aloud right now, especially with the little devil on my shoulder telling me to ask him to scrub my back. He slowly moved forwards, his lips pursing, and I could feel mine doing the same. Just as I could feel the heat of his breath on them, he veered upwards and lay a kiss on my forehead, causing my heart to plummet.

'Take your time, I'll be outside if you need me. Help yourself to my shampoo and body wash, it's in the shower.' He spun on his heels and headed out, pulling the door shut without a backwards glance.

Ok, what was that all about?

I scrubbed myself like I never had before, but when I stepped out of the shower, I sighed to see that I still had blotchy patches of multi-coloured dye on my arms, torso, and legs. That damn dress was never seeing my attic. In fact, I could "accidentally" leave it here and never have to see it again.

'Are you ready for towels?' came Miller's deep and seductive voice. I had a feeling I could be ready for anything he offered. I hurried across to stand behind the door, opening it and using it to shield my naked body. He was true to his word. His eyes were tightly closed and he stretched out his arms with a bundle of black towels balanced on them, along with the shirt he'd promised. I quickly snatched them off him and shut the door, letting out a tense sigh. Why was I letting myself like him so much? He lived in America. I couldn't make a relationship with a guy in my village work, so what chance did I have with a pretty ginormous ocean separating us? Plus, he wasn't the settling-down kind from what I'd heard earlier. 'I put one of my spare pairs of boxers there for you as well, as I figured your panties would be wet,' he called.

'Seriously soaked,' I yelled back, then cringed, wondering what he'd have made of that stupid comment.

I dried myself off, then wrapped my pretty underwear set in a towel and tried to squeeze as much moisture out as I could before stuffing them into my clutch. Giggling, I pulled on his pair of tight black jersey boxers and said a silent prayer of thanks that my boobs were still pert enough to go braless under this shirt. I picked up the wet dress from where I'd abandoned it on the tiled floor and draped it over the heated towel rail, glad to be seeing the last of it. I emerged from the bathroom in a plume of steam, a towel turban around my damp hair and face scrubbed free of make-up and wondered if he'd run screaming for the hills to see me like this.

'Jesus,' I gasped. 'Biteable.'

I should have knocked on the door first, as he was stripping off with his back to me. He'd discarded his wet jacket, waistcoat, and shirt, and was just bending over to remove his trousers. However good his pert bottom had looked in the church, encased in a suit, was nothing compared to seeing it now, waving in my face in just a pair of tight white boxers.

'What did you say?' he asked as he straightened up and turned around.

'Bot … damn … gorge … holy hell … Jesus .... body … firm … blahhh. Can't speak!' I stuttered, squeezing my eyes tightly shut as I nearly hyperventilated. His chest and abs were a work of art. My God! With the exception of some of the half-naked men I'd ogled during the Olympics on TV, pausing and moving forward frame by frame, I'd never seen such a toned body in my life. 'You're beautiful.'

'Exactly my thoughts when I saw you in the church, Abbie Carter,' he chuckled as I felt him waft past, the scent of cinnamon assaulting my nostrils as I heard the bathroom door close behind me. I made it over to his large bed and plonked my backside on it, then flopped back in a daze. I was in lust at first sight. That was all it was on my part. Pure lust. But then why did I feel so at ease in his company? I took some long, slow, deep breaths as I heard the shower turn on, then the sound of him singing along to one of Nevada 6's latest hits, and tried to drag my mind out of the gutter as I imagined him naked in there.

'Thank God,' I stated when there was a knock on the suite door. Something other than Miller for me to focus on. I padded over to open it and found Georgie outside.

'Interrupting?' she asked, angling her head to try and see in the room.

'He's in the shower, alone.'

'Naked?' she gasped, putting a hand to her chest. 'Oh my!'

'Tell me about it,' I groaned.

'Why aren't you in there with him?'

'Hello, stranger, Abbie Carter, nice to meet you.' I held out my hand in greeting and she swatted it away, laughing. 'How long have you known me? I'm not a one-night-stand kind of girl.'

'Me neither, but I might be persuaded to change my mind for him,' she grinned. 'Anyway, here's some mascara and grey eye shadow, and they've dried out your shoes, they're both here in the hall. Come down when you're ready. They're setting up the dance floor and I'm already on my way to being pleasantly drunk. I see a bit of a shimmy coming on, a little shake of the old boot-*tey*. Hmmm, loving this sexy shirt-dress look on you, sweetie. See you in a while, and if I don't, have fun!'

'Georgie,' I called after her retreating back, needing some advice right now. She just waved and disappeared up the corridor. I carried the shoes inside and headed over to the dressing table to rummage out the hairdryer, using Miller's comb to detangle my hair as I set to work. Ten minutes later, I was looking a bit more respectable, and he was still in the bathroom. I felt kind of awkward standing here, so I put on my shoes and stuffed the borrowed make-up in my clutch, then went to knock on the bathroom door. 'Miller? Are you ok in there?'

'Sorry, just shaving. I'll be out in a minute.'

'Ermmm, I think I'll head down and let you get dressed in private. Plus, I need a drink. What's your tipple?'

'My what?'

'Your favourite drink.'

'Oh right. Jack Daniels and Coke on the rocks. I won't be long though, why don't you wait?'

'No, I'll see you down there,' I replied, and hurried to the door before I changed my mind. I'd had more than enough excitement for one day. Seeing him shower fresh in his boxers again would probably finish me off.

'I scared him off, he's not coming back,' I sighed as I sat at the bar, the ice in his drink having melted already.

'He's coming back. How were you supposed to know there were two bars open for the reception tonight? He's also the best man, remember? He's probably schmoozing with the other guests as he tries to find you,' Georgie said in a reassuring tone. 'His actions aren't that of a guy who's not interested, Abbie.'

'Even if that was true, look at me now. I look like an entrant to a body-painting exhibition with all this damn dye staining my skin. In fact, I look like Joseph in his technicolour dream coat, without the damn coat. And I'm wearing men's boxers!'

35

'Got to say I'm finding it all very amusing. Thank God you brought me along.'

'I'm so happy I've provided the entertainment for you today.'

'Excuse me, are you Miss Abbie Carter?' the barman interrupted.

'Yes,' I drew out, giving him a puzzled look.

'I have this for you,' he replied, handing over a letter on luxury Severn Manor stationery. He smiled and headed off to serve someone else.

'Intriguing,' Georgie stated, as I saw my name written on the front in small, neat script. I ripped it open and pulled out a short letter, inhaling sharply as I started to read, and disappointment slammed into me. I suddenly felt really down. 'What, what is it?' she asked. I shook my head, and she snatched the letter off me and started to read it.

'Dear Abbie, I'm so sorry to do this to you, but I've had to leave unexpectedly … Oh no, he's gone?' she gasped.

'Told you it was too good to be true,' I replied, feeling dejected and rejected. Apparently some business crisis had demanded his attention and he'd had to rush to the airport to head back to New York. He'd written how much he'd enjoyed my company, and had included his phone number, asking me to call him as he'd like to keep in touch, and that we could swap clothes when we next saw each other, as he still had my dress. 'I mean, he's the best man. Who runs out on a best friend's wedding?'

'It must be life or death stuff,' Georgie suggested.

'He designs video games, hardly the same as being needed to carry out major heart surgery,' I huffed.

'Don't take it personally. He made the effort to write a letter before he left,' she reminded me, shoving the letter back in the envelope and offering it to me. I shook my head.

'Bin it.'

'What?'

'Bin it. What's the point of me having his number? He lives over there, I live here. He's hot, I'm not. So we had a moment, but he's going to forget all about the clumsy, wet, tie-dyed girl when he's settled back into his life over there.'

'Abbie, you really like him and from what I saw, he really likes you, and stop with the Abbie bashing. You're beautiful. Ok, granted, you may not end up walking down the aisle with him, but don't stop something before it's even had a chance to begin. I've not seen you this interested in a guy before. At least communicate with him, see what he wants.'

'Sweetie, I can't make a relationship with Mr. Sumo work, and we've lived together for seven years. I've got no chance with a hot American. So I liked him, I felt a spark, but it was what it was. A fleeting moment. There must be loads of local guys I could spark with, I just have to get out there and start looking again. Now drink your drink and let's go dance. I need a bit of fun after the disaster of today,' I stated firmly, not entirely convinced I meant it.

'Abbie,' she pleaded, waving the envelope at me. I pulled it out of her hand and slid it across the bar towards the guy that had given it to me.

'Can you bin this for me please?' I asked, and he nodded and took it off me. I grabbed Georgie's hand, blanking out her protests, and dragged her away towards the dance floor before I had a chance to change my mind.

I had really liked him. How many times did you feel a pull to someone so strongly within seconds of meeting them? Not often in my case. But even if there wasn't the Atlantic between us, he was out of my league. And I'd heard what the girls had said earlier. He was single for a reason. He was a serial dater and he wasn't the settling-down type. I was living in fantasyland, and as an accountant, I should know better.

Miller Davis plus Abbie Carter was one mathematical equation that would never work out.

Chapter Three
The Bush Trimmer
August

'OK, OK, I'M COMING,' I yelled, trying to rake my fingers through my bed-matted hair while I jogged down the stairs, quickly doing up the buttons on the pyjamas I'd just grabbed from my chest of drawers. It had been two weeks since my Miller encounter and Georgie had come over to help me drown my sorrows in my subsequent slump. I was seriously regretting having thrown away his number now. I couldn't stop thinking about him. I knew that I could always ring Rachel to ask for it, but so could he if he wanted to get mine, and he hadn't. I was kind of old-fashioned, I liked a guy to do the chasing. Again, in his case. I didn't want to come across as some desperate, panting groupie, which of course I was. Then there was the whole he-didn't-do-relationships thing, against my not-looking-for-a-fling thing, not to mention the whole ocean thing. There were too many "things" to even consider dating a man like him. I heard Sumo grumbling in the lounge, as annoyed as I was to be woken up at eight a.m. on a Saturday. Who the hell was it?

I paused with my fingers wrapped around the door handle, my heart suddenly racing. What if it was him? He could have flown all the way over an ocean, traversed the countryside lanes, dodging badgers and the odd stray sheep that wandered into the road, to come and claim me in some kind of romantic-comedy movie moment. My fingers were shaking as I unlocked the top half of the door and threw it open, sighing heavily to find a complete stranger staring back at me.

'Good morning. Abbie Carter?' came the deep male voice with a noticeable Welsh twang to it.

'Yes?'

'I've come to trim your bush.'

'I'm sorry, I'm half-asleep. Did you say you've come to trim my ... *bush*?' I was having a déjà vu of the conversation, but not of the admittedly cute, strapping guy standing in front of me. He was dressed in a pair of honey-coloured Timberland boots, black combats, and a khaki Henley shirt, which was rolled up to his elbows, exposing some sexily tanned, strong-looking forearms.

'Sorry, I'm an early riser, I like to get as much done as possible before it gets too hot in the afternoon. David, your neighbour, said it's got out of hand, and you might need some other jobs doing?'

'Oh, you're the bush trimmer, sorry, gardener.'

'Heath Jones, nice to meet you,' he said, extending his hand.

'Abbie Carter, obviously,' I replied, giving it a shake. Wow, he had a firm grip. And unlike the businessmen I usually shook hands with, his hands were rough and slightly calloused. 'So, Heath Jones, how much do you charge for bush trimming, sorry, sorry, gardening?'

'Twelve pounds an hour, but I don't just do bushes.' He gave me a lopsided grin, showing a set of nice, even teeth and a solitary dimple. Was he flirting with me?

'Tell me more.' I smiled, folding my arms across my chest. I was suddenly acutely aware that I was standing in front of a very cute guy wearing just my emergency hot pink pyjamas with a huge Hello Kitty face on my chest and a small white one on my backside.

'I'm a jack-of-all-trades, really. Landscaping, plumbing, odd jobs around the house like painting, putting up shelves, and assembling furniture. I'm a trained carpenter too. I made the tree house in the Weathers' garden for their grandchildren, and those custom-made struts to hold up the branches of my uncle's plum tree, which were hanging too low with the heavy load.'

'Oh,' I nodded, having a light bulb moment. '*Those* are the plums that gave Daphne the black eye. Got to say that's a relief.' Well, this Heath was cute, and now that I knew he wasn't a bisexual, old-aged-pensioner romancer, his stock was rising rapidly. He gave me a puzzled look and went to say something, then changed his mind. 'Ok, Heath, I obviously need the holly bush doing, the hedge trimming, and some general tidying up in the back garden. But I have some jobs around the house that need doing too.'

'What kind?' he asked, folding his strong arms across a very broad chest as he angled his head.

'Well, I have a slight leak under the kitchen sink, the front door sticks and squeaks, I've had a shelf unit to put up in my bedroom forever, and the house, as well as the windows and doors, are overdue painting. Then my chimney in the lounge needs sweeping.'

'Ok well, I can do the bush and hedge today, and the odd jobs in the house. I'd have to come back to do the back garden another day, if it's as large as next door's. The house painting I'd have to schedule in, but obviously it will depend on the weather, and I can give you a number for the chimney sweep, as that's not something I do.' He smiled again, some fine creases appearing around a pair of bright emerald eyes, and ran a hand through his short, very dark brown hair. I needed to upgrade him from cute to very cute.

'Great. Well, give me a minute to get out of these pyjamas and I can show you how I want my bush done. I kind of like a shape to it, you know? It makes it look more pretty,' I told him. He chuckled and put a hand up to his mouth as he tried to keep in his laughter, while I felt my cheeks flush when I realised how that must have sounded.

'I'll go and get my tools out of my van,' he nodded, his eyes still sparkling with amusement. 'Nice pussy, by the way,' he added. I gasped, and he dropped his hand as he flicked his chin at me. 'On your chest. My niece loves Hello Kitty.'

'They're emergency pyjamas only, I'm not some kind of woman who thinks she's still a teenager,' I advised him in a rush. 'Trust me, I'm *all* woman. I happen to sleep naked and when you knocked on the door, I grabbed these to put on. And now I'm telling you totally inappropriate things. I'm going to shut the door and go and get changed and come back when I'm more respectable.' My cheeks burning, I didn't give him a chance to respond and quickly pushed the top half of the stable door, ramming it a couple of times to get it to shut, then locked it. 'Idiot, Abbie,' I muttered to myself as I took the stairs two at a time.

'Seriously, Sumo,' I griped as he waddled out of the kitchen, leaving the utility room in carnage. His breakfast bowl was upside down, there were drops of stray gravy on the floor where it had dripped off his head, and he'd managed to put his foot in his water bowl in his enthusiasm to chow down his food, leaving a puddle of water everywhere. Not to mention the wet paw prints he was leaving as he headed back for his après-breakfast snooze. I grabbed him first, much to his bemusement, and dried his paws with an old towel. I then tried to hold him still, struggling to keep my grip while he wriggled to escape, as I attempted to wipe the gravy out of the deep, hairy creases in his forehead. 'I'm feeling very under-appreciated as a mother right now, you know.'

His dark, moist eyes just held my gaze, as his pink tongue hung from the side of his mouth while he panted. I was going to have to ask Georgie if she offered teeth cleaning as part of her services, as he was in desperate need of some breath freshening.

'Go on then, go sleep while I clean up your mess, then after lunch we'll go for a walk, ok?'

He gave me a grunt of disapproval, then wheezed as he trundled away towards the lounge, his chubby bottom swaying like he was doing the samba. After cleaning up the kitchen, I put the kettle on. I needed more coffee and a bacon sandwich to soak up some of last night's alcohol. I leaned over the sink to look out of the kitchen window and saw Heath bending over as he finished shaping the bottom of my holly bush. *How had I not seen him in the village before?* Especially if he did the gardening next door. I mean, Miller's bottom would have taken gold medal in the sexy arse Olympics, but Heath's definitely ranked of all of the male bottoms I'd ogled. Which I did more times than was probably healthy. I'd say a definite bronze medal. He didn't have quite as much curve as my former gold medallist, Alec Wright, who'd now slipped to silver medal position.

I sighed as I thought of Alec. I'd admired him from afar for years when I'd been in young farmers', but he was five years older than me and had gone away to university, then moved to London, and finally relocated to New York by the time I came of dating age. He'd settled back near Dilbury and I still saw him now and then, usually on a Thursday night in The Cock & Bull, but he only had eyes for his great love. It was high time I found my own. I opened the kitchen window.

'Want a cup of tea?' I called. Heath straightened up and turned to look for me, smiling when he saw me framed by the window.

'I'd prefer a coffee, if that's ok? Black, no sugar.'

'Of course it is. I'm making a bacon sandwich if you want one, too,' I offered.

'I'd love one if you don't mind.'

'Crispy?'

'Is there any other way to eat bacon?' he scoffed, running the back of his hand over his forehead, where a slight sheen of perspiration was forming as the sun moved higher in the sky.

'Exactly!' I nodded. How people could eat flaccid bacon, with the fat still raw and chewy, was beyond me. That was one of my secret tests for a man, after meeting the bottom-approval criteria. Did he like crispy bacon? Maybe I ought to check Heath out against my other criteria. 'I'm thinking we'd better head to the bedroom next, before you get all hot, sweaty, and dirty out there.'

'I have been known to get hot, sweaty, and dirty in the bedroom too, you know,' he chuckled. Humorous. Tick. Another item off my list.

'Do you flirt with all of your customers?' I called.

'Only the pretty ones who offer me bacon sandwiches,' he replied with a wink. Tick, tick. What girl didn't love a good wink from an attractive guy? Hmmm, maybe I should forget about Miller, who lived thousands of miles away. Heath hadn't knocked the air out of my lungs like Miller had when I'd first seen him, but I was beginning to really like him.

I made our drinks and smiled shyly when his fingers brushed mine as I handed his over, then I returned to the kitchen to busy myself with breakfast. I berated myself for running through my remaining criteria. On the one hand, it was so shallow to have a list when it came to a potential mate, but on the other, who didn't have a preconceived idea of their ideal match? You had to find them attractive, and there had to be key personality traits that told you if you were likely to be compatible. It was just odd that I hadn't met anyone who even came close in the last eighteen months, and suddenly, in the space of two weeks, I'd met two.

As breakfast was ready so quickly, Heath didn't have a chance to go and sort my shelving unit first. He'd wolfed down his sandwich and was lying on his back on the floor, his head and shoulders in my cupboard under the sink, before I'd had a chance to start on the second half of mine. Eating that portion took a lot longer as I sat staring at his toned body while he worked to fix my leak. I blushed as he suddenly slid out and caught me staring at him, and I started choking on some of my sandwich.

'Done. You just had a loose connection on the pipework, so I tightened it for you.'

'Great, thanks,' I spluttered, banging my chest as I tried to catch my breath. He shot to his feet and grabbed a glass off the long shelving unit, which displayed all my mugs and glasses, then poured me some water and handed it to me to gulp down as he patted my back.

'Ok?' he eventually asked. I nodded and gave him a grateful smile. 'Let's get these shelves done in your bedroom, then I can sort the door and do your hedge. I'll make some notes on what needs doing in the back garden and we can agree on a time for me to come back and do that, then fix a regular schedule.'

I was sitting with my feet up, MacBook on my knees as I ran through Georgie's accounts, when the sound of the noisy hedge trimmer starting up made me jump, breaking the usual tranquillity of my countryside home. I pushed my lap tray to the side and went to look out of the lounge window.

'Holy hotness, bush trimmer,' I murmured. He'd stripped off his top and was hard at work, bare-chested. I quickly tapped out a message to Georgie.

Get yourself over here ASAP. Take the field footpath and come in the back way, through the lounge patio doors x

What's up? I'm just finishing off Portia the poodle's blow-dry! she replied.

Well, if doing that is more interesting than a half-naked man in my front garden, one who could audition for The Chippendales, then I guess I'll just have to enjoy the view all on my own!

'What do you think, Chubbers?' I asked, as I shoved my phone back in my pocket and went to give him a head scratch after he snorted himself awake. I got the usual blank, uninterested expression I always got, unless food was involved. 'Fat lot of use you are,' I huffed, then moved back to the window to enjoy the view. Phew, this was one vista I could get used to. I began to curse myself for not making more of an effort when I hastily dressed in a pair of leggings and a loose-fit t-shirt this morning, desperate to get rid of my childish pyjamas.

'Ok, ok, I made it, and Portia's not happy to be abandoned and put in a cage mid-pamper,' came Georgie's voice, panting hard behind me as she burst through the open doors. 'Please tell me I didn't just race around here for David Jones with his shirt off?'

'Oh, I think you'll find it worth the journey,' I confirmed without breaking my gaze to turn and look at her.

'Oh, hello!' she uttered as she came to stand next to me. 'It's like we're in the middle of a Diet Coke commercial. Who's *that*??!!'

'My new gardener, Heath. And he's been flirting with me.'

'Please tell me you flirted back, because if you didn't, I could be tempted.'

'Sort of, but you know my flirting skills are pretty non-existent.'

'Is he single?' she asked, hip-bumping me over so she could get a better view.

'Hey, my view and my gardener,' I protested as I jostled her back over.

'You invited me, so don't be a mean hostess,' she countered, giving me a shove.

'Oi!' I cried as she braced herself at my window, palms planted firmly on the windowsill, legs straight and strong. I grabbed her from behind and started tickling her ribs, where I knew she was sensitive.

'You've had him all morning,' she shrieked as we tussled for pole position. 'Give me a minute to enjoy it. Oh no, he's looking over at us staring at him,' she giggled, dropping like a stone to hide under the window and dragging me down with her.

'Way to embarrass me,' I moaned as I crouched down next to her, both of us palming the wall.

'So what's the deal? Is he single? Are you going to forget about this whole Miller thing and go on a date with this hottie?'

'I haven't asked him. It's not exactly the sort of question you can ease into casual conversation with someone you just met.'

'Not the sort of question the old Abbie would ask. But after our discussion last night, where you were going to forget all about the delectable Mr. Davis and find someone closer to home, the new Abbie should be getting right in there.'

'You don't go from shy girl to shameless flirt overnight, Georgie Basset. It takes time.'

'It's not like I'm suggesting you turn into the village slut, particularly as that position's already taken by Rowena the barmaid, but what's the harm in asking if he's seeing anyone, seeing if he fancies a drink one night?' she asked.

'Well, David told me he is, but what if he's some kind of gardening lothario, with a woman at every job? I don't want to look desperate. I mean, he must get women throwing themselves at him.'

'I can see why,' Georgie nodded. 'How are my accounts looking? Can I afford a gardener?'

'Hey, I saw him first, go get your own,' I scowled, reaching up to grip the windowsill with my fingers and slowly pulling myself up to peek over the sill to see what he was doing. Georgie popped up beside me.

'Where did he go?' she pouted, as we craned our heads left and right, only to find he was nowhere to be seen. 'Me want more.'

'Maybe he needed a bigger tool,' I suggested, waggling my eyebrows at her. 'I did have a big bush.'

'I reckon he's already got an exceptionally big tool,' Georgie giggled, bumping my shoulder. 'He looks the type.' We both froze as we heard a polite cough from behind us.

'Please tell me he hasn't come around the back and has been standing there, watching us watching him, and is now listening to us talking about him,' I whispered, too embarrassed to stand up and turn around.

'You look,' Georgie whispered back.

'No, you look,' I pleaded, wanting the earth to swallow me whole.

'What happened to "I saw him first, go get your own?"' she protested under her breath.

'Are you both ok?' came Heath's voice from behind us.

'Damn,' I muttered, screwing up my face as Georgie broke into a fit of the giggles next to me and dropped her forehead to the windowsill. 'Ermmm, yes, just doing a … woodworm check. You know old cottages, all kinds of problems.'

'Woodworm check?'

'Yep, that's right,' I called as I dragged myself up and dusted off my knees. 'Happy to report I couldn't see any wriggly worms anywhere. No, sir. Not a single worm in sight. How about you, Georgie?'

'No, pleased to report no worms here,' she confirmed, rising up to join me. 'I pronounce this window woodworm free.'

'You both know that woodworms are actually beetles, right? The maggots only live in the wood before they transform, so if you had woodworm, you'd only see the beetles crawling around on the windowsill.'

'Ermmm, no, didn't actually know that. Very helpful tip though, thank you, Heath,' I nodded, plucking up the courage to turn and face him to find him standing with his hands on his hips, a knowing smile on his face. Damn, he definitely knew we'd been checking him out.

And why wouldn't we? I was finding it hard to keep my eyes on his and not wandering down that chest and six-pack he was sporting. 'Can I help you with something?' I asked, trying to erase the excited squeak from my voice.

'Like his big tool,' Georgie muttered quietly as she turned around to stand next to me.

'I wanted you to come and look at the hedge, to see if you wanted me to take it back any further. But it err ... looks like you already got a good look, as you were ... woodworm hunting.'

'An excellent look,' I nodded vigorously. 'I mean, an excellent trim, it looks gorgeous, I mean fine. Fine, the hedge looks fine.'

'Great,' he grinned. 'I'll go and shape it, then I'm done and we can discuss a date.'

'A date?' I squeaked, as Georgie elbowed my side.

'To come back and do your back garden and the painting,' he reminded me.

'Oh right, sure,' I replied, feeling mildly disappointed. 'Can I get you another coffee?'

'I'd love one please. I'll leave you and your friend to your ... err, woodworm hunt.'

'Great, thanks,' I nodded, feeling my cheeks flame.

'Nice to meet you,' Georgie called. He did that cute lopsided grin and winked before striding off, my shoulders slumping immediately.

'Oh God, could that have gone any worse?'

'On the plus side, you didn't end up wet like you did with Miller,' Georgie reminded me as we headed to the kitchen and I flicked on the kettle. 'So, he seems nice, good looking, hot body. Are you going to ask him out?'

'If you can find the balls and courage that I seem to have misplaced lately, sure. Are you having a coffee?'

'I'd love to, I'd love nothing better than to be here to see how you handle this, but I really have to get back. Portia's mum will be coming to pick her up in a while and I haven't finished styling her.'

'Go, go, then,' I retorted, shooing her towards the open French doors in the kitchen. 'Abandon your best friend in her time of need, in favour of a poodle named Portia. I know where I stand now.'

'You know I'd stay if I could,' she replied, giving me a peck on the cheek. 'I'll pop over as soon as I'm done, see how it went. Don't back out, Abbie, I like him. And if he is single, he won't stay that way for long, not looking like that.'

I rolled my eyes, then gave her a parting kiss and watched her hurry out and down the back garden towards the gate to the field behind. I let out a sigh, then made the coffees and went to stand by the stable door, which he'd fixed in a matter of minutes by shaving off some of the

45

wood down the sides. I just needed to buy some matching paint to touch it up and it would be as good as new.

'Coffee,' I yelled, not wanting to get near him while he was wielding a chainsaw-looking device. He turned it off and ambled over, stripping off the thick gloves he was wearing. I had to admit I'd always been a Naval Officer fantasy sort of girl, but this rough and ready lumberjack-style look was really doing it for me. Then again, after eighteen months of being single, pretty much anything did it for me. He took his cup from me with a smile, and I leaned on the lower stable door as we both sipped in silence. Embarrassed as I was, it seemed rude to walk away to leave him to drink on his own.

'What exactly is that?' he eventually said, flicking his head to Mr. Sumo's walker. He burst out laughing when I told him. 'Seriously? He doesn't walk? You pull him along on that?'

'Seriously,' I nodded.

'Does he fit on it?'

'Barely. He's a bit overweight and those extra bits I tried to fix on to accommodate him are starting to come loose.'

'I could build you a new one if you like,' he offered.

'I should say yes, but ...' I blew out a deep breath. 'I can't bear to part with it. My dad made it for me and he ... he passed away and ...' I shook my head and sucked my lips into my mouth, feeling emotional at the reminder.

'It has memories for you,' he suggested in a soft tone. I nodded. 'How about I create a larger seating area, a tray of sorts, and we attach that to the existing skateboard instead of these two bits of wood that you've tacked onto the sides. The rest looks pretty sound. I can even put some sides on it to make sure he doesn't fall out, and hinge one to make it easy for him to walk in and out. It could be a sort of ramp that you could then lift up and secure shut.'

'You can do that?'

'I'm good with wood,' he smiled, almost making me choke again at the reminder of mine and Georgie's conversation about his tool.

'Ok, as long as the skateboard stays, and he can still see over the sides, let's do it,' I nodded.

'I'll finish the hedge, then measure it up, and then I'd better get going. I've got another job this afternoon.'

I took his cup off him and headed back to the kitchen to wash it up, trying not to look at him as he started up his trimmer again. I went to carry on with Georgie's accounts in the lounge, where Sumo was snoring loudly. What a life. Eat, sleep, fart, get pulled around on a trolley, and be subjected to a bi-monthly doggie spa experience. He had no idea how easy he had things.

I handed over Heath's cash when he came to tell me he was done, his tight khaki top back in place, but not erasing my memories of what I knew lay under it. Could I really do this, ask a guy on a date? I'd never done it before and my stomach was churning at the thought of it. But what if I didn't? Would I kick myself for a missed opportunity, just like I'd been doing for the last two weeks with Miller?

'I'll see you in few weeks then, Abbie,' Heath smiled.

'Are you seeing anyone?' I blurted out before I had a chance to talk myself out of it. He looked surprised and blinked a few times.

'No, actually I'm not.'

'Oh, ok,' I nodded. I bit my lower lip as he gave me a puzzled look. Was I supposed to do more? Did I need to make it clearer? 'My friend Georgie thinks you're really cute, that's all, and I wondered if you were available.' *Way to go, total cop out, Abbie Carter*, I scolded myself. And now he was going to say, "Actually, I really fancy her. Can I have her number?"

'Oh, right. Well, as it happens, I just got out of a ten-year relationship with a girl I'd been with since college, so I really wasn't looking to rush back into dating quite yet.'

'I'm really sorry to hear that, but I'll let her know,' I nodded, feeling a touch relieved. 'See you in a few weeks.'

'Sure,' he smiled. He turned around and started walking up my path, then hesitated and turned back. 'Abbie?'

'Yes,' I answered.

'I was kind of hoping it might be you that was interested, you know, for when I am ready to get out there again.'

'Oh.' My eyebrows raised in surprise. What were the odds? Two guys that I found attractive in two weeks, and they both preferred me to Georgie. This was unheard of. *Tell him, Abbie.* 'Well, when you feel like it's the right time, if you come to ask me if I want to go on a date, and I'm still single too, I …' I hesitated, feeling shy again all of a sudden. I was used to men doing this, taking charge and asking me out.

'Would you say yes?' he asked, a hopeful look on his face. *Damn it, Abbie, you're twenty-eight years old, not twelve.*

'I'd say yes,' I confirmed, feeling a familiar blush spreading across my cheeks. He broke into a wide grin.

'Then I'd better hope you're still single by the time I sort myself out. See you in a few weeks.'

'See you,' I waved. I shut the top door and flopped back against it, feeling a little giddy. Wow, I was on fire this month.

Chapter Four
Dress Ten
December

'GREAT, TODAY OF ALL days you want to go for a walk, when there's a few inches of snow on the ground. Uh-uh,' I advised him with a waving finger as he stood by the front door. His little curled and stumpy tail hadn't mastered the art of the wag, so instead he shimmied his whole butt in time to his wheezy panting.

I'd just come down, dressed in my black skinny jeans and warm, fleecy black Ugg boots. I was also wrapped up in a grey V-neck jumper over a loose white shirt, a grey felt cloche hat, and grey wool fingerless gloves. Sumo whined at me, giving me his best pleading face, but I didn't have time. Today I was putting on bridesmaid dress ten for Julia, and the taxi was due any minute. Georgie had been invited as my plus-one, but couldn't make it. And as much as the flirting and banter was going well with Heath, he still didn't seem anywhere near over his ex. He talked about her a lot in casual conversation whenever he came to do his bi-monthly gardening work, which had made me wary. No one wanted to go out with someone who was still in love with someone else. Even I wasn't that stupid. So I was going to this wedding on my own.

'I'm sorry, Mr. Su,' I advised, crouching down to rub his head, 'but there's no way I'm having Daphne take you out in this either. She's in her eighties. She could slip and break a hip, and you'd both freeze to death out there. She'll be over in a while to give you some dinner, and I'll be back later tonight, ok? Be a good boy for me.' I grasped his head and tried to give him a quick peck between the ears, but as usual, he wriggled out of my grasp and strutted off in a sulk back to his armchair. I grabbed my bag as I heard the taxi hoot outside and managed to make it up the path without slipping over. 'Hi, Andy.'

'Afternoon, Abbie. Severn Manor, right?'

'You got it,' I confirmed. Julia was having a late afternoon wedding, followed by an evening reception there too, thankfully indoors. It was seriously cold and the snow was falling thick and fast. It would make for a magical wedding. Great for pictures, but not so great for standing around in a strapless bustier bridesmaid dress. And I knew they were wanting outdoor night-time pictures.

'I know I'm supposed to be picking you up at midnight, Abbie, and it's only just up the road, but if this snow keeps falling the way it is, it might be too dangerous for me to come out,' Andy advised as he drove steadily up the lane, skidding slightly as he turned the corner to head up to the main road. 'I'll give you a call if I think I'm going to have to cancel. I've got no other bookings, so I could come and get you early. Otherwise, you'll have to try and find another way back or stay over.'

'Thanks, Andy,' I nodded. That seemed a sensible solution. I wouldn't want to be driving in this. We were hardly suffering from Russian tundra-like conditions, but us British just weren't equipped to handle anything more than a couple of inches. Of snow, anyway.

Even with a more cautious drive, it didn't take long to get there. I only lived two miles away, and the trek was along a winding country lane that veered off the main road that I lived just off of. It was already getting dark, and all of the lights in the manor were on, including the ones under the huge cedar tree out on the front lawn and the twinkling outdoor Christmas tree. It really was a beautiful location. Dad had always said how he wanted to see me have my reception here. Like that was ever going to happen. I paid Andy, including a generous tip for driving me in this weather, then scurried into the warmth of the welcoming reception hall, complete with roaring log fire and decked out in sumptuous gold, green, red, and white Christmas decorations. The scent of the mulled wine and minced pies being prepared wafted through, making my tummy rumble. I was soon shown up to the huge, specially designed bridal party suite, where Julia and her team of twelve bridesmaids, matron of honour, and flower girl were being dressed, preened, and pampered by hair and make-up stylists.

The air was a buzz of excitement, girlish laughter, and chatter as I was shown to a changing room to slip into my dress, which for once I loved. It was a gorgeous scarlet red shade, with a fitted bustier, tight to the waist then flared out to the knee, and was teamed with a pair of black high heels. Julia's dress, in traditional white, had a red tartan bow, in homage to her Scottish soon-to-be husband, who I sincerely hoped didn't come to speak to me tonight. His accent was so thick, I could never understand what he was saying and frequently just smiled, nodded, and laughed. He could be telling me, "Och aye, my gran's got a bad case of syphilis, lass, she's a bit of an OAP bike around the town, and I dunnie know what to do about it," and I'd just laugh and smile with a nodding dog head.

'So, Abbie, dish the dirt,' Fi-Fi squeaked, as I took one of the vacated seats next to her at the make-up and hair section of the suite, ready to be styled next.

'What dirt?' I asked, sipping on a glass of prosecco that had been handed to me.

'You and Miller Davis at Rachel's wedding. I heard you got wet and steamy in his bedroom, but you obviously disappointed him as he fled back to America.'

49

'Then you heard wrong,' I retorted, feeling my hackles going up. She had always been a bitchy gossip at school. 'We had separate showers after getting soaked by the sprinklers. While he took his, I came to the bar, and he left at some point on an urgent business matter.'

'Oh,' she replied, looking a combination of disappointed that her gossip radar had failed her and relieved that nothing had happened. 'So there's nothing going on with you both?'

'No,' I huffed, shooting the hair stylist a smile as she moved into place behind me and started to brush.

'Excellent. I might take a run at him myself later.'

'Not married to Dave anymore, Fi-Fi?'

'Oh yes, but he's not here tonight, and what he doesn't know won't hurt him,' she giggled. Crikey, her voice was irritating, even more than at school. Hang on a second, was she implying what I thought she was implying?

'Miller's here? He's attending the wedding?' I felt my heart start to race at the thought of seeing him again.

'Oh, yes. Julia and Jock are good friends with Rachel, Dean, and Miller. Well, wish me luck with him.' She beamed as she stood up and trotted off with her empty glass in hand, looking for a refill of prosecco. I was not going to wish her luck with him. I didn't want to wish anyone luck with him. I wondered what he'd been up to since I last saw him. Had the fact I'd not rung him even bothered him? Probably not. Not when he had women throwing themselves at him. Even with her annoying voice, Fi-Fi was a blonde bombshell. What red-blooded man would say no when it was offered on a plate?

'Can you do my eyes as dark as you can get away with, that sort of sexy smoky-eyed look?' I asked the girl.

'Single, huh?' she replied with a smile.

'How did you guess?'

'All the single ones have been asking for a sexy look today and all I've heard about is the gorgeous Miller Davis. I kind of wish I was coming to this wedding myself. Is he all that?'

'All that and more,' I nodded firmly.

I was a bag of nerves as I stood at the entrance to the indoor ceremony suite. The wedding itself was going to be very small and intimate, immediate family and close friends only, with the exception of the ridiculously sized bridesmaid and usher party.

I started my walk, clutching my red and white roses in front of me, refusing to allow my eyes to scan the guests for a sight of him. I was not letting myself down at this wedding. I made it to the top in one piece and took my position, trying to focus my gaze on the ornate wall lights, but curiosity got the better of me and my eyes started to wander.

I soon found him, and my breath hitched to see his handsome face again, my heart rate picking up speed as I found those gorgeous tempered-chocolate eyes staring at me. I smiled, but he frowned and looked away, focussing on the soon-to-be happy couple. Ok, not exactly the reaction I'd been hoping for, but seeing as how I didn't call him, or return his shirt, boxers, or belt, I could hardly complain. I'd slept in his shirt a few times, liking to imagine he'd worn it at some stage and wishing I could smell his tantalising cinnamon aroma on it.

There were polite claps as the bride and groom kissed, then we all filtered out and were served mince pies and mulled wine, with soft Christmas music in the background. It was so romantic and magical. I stopped and chatted to people, wishing I had Georgie with me for some company, but she'd gone away on a spa break for her mum's early Christmas present. Every time I plucked up the courage to inch nearer to Miller, it seemed like he moved further away.

The wedding feast was lobster tails in truffle oil, followed by a traditional roast turkey dinner, rounded off with Christmas pudding and brandy butter. I'd barely been able to eat, though, pushing my food around my plate with my fork as I tried to catch Miller's gaze at the table opposite. It seemed like he was deliberately avoiding looking at me, or if our eyes met, he quickly looked away.

When we were moved to another room so they could set up for the much larger evening reception, I slipped away to the powder room, wondering if it would be rude to sneak away early after the first dance. It was miserable being at a wedding on your own. Especially when someone you'd only just been reminded how much you liked was there too and ignoring you. I hitched up my skirt and sat on the toilet, too many glasses of prosecco tinkling out at speed. I could be sitting at home in a fleecy onesie in front of a log fire right now, watching *Love Actually* with a box of chocolates in my lap, a bottle of wine at my side, and a box of tissues. It was a Christmas tradition, and it always made me cry. Sumo would be snoring and farting in his chair as usual. I suddenly felt lonely and homesick. Was that normal when you'd only been gone a few hours?

I made an effort and had a few dances, feeling like Miller's eyes were on me the whole time. But whenever I took a sneaky a look at him, I found him looking elsewhere. Checking my watch, I was surprised to find it was already ten o'clock. I pulled my phone out of my black satin clutch and groaned to see I'd been so busy dancing, or Miller watching, that I'd totally missed a call from Andy. He'd texted me about two hours after dropping me off to say that the snow was too bad to come out now. Damn it! I hurried out to reception and asked if they could try some taxi firms for me, but was told that due to the festive season and the weather, they were having trouble booking any, especially to come out this far into the country. I looked out at the white blanket covering the ground as I considered my options.

Half an hour later, I was back in my own clothes, standing at reception and giving them my carefully folded dress and shoes, which they'd agreed to look after for me. They'd also been kind enough to lend me a torch. I took a deep breath and headed out of the front door, ready to start my slightly drunken trek home.

'Where the hell are you going?' came an annoyed American voice. Miller! I turned around to face him, and my heart skipped a beat as he held my gaze this time. My God, he was just stunning.

'Ermmm, hello, Miller. So nice to see you again. How have you been?' I replied, with a little more sarcasm than I'd intended.

'Well, you'd know if you'd called me. And don't try to tell me you didn't get my letter. I called the hotel when I didn't hear from you and tracked down the barman who gave it to you, then threw it out at your request. After you read it!' he shot back.

'So that's why you've avoided me all night? You're mad I didn't call you?'

'Well … yeah!' he scoffed, folding his arms across his chest and looking at me like I was stupid.

'What was the point of me calling you? You live there, I live here, and from what I've heard, you're not looking for a relationship, and I'm not looking for a one-night stand. We had a fun afternoon, but there was no point trying to make it into something it wasn't.'

'Who said I was looking for a one-night stand?'

'I've heard your reputation. I'm not the sort of girl who goes for that.'

'Well, you heard wrong, because I'm not into one-night stands either. I just haven't met a girl I want to settle down with yet, so I date a lot. Maybe, just maybe, you're exactly the kind of girl I'd like to get serious with, but you didn't even give me a God damn chance, did you?' He glowered at me, all six-foot-odd prime muscular male, simmering with tension. My God, suddenly I was feeling super hot out here on the doorstep in the freezing cold.

'Why me? What's so special about me?' I asked hesitantly.

'I don't know, Abbie,' he admitted with a shrug, relaxing his posture a little. 'All I'm asking for is the chance to find out. I'd just like to get to know you better, spend some time with you. I thought we had a connection that day, then you blew me off.'

'Maybe your ego is wounded that I didn't call, as I can't imagine you having to chase many women. Maybe that's the only reason you're interested, you see me as a challenge.' I half-believed my comeback. I mean sure, I was hard on myself. I was attractive enough, but I wasn't a stunning, glamorous model type, the type I could see him with. He was so far out of my league, I was getting vertigo from looking up at him.

'I liked you the moment I met you, Abbie. Was I annoyed that you didn't call me? Sure. I've never chased a woman in my life, and you have no idea how many times I went to ask Rachel for your number, then stopped myself. But when I heard you were going to be here, I decided I'd come and wait to see if you'd apologise to me. And you didn't, which annoyed me even more.'

'Well, it's not like I had a chance,' I bit back. 'You had Fi-Fi hanging on you most of the time, and every time I got near you, you moved away.'

'First of all, I never encouraged her, and secondly, I was supposed to make it easy for you? Like hell. And now I find you running away, to God knows where.'

'I'm not running, but I need to get home. I can't get a taxi so I'm going to walk.'

'In this weather?' he frowned, his look of annoyance turning to one of concern. 'Do you live nearby?'

'Two miles away.'

'No way,' he stated firmly, reaching out to grab my arm before hustling me back into the reception hall. 'You can stay here.'

'I can't. For one, they have no rooms and for another, I *have* to get home.'

'Well, you're not walking on your own.'

'It's two miles in the Shropshire countryside on a snowy night. It's hardly a "Scott of the Antarctic" expedition. I'm not going to be mauled by a vicious polar bear or develop frost bite,' I muttered stubbornly, sure I could smell cinnamon on him again. It made the butterflies in my tummy go crazy.

'Well, I should hope not,' he laughed.

'What's so funny?' I demanded as I pulled my arm from his grasp, annoyed with him now. He'd ignored me all night, and now he was trying to lay down the law? I had no idea what was going on with us, but the chemistry sizzling between us now was unmistakable.

'Polar bears don't live in the Antarctic, completely different side of the globe. You'd be more likely to be eaten by penguins,' he chuckled.

'Flesh-eating ones?' I asked as I softened to see his smile.

'Well no, not this time. Penguins are too cute to be made into flesh-eating creatures,' he replied. 'Look, I'm sorry, ok? You didn't call, it threw me. I came here spoiling for a fight instead of talking to you like an adult. But regardless, there's no way I'm letting you walk home.

You can stay here. I have a large suite, I can sleep on the couch if you don't want to share a bed.'

'I can't,' I replied with a shake of my head, thinking how much I would love to share a bed with him. 'I *have* to get home.'

'Do you have some children I don't know about?'

'Sort of. An elderly bulldog. My neighbours will have been to feed him this afternoon, but they were going away for a pre-Christmas break with their son straight after. I can't leave him alone until the morning.'

'Surely he won't starve overnight?' Miller questioned.

'No, he has enough fat to live on for at least a few weeks,' I giggled. 'But he'll need a poo, and you have no idea how flatulent and gassy this dog is. Sometimes when I take him out for his night-time tinkle and dinner expulsion, it's like someone making a poop smoothie without the lid on the blender, crap flies everywhere. There's no way I want to come back to a house that's been redecorated a lovely shade of brown, thank you very much!'

'He can't be that bad,' Miller laughed, his eyes sparkling with amusement.

'Trust me, I'm under-exaggerating. Besides, he's old and he loves his routines. Even though he's a cantankerous old bugger who doesn't appreciate me, I don't like the thought of him being alone all night.'

'Ok then, give me five minutes,' Miller relented.

'For what?'

'To get changed into something more appropriate to escort the damsel in distress home.'

'I can't ask you to do that, it's miles!' I gasped, stunned at the offer.

'According to you, it's an easy walk, or were you under-exaggerating that as well?' he asked, a disapproving tone in his voice.

'No, it's two miles, mainly on the flat, apart from one quite sharp uphill, but it's too far to ask you to come.'

'You didn't ask, I'm volunteering. And if it's too far for me, it's definitely too far for you, especially alone. You can either sit here and wait or come up with me, but either way, I'm walking you home, Abbie Carter. It will be a good chance for us to get to know each other a little better.'

'Why are you being so nice? I'm not going to put out, if that's what you're hoping,' I warned. He chuckled again and ran a hand through his hair.

'I already told you I'm not that kind of guy. Are you always so cynical of men?'

'Ones who are too good looking for their own good, yes,' I nodded with a smile.

'Well, even good-looking guys can be chivalrous. Maybe I'm hoping that after I've rescued you and your gassy dog, you'll accept my number this time and call me after I leave.'

'Go get changed then,' I sighed, finally relenting. He grinned, then turned and took the stairs three at a time while I openly ogled his peachy backside in his fitted suit as he went.

He was right. This was the perfect chance to get to know him better, to try and fathom why on earth he was interested in a girl like me. I'd seen Fi-Fi flirting outrageously with him for most of the night. It seemed the harder she tried, the more turned off he got. Maybe that really was his thing, he loved a challenge. Well, I was definitely that. There was a reason I was still single at twenty-eight.

'God damn it,' I screeched, laughing my head off as I lost my footing again, my legs shooting out from under me. I landed with a thud on my backside and started sliding backwards down the hill. Miller laughed, his hands on his hips, as I tipped sideways into the hedge, and it dumped a heavy load of snow on me. I was soaked. Again. This was getting to be a theme around him. My Uggs, which had kept my feet beautifully warm for a while, weren't snow protected and were starting to soak up the cold moisture, and they weren't exactly designed for climbing up a steep and icy hill. The snow on the main road had been compacted by cars earlier, making it like glass, then it had been covered with more snow, so you couldn't even see where the worst patches of ice were, and there was no pavement to try and traverse up. I spat a load of snow out of my mouth as Miller approached, hauled me up, and dusted me off. 'This hill will be the death of me, I'm never going to make it up.'

'Then hop on,' he advised, turning around and crouching down. 'My boots have more grip. I'll give you a piggyback to the top.'

'I weigh a tonne,' I protested.

'Don't be ridiculous. Come on, get on. You don't have enough layers on. You're wet now and you'll freeze soon. We're closer to your place than the hotel, right?'

'Right,' I sighed, giving in to his insane plan and climbing on board. He hooked his hands under my knees and I wrapped my arms around his neck, putting my chin on his shoulder. Maybe there were some advantages to a slippery hill. I could breathe in that cinnamon scent to my heart's content now.

He struck out, taking it slowly as we inched our way up the bank. A walk that would normally take me around three-quarters of an hour had taken us over an hour so far, as the lane, and now the road and hill, were so treacherous. We'd had time to talk though, and we'd made the most of it. In fact, we'd chatted like old friends, comfortably, like

Georgie and I did. I'd filled him in on my work and my family, or rather lack of one now, at which point he'd reached out his hand and held mine without saying anything. It had made me feel so warm in that moment, we could almost have been snuggled under my fur blankets in front of the lounge log burner. He just seemed to get how painful it was for me to tell him my past, without offering words of condolence or pitying me, but just taking my hand and being there for me. It made me more curious to know his backstory, as he hadn't mentioned a family yet, and that kind of reaction usually only came from people who'd suffered loss themselves. This last part of the journey, he'd been telling me about his love of New York.

'Damn it,' he grunted, as his foot slipped and he staggered slightly, making me scream, before he righted himself. 'There is *no way* we're ending up at the bottom of this hill again,' he said in a determined voice. 'I feel like I'm in some badly designed adventure game, where there's actually no way up and we're just going to keep repeating this over and over.'

'Don't say that. I'm getting cold, hungry, and thirsty, and it will be poo city if we don't make it back soon,' I warned. He burst out laughing, then yelled, coinciding with my scream, as he completely lost his footing and fell flat on his face, me going down with him and landing on him with an "Oomph."

Seconds later he was sliding, me lying on top of him, as we did a backwards human toboggan down the hill, picking up speed rapidly as I shrieked. We ended up in a tangled heap in a pile of snow where the main road forked off to the lane back up to Severn Manor. We were both panting, trying to catch our breath from the shock.

'Are you ok?' he huffed.

'I ... I think so,' I uttered, gently moving all my limbs and checking for pain. I winced as I straightened my legs. My knees had taken quite a bashing. 'You?'

'I think my face is bleeding, but other than bruised knees and scuffed hands, I think so,' he confirmed. He managed to extract himself from under me, then quickly rolled onto his side and reached out to clasp my chin, turning my face to his as he checked it for damage. He really was quite the gentleman.

'Oh God, your chin, you have a really nasty cut.' I sat up, groaning as my muscles uttered a protest, and put my cold wet hands in my pocket to find a tissue. 'Here, stay still while I dab it. We need to get back so I can clean and patch you up, but I can't see us making it up this damn hill.'

'Me neither,' he responded, wincing as I tended to his cut. His lips were so close, I could lean in and kiss him right now. Our wispy white breaths were mingling, swirling as we both breathed heavily, inches apart. 'Come on, we really will freeze out here if we don't get dry and warm soon.' He stood up abruptly and hauled me to my feet.

'How? This hill is going to kill us,' I reminded him.

'This way,' he pointed, ushering me towards a stile into the field that ran alongside the road. 'The snow here will be powdery, easier to walk on. We can follow the hedge and re-join the road when we level out.'

'As long as there's no flesh-eating sheep or cows,' I joked as he helped me over the wooden structure.

'True,' he grinned, then winced at the reminder of his chin injury.

He joined me and automatically took my hand as we made our way, much more easily, up the hill. My knees really weren't happy though, and throbbed as we climbed. We didn't speak this time, both still slightly winded from the fall and concentrating on our ascent. But it was a comfortable silence. The lights were still on in The Cock & Bull on the opposite side of the road at the top of the hill, the sound of the locals enjoying themselves drifting out to meet us. We stayed in the field until we reached the village hall, and used another stile to cross over into the car park.

'Not far now,' I reassured him.

'Great,' he nodded.

I pointed out the local royalty's manor and the deer park as we turned right at the stone cross on the village green to take Church Lane. We carried on past the farmworkers' terraced houses on the right, the church up ahead as we turned right onto my lane. Apart from the church, there were only four detached cottages along here. First was Holly Cottage, which was mine. Honeysuckle Cottage, which was the Joneses, was next door, then Georgie lived in Ivy Cottage, and Jasmine Cottage was at the far end. That one was for sale, the current owners having decided to emigrate to Australia. I smiled as I saw the outside light on my front porch burning brightly. I didn't think I'd ever been so happy to return home.

'This is me,' I confirmed, swinging open the gate.

'Cute place. It looks really old,' Miller said, his eyes scanning it with interest.

'It is. I'll give you the tour in the morning,' I said bravely.

'Morning?' he queried, his voice full of surprise. I let go of his hand to lift up the plant pot on the left of the door to retrieve my front door key.

'Like I'd let you walk back on your own, when you're cold, wet, and bleeding. You can sleep in the spare room, ok?'

'Ok,' he grinned. 'But we seriously need to have words about security if that's where you leave your keys.'

'I'm in the country, in a sleepy village, not the centre of New York. It's safe out here.' I opened the door to find Sumo waiting in the hall, his stubby little legs firmly rooted on the oak floor as he eyed up the new arrival.

'I'd better warn you that Mr. Sumo can be quite cantankerous with people he doesn't kno–' I gasped, unable to believe my eyes or ears, when he barked and scuttled forwards, then put his paws up on Miller's legs, snuffling and licking his hand as his bottom wagged.

'Is this the same dog you told me about?' Miller laughed, as Sumo slobbered all over him.

'Apparently not,' I uttered, completely bewildered. 'He's never been like that with anyone since my dad.'

'Then he obviously has good taste. Are you hungry?'

'Starving,' I confirmed as I shut and locked the door.

'I was actually talking to the dog.'

'Charming,' I replied, heading into the kitchen as I stripped off my wet gloves and hat, then shivered. 'Why don't you head upstairs and take a hot shower and clean your face before you get an infection. There's clean towels on the rail.'

'What about you, you're cold too.'

'I'll just feed Sumo, then I'll go up and change. I still have your shirt and boxers here, I'll put them on the spare bed, door on the left as you come out of the bathroom. I'll try and find some jogging bottoms for you, but they may be a short, snug fit,' I warned.

'Thanks, Abbie,' he nodded, rubbing his hands together to try to get them warm.

'I'll turn up the heating and when we come down, I can make us something to eat, as we missed the buffet.'

He flashed me a smile, then gave a way-too-excited Sumo a pat on the head and made his way upstairs.

'You traitor!' I glared at my dog as he finally headed through to get his dinner. 'Why don't I ever get that welcome?' He just yawned at me, then licked his lips. I warmed my hands up under the hot tap first, then put his dinner down and left him to trough it while I ran upstairs.

I quickly stripped out of my damp clothes and riffled through my wardrobe. What the hell was I supposed to wear? No matter how much my body might be screaming at me to wear something sexy, I didn't want to give the wrong impression. Equally my Hello Kitty pyjamas weren't going to give the right impression either. I settled on a pair of tight black jeggings and a fluffy, cosy, baggy cream jumper, with a pair of toasty cream eyelash socks. I dug out Miller's clean shirt and boxers, then a pair of my baggiest black jogging bottoms. I only had size five feet, there was no way my socks were going to fit him. Not that I'd really paid much attention to his feet, but most men weren't a size eight, let alone a five. I headed out of my room to cross the landing just as Miller appeared from the bathroom, with nothing but one of my white towels wrapped around his waist.

'Hey,' I squeaked. My God, his body looked even better with a sheen of water still clinging to it.

'Hey,' he grinned, the look in his eyes telling me he knew that I was checking him out and liking what I saw.

'Here.' I shoved the clothes into his arms and shot down the stairs before my hands had a chance to reach out and do something totally inappropriate. 'Sumo, poop time,' I called.

For once, he came obligingly, looking a little disappointed to find it was only me and not Miller. I undid the dog flap and pushed him out, then flicked on the kettle. Going for a poo was the most exercise he had, though he never ventured far. I usually went out with him and scooped up the mess, as best I could when he was extra gassy, but I was too cold to accompany him tonight. Especially not when he sometimes liked to take his time, pulling a face as he strained for ten minutes before it all shot out like a cork from a bottle of champagne.

Tonight he was super fast and scurried in panting, then went to sit in the hall. I angled my head to give him a curious look. He was wagging his butt, his eyes focussed on the turn of the stairs. He was waiting for Miller to come down. *What the hell?* Seven years of love and I'd never once got that reaction from him. Miserable mutt.

I decided bacon and egg sandwiches would be quick and hot and should hit the mark, so I busied myself making them.

'He's a friendly little guy,' came Miller's voice as he padded into the kitchen, his legs bare, wearing just his black shirt. I swallowed hard as I ran my eyes up and down his firm thighs. He had the build of a rugby player. 'Sorry, I tried your pants, but they were too tight.'

'My pants? You found a pair of my pants and tried them on?' I gasped. Crap. Had I left a pair lying around in the bathroom? Oh no! Had he rummaged in the laundry bin for a used pair? I was mortified. Why the hell would he need a pair of my pants when I'd given him his own? I knew he was too good to be true. He was a damn cross-dresser.

'No, you gave them to me.'

'I did not! Like I'd just hand out a pair of my smalls to some … some … virtual stranger, even if he did act chivalrously the once, ok twice, actually three times,' I shot back, trying to remember which knickers I'd been wearing yesterday that would have been on the top of the laundry pile. 'Oh God, the big pink granny ones?' I groaned. I'd been in my comfy knickers. Not that I possessed many sexy lacy ones, but these were the extra big, extra comfy ones for lounging around at home in. They encased everything.

'No, the small black ones you handed to me outside the bathroom. Do you have color blindness?'

'No. Are you telling me you're not wearing the ones I gave you?' I asked, my eyes flicking down to see if I could spot anything hanging out. Sadly not.

'Well, you can see I'm not. Good thing too because I'm bleeding. I'd have ruined them.'

'Are we having the same conversation here?' I asked, covering my eyes and feeling very confused. Now he was telling me he had a period? Did that mean he was a transsexual? No, hang on a second, they didn't have periods.

'Oh God,' he uttered, completely aghast. 'You thought I meant I was wearing your panties? What do you English call them, knuckers?'

'Knickers,' I whispered, still not sure what was going on. He burst out laughing, and I dropped my hands in time to see him stride over.

'No, I definitely didn't try your "knickers" on, Abbie. I meant these,' he chuckled, reaching down to rub my covered leg. 'We call them pants.'

'Oh, thank God.' I let out a sigh of relief as I finally smiled again. 'I was having a whole visual there that I really didn't want to have. But I dread to ask what's bleeding, other than your chin.'

'My knees,' he confirmed, pointing down to where they were looking red and raw. 'Scuffed them up a bit when we fell, but they're fine. You really call your panties knickers, not knuckers?'

'Ermmm, I should know. Not that knickers makes any more sense than knuckers. Damn it, the eggs,' I exclaimed as I heard them spitting in the pan. 'Sit down, we'll eat, then I'll sort out your knees and chin. Are you warm enough?'

'I am, thanks,' he replied.

'Well, after we've eaten, you can head to bed if you're tired, or I can make a fire if you want to stay up and talk, or we can watch TV or something.' I flashed him a hopeful look over my shoulder.

'I'm not tired, surprisingly wide awake actually.' He gave me one of those slow smiles, the kind that could melt a girl's heart.

'Great,' I replied, sliding the eggs onto the buttered bread then reaching for the pan of grilled crispy bacon.

I was far from tired and wasn't in any hurry to have this evening end.

'Hmmm,' I moaned, snuggling down in my warm bed as flashes of the evening in front of the fire with Miller came back to me.

We'd sat on the long sofa, feet up and tucked under each other's thighs to keep warm, as we'd talked about differences in our language. We'd laughed more often than not while we drank a few glasses of whisky to warm us up from the inside. I'd still been shivering, not seeming to be able to get warm despite the central heating being on and the fire roaring. So Miller had made me turn around and settle back between his outstretched legs, my back to his chest. He'd pulled my cream fleecy blanket over us, then wrapped his arms around my waist as we'd continued to talk. Injuries aside, it had been the perfect night. Even Sumo had displayed uncharacteristic happiness, venturing off his armchair to lie on his back on the floor next to us, whining now and then for a belly rub from Miller.

I smiled to myself. Was it normal to like a guy so fast? I mean *really* like. He just seemed to accept me as I was. I didn't feel like I had to try and make myself better for him to be interested in me. And he really seemed to be. Each minute I spent with him, the less I worried that he was only satisfying curiosity over someone who wasn't his usual type. But there was still that thing, the "he hadn't found the kind of girl he wanted to get serious with." For most guys, that was usually an admission that they really weren't into relationships. So why would he change for me? And if he did, how the hell would it work with him so far away?

I heard a load of snuffling, then a grunt, and frowned. That sounded like Sumo. How had he got into my bedroom? He struggled with the doorsteps to the garden to do his business, and he'd definitely never made it upstairs. And thinking about it more, why did my pillow feel so firm, and why didn't I remember going up to bed?

I opened my eyes, surprised to see the patterned cream material of my squashy sofa instead of my high, vaulted ceiling in my bedroom. I soon realised I was in the lounge, curled up against Miller, my head on his firm chest. I held my breath, not wanting to wake him, as I desperately tried to remember what had happened before I must have fallen asleep on him last night.

'Oh my God,' Miller groaned loudly. 'Please tell me that isn't you?'

'What?' I gasped, taking a huge gulp of air when I realised he was awake, only to choke on a Sumo morning special. I buried my face in Miller's chest, giggling as he started to gag.

'It's the dog, right? Tell me it's the dog, or it will ruin this whole "Abbie's really cute" thing I have going on.'

'Well, it's *not* me, thank you very much,' I mumbled, homing in on him thinking I was cute and feeling my stomach flutter deliciously. 'Close your eyes, it'll melt them. His morning trumps are always the worst.'

'Trust me, I'm closing … everything.' He gagged again and quickly pulled the blanket over our heads. 'Is that normal for him?' he eventually asked when he'd finished choking.

'Pretty much. I did warn you he was gassy.'

'That's not gassy, that's nuclear. You need an exclusion perimeter set up around him.'

'Bet you wish you'd stayed in your expensive hotel suite right now, don't you?' I asked, angling my face up to meet his gaze. He shook his head and reached up to hold my chin, sweeping his thumb over my lower lip, which made a shiver run down my spine, that giddy feeling I'd felt when I first set eyes on him returning full force.

'I'm right where I want to be, Abbie, and I'm not waiting any longer.'

'For what?' I whispered, drowning in his deep, rich brown eyes, which were holding me captive, the tension between us rising with each passing second as our chests rose and fell in unison.

'For this,' he murmured, dipping his head and brushing his lips across mine. I closed my eyes, the butterflies in my stomach soaring, fluttering madly. He repeated the move more firmly, sparks of high voltage stimulating my lips. The next time he kissed me properly, I returned it, making him groan and tighten his arm around me, his other hand firmly gripping my chin to stop me from going anywhere. I was ready to swoon. No one had ever kissed me like this, so full of determination and passion, or coaxed such an incredible response from me. He kissed like a man, a proper alpha-male *man*. I snuck a hand down to grip his firm bottom, right as Sumo scared himself with a gurgling rumbling trump, which made us break our lip lock and laugh.

'Sorry,' I said quietly, holding his gaze. 'But it will get worse if I don't let him out for his morning business.'

'I'm not going anywhere. I want to keep kissing you, but we need to talk.'

'About what?'

'About how we're going to do this.'

'Keep kissing? Well, I think you just put your lips on mine again. Feel free to practice, over and over, until you get it right.'

'You think you're funny, huh?' he laughed, planting another kiss on my lips, making me melt in his arms. 'I mean us.'

'There's an us?' My voice was barely a whisper. The thought of it excited and terrified me at the same time.

'There is,' he stated firmly. 'I can't explain it, Abbie. The moment I saw you, it was like I was looking at a missing part of myself. Like I've been alone all of my life, and suddenly I wasn't anymore. I've thought about you every day since we met. I don't know how we're going to do this, with me in New York and you here, wherever the hell we are because I have no idea. I just know that I've got to try. The question is whether you're willing to?'

I swallowed hard as I considered his question. I didn't want a long-distance relationship. I was twenty-eight years old, I wanted someone to share my life with. But equally, I'd spent the last few months kicking myself for letting him go the last time. Even a very nice flirtation with Heath hadn't erased Miller from my thoughts. He was embedded deep. Sumo whined, then somehow scrambled up onto the sofa and nudged his way under the blanket to nestle between us. He stuck out his long tongue, trying to lick Miller's face, and broke our intense moment as we both laughed. How could I refuse trying this? Even my moody dog seemed to love him. He'd never jumped on the sofa for me.

'I'm willing,' I breathed softly, as I jumped into unknown territory without a parachute. The smile that lit up his face as he bent his head to kiss me again told me that I'd made the right decision. Sadly, Miller hadn't, as when he parted his lips a fraction of a second too soon, he got a mouthful of Sumo's over-enthusiastic tongue and the French kiss to end all French kisses.

'God damn it,' he groaned, pulling back to furiously wipe his mouth as I burst into uncontrollable laughter.

Chapter Five
The Long Distance Thing
February

'HELLO,' I CALLED, AS I stuck my head around Georgie's grooming parlour door to find Sumo lying on his back, mouth ajar, tongue out, tiny tail swinging as he waggled his butt while Georgie massaged his belly. 'How was he?'

'Except for that one time, which we're never discussing again, he's always the perfect pooch in here,' she smiled, looking up.

'For everyone but me. I'm the one who puts a roof over his head, feeds him, walks him, picks up his poop. What did I do to make him hate me so much?' I asked with a heavy sigh. 'I've never been mean to him. I try and give him love and he walks off. I just don't understand where I've gone wrong with him.'

'You've done nothing wrong, and I'm sure, despite his standoffishness with you, he knows how much you love him. It's like humans, we don't all gel with everyone. Look at you and me. The first time we met, we got on so well, we just clicked. I meet loads of people doing this job and I haven't become best friends with them all. Some people are just a good fit. Maybe your dad chose Sumo as they were the perfect fit, not thinking that he was going to be your dog.'

'I guess, I just … it would be nice for him to greet me the way he does you and Miller, to try and give me a kiss from time to time.'

'With his breath?' she grimaced, patting his tummy one final time before picking him up and placing him on the floor, to much whining on his part. 'Trust me, you don't want to be anywhere near there. I've cleaned his teeth, but I think you ought to take him to the vet. All dogs' breath smells, but his is really ripe, not to mention the other end.'

'He didn't shart again, did he?' He'd farted and followed through a few sessions ago, splattering Georgie's walls, which had taken her ages to scrub down.

'No,' she giggled, finally able to see the funny side. She stuck her hands into the sink and started to scrub them. 'I can't believe I'm about to say I'm thankful it was only a fart, as this is Mr. Sumo, fart master, we're talking about. But seriously, sweetie, I'm worried there's something wrong with him.'

'What do you mean? Did you find something?' I asked, my heart sinking.

'No, I checked him really carefully for any lumps or bumps, but sometimes things like this can be internal. His wind has been a problem for years, but this … sharting, it's not normal.' She shot me a sympathetic look as she grabbed a towel to dry her hands. I looked down at Sumo, who was just staring up at me as if to say, "Come on then, take me home for my nap." 'Is he off his food?'

'Does he look like he's suffering from appetite loss?' I asked, as I pulled my phone out of the back pocket of my jeans and dialled the vet's number.

'Good point,' she agreed, eyeing my rotund little guy. I had a ball of acid in my throat as I told the receptionist that I needed him to be checked as soon as possible.

'We've had a cancellation, can you get him here in ten minutes time?' she asked.

'I can do fifteen,' I suggested, checking my watch.

'We'll see you both then, Miss Carter.'

'Thanks.' I ended the call and looked back down at Sumo, who was completely oblivious to me suddenly wanting to burst into tears.

'Give me a few minutes,' Georgie said. 'I'll try and ring to cancel Boomer's cut and blow-dry.'

'Don't be silly. This is your business, you can't cancel. I'll be fine, it's just a check-up.'

'Well, how about I come over later and see how you got on? I'll be done by six.'

'That would be great,' I nodded. 'I'd better get him back home and into the car.'

'Call me,' Georgie stated, coming to pull me into a tight hug, which I returned. 'And call Miller, he'd want to know. I think he loves that mutt as much as he loves you.'

'Steady on, we haven't said the "L" word yet. This long-distance thing means we're taking it slowly.'

'Sometimes words aren't needed, Abbie,' she said seriously as she let me go to scratch Sumo's head. 'I've seen the way you look at each other. Now go. I'll see you later.'

I was grateful for the new four-sided box that Heath had built and attached securely to the skateboard. I lowered the one side, creating a ramp for Sumo to shuffle up, then closed and latched it and started to make my way up Georgie's paved path to head back to the lane, feeling like I had lead in my shoes. He needed to be checked, but I was scared to take him in case it was bad news. We rumbled our way up the lane and turned right into my block-paved drive, then headed straight to the car. He gave me his sad face, knowing a car trip usually meant a trip to the vet, but he didn't complain when I opened the back door of my 4x4, then the dog cage door, and nearly put my back out when I heaved him up to put him inside.

We arrived at the vet soon after. It was only a few villages away and they were so nice to him whenever he came in for a check-up. Bradley gave him a full examination and questioned me extensively on his toilet and eating habits, then took him away to draw some blood. I decided to wait for the results, so I took a seat in the waiting area and checked my watch. It was still too early to call Miller in New York, but I so wanted to hear his voice right now. I closed my eyes as I tried to imagine what he'd say to me. He'd tell me to try and stay calm, as Sumo would sense if I was tense. Well, I'd done a crappy job in the car driving over here, crying every few minutes when I didn't even know if anything was wrong.

It was times like this that I found our relationship really hard. Both of us had gone in eyes wide open, knowing that we wouldn't get to see each other very often, that even a simple thing like a FaceTime call or text would be affected by the time zone difference, but we were making it work. He'd been over for a long weekend every other week, saying he had flexibility with his job and not to worry about the money as he was paid well. But it was getting harder and harder to say goodbye to him each time. Neither of us could say why we'd clicked so fast, or why we were so drawn to each other. The only similarity we had was that we were orphaned and had no siblings. He'd been given up as a baby and passed around the foster system. He hadn't managed to trace his parents yet, though he was still trying. He said he'd been drawn to me as he sensed a sadness in me that matched his own. Except it didn't. I'd had my dad for many happy years, while he'd had no one, a thought that made my heart ache for him.

'Miss Carter,' a voice interrupted, snapping me from my thoughts and making me open my eyes. 'Bradley's ready to see you now.'

The receptionist gave me the smile.

The smile that said, "I'm so sorry."

The smile that told me that whatever Bradley was about to tell me wasn't what I'd want to hear.

I threw my handbag on the floor as I walked in the door and sat on the bottom step of the stairs in a daze. And that was where Georgie found me when she burst through the front door huffing, out of breath, goodness knows how much later.

'You didn't call me. What's happened, where is he?' she demanded. I shook my head, tears filling my eyes.

'His blood tests showed abnormal enzymes, so they've kept him in to run scans and X-rays tomorrow, as they need to anaesthetise him. Oh, Georgie, it broke my heart to leave him there. He looked so sad and scared,' I sobbed, letting my tears flow freely at the reminder of the look in his eyes and the whine he made as I walked away. He'd never done that with me before, like he was pleading with me not to abandon him.

'Oh, sweetie, I'm sorry,' Georgie soothed, pulling me into her arms as she wrapped me in a much needed hug and ran her hand over my hair as she kissed my temple. 'But this is necessary. If they find something, they can treat it. It's better than not knowing.'

'I know,' I sniffed, trying to pull myself together. 'It just doesn't feel like it right now. And I want to ring Miller and I can't. He'll still be sleeping.'

'Then wake him up. You need to hear his voice and he needs to know. I'll make a coffee and put some whisky in it, then we're going to curl up on the sofa with a takeaway and a bottle of wine or two, and watch something to take your mind off it, as it's out of your hands, ok? Ok?' she repeated, forcing me to look up at her.

'Ok,' I nodded, wiping my eyes. She was right, there was nothing I could do. He was in the best place he could be right now. I shuffled through to the lounge, sighing as I looked at his empty armchair. I took a deep breath and dialled Miller's cell, but as expected, it went to voicemail, as it was only five a.m. over there.

'Hey, it's me, Abbie,' I said to his answering machine, at least grateful to hear his voice, even if it was only telling me to leave a message after the tone. I filled him in on what was happening, then told him how much I missed him and how I wished he was here.

Sunday

The alarm sounded and I went to roll over to turn it off, but found I couldn't move.

'Hey, baby,' Miller's voice whispered in my ear, as a soft kiss was planted on my neck.

'Miller?' I cried, struggling to spin in his arms, needing to see him to make sure I wasn't dreaming. I laughed and reached up to clutch his handsome face when I realised I wasn't, then kissed him repeatedly. 'What are you doing here?'

'You called. You said you missed me and wished I was here, so here I am. That's what normal boyfriends would do, isn't it?' he smiled, lifting his hand to tuck my hair behind my ear as I nodded, beyond happy to have him lying there. We were both new at this relationship thing, this being the longest for both of us, but we just gelled. We were passionate about our work, loved dogs, had the same sense of humour, music and film taste. We were content just being together or with friends, nothing flash or extravagant. 'Besides, I missed you too.'

'This is getting so hard,' I whispered, tracing the scar on his chin from our eventful trek home at Christmas, then following the line of his sexy lips with my fingers, still in awe that he was mine. He nipped one of my fingers gently, then kissed it.

'I know, I feel it too. So before I ravish you the way I've been dreaming of since I last saw you, how's our boy?'

'I won't know until this afternoon. They'll call me when they're done after lunch,' I replied. 'And speaking of, I'm so sorry, but it's the Joneses' day to come over for Sunday dinner and they were so looking forward to it. I had no idea you'd be here.'

'Would I rather have you to myself, to spend the day in bed with you?' he whispered against my lips, my body heating up in an instant. 'Sure, but I know how fond you are of them. When I come here, I fit into your life, and vice versa. That was the deal, right?'

'Right,' I sighed, as he started kissing my neck and made me forget my worries about my fur baby for a welcome moment.

'So, let me work some of this tension out of … us both, then we can cook together while we wait for the news.'

'I'm *very* tense,' I warned him with a giggle.

'Hmmm, me too,' he chuckled. 'This could take some time,' he added, as his lips found mine and he pressed me back into the mattress. God, Miller Davis was all man, and waiting for him for weeks, insisting we get to know each other first, had only made our first time all the more explosive. And so far each time since had been as well, so I had no doubt this time would be either. I switched off my mind for a while and let myself be in the moment with him. After all, they were so fleeting.

'Get off, you randy old fool,' Daphne scolded, slapping her husband's hand away as he tried to cop a feel of her arse when she came back from the cloakroom. He chuckled, then picked up her hand when she sat down and kissed it, making her bat her eyelashes as her face softened. Miller and I exchanged a smile as we watched them while we made some tea and coffee. It was so lovely to see a couple, who'd been together for the best part of sixty years, still so in love. I wished I had more free time to spend with them. They were almost surrogate parents, offering well-meaning advice, often without prompting. But with me having a job and an overseas boyfriend, life was so hectic. I saw Daphne more regularly, as she'd join Georgie and

I on some of our girls' nights in, but every other week I did a Sunday roast and invited them both over. Georgie did the same on the alternate weeks, and we took it in turn to check on them and help with the ironing or shopping.

'So, what was wrong with Heath?' David asked, still holding his wife's hand as I set them both a cup of tea on the kitchen table.

'Nothing, he's an amazing gardener and handyman. He's really tidied up the place,' I replied.

'I meant to court. You had a perfectly nice, single young man, a local too, and you had to go and pick a foreigner.' I saw Daphne roll her eyes, knowing he was about to go off on a rant, as I stood there open-mouthed. Miller leaned back against the kitchen island and folded one arm across his chest, a bemused look on his face as he took a swig of his coffee. David had always been to the point, but honestly, in front of Miller? 'And after he sorted out your bush so well. Youngsters today, isn't it,' he added with a tut.

'He did *what*?' Miller spluttered, setting down his cup of coffee.

'My holly bush, not my actual … David, honestly, can we just put the whole bush nightmare to bed?' I begged.

'What did I say?' he objected. 'He sorted it out good and proper. At least it's not attacking Fred every time he tries to stick something in your box anymore, isn't it.'

'Who the hell is Fred?' Miller demanded, getting more annoyed by the second.

'The postman, and he means my letterbox. My God, it just turns into double entendre city around him, without him even knowing,' I groaned.

'Well, I think he's a lovely guy. Didn't I say that to you, Daphne, didn't I say our Heath would be perfect for Abbie?'

'You did, dear, and I know as he's your nephew, you were extra keen to match them, but the heart wants what the heart wants, you can't force these things. You tried to set them up, it didn't work, and now she's happy with Miller. Let it go.'

'Just saying. Perfectly good man on her doorstep, don't know why she had to pick some Yank,' he muttered.

'Now, now, dear, no need to get racist. Nothing wrong with the Americans, and Miller's a very nice young man. Very easy on the eye, too,' she mouthed at me, making me giggle.

'As a matter of fact, I actually asked Heath out on a date and he turned me down, saying he wasn't over his ex. But–'

'So I was a second choice, was I?' Miller interrupted, flashing me an unimpressed scowl. Wow, jealousy was a seriously hot look on him.

'If you'd let me finish, I was about to say that I made a mistake. I realised I was only asking him out as I was annoyed at myself for not ringing you back the first time we met. For those months that followed, it was you that I was thinking about, not Heath,' I said firmly.

'So what was wrong with Heath?' pressed David, obviously not willing to let this go. 'He's a looker, keeps himself in shape, and has a lovely sense of humour. And he's really good with his hands. I told you how he sorted my plums out for me.'

'I can't believe what I'm hearing here,' Miller mumbled as he swallowed another mouthful of coffee. 'Are Brits normally so … open about their sexual practices?'

'He means his plum tree, not his … can we just move on from the whole bush, plum, Heath thing? Please?' I pleaded. 'I'm with Miller and I'm very happy to have Heath as my gardener.'

'Dear, it's time to let it go,' Daphne warned, shooting him a look when he opened his mouth to say something else that said she wasn't going to take any more nonsense from him. It was obvious who wore the trousers in that relationship.

'Just saying he's a nice boy, that's all,' David grumbled.

'Man,' corrected Daphne. 'And just because he's your nephew, he doesn't need you setting him up on dates. He needs some time to get over Rhiannon. Anyway, it's time we were getting back. You need your afternoon sleep and I'm sure Abbie and Miller don't want us oldies cramping their style all day.'

'You're welcome to stay as long as you'd like,' I offered. I felt bad for upsetting our routine, even though I wanted to spend some time alone with Miller.

'And that's why you're such a sweet girl, Abbie Carter,' she beamed, gripping the oak table as she stood up. Miller strode around to take her arm when she wobbled on her feet. 'But he's come all the way to see you, not us. You'll ring us as soon as you get any news on Mr. Sumo, won't you?'

'Yes, of course.' My heart ached at the reminder.

'I'll walk them home,' Miller offered. 'Why don't you call the vet and see if there's any update?'

We curled up on the sofa in front of the crackling fire, Miller spooning me as I reached down to pull another tissue from the box to wipe my tear-puffed eyes and honk my nose loudly. Sexy Abbie, or at least my best attempts to be her, had totally left the building. This was red-eyed, blotchy-faced, snotty-nosed, sobbing Abbie. Mr. Sumo had bowel cancer. I took in a juddery, chest-shaking gasp as I recalled the telephone conversation. It was in the early stages, but it was still cancer and there was a risk of it spreading, so they were keeping him in overnight to administer chemotherapy in the morning. Miller had driven us down in my car so that we could give Sumo some fuss and attention. Of course, I was virtually ignored, as Sumo was so excited to see his favourite man. And it had broken my heart all over again to have to drive away and leave him there.

'Sssshhhh,' soothed Miller, kissing the top of my head softly. 'You'll make yourself sick.'

'I can't help it,' I whimpered. 'I should have taken him sooner. I should have known, but in fairness, he's always been flatulent and pooey. It wasn't like there was that much of a change.'

'You couldn't know, Abbie. You heard the vet. You got him there sooner than most, thanks to Georgie suggesting he get checked over. You've done everything you can. And the chemo may work.'

'He's going to look awful. I mean, he's ugly as it is, his gold and white coat is all he has going for him. How's he going to look with no hair?' I howled, giving my nose another unladylike honk. 'He'll be pink and wrinkly, like a really, *really* old penis!'

'He won't lose it all,' Miller chuckled. 'It will just thin a bit. And it's not like he's strutting around the village on a daily basis sniffing out a girlfriend and needs to look his best.'

'I guess. But what about the poo if he has an upset tummy? It's not like he has the best control as it is. Do they do doggie nappies? Will he have to waddle around in one and I'll have to lift him up to sniff his butt to see if he's filled it? I'll end up needing surgery to my nose, his normal poos are toxic enough. And what about his walks to the village shop? He's a laughing stock on his skateboard as it is. I don't want people making fun of him when he's wearing a nappy too.'

'Turn around,' Miller demanded, as I blew my nose again.

'I look hideous,' I moaned.

'You love him, there's nothing to be embarrassed about. Turn around and look at me.'

'Promise not to laugh?'

'I promise,' he stated sincerely. I shuffled over, avoiding looking up at him, but he grasped my chin and tipped it up to his, then smiled. 'You look as beautiful as ever, Abbie. You think you look hideous, but I don't see that. I see someone who loves her dog with all of her heart and isn't afraid to show it. If you get like this over a pet, imagine how you'll get if we have children. Knowing that, seeing you like this now, just tells me that I made the right choice. I was going to wait until Valentine's Day to say this, to try and be romantic, but screw it. I love you, Abbie Carter.'

'You love me?' I whimpered, more tears battering at my eyes. He grinned and nodded, and I started sobbing again. 'I … love … you … too,' I wailed. 'And now I've just snotted all over your shirt.'

'Ok, Chubbers, let's say hello to Miller,' I told Sumo as he lay forlorn on his armchair, which I'd covered with a huge waterproof pet pad, then a warm blanket. He was also wearing a purple and white doggie nappy, just in case, which he was none too happy about, but I was taking no chances. I'd been amazed at how normal he'd been when Miller and I picked him up on Monday afternoon after his first chemo session. He'd eaten more than his usual amount of dinner, and when my back had been turned as I put some milk in my coffee, he'd stuck his head in the fridge and trotted off with a trail of best butcher's uncooked sausages streaming behind him. It had turned into a battle of wills, an all-out tug of war, me at one end of the sausage chain and Sumo the other. He'd won, and he'd even growled at me in warning not to follow him when he'd scurried off into the lounge with them. But I'd had the last laugh by grabbing a pair of scissors from the kitchen and chopping them so he was only left with the one he had in a death grip. The rest I'd cooked and chopped up into small pieces for him, offering them as treats from time to time.

Miller had had to fly back to America on Tuesday afternoon, and Sumo had pined for him. But yesterday and today, he was really suffering. He was even more lethargic, he'd lost his appetite for the first time ever, and he'd growled and gave me a warning nip when I'd tried to pick him up to take him out on his skateboard for some fresh air. Even Georgie coming over to give him a massage wasn't cheering him up in the slightest. His ears did prick up a little at the sound of Miller's name, and I managed to plant a kiss on the top of his head as I waited for the call to connect.

'Hey, you,' I smiled, as Miller's face appeared on screen.

'Hey, how are things?' Miller asked, reaching up to adjust his tie after angling the screen of his iPad. 'This long-distance thing sucks. I wish—'

'Sumo,' I laughed, as he cut Miller off by climbing onto my shoulder and sliding down my chest to lick my iPad screen. I'd propped it up against my bent legs as I sat on the floor leaning back against his armchair. 'Honestly, he's been moping and miserable for two days, but one look at your face and he turns into an excited puppy,' I called. I tried to move him so I could see Miller, but he dug in his stumpy front legs on the top of my thighs and refused to budge.

'I wish I could be there,' came Miller's voice.

'Me too. It looks like you'll be having a long-distance relationship with my dog now instead of me, as he's not going to let me get any screen time from now on.'

'I'll be back as soon as I can take some more time off work.'

'Well, I've also got Annabelle's wedding coming up in July.'

'July's months away, Abbie.'

'I know, I'm sorry, but I can't make a trip from March to May as it's my peak time with end-of-year accounts. Plus with Sumo's chemo for the next few months, I need to be here with him. You know I'd come if I could. Sumo, please move, I'd like to see Miller's face. And having your bottom so close to my face, nappy clad or not, is making me nervous.' I tried to lift him up, but he growled again and relaxed all of his muscles, making himself a dead weight in my hands. I huffed and gave up.

'I've got to go anyway, you just caught me on my way out of the door. I'll try you at lunchtime if it's not too hectic,' Miller called. 'Go easy on the little guy.'

'You wouldn't be calling him little if you had him slumped on you right now,' I grumbled.

We said our goodbyes, still unable to see each other's faces, and Sumo refused to move until Miller terminated the call and his face disappeared. He let out a low whine and pawed at the screen, then wiggled and wriggled on me as he tried to get down, but he was stuck with his back legs stretched out over my shoulder. This time he didn't object when I picked him up and settled him back down into his chair, gently stroking him while his face settled back into a miserable-looking one. He was missing Miller too.

This long-distance thing sucked for us all.

Chapter Six
Dress Eleven
July

I LOOKED AT THE pictures Georgie had sent of Sumo. She was taking care of him for me while I was in New York for the next couple of weeks. I was tying in some time with Miller with my bridesmaid duties for Annabelle, who'd moved out here after finishing university. Sumo had received a number of courses of chemo, and while the vet had sadly confirmed that his cancer was incurable, the treatment he'd had should extend his life. As long as he wasn't suffering, I was happy. And other than when he lost his appetite a few days after his treatment, he was his usual miserable, farting, gluttonous self. He was obviously in doggie heaven living at Georgie's, and he was virtually smiling in every picture. I would be too if I was getting multiple massages a day. He wasn't going to want to come home to me when I returned.

'Ok, everyone to the elevator,' called Martine, the super-organised wedding planner at The New York Domville. The actual ceremony and following sit-down reception were being held at the luxurious and iconic six-star hotel, up on the huge roof terrace, complete with patio areas, swimming pool, and lush, manicured garden sections. I turned off my phone, tucked it into my clutch, and stood up, smoothing down my elegant black Grecian-style, one-shouldered dress. The whole theme was black and white elegance, and nothing was over the top. Annabelle had admitted she was thrilled when most of the school clan had said they were unable to attend as the wedding was being held in New York. So she just had myself, Rachel, Fi-Fi, and her own best friend as bridesmaids. I was going to be on my best behaviour, again. Ten weddings ticked off so far, and I'd only screwed up Rachel's. I planned to keep it that way.

'I hear you're seeing Miller Davis,' Fi-Fi stated as we all followed Martine from one of the Signature suite bedrooms that had been used as the dressing area.

'I am,' I confirmed, my heart warming at the reminder. It had been so good to see him waiting for me at JFK when I'd landed yesterday morning, then to feel his strong arms around me and to breathe him in. We'd come straight to a suite here and hadn't left it until I'd come to Annabelle's to get ready, both of us eager to make up for lost time. And we had. I was amazed I wasn't walking with a cowboy-like strut this afternoon.

'Huh.' Fi-Fi let out a squeaky huff of surprise, which immediately irritated me. 'Lasted longer than I'd expected. I don't know what he sees in you, you were always a bit of a plain Jane,' she sneered, making me take a deep breath as I tried to stay calm. She'd grated on me from the moment we'd met as kids at school, and she still did now.

'Well, luckily for me, beauty is in the eye of the beholder. And I'd much rather be plain than a bitch.'

'What are you trying to say?'

'I'm not trying, I just said it,' I retorted, turning to give her my full-on glare. I was sick of being nice all of the time, and she'd just worn down all of my years of restraint with her. 'In case I wasn't clear enough for you, Fi-Fi, I'll repeat myself. You're a bitch. You always were at school, and you always will be.'

'Well, look who finally grew a pair. Let's see if you're so full of it when I've convinced your boyfriend that he's wasting his time with you. You're beneath a man like Miller.'

'Yes, as a matter of fact, I've been beneath him on a regular basis. He just can't get enough of me.' I gave her a smug smile, hating that I'd resorted to lowering myself to her level. 'Now please drop it. I'm remaining dignified because I refuse to ruin Annabelle's day,' I warned her, poking her chest forcibly. 'But if you so much as look at Miller the wrong way, or make any nasty comments to me again, all bets are off from tomorrow.'

'Ooooh, colour me scared,' she taunted. 'What are you going to do? Sit on me with that fat arse of yours?'

'Grow up, Fi. We're twenty-eight, not eleven anymore.' I gritted my teeth, trying to let her continuing catty remarks fade to white noise in the background.

'Well, you wouldn't know it from the way you—'

'For God's sake, Fi-Fi, just shut up!' snapped Rachel as she forced her way between us in the elevator. 'Abbie's right. We're grown women, there's no need for this playground mentality anymore. Just because you went on a date with Miller years ago and he dumped you straight after doesn't mean you need to take it out on her. You've got Dave now. Move on and let it go.'

Fi-Fi muttered something under her breath as I mouthed, "Thank you" at Rachel. She smiled back at me. I'd sent her and her mother an apology gift after the debacle at her wedding, and she'd accepted it was just an unfortunate mishap. Fi-Fi, though, obviously wasn't one to let things go. I'd been devastated when Miller had confessed he'd asked her out when he'd met her on one of his trips over to the UK. He'd admitted he'd been shallow back then, easily impressed by looks, but he'd soon realised how toxic she was. Plus, he said, after five minutes the high-pitched whining voice was enough to put him off. He'd assured me that they hadn't even kissed. But I still hated her.

With a passion.

'Ok, Annabelle?' I asked the bride, as I noticed her hands shaking when the lift started to glide upstairs.

'I'm terrified,' she admitted. 'Months and months of planning and it's here. I just want it all to be perfect, it *has* to be perfect.'

'Take a deep breath. It doesn't have to be perfect, because your wedding isn't the important thing, Annabelle. Your marriage is. Today is the day you start a new chapter with the love of your life. That's what you need to focus on, all the days you'll get to spend together now, not just this one day.'

'Oh, Abbie, that's *so* sweet, and so typically you,' she smiled, reaching out to take my hand. 'But you've never been engaged. You've no idea how much my parents have spent on this event. The rest we can muddle through, but this *has* to be perfect,' she repeated, letting go of my hand as she faced the doors, the lift settling into position. Well, that told me, didn't it? Was I stupid to think that the relationship was more important than the day? The more time I spent with some of my ex-school friends, the more shallow they seemed to become. I was so grateful that Georgie was my best friend. She'd never be like some of these girls.

'Right, Juliet, you're first, then Rachel, followed by Abbie, then Fi-Fi. Keep close, a step or two behind. Annabelle and her father will bring up the rear. Remember, shoulders back, heads up, and smile,' Martine ordered as she shuffled us into position.

The doors parted, sunlight filling the space as we were presented with the most breathtaking view of Manhattan. Polished marble steps led from the lift down to the roof terrace, where rows and rows of guests were seated under billowing muslin sails, protecting them from the glare of a relentless New York summer sun. The swimming pool, a crystalline turquoise, shimmered in front of them, cutting the roof terrace in half. A narrow wooden bridge spanned it, leading to a lush green lawn on the other side, surrounded by potted bay trees interspersed with black and white rose bushes. A muslin gazebo stood at the top, with a celebrant waiting with the groom and his best man and ushers, while a string quartet played in the background. Very classy, very Annabelle.

Juliet stepped forwards, gliding down the steps with poise, and we all followed suit. I kept my eyes firmly ahead of me, not wanting to be distracted by Miller, who was sitting somewhere in the congregation. *Was I pathetic to be missing him already,* I wondered. The sound of our high heels clip-clopped along the marble floor, then dulled as one by one, we stepped onto the wooden bridge. I took a deep breath, clutching my white rose bouquet tightly. It was hard to breathe out here, it was so hot and humid. Miller had warned me that New York suffered extremes of temperature in summer and winter, but I'd really had no idea. What I'd give to just go and change into my bikini, then dive head first into that pool and frolic with Miller and some cocktails.

'What the–' I gasped as I went to step forwards and was yanked backwards by my dress tightening around my chest. I staggered, flashbacks to Rachel's wedding rushing into my mind, forcing me to cling to my bouquet for dear life instead of flinging it. I tried to find my centre of gravity, but without my arms to balance me, I was useless. I felt myself tipping, Annabelle's last words of "It *has* to be perfect" ringing in my ears, along with that damn annoying song of the same title.

I could have sworn I heard Fi-Fi's squeaky snigger as my wish for a swim came true. I landed on my side in the cold water with a shrill scream, then quickly went under, the weight of my dress and small train pulling me down. I finally let go of my bouquet and opened my eyes, then struck out for the surface as I heard a muffled noise and saw the water churn above me. The bridge was just visible, with distorted faces peering down at me, as I felt someone's arms wrap around my waist. We shot to the surface, both gasping for air.

'Are you ok, baby?' came Miller's concerned voice as he let go of me.

'What the hell just happened?' I spluttered, treading water as I tried to wipe the water and hair out of my eyes.

'I think she deliberately stepped on your dress,' Miller panted, scrubbing his face as he bobbed in front of me.

'That bitc–' He cut me off by clamping his hand over my mouth.

'We'll deal with her later. We'd better get out, we're causing a bit of a scene,' he whispered. I nodded, but my eyes darted over to Fi-Fi's far-too-gleeful ones while Martine urged everyone to keep moving, announcing the wedding must go on. 'Come on, let's swim down to the shallow end and we can try and sneak out with minimal disruption.'

'Why do weddings with you always end up with us cold and wet?' I asked as we started to climb the steps. Miller offered me his hand as my dress hung heavy around me. Most of the crowd was focussed on us instead of the soon-to-be happy couple.

'I'd rather a wet wedding with you than a dry one with anyone else, Abbie,' Miller grinned. He was still in his suit trousers, but he'd obviously managed to strip off his jacket before he'd dived in after me, as his white shirt was clinging to his chest and toned stomach.

'And me you, Mr. Darcy,' I whispered, eyeing him up. He shook his head and chuckled, then gasped and grabbed both of my breasts as the laughter and chatter from the guests at the back of the congregation grew louder. 'Oh no,' I groaned.

As if I thought my humiliation at ruining Annabelle's perfect day couldn't get any worse, the weight of the water had pulled my dress down as I'd stepped out of the pool and both of my tits were out, flashing everyone whose eyes were on us.

'Quick! You know I love them, but pop them back in,' Miller laughed.

'I swear I'm going to kill her. I'm going to push her over the edge of the building. I'm going to bottle Sumo's farts and send it to her as a new designer perfume. I'm going to pop her over-inflated tits with one of Daphne's knitting needles,' I ranted, as I dragged my dress back up and scooped my breasts into the cups. 'I'll make her walk barefoot on sharp gravel. I'll make her rue the day she—'

Miller cut me off again by yanking me to him and kissing me until I sagged against him in a happy, relaxed heap. He then swooped down to scoop me up into his arms.

'You can exact your revenge later. Right now I want you out of this wet dress.'

'Oh, hello,' I giggled.

'That wasn't what I was thinking, Abbie Carter,' he grinned. 'I can't have you slipping and breaking anything, not when we have another week of sight-seeing to do,' he advised.

'Come, come,' Martine ordered as she scurried up to us, holding Miller's suit jacket. 'Let's get you out of here. Bernard will be waiting for you when you exit the elevator to escort you to a vacant suite so you don't drip water all over your own. You can shower, then relax in the bathrobes with some complimentary champagne and truffles. We'll wash, dry, and press your clothes within the hour and he'll return them to you. Abbie, I'll send up a beautician from the spa to redo your hair and make-up. You'll miss the wedding itself, but should make it back in time for the champagne reception before the sit-down meal.'

'I'm so sorry,' I grimaced as I gave her an apologetic smile.

'Pfft,' she huffed with a flick of her wrist as we climbed the steps to the lift. 'Trust me, as wedding disasters go, this is nothing. Anyway, don't blame yourself. I was watching, this was no accident.'

'She *did* step on my dress! I'm so going to be having words with her later,' I hissed. A hiss seemed appropriate as visuals of a catfight with her filled my head. She was well overdue being put in her place.

'Trust me, *I* will be having words with her later,' Martine stated, with a scary, stern schoolmistress face.

'Me too,' added a furious-looking Miller.

'And I will let the bride know that this catastrophe was not your fault,' she added, softening her face to give me a smile as she ushered us into the lift and pressed for it to go down.

'Catastrophe,' I groaned loudly as the doors slid shut. 'Annabelle's going to kill me, but on the plus side, I don't think I'll be asked to be a bridesmaid again, not after two total disasters.'

'And on another plus side, this dress isn't running, so you won't be returning with black, blotchy skin.'

'Oh, God, can you imagine?' I laughed, burying my face in his wet chest. 'That would be even worse than my multi-coloured one.'

Martine was true to her word, leaving me marvelling at the efficiency of The Domville. Bernard showed us to a suite opposite the lift and straight into the bathroom, where piles of fluffy white towels were waiting, along with some toiletries. By the time we'd emerged from the shower, a bottle of champagne on ice was waiting for us in the lounge, with chocolate-dipped strawberries coated in edible gold leaf. There was also a note to say that one of the girls from the spa would arrive soon and our clothes would be returned within the hour.

'I could get used to this,' I grinned, as Miller pulled me down onto his lap and fed me a strawberry.

'I didn't think you were that sort of girl,' he said, biting down on one of his own.

'I'm a girl full stop. Show me any girl that doesn't like being pampered from time to time.'

'I meant all this. The luxury, the money, the glitz of it all. Beautiful as you looked in that dress, and you really did, deep down you're Abbie Carter, simple jeans-and-tee country girl. Aren't you?'

'I am, but a little glitz and glamour is nice from time to time,' I confirmed, feeding him a strawberry this time, then licking some stray juice off his lower lip.

'Could you ever see yourself leaving the country, living somewhere like this?' he asked.

'The Domville?'

'No, a big city like New York.'

'No way!' I scoffed immediately. 'I think it would be like London, fun for a while, but then the noise and hustle and bustle and constant crowds would get on my nerves. And can you see me taking Sumo for a walk on his skateboard here?'

'Hmmm,' he responded, picking up his flute of champagne with a frown on his handsome face.

'Oh God, you weren't …' I felt myself starting to panic. Was he asking me to move here, and I'd just unknowingly shot him down? 'Was that a subtle proposition? As I'm not good with subtle. I've lived with Sumo's gas for too long, and as you know, subtle isn't his style.

He goes for the smack-you-in-the-face method of subtlety, just like that time he redecorated Georgie's salon brown. So if you were–'

'Hey, take a breath,' Miller laughed, putting his fingers over my lips. 'I wasn't trying to be subtle, I wasn't trying to be anything. It's just being back together reminds me how much I've missed you, and sometimes I try and imagine where we're going to end up, that's all.'

'I've missed you too,' I mumbled against his fingers.

'So, how is the little guy?' Miller asked, changing the conversation. But I was sure he was as aware as I was that it was one conversation we couldn't avoid forever. Not if we didn't want to have an ocean separating us for all eternity.

'Should I wait, or see you up there,' he asked as he shrugged on his navy jacket and tugged the white cuffs of his shirt down. I looked up at the girl doing my hair and make-up.

'I'll be done in ten minutes,' she responded.

'Go up then,' I suggested, licking some drool from my lower lip. He looked so hot in his suit. 'I'll find you.'

He flashed me a smile and one of his sexy winks, and I swore I heard my helper sigh breathlessly. I was getting used to that reaction from women when they saw my man. She gave me a sexier, smoky-eyed look ready for the evening and turned my straight hair into some kind of movie starlet's, with tumbling waves and body. I gave her a tip and went to twirl in the mirror, thinking I didn't look half bad. By the time I made it back up onto the roof terrace, everyone was milling around with champagne and nibbles. I spotted Miller over in the corner, talking to none other than my sworn nemesis, Fi-Fi. Well, if she hadn't been before, she was now.

I headed over, wishing I'd learned some kung-fu moves so I could flip her up into the air and smack her down on her arse, then pin her to the floor until she screamed for forgiveness. The two of them were oblivious to me as I approached, seeming to be in the middle of a heated debate, so I swiped a glass of champagne from one of the waiters and stayed a discreet distance, but within earshot. I felt like 007 on a secret mission, and idly wondered why there wasn't a female 007. Bond, *Abbie Bond*. No, didn't really have the same ring to it.

'Stop trying to deny it, Fi. I've spoken to half a dozen people who all confirmed you stepped on her dress deliberately. I don't know what you thought you'd achieve by humiliating her in public, not to mention the stress you caused Annabelle, but if this was some sort of ploy to make me ditch Abbie and come running into your arms, you're sadly mistaken.'

'You're telling me you're happy with that … that … *bore*? Squeaky-clean Abbie, the stuffy accountant? She has no idea how to satisfy a man like you, Miller.'

'Well, she does. It's not all about appearances, Fi, and the sooner you realise that and grow up, the happier you'll be.'

'Haven't you changed,' she sneered, as I stepped back a few paces when someone blocked my view of them. 'There was a time when you'd have accepted any offer.'

'That was the old me, I've changed. Maybe it's time for you to as well.'

'Have you changed, Miller, I mean *really* changed? Does she even have any idea of the kind of sexually active man you were? Does she even know *who* you are?'

'She knows me better than most,' Miller stated firmly.

'That's not saying much though, is it? You always kept your cards close to your chest. I wonder if I went and had a chat with her about who you really are, though, about what you've hidden from her, how would she feel about you then?'

'I'm warning you, Fi,' Miller growled, and I frowned, wondering what she was talking about. 'Stay away from her!'

'So, she doesn't know. Well, well, well. I wonder how Miss Perfect, Miss "It's wrong to tell lies, Fi-Fi" Carter, will react when she finds out the very man she's trusted has been lying to her all along. I might just have to go and whisper the truth in her ear.'

I gasped as I watched her put her hand on Miller's chest and move closer, pressing herself against him as she licked her lips. My God, she was like a lioness, sizing up her next meal. I was so close to marching over and slapping her, but I wanted to know what was going on. What had Miller lied to me about? What was he hiding from me? I suddenly felt sick.

'Back. Off,' Miller warned, reaching up to grip her wrist.

'Make me. You know what I want, what I've always wanted, Miller. *You,*' she added breathlessly, making me grit my teeth. I put up my palm and blew out a harsh "Sssshhhh" as someone came to make polite conversation with me, receiving a startled look in response.

'Even if you were the last woman on earth, Fi, my answer would still be no. And you're right, I haven't been honest with her, but that was something I was going to rectify tomorrow anyway, because she deserves to know the truth. You know why? Because unlike all of you gold diggers who came after me knowing exactly who I was, she fell in love with me without having a clue. I'd take a thousand Abbie Carters over one vapid, vacuous whore like you.'

I gasped at the same time as Fi-Fi, then winced as she ripped her hand from his grasp and slapped him sharply across the face before stalking off. Miller rubbed his cheek as he frowned, then turned to scan the crowd and saw me standing there, my mouth ajar.

'How much of that did you hear?' he demanded as he marched over to me.

'Enough to know that you've been honest with me about your feelings for me, but also enough to know that you've apparently lied to me about who I'm dating.'

'Damn it,' he muttered, wiping his hands up over his face and into his hair. 'It's not what you think, and what I was going to share with you tomorrow isn't some deep, dark secret that would have you fleeing from me in horror, but I'm worried that you're going to hold it against me for not being upfront with you.'

'Then maybe you should tell me and let me decide for myself,' I suggested as I set down my empty glass. 'Until I know, I can't gauge how I'm going to react, but I hate lies and I'm feeling a bit let down right now if that's what you've done.'

'Not exactly,' he replied, taking my hand as he led me to a section of the garden that wasn't quite as crowded. 'I think the phrase is "economical with the truth."'

'Are you married?' I asked, my stomach churning as I waited for his response. That would kill me, to find out I'd unwittingly become "the other woman."

'No.'

'Engaged?'

'No,' he replied, a little more firmly.

'Seeing anyone else?'

'No.'

'You're transgender?' I shot back.

'No!' he exclaimed.

'An ex-serial killer?'

'Again, no. And how do you become an *ex*-serial killer?'

'I don't know, I'm thrown as you've not been honest with me and I've no idea about what.'

'How about you just let me tell you?' he huffed, full of exasperation.

'Well, I'm not getting any younger, just spit it out,' I suggested.

'I don't just design video games, Abbie. I'm the Davis of the August Miller Davis Corporation, better known as AMD,' he stated, then folded his arms across his chest as he waited for my reaction.

'Ermmm, great?' I offered. His brow furrowed into a puzzled frown. 'Sorry, is that supposed to mean something to me?'

'Yes,' he chuckled, shaking his head with a look of astonishment on his face. 'It's the reason women tend to throw themselves at me.'

'Oh my God, you're a stripper! Your group AMD rivals The Chippendales!'

'No!' he laughed, his shoulders shaking violently as he tried to contain himself. 'See, this is part of the reason I love you, Abbie. You have no idea who I am. You're with me for me, the man, not the business mogul.'

'You're a mogul? Fancy. So this is your big secret, you own a business or something?' I asked, the overwhelming feeling of relief at it being nothing untoward calming me.

'Or something,' he chuckled with another disbelieving shake of his head. 'Just when I thought I couldn't love you any more, you prove me wrong. I'm August Miller Davis, founder and owner of the largest gaming company in America.'

'Your first name is August?' I giggled.

'*That's* what you're taking from that statement?' he asked, looking surprised.

'So you're worth a few bob, is that what you're telling me?'

'Who's Bob?'

'It's a phrase, like … bucks. You're worth a few bucks?'

'Yes,' he said slowly, elongating the word. 'A few … billion bucks.'

'Billion?! Damn. I've got to end this relationship right now then, I only like to date penniless losers. Now that I know you're a billionaire, this is never going to work out.'

'Abbie,' he scolded, yanking me to him and lifting me up off my feet to plant a kiss on my lips. 'You're not angry that I kept this from you?'

'No,' I replied, putting my arms around his neck. 'As a single woman who owns her own car and house and has a pension and savings, I get being cautious in case someone's only after what you have. But I mean, you need to be on a whole other level. Or billion levels even.'

'You could have looked me up on the internet anytime, but you seemed so clueless when we first met, unlike most of the women I meet, I just wanted to see if you'd like me, plain old Miller Davis, not because you thought I was worth a few … Toms.'

'Bobs. Actually bob, singular. Don't ask, English is confusing, and I'm English. And you, August Miller Davis, will never be plain old anything to me. You're the most handsome man I've ever set eyes on. You made me fall for you the first time that I saw you, remember?'

'I remember,' he nodded, with a soft smile full of emotion.

'Just tell me I don't have to call you August from now on, as that's a ridiculous name!'

'It is,' he laughed. 'I was found in August, and since no one knew my name, that's what they chose.'

'Good thing they didn't find you in June,' I giggled. 'That wouldn't have been a manly name at all. Where did the Miller Davis come from?'

'The male nurse who found me. I'm only called August in the boardroom, which I want to show you this week. I promise I was going to come clean. When we checked out of the hotel tomorrow morning, I was going to take you to my penthouse, then show you around my company on Monday.'

'As long as I don't have to play any video games, which so aren't my thing, I forgive you,' I murmured, letting my lips linger on his for as long as was polite at a high society function. 'But there's someone I'm not forgiving any time soon.' My brow furrowed as my mind whirled, trying to think of a way of getting her back.

'The bitch!' Georgie gasped as I filled her in from my suite during a quick break before our evening sit-down meal.

'I can't think of a way of getting her back that won't ruin Annabelle's function,' I sighed. 'Pushing Fi-Fi in the pool would cause a scene, or more likely a catfight. Making sure the waiters didn't give her lactose-free meals could end up with her being sick or sharting at the table, and anything I do in public would make me look like a malicious, vindictive bitch myself. Which I so want to be, but not at the risk of my own reputation.'

'Can you get in her room? Switch her shampoo for hair removal cream or something?' Georgie suggested.

'That's a bit harsh!' I exclaimed.

'No more harsh than she deserves, coming on to your boyfriend and shoving you in the pool, making you look like a drowned cat.'

'Cat ... hmmm, cat ... otherwise known as pussy,' I mused.

'Yes, where are you going with this? You have an idea, don't you?'

'I do, but it all hinges on access to her room and whether I can get hold of a certain product out here. Give Mr. Sumo a kiss from me, sweetie, got to go.'

'What about a kiss for–'

I cut her off and dialled the concierge to ask if he could get me a pot of Vicks Vaporub, a sealable plastic food bag, and some disposable gloves, which he appeared with less than ten minutes later, receiving a large tip for his efforts. I shoved all of the items in my clutch bag, then went in search of Martine, the wedding planner.

'I can't allow any guests into a suite that doesn't belong to them, Miss Carter. Absolutely not,' she replied when I asked the question.

'You saw what she did. Doesn't she deserve a little payback?' I moaned, pulling my best pleading pout and big watery eyes.

'Even if my key card allowed me access anywhere in the hotel, even into suite *six-hundred and sixty-five* where the lady in question is staying, I would be sacked on the spot if I simply gave it to you. I'm sorry. While I sympathise and understand how you might want to exact a little revenge, I can't be complicit. Now if you'll excuse me,' she retorted, 'I need to make sure that the entrées are on their way up. We'll be serving in less than ten minutes.'

'Ok,' I sighed. Damn. *Mission Impossible* really was mission impossible. Tom Cruise made it all look so easy. My cunning plan had been thwarted. I watched Martine as she walked away and saw something fall from her hand, clattering on the marble floor. I went to pick it up and frowned to find it was a key card. I looked back up and saw her smile at me over her shoulder, then give me a quick wink before she strode away. Good old Martine. Mission impossible had just become mission … on!

I headed up the steps towards the lift and scanned the area, where I spotted Fi-Fi flirting outrageously with another guest, her inflated beach ball tits virtually spilling out of her dress. Hussy! Pushing her in the pool would have been no payback at all, she'd have floated with those ridiculously large buoyancy aids. I hurried to the lift and took it down to the sixth floor, looking left and right up the corridor. The coast was clear.

I pulled on my gloves, then flattened myself against the wall and pulled my hair forwards over my face. I was hoping that would disguise me in case any cameras were watching and I got into trouble if this was reported. I moved sideways up the corridor, my back to the wall, occasionally pulling my hair aside to see what progress I'd made towards her suite. When I finally made it to number six-six-five, I did wonder why she hadn't been put in suite six-six-six, seeing as she was the devil incarnate. I peeked through my mane to check that the coast was clear again and entered her suite, quickly closing the door behind me.

I searched the bathroom first, looking through all of her toiletries, but came up empty handed.

'Georgie, it's me,' I whispered as she answered her phone.

'The fact that you rang me from your number and your face came up on my screen sort of gave it away,' she grinned. 'Why are you whispering?'

'I'm in her suite, looking for something. If you were a pot of vaginal orgasm enhancer, where would you hide if you weren't in the bathroom?'

'What's vaginal orgasm enhancer?' she asked, her blue eyes widening.

'The name's not clear enough?' I scoffed. 'You know, *stuff* you rub down there to make your lady parts tingle.'

'Oooooh, where do you get that? Does it work?'

'I've never tried it to be honest, but as part of Julia's spa-break hen weekend, we were all given a saucy bag, and there was some in it. At Annabelle's hen night, Fi-Fi was raving about it, saying she carries a pot with her all the time, it's that good. She called it "women's Viagra." Swears by it.'

'So you've gone in her suite to steal it? Ewww! Go buy your own pot, you cheapskate!'

'I'm not looking for me, Georgie. Like I need to when I have Miller.'

'Oh right, good point. So what are you doing with it?' she asked. I started giggling and had to take a few deep breaths to calm myself down at the thought of it.

'Remember that really bad cold I had in November?'

'Hmmm.'

'Well, I was using Vicks Vaporub on my chest and I mustn't have washed my hands properly, as I was needing a little … tension relief that night and *boy*, does it have an extra effect they don't advertise on the pot!'

'What effect?' she gasped.

'Do I have to spell it out?'

'Obviously!'

'It made me tingly, you know, down *there.*'

'Oh! How tingly are we talking?'

'Very excitingly tingly for the first thirty seconds, then owww-this-stings-like-a-mofo for about an hour afterwards. I had to sit in a cold bath to try and cool my … you-know-what down.' I winced at the reminder.

'You're going to swap her orgasm cream for Vaporub?' she shrieked.

'Sssshhhh,' I giggled. 'Am I taking it too far?'

'Hell no!' she shot back. 'I'd try and find her vibrator and smother that in it as well.'

'Now it's my turn to say "Ewww." I don't want to touch that, thank you very much!'

'Excellent point,' she nodded. 'Ok, ok, if I was a pot of orgasm cream that might be needed for a spur-of-the-moment urge, where would I hide?' She bit her lower lip as we both had a think.

'Bedside table!' we shouted at once. I scurried over and opened the drawer, and sure enough, there it was, hidden behind the Bible.

'I'm going to go to hell for this,' I moaned as I set the Bible aside and pulled out her pot. I scooped out the cream, praying I wouldn't see any stray pubic hairs in there, then dumped it in the ziplock bag. When I was done, I transferred the Vaporub into the orgasm cream tub and shut it tightly, then shoved it back in place.

'What if she smells it first? That eucalyptus scent is pretty powerful.'

'Please. The amount of nose reconstructions she's had, not to mention drugs she's snorted over the years, I'd be amazed if she has any sense of smell left. Besides, I may not have any of this cream, but I doubt you stick your nose in it first. I just have to hope that she's slathered it on before she notices something's amiss.'

'Oh, she'll soon notice something's amiss if she does rub it in. The hotel staff are going to find her, legs akimbo, in the ice dispensing machine,' Georgie cackled, setting me off again. I made sure I peeled the gloves off, turning them inside out as I did to avoid getting any of the sticky mixture on my fingers, before I wiped my eyes. 'You just have to hope she's feeling in a frisky mood soon.'

'If only I knew a man she'd give her eye teeth to sleep with,' I grinned. 'Miller's going to have to pull out all of the flirtation stops with her tonight. Wind her up, then walk away, leave her panting for some relief.'

'You're evil, Abbie Carter. *Evil.* And I love it! Where were you when I needed revenge on my cheating partner?'

'Too busy consoling you, sweetie, but it's never too late. Crap, speaking of late, they'll be serving the food upstairs. I'd better go back before I'm missed.'

'I wish I could be a fly on the wall in that room tonight,' Georgie pouted.

'Me too,' I agreed.

I disposed of the gloves and bag in one of the receptacles outside the lift and headed up to find everyone was taking their seats. I hurried over to where Martine was barking orders into her Bluetooth device, ticking items off the huge list on her clipboard. She raised her eyebrows in an unspoken question when she saw me. I gave her a discreet nod and slipped the card into her jacket pocket as I asked which table I was supposed to be at.

'Thank you,' I over-emphasised

'You're welcome,' she smiled.

'Where have you been?' Miller asked as he held out my seat for me.

'Let's just say if payback's a bitch, you're looking right at her.'

'What did you do?' he groaned.

'We'll talk after dinner, but you owe me a favour for hiding who you were from me, and I intend to collect.'

'You said you understood and it wasn't an issue,' he reminded me as he took his seat.

'Do you know *nothing* about women?' I uttered. 'We tell you all is forgiven and that something won't be brought up again, when really we have every intention of blackmailing you with it time and time again for the rest of eternity.'

'Am I going to regret this favour?' he sighed.

'She will,' I grinned. I just about stopped myself from rubbing my hands together in glee, Dr. Evil style.

Chapter Seven

Doing The Locomotion
August

'I CAN'T BELIEVE I'VE never been out here,' Miller observed as he carried Sumo out through the kitchen French doors while I followed, carefully balancing a tray with our lunch on it.

'Well, you're experiencing the rare phenomenon of a British summer. And on a Saturday for everyone to enjoy, too. If we're really lucky, it will last all day before the rain returns or it starts hailing or snowing.'

'It's an amazing view,' he nodded as he looked around.

'Hardly Central Park,' I scoffed. I was still adjusting to the news he'd shared with me in New York. Telling someone you were wealthy was one thing. Showing them was something completely different. I swore I already had a bruise on my chin from the amount of times it had hit the floor before I'd headed home with him last weekend, in his private jet no less.

'Still stunning, in a very different way. There you go, boy,' he added, setting Sumo down on the blanket he'd spread out on the grass earlier, next to my patio table and chairs. 'Some fresh air and sunshine will do you good.'

I smiled even more when Sumo started wiggling his big butt, signalling his delight in this plan, then turned around and around, circling incessantly as he panted before finally flopping down and rolling onto his back for a tummy rub. He just adored Miller, and it made me happy to see my pooch so content, even if he was never like that with me. I swore he pined for Miller when he left, even more than I did. I dished up the grilled chicken salad and opened a couple of bottles of cold beer as Miller gave Sumo the fuss he was demanding.

'Abbie?'

'Miller?'

'Why do you have a set of train tracks in your backyard?'

'Garden. A backyard sounds like something that's been filled in with concrete.'

'Don't overload me, I'm still getting over the whole pants, fanny-pack, and vest misunderstandings,' he chuckled. 'So?'

'My dad,' I nodded, taking in a deep breath as my eyes automatically drifted towards the large studio room down at the bottom of the garden. The one he'd done up to look like a country station, complete with signals and station name. 'He was a train enthusiast and when he retired, he purchased a working miniature train and some carriages to attach to it, and he could sit on it and go all of the way around the back garden. That was the main station down there,' I advised, pointing to it. 'He spent most of his free time in there tinkering. Sumo loved it. Dad adapted it with a flat-bed carriage that Sumo used to sit on as he circled the garden. He even put on a large starter switch that he taught Sumo to press so he could go for a ride without us.'

'Seriously?' Miller laughed.

'Seriously,' I nodded. 'Whenever we visited, he'd waddle out of the dog flap, climb onto the train, and press the switch. He'd stop it himself wherever he fancied getting off for a sniff, or a poo, then he'd climb back on it again to come home. Or he'd just circle the garden again and again, panting like he was doing doggy circuit training. I swear that train was the reason he started refusing to go for a walk. He got lazy.'

'Now I get why he loves his pull-along contraption so much. Does the train still work?' Miller asked, taking the beer I offered.

'No,' I sighed, sitting down next to him and taking a swig of my own. 'Dad was the mechanical genius, I'm the mathematical one. It worked for a few years after I moved in, but when it stopped one winter, I put the train away in his studio. I meant to get it repaired, but … I just never got around to it. To be honest, it's a bit of a specialised thing, I wouldn't know where to start.'

'I'd love to see it, if you don't mind me looking in your dad's studio?'

'I'll get you the key after lunch. I'm not sure I'm ready to go back in there though,' I confessed. Even just talking about Dad, being hit with visuals of him on the train and Sumo grunting with delight as they'd trundled around the garden together on it while I'd sat with a glass of wine and watched, was painful.

Wednesday

I kissed Miller goodbye over the half-stable door, and he waved me off as he stood with Sumo in his arms. He was only here for a couple of weeks and I really wanted to spend every day with him, but I'd already promised the Joneses a trip up to the coast. They were too doddery now to drive themselves. In fact, the last time David had gone out in their car, he'd managed to hit three others as he tried to park. I'd suggested Miller come, but he'd told me he could do with using my office to deal with some business-related matters. Instead, Georgie had asked if she could come, so I'd packed up a large picnic hamper and a few blankets so that we could have lunch on the beach. The old couple loved to play the slot machines, so that was the plan for the afternoon, out of the glare of the sun, followed by a fish and chip supper as we listened to the tide coming in, before we headed home.

'Ok, everyone buckled up?' I asked as I put the car in reverse.

'Aye-aye, Captain,' Georgie nodded next to me.

'This is so good of you, Abbie,' Daphne smiled as I looked over my shoulder to check on them.

'No trouble at all. I've been looking forward to it.'

'Should have asked Heath to come. I think he'd get on really well with Georgie, isn't it,' David stated.

'First you were trying to fix him up with Abbie, now Georgie, just let it rest. He's a grown man, he can find his own dates,' Daphne scolded, as Georgie and I grinned at each other with a roll of our eyes.

We settled the couple down in their deck chairs, sitting on the blankets on the sand. I'd managed to nab a spot right next to the steps up to the car park that bordered the beach, so they didn't have to walk too far. They had parasols to protect them from the sun, and a few bottles of beer in the cooler box for David and a small bottle of Daphne's favourite wine. Georgie and I kicked off our shoes and raced each other down the beach to the water, screeching at how cold it was as we waded out, knee deep, having come prepared in our shorts.

'How amazing is it that we have this an hour from our house?' she exclaimed in awe as we looked up and down the Welsh coastline, the rugged coastal view stretching on for miles.

'Sumo used to love coming here as a puppy. Dad would throw a stick and Sumo's little legs would work overtime to go fetch it and repeat, over and over. He'd paddle in the water and come and shake it all over me while I lay reading a book and sunbathing.' I sighed at the memories.

'The vet has no idea how long he has?' Georgie asked gently.

'No,' I replied, blinking back some tears. 'He doesn't seem to be in any pain. I've just got to watch for signs of him deteriorating and make a decision then.'

'As long as he's happy, you're doing all that you can,' she said reassuringly, and I nodded.

'Do you think Miller's happy?' I asked hesitantly.

'What? Where did that come from?' she responded, shooting me a concerned look. I shrugged and averted my gaze, looking out to sea.

'He's some huge … mogul, Georgie. I was stupid the other night, I looked him up on the internet and there were hundreds of pictures of him with glamorous women dripping from his arm. I'm so not his type. Then there's …' I shook my head. I was making more of a throwaway question than there was to make.

'He chose you, sweetie. He even admitted to me that he'd never had a relationship before. They were arm candy, one-night stands for a guy that didn't want any more at the time. Who wouldn't have their head spun earning the sort of money he has at his young age? He's grown up now though, he wants more. He wants you.'

'I guess,' I nodded, my old insecurity of being "undateable Abbie Carter" rearing its head again.

'What were you going to say?'

'Huh?' I gave her a puzzled look.

'You made your very incorrect observations, then said, "Then there's" and never finished,' she reminded me.

'He asked me if I could ever see myself living in a city like New York.'

'He did? You think he's testing the water before he asks you to move there with him? What did you say?'

'I didn't think when he asked it. I think I said something along the lines of "Hell, no," then I realised he might have been seeing how I felt and I'd just completely shot him down.'

'Would you move there?'

'I love him, Georgie, like crazy "I want to scream his name from the rooftops" love him, but even for him …' I took a deep breath as I admitted it to myself for the first time. 'No, I don't want to live in New York. I love the peace and quiet too much. I'm a country girl at heart, I always will be. There's Sumo to consider, and my best friend who needs me as much as I need her.' I flashed her a smile, which she returned. 'The Joneses too, then all of the memories of Dad here. But Miller's business is over there. He's not going to move to a sleepy village like Dilbury. It's hardly the commercial capital of Shropshire, let alone England.'

'Well, selfishly I'm happy to hear you're staying put, but keep an open mind. Maybe one day you'll want a new adventure, and we'll be friends wherever you live. I'm not that easy to shake off. Besides, "trout pout" Abbie has been laid to rest. I haven't seen you looking so happy since I met you.'

'I'll give you "trout pout,"' I scoffed, as I bent down to scoop a load of seawater in my hands and chucked it at her. She shrieked and splashed me back, so I started kicking water in her direction and she retaliated until we were both soaked and laughing so hard we were crying. 'Come on, I need to sit down and dry off, and I'm starving.'

We linked arms as we headed back to the old couple. David's head had flopped back, his mouth ajar as he snored like a steam locomotive. Daphne had her half-moon glasses on, looking like Professor McGonagall from *Harry Potter*, as she knitted a tiny, brightly coloured striped jumper.

'What are you making?' I asked.

'A jumper for Mr. Sumo,' she smiled, peering at me over the top of her glasses as we sat cross-legged on the picnic blanket in front of her. 'He's going to feel the cold even more this winter, now that he's not very well.'

'You're so good to me, Daphne.'

'Nonsense. You and Georgie are so good to David and me. You're young, you should be out having fun, not taking us old fogies on beach trips, cooking us Sunday dinners, doing our shopping and heavy lifting.'

'We don't mind,' Georgie said, and I shook my head in agreement. 'You're as good as family to Abbie, and I know I haven't known you that long, but you feel like it to me, too.'

'Don't make an old lady cry, girls,' she moaned, putting her knitting down in her lap. 'What say we wake up the old codger and have something to eat? I'm feeling a bit peckish.'

'Me too,' I agreed. 'Has he always snored so loudly?'

'It started when he hit forty. Trust me, it's all downhill from there. One minute he went like a locomotive, the next he was snoring like one.' She smiled as we burst out laughing.

'Gosh, as Miller's just hit thirty, I've only got ten more years of steam left in him then. I'd better make the most of it.'

'It's about time you thought about settling down and starting a family, Abbie Carter,' Daphne warned with a pointed look at me, before she turned to shake David's arm. He jumped in his seat, a startled grunt erupting that had all three of us giggling like schoolgirls.

We were chatting away, eating our picnic of delicatessen meats and cheeses, along with nice pâté on crusty bread, when I gasped in horror as a stream of seagull poo fell from the sky and landed on the peak of David's cap. It was the consistency of warm, runny icing, in shades of grey and white, and just as he parted his lips to push a morsel of the loaded bread into his mouth, a dollop of poo slithered over the edge of his cap and landed straight on the pâté. He shoved it in and started chewing before I had a chance to do anything to stop him. I froze mid-conversation as my jaw dropped, waiting for some kind of reaction from him to it, but he swallowed it down and smacked his lips.

'Where did you get that pâté again, Abbie? Best I've ever had, real creamy texture to it, isn't it.'

I sucked my lips into my mouth, clamping down on them furiously as I tried to hold in my laughter.

'You think, David? Personally I thought it was a bit shitty,' Georgie giggled next to me. I shot her a look as she put her head down, her shoulders shaking, and I couldn't keep it in any longer. I roared with laughter and fell backwards onto the picnic blanket, clutching my sides. Georgie's laughter, interspersed with her one flaw, a loud piggy-like snort every few gasps for air, made me laugh even harder.

'Youngsters. I don't get them, nothing shitty about that pâté at all,' I heard David mutter in the background, Daphne agreeing, as Georgie collapsed next to me, crying so hard her mascara was running down her cheeks.

'Oh my God,' she moaned under her breath after we'd tried to compose ourselves. 'I nearly died, and the look on your face was priceless.'

'If he dies from bird flu, you won't be laughing so hard!'

'Bird flu! Stop it, my sides are hurting.'

'I'm serious. It's a well-known fact that eating bird shit transmits bird flu in humans.'

'I never heard that before. You're a mine of information, Abbie Carter,' she exclaimed.

'And you're so gullible,' I teased.

'Gullible, ha-ha, nicely punned. So it's not true? Flu from poo?'

'Honestly, I've no idea,' I giggled, trying to pull myself together. 'We should get him checked at the hospital, right? It can't be good for you to eat poop.'

'I don't know, I was fed shit for the last year of my engagement and I'm doing ok,' she winked.

'Yes, you are, aren't you?' I beamed, flashing her a wide smile. 'It will be time to get you out dating soon. You're too fabulous to stay single, Georgie Basset. But seriously, we should get him checked over, right?'

'Stop flapping,' she winked. 'You could always ring the hospital, tell them what happened and ask if it's tweetable.'

'Stop it,' I laughed, batting her shoulder as she started giggling again. I sat up, avoiding eye contact with the Joneses as I rummaged in my bag for my phone, and excused myself to call the hospital for some advice. I was soon reassured to hear that unless he became sick in the next twenty-four hours, he should be fine.

'I'm home,' I called.

'Stay in the hall,' Miller yelled.

'Oh no, what did he do?' I groaned. 'I've had my fill of poo-related disasters today.'

94

'What?' Miller asked as he appeared in the kitchen doorway, looking delectable in a pair of knee-length, dark indigo denim shorts, some flip flops, and a white t-shirt, which showed off his gym-buffed body and bronzed skin. My God, what did this man see in me? I was a hot, sticky mess from the journey home, and had salt stains on my shorts and t-shirt from splashing about in the sea.

'Don't ask. Is he ok?' I looked up at Miller as he put his arms around my waist and dipped his head to leave me breathless with a soft, deep kiss.

'He's fine, happy as a ... what's the phrase?'

'Pig in muck,' I smiled, wondering if my poo-related day would ever end. 'So why am I out here in the hall?'

'I have a surprise for you,' he grinned, then reached behind him to pull out a dark grey tie.

'Oooh, hello, Mr. Grey,' I giggled.

'What?'

'Maybe you should read a book now and then instead of playing video games.'

'Designing and testing,' he protested.

'Hmmm, right, boys and their toys.'

'There has to be some perks to owning a global corporation,' he smirked, planting a quick kiss on my lips again. 'Now turn around and do as you're told.'

'Yes, sir. You're so Mr. Grey right now and you have no idea!'

I let him blindfold me, then he spun me around and around until I begged him to stop when I started feeling giddy. I had no idea which way was up, let alone my left from my right or what direction he was gently pushing me in.

'Ok, there's a step down here, take my hands,' he ordered, as I felt him squeeze past to get in front of me. I deduced that we'd gone outside onto the patio from the feel of the late evening sun and breeze on my face, and the solidness under my feet from the hard surface I was walking on. 'Keep your eyes closed until I tell you to open them,' he warned as he forced me to stop, then positioned me.

He made me jump when he did a shrill wolf-whistle. I twisted my head left and right, trying to see if I could hear anything. It wasn't my birthday yet, so I was pretty sure there wasn't a patio full of guests about to shout, "Surprise!" at me and give me an early coronary. 'Sumo?' I whispered, as I heard the unmistakable sound of the dog flap in the back door clatter. He was snuffling and grunting so loudly, just like he used to do when Dad got him overexcited. I could just picture his fat little butt wagging from side to side.

'Stay, boy, just like we practiced all afternoon,' Miller warned as he pulled the tie off over my head. 'Ok, open your eyes, baby.'

I did slowly, blinking a few times to adjust to the light, and my heart warmed to see Sumo doing exactly what I thought he'd be doing as he stood on the doorstep, with a super-cute red baseball cap on his head and a red and white checked scarf tied around his neck. I hadn't seen him so excited in years, not even with Miller, not since Dad had died. He started bouncing; his front paws lifting off the ground and then dropping as he let out a few uncharacteristic barks. Then the tears in my eyes started to form as I heard an unmistakable noise. A sound that took me straight back to my childhood. The rattle of train wheels on a track. I spun around, my hand over my mouth to see Dad's prized, electrically powered fake steam engine chugging up the garden towards us, Sumo's carriage hooked on behind it. I shook my head in disbelief, for once words failing me as I turned to watch it curve around the top of the garden, pass the back of the house, then gently draw to a stop opposite Sumo.

'Oh my God,' I whispered, tears starting to stream down my face as he climbed onto it and stuck his front paw on the pad that had been designed for him to start it up again. He sat down as the train pulled away to do another circuit, his head held high, his floppy pink tongue hanging from the side of his mouth, with an unmistakable smile on his wrinkled old face. He *was* the proverbial pig in muck. I hadn't seen him look so happy in years. 'How ... how did you ... *Miller*!' I turned and buried my face in his chest as I started to cry properly.

'Please tell me these are tears of happiness, that I didn't make a huge mistake, overstep my bounds and upset you?' he said softly as he held me tightly to him.

'Happy ... tears,' I sobbed. 'How ... how ...' I gave up, too emotional to form any more words for a while.

'Let's just say there are perks to having money, like making skilled craftsmen drop everything to work on your project at a moment's notice.' He planted a kiss on the top of my head, then forced me back at arm's length as he wiped my eyes for me and spun me around. He pulled me back against his chest, his arms around my waist, and I covered his hands with mine as we both watched Sumo surveying his garden from his vantage point as he did a full tour. We both laughed as the train came to a stop at the back door and instead of getting off, my happy boy whacked the starter pad again, letting out a woof of delight.

'We'll never get him back in the house,' I laughed.

'As long as he's happy, right?'

'Right,' I nodded, tipping my head back to look up at my thoughtful man. 'And you've no idea how happy you've just made me, Miller. How can I ever thank you?'

'I can think of a few ways,' he grinned with a wink and a wicked twinkle in his eye.

Chapter Eight

Knocking On Heaven's Door
December

'DO YOU THINK THAT will be us one day?' I asked Miller as I sat in his lap in one armchair, Sumo snoring in his, and the Joneses asleep, sitting upright on the sofa, holding hands as Daphne's head rested on David's shoulder. It was Christmas Day, or rather Christmas evening. We'd had a huge Christmas dinner, plenty of good conversation, and had then all sat around in front of the fire to watch the latest Bond film. They'd both fallen asleep within minutes of it starting, even after David had complained of indigestion as they'd hobbled through from the kitchen.

'Do you want that to be us one day?' he asked, reaching up to cup my face with one hand, his thumb sweeping backwards and forwards across my cheek.

'Will I scare you if I'm honest with you?' I held his liquid chocolate gaze, trying to see any flicker of fear, but didn't spot any.

'No, I want to know what you're thinking.'

'Ok,' I nodded, swallowing a lump in my throat. We'd been dating, albeit long distance, snatching long weekends here and there between holidays, for a year now. It was a relationship record for both of us. 'When I think about the future, I imagine myself sitting here with you at Christmas as we watch our children opening their presents in front of the tree, but …' I hesitated and saw a flicker of a frown grace his face.

'But?'

'I'm not sure you see that future, or if you do, it's a different version of it.'

'I do see that future, Abbie, but I'd be lying if I said you weren't right.'

'You see that picture in New York, don't you?' I whispered, breaking his gaze as I looked down at my fingers, knotting them together anxiously.

'Yes,' he said quietly, gripping my chin and forcing my head up to hold my disappointed gaze.

'Where does that leave us?' I asked, my eyes searching his, hoping he'd have some answers.

'I don't know,' he sighed. 'You really won't consider moving over with me, even just to try it for a while?'

'How can I, Miller? There's my job for a start, I–'

'You can be an accountant in New York.'

'You have different tax laws, rules and regulations. I'd have to retrain,' I reminded him. 'And what about Sumo?'

'We could fly him over.'

'He's a British bulldog.'

'So?'

'They have snub noses, which means their breathing is already compromised. They're classed as flight risks, as too high a percentage of them have died in transit.'

'So we wait until ... until ...' Miller broke off and looked over at where my boy was oblivious, sleeping off his turkey and gravy dinner.

'Until he dies?' I exclaimed, stiffening up on Miller's lap. 'That's a bit heartless.'

'That's unfair, you know how much I love him. I'd never wish for it to happen faster to suit my own purposes, but we both know it's inevitable. His cancer's incurable, Abbie. I'm just trying to say that whatever objections you have, there's an answer. I'm not saying now, I'm saying someday.'

'And what about them?' I suggested, tipping my head in our guests' direction. 'Or Georgie? They're as good as family to me. I can't just leave them, leave the place that's been my home for as long as I can remember.'

'So you just expect me to leave mine?' he bit, full of frustration, as I scowled at him.

'You spend more time here than I do in America, Miller,' I reminded him. He'd even purchased a private hanger at the local airport, and his own car, which was left there when he was out of the country. 'And who is over there to tie you to them?'

'That's a low blow,' he grated, suddenly lifting me up as he stood and firmly set me down.

'I wasn't trying to be nasty,' I replied, softening my tone as I reached for his hand, then winced when he pulled it away.

'So my best friend moved here, and I don't have any family in America, but that might change one day.'

'Not if we can't agree on where we're going to live.'

'I wasn't talking about us,' he responded, pulling his grey sweater into position as he stalked across the room and out into the hall. I quickly followed him, checking that our guests were none the wiser to our little disagreement, but David was snoring, in competition with Sumo, and Daphne was still asleep too. How she managed it with that racket going on was beyond me.

'What was that supposed to mean?' I asked as I pulled the lounge door behind me.

'Nothing,' Miller stated, as he grabbed his long wool coat from the rack and pulled it on.

'Where are you going?'

'I need to stretch my legs and clear my head,' he replied, avoiding looking at me.

'Let me write a note in case they worry where we are then,' I suggested.

'I meant on my own, Abbie.' He flashed me an apologetic look as I drew in a sharp breath. Was this a fight? Were we having our first fight?

'Where? For how long? What if you fall over and hurt yourself and I don't know where to find you?' I reached out and grabbed his arm as he went for the door handle. 'Don't leave like this, please,' I urged.

'I'll be fine, I've got my phone.' He picked up my hand and removed it from his arm, giving it a slight squeeze as he did.

'Are you coming back?' I asked, almost choking on the words. The thought that this was it, that we were breaking up over our first disagreement, made my chest hurt. He finally looked at me properly, his serious brown eyes scanning my teary green ones, and he gave me a soft smile, then sighed.

'Of course I am. I'm … *frustrated*, that's all. I'm finding it harder and harder to say goodbye, Abbie, whatever country I'm doing it in. I don't want this for us. I don't know how much longer we can keep doing this long-distance thing. All I know is that I want to keep doing this, *us*,' he added gently as he grabbed my face and kissed me hard.

'I want to keep doing this, us, too,' I replied, kissing him back forcefully.

'Then let's agree to put this conversation on hold, but I still need to clear my head. I won't be too long.'

'Promise?'

'Promise,' he nodded seriously. He dropped his forehead to mine and I closed my eyes, inhaling him. He'd always smelled like Christmas to me, that deep, musky cinnamon scent that was so comforting and homely. 'See you later,' he breathed.

He planted a delicate kiss on my nose, then his warmth was replaced by an icy chill as he threw open the front door and stepped out onto a blanket of crisp, white snow. He tucked his hands in his pockets and put his head down as he trudged up to the gate. I stood shivering with my arms around me, waiting for him to look back as he passed through the gate and shut it. But he didn't. It was like someone had just sucked all of the joy out of Christmas at once.

I felt completely deflated as I shut the front door, then headed straight for my drinks stash in the kitchen and poured myself a glass of whisky. I leaned back against the sink and nursed my drink as I tried to use the warmth of the alcohol to breathe some life back into me.

'Abbie, is everything ok?' Daphne's voice startled me, and I looked up to see her holding the doorframe.

'I've no idea,' I admitted, my bottom lip wobbling.

'Pour me one of those, then come and sit down and tell me all about it,' she ordered as she shuffled into the kitchen and settled herself down on one of the dining room chairs. I sat down and started to tell her my fears that Miller and I wouldn't be able to work out our differences.

'If love was easy, there wouldn't be any single people or divorce,' she said wisely as she patted my hand, while I wiped away the last of my tears.

'If we can't agree on this, though ...' I trailed off, shaking my head.

'When the time comes that you have to make the decision, you will.'

'And what if I make the wrong decision?'

'Take some advice from an old woman, Abbie. There's no such thing as a wrong decision. You make your choices in life based on the cards played to you and your emotions at the time. Whatever will be will be, you can't change fate.'

'Thank you,' I sighed, leaning in to give her a kiss on the cheek.

'Right. Well, I'd better go and empty my bladder, then wake up his lordship and get him home. We've had a lovely day, thank you so much for having us. Again.'

'You know you're welcome anytime. I'll just plate up some food for you to stick in the microwave tomorrow while you go and wake him up and get your coats on,' I suggested, helping her up off the chair. It was scary to see how less mobile the old couple was getting. There was a noticeable difference in her movement and speed compared to last year and the year before that.

I put together two large plates for them and covered them in cling film, then did another bowl of scraps for Sumo, making sure to leave off any hint of Brussels sprouts or cabbage. He didn't need any encouragement in that department, that was for sure. I whipped my head around when I heard a cry from the lounge.

'Are you ok?' I called as I set his bowl to the side. 'Daphne?'

I got no reply and scurried across the hall. I bet Sumo had got under her feet and tripped her up. I had visions of her lying on the floor with a broken hip. Instead, I found her sitting on the sofa, sobbing, as she held David's hand. He was completely oblivious, as was Sumo, still fast asleep.

'What's happened, what's wrong?'

'I can't … I can't wake him up,' she whimpered. 'David, David, please wake up. It's time to go home.'

My heart sank as I rushed over and paid more than a cursory glance at him. He wasn't snoring, his chest wasn't heaving, and his lips had a blue tinge to them. I grabbed the phone and dialled 999 for the emergency services as I put my fingers on the pulse point on his neck. Daphne gave me a hopeful look through her tears, both of her hands firmly wrapped around one of his.

Nothing.

I looked up as Miller burst through the doors of the hospital waiting room at Accident and Emergency in Shrewsbury, then stalled in his tracks as he saw me sitting with Daphne, my arm around her shoulders, my other hand holding hers tightly as she sobbed. The ambulance had arrived so quickly, I'd barely had time to scribble a note and stick it on the kitchen island to say the words "Hospital. Emergency. David."

I swallowed a lump in my throat and shook my head. Of all the days to suffer a fatal heart attack, David had chosen to do it on Christmas Day. Sixty years of marriage ended in the blink of an eye, while she'd been sitting comforting me. I fought back my tears. I had no right to cry right now. No matter how fond I'd been of David, how guilty I felt that he'd been all alone when it happened, it wasn't about me. Daphne had just lost her soul mate and the love of her life. Her grief was what mattered right now.

'Damn it,' Miller uttered, before turning around and punching the wall. He held his hands up in apology as the receptionist snapped her head up and the security guard gave him a warning glance. 'What can I do?' he whispered, as he crouched in front of me and placed a hand on my knee, squeezing it gently.

'Can you sit with her while I sort out some of the paperwork? They said it shouldn't be long, then I think we need to get her home. How did you get here?'

'I'd had too much to drink to risk driving your car, so I headed up to The Cock & Bull. Tony the landlord hadn't been drinking, so he offered to bring me in. He's waiting outside.'

'That's good of him,' I nodded, tightening my arm around Daphne as her sobs started to slow. 'Do you think he'll wait a while? I'd really like to take her home as soon as possible.'

'I'll check.' Miller stood up, then hesitated and bent down and kissed me quickly, then clasped Daphne's face and gently kissed her forehead. 'I'm so sorry,' he whispered. She nodded and sniffed as we watched him walk away.

'What am I supposed to do without him?' she said quietly. 'He was my reason, you know.'

'I know, and honestly, I've no idea,' I said sadly. 'But however you face this, you won't be doing it alone, and we're going to take it day by day, ok? I'm just so sorry that you were … with me when …'

'Don't you dare, Abbie,' Daphne warned as she straightened herself in her chair. 'This wasn't your fault. It was his time to go and nothing either of us did or didn't do will ever change that. I told you that there's no arguing with fate,' she reminded me, her old arthritic hands curling tightly around mine. 'As last days went, it couldn't have been better, thanks to you mollycoddling an old couple out of the goodness of your heart. You have nothing to apologise for, do you hear me?'

I nodded, hoping she really meant that. The only consolation was that the doctors had said he'd likely have had no idea what was happening to him. To all intents and purposes, he'd slipped away peacefully in his sleep after a bellyful of Christmas dinner and a few glasses of his favourite whisky. Right now David Jones had it easy. It was Daphne and me who had it hard. Not to mention poor Georgie, how was I going to tell her?

Chapter Nine

Hello And Goodbye
January

'I'M SORRY, ROGER, BUT this is your mother we're talking about! I never had the chance to get to know mine, so trust me when I say that you taking your relationship with yours for granted makes me see red. You've been here *once* since the funeral and it's unacceptable. She has Georgie and me, she'll always have Georgie and me, but you're family and it's time you took some damn responsibility and took care of the woman who needs you more than ever right now.' I slammed the phone down on him, with steam coming out of my ears. Georgie was sitting on the sofa, watching me with her mouth ajar and a stunned expression on her face.

'I don't think you should have sugar coated it, Abbie. Why not try telling him what you really think?' she suggested, her tone laced with sarcasm.

'Well, honestly! He's her son, her only child. I love her like she's my own family, you know I do, and I'd do anything for her, but she needs *him* right now. She needs her flesh and blood. He's a pathetic excuse for a son, only turning up once or twice a year when it suits him. Begrudgingly having them for a few days before Christmas. Where has he been when they needed help, when the heating broke down, when David fell down the stairs and broke his ankle, when Daphne gave them food poisoning by using food from tins that were ten years out of date? Huh? Huh?!' I ranted, pausing for breath as I put my hands on my hips.

'I totally agree, but this anger you have needs another outlet, Abbie. You haven't cried since it happened, not even at the funeral. I get that you've wanted to be strong for Daphne, but you need to let someone else be strong while you grieve, too. He was like a father to you.'

'I don't have time to cry,' I muttered stubbornly. 'With Roger … *arsewipe* out of the picture, who else does she have?'

'Ermmm, hello, am I not much cop? Come and sit down, sweetie, it's ok to stop for a moment and think about what you've lost, too,' she urged.

'I don't want to, Georgie! I've experienced too much loss and I don't think I can take anymore. If I let myself cry, I'm not sure I'll stop. Come on, let's go and check on her. I made some lovely fruit scones and strawberry jam, and got some clotted cream, as it's her favourite snack. We can go and have a nice Sunday afternoon tea with her, take her mind off it.'

Georgie sighed with a nod and held her hands up in defeat as I busied myself in the kitchen. Truth be told, I needed my mind taken off it. I'd been miserable since it had happened, finding it difficult to remember the last time I'd laughed. I was tired and irritable, and lately this long-distance thing with Miller was getting me down. I'd turned twenty-nine in June, and eleven bridesmaid dresses were now residing in my attic as my biological clock continued to count down. Sixty years the Joneses had been married. Was it wrong to want a love like that? To want to be with that person permanently, for your love to be so strong it would last a lifetime? I'd fallen for Miller so hard, I'd been so sure he was the one, but lately I was questioning that. How could we build a foundation as solid as Daphne and David's when we were constantly chasing time with each other, with long breaks in between?

I hugged Daphne as tightly as I could when she opened the door, causing her to remind me that at her age, she was likely to suffer from brittle bones and I might break her if I didn't let her go. How pathetic was I that she was handling the loss of her husband better than I was? I blinked away some tears and busied myself putting together our cream tea while Georgie went to light a fire in the lounge. I laid out the tray, with Daphne's pretty blue and white Wedgewood fine china tea service. I put doilies under the pile of freshly baked scones and little pots filled to the brim with sticky jam and thick yellow cream with that crust that just made the English treat so delightful. Except right now it was looking as tempting as cardboard. I carried it through and put it on the coffee table, then took charge of the teapot and poured a cup of aromatic Earl Grey for us all.

'Well, this is lovely,' Daphne smiled, reaching over to squeeze my knee as I took my place on the sofa next to her.

'Hmmm,' agreed Georgie, 'nothing beats Abbie's scones in front of a nice fire on a winter's afternoon.'

'Aren't you having any, dear?' Daphne asked, as she loaded one with jam and cream.

'No, I'm not really feeling hungry right now. But you two tuck in,' I suggested. I sat back with my cup and saucer and absentmindedly sipped the steaming hot tea, glancing up when I heard Georgie splutter, then choke.

'Jesus,' she muttered, screwing up her face as Daphne began to cough and pat her chest.

'What? What's wrong?' I asked, my eyes darting between them as they both set their plates of food down and gulped at their tea.

'Ermmm, have you been trying out a new recipe?' Georgie asked.

'No, it's my usual one, I know it by heart. Why?'

'You were a bit heavy handed with the–'

'Currants,' Daphne interrupted. 'Lots and lots of currants. They just took us by surprise, went down the wrong way.'

'Currants?' I looked down at my scones in surprise. If anything, I'd put less in. I hadn't had many left in my cupboard and couldn't be bothered to walk up to the village store.

'Yes, currants,' Georgie agreed, nodding very emphatically when I looked up at her. 'Down … the wrong way.'

'Are you sure? I didn't put in as many as normal. Don't they taste good?'

'De-li-cious,' Daphne stated, over-pronouncing each syllable and flashing Georgie a look that I couldn't quite work out, before she lifted up the piece she'd started and carried on tucking in.

'Mmmm-hmmm,' Georgie agreed, nodding so hard her head was at risk of falling off as she nearly emptied her pot of jam on the small morsel she lifted up to her lips and started to chew.

'Want a bit of scone with your jam?' I asked, raising my eyebrows as she chewed. Her blue eyes went wide as Daphne's patterned cake plate as she made a meal of swallowing and forced back another cough.

'How about another pot of tea, dear?' Daphne suggested, giving me a poignant look.

'There's plenty left, let me pour you another cup,' I offered, picking up the teapot.

'I'm not feeling in an Earl Grey mood today. How about some plain breakfast tea? It's in the top cupboard above the kettle.'

'Hmmm, I'd love some breakfast tea to go with these really, *really*, delicious scones,' Georgie nodded. I gave her a strange look, wondering if she'd suddenly developed some rare nodding illness, as her head just continued to bob up and down.

'Ok.' I gave them both another look. I was getting the feeling I was missing something here, but I picked up the teapot and headed back out to the kitchen.

I flicked on the kettle as I rinsed out the dregs of Earl Grey and sighed. Even spending yesterday working hadn't cheered me up, and I usually loved a good spreadsheet. Messing around with numbers always made me happy, but it was like someone had sucked out my happiness these last few weeks. I felt like I was living under a permanent stormy black cloud, waiting for the heavens to open. I rummaged in the cupboard, but couldn't find the tea leaves Daphne had mentioned anywhere, nor in the cupboard to the left of the sink. I padded back to the lounge to find the two of them with their backs to me, bent over the fire.

'They're not burning. Quick, cover them with another log,' Daphne ordered.

'She'll know. I mean, there were six on the plate, no one eats three scones each that quickly,' Georgie replied, grabbing a piece of wood as I folded my arms over my chest.

'She won't if we just say how delicious they were.'

'I can't believe you're advocating lying!'

'You were the one who said burn them. Don't lay this on me, Georgie Basset. I was all for eating them regardless,' Daphne retorted. 'Besides, we're doing a kindness. She's down as it is, I don't want to see her any more unhappy.'

'Ok, what's going on?' I demanded, making them both jump, then turn to face me with grimaces. Georgie swallowed hard as her cheeks went pink.

'Nothing, just a bit chilly, that's all.'

'Don't give me that. You're both hiding something from me. What was wrong with my scones?'

'Nothing,' they both chorused. I narrowed my eyes at them and Georgie wilted, then covered her eyes.

'Stop, stop. That's the stare, the terrifying accountant stare that says you've found a discrepancy and has me visualising a life behind bars for a one pence tax fraud. Or the one that says my tax bill's going to be so high, I need to sell my house and leave Dilbury. You know it puts me on edge.'

'Georgie Basset,' I warned.

'Your scones were disgusting. There, I've said it!' she expelled in a rush. I gasped as Daphne groaned and covered her face with her hands.

'My scones have won first place at the village fête for the last seven years,' I protested. 'And my jam and my cookies.'

'Well, these wouldn't have, sweetie. It was like swallowing seawater. Except I've done that and that was more pleasant. In fact, I'd rather stick my hand in the fire and pull them out than try and eat another crumb of one.'

'Georgie, what happened to our plan not to upset her?' Daphne scolded.

'They were salty? Seriously?' I uttered, stunned.

'The jam too, which I didn't discover until I put a mountain of it on a tiny piece of scone, hoping to ease it down,' Georgie confirmed, nodding vigorously again.

'Really?' I plopped down onto the sofa, shaking my head.

'I think you must have mixed up the sugar and salt, my dear. It's not the end of the world,' Daphne said softly as she shuffled back over to ease herself down next to me.

'But other than maths and accounting, cookies, scones, and jam are what I'm good at,' I moaned. 'If I can't even make those right, what kind of mess have I been making of my customers' accounts? Why didn't you just say, instead of trying to eat ... then burn them?'

'You've been so depressed lately, we didn't want to add to your burdens.' Daphne took my hand and stroked it as she smiled at me.

'But ... but ... I have no right to be depressed. You ... you ...' I shook my head, feeling the sting of tears prickling the back of my eyes.

'You lost him too, dear,' she stated gently. 'Grief can remind us of other people in our lives that we've lost, and I know you've been blaming yourself for it happening at your house while I was with you, which is ridiculous. Then there's poor Mr. Sumo's cancer, your American boyfriend who you barely see, and you've taken on too many clients and are working too hard. It's all caught up with you.'

'She's right, Abbie. And I know this always-the-bridesmaid thing is getting to you as well. We need to inject more fun in your life.'

'Well, I know something that will cheer you up,' Daphne announced, giving us both a so-there nod.

'Liam Hemsworth is moving to Dilbury?' I offered as I sipped on the remains of my nearly cold tea, but even the thought of my go-to celebrity hunk didn't raise any excitement in me. Wow, I really did have the blues.

'No, but our new neighbour has moved in, and I have all the gossip.'

'Why doesn't that surprise me?' Georgie whispered as she flashed me a knowing smile. Daphne beckoned us in closer, then took a look around her before whispering the news.

'She's an author. Of *very* salacious material. I've not read any of her books yet, but I've heard they make Fifty Shakes read like a children's novel.'

'Fifty Shakes?' Georgie giggled, and I couldn't help but smile a bit too. 'Do you mean Fifty Shades?'

'No, I'm sure it's Fifty Shakes.'

'Well, I'm pretty sure I could write a novel more saucy than one about milkshakes,' Georgie stated emphatically.

'Milkshakes? Oh no,' Daphne rebutted with a shake of her head. 'It's all about sex, my dear. With whips and handcuffs. Of course, it may be shocking to some, but some of us have had a slightly more colourful life.' She gave me a wink, and I choked and sprayed my mouthful of tea all over myself, making Georgie do her unladylike snorting laugh.

'You and ... David ... handcuffs ... kink ... need bleach for my mind,' I groaned, slamming my cup and saucer down as I covered my eyes and tried to blot out that disturbing visual.

'Like you youngsters have the monopoly on sexy bedroom shenanigans,' Daphne chuckled. 'That book injected a bit of passion back into our lives and led to David's hip replacement operation being moved forward. They couldn't understand how it had worn down so fast from his last X-ray.'

'Oh my God,' I moaned, as Georgie continued to snort.

'I'm pretty sure you mean the book Fifty Shades, Daphne, but if there really is a saucy one called Fifty Shakes, I might have to look it up,' she added.

'Really, it's shades and not shakes?' Daphne mused as I finally uncovered my eyes, wondering if I was dreaming this frankly awkward conversation. 'I thought it was shakes because it was the amount of times his penis was milked. I did try keeping count of all of the sex scenes, but was too busy trying to re-enact some of them.'

'Hahaha,' Georgie screeched, throwing herself back in the armchair and clutching her sides as some tears rolled down her face, while I sat with my mouth ajar. 'Please … stop, you're … killing me,' she gasped, trying to wipe her eyes. 'So I have a saucy author living next door to me? What does she look like? You'd imagine them to be sexy minxes, but I've heard some of them look like butter wouldn't melt in their mouths.'

'No idea, dear,' Daphne replied, picking up her knitting and sitting back in the chair. 'She moved in while I was having my afternoon nap yesterday. Why don't you nip around and introduce yourselves?'

'I think we ought to. Come on, Abbie. It's not like we can eat the rest of our cream tea.'

'Not since you burned it,' I reminded her.

'True.'

'I'm not in the mood to be nice. Can't we just look over the hedge and see if we can spot her first? It'll give me time to adjust to this disturbing news about … *all* of our neighbours.'

'Don't tell me you haven't read those kind of books, Abbie Carter,' Daphne scoffed as her knitting needles clacked together, and she gave me a look over the top of her glasses. 'We've all heard the noises coming from your bedroom in the hot summer months, when Miller stayed over and you left your windows open.'

'Ok, that's it. Disturbing sex talk tolerance has reached its maximum quota,' I said firmly, shooting up from my seat as Georgie giggled and nodded her agreement. 'Let's go check out this mistress of erotica, then I'm going to bake a fresh batch of scones and we can start this weird afternoon all over again and erase it from my mind with our usual afternoon tea banter.'

'I quite enjoyed this, I haven't laughed so much in ages,' Georgie stated as she stood up. 'You're not coming to spy on our neighbour, Daphne?'

'Much as I'm dying to meet her and grill her, I'll invite her over one afternoon. Or better yet, invite her around now, or at least come back with the gossip for me. I'm warm and comfortable and I want to finish this new jumper for Mr. Sumo. They've forecast snow for tomorrow.'

'He does love them,' I agreed, bending to give her a quick peck on the cheek. She smiled back at me and I felt my cheeks flush. I wasn't sure if I was more embarrassed at her hearing my sex noises or at the thought of her and David with handcuffs ... *no, don't go there, Abbie.*

'Why are we doing this?' Georgie complained as we crawled on our hands and knees along the thin strip of green grass that bordered the naked field running along the back of all of our cottages.

'We don't want her to see us watching her,' I replied as we approached her garden.

'Why can't we just knock on the door with a cup of sugar, like most neighbours would do?'

'Because apparently I'm so out of sorts, I'd give her a cup of salt and likely poison her!' I retorted, still annoyed with myself. 'Besides, she's probably sexy and glamorous. I don't want to meet her when I'm looking like crap, dressed in my leggings and a baggy jumper.'

'Honestly,' Georgie huffed, then squealed when I pushed her flat onto her front. I'd found a gap in the hedge which would be perfect for spying, as our new neighbour was the only one of us that didn't have a back gate. 'What now?'

'We watch and we wait,' I replied as I lay next to her, our eyes trained on the back of the cottage. The plot of land that all four cottages had been built on was a sort of triangular shape, with this cottage having the smallest rear garden, and mine, at the other end of the lane, the largest. We were much closer to her house and could see right into her lounge and kitchen through the expanse of modern glass bi-fold doors the previous owners had put in. We could see piles of boxes in the middle of each room, and I felt sorry for this woman. I remembered being surrounded by them when I moved into Dad's cottage and not knowing where to start.

'I can hear a tractor in the field next door,' Georgie whispered. 'It'll be all around the village if we're spotted lying here, spying on our neighbour.'

'Sssshhhh,' I warned, spotting movement in the kitchen. 'You know old Richard Davies is as blind as a bat. He won't spot us over the hedge as he goes past.'

'He shouldn't be driving full stop with that eyesight. Have you seen his glasses? Like the bottom of beer bottles. Honestly, I'm more worried about him missing the hedge and ploughing right through it. And us!'

'Sssshhhh, look, she's there.' I nudged Georgie as our new neighbour came and stood at the glass doors of her kitchen diner to look out over the garden.

'Wow, so not what I expected.'

'Me neither,' I agreed, as we looked at the very pretty blonde around our age. She was shorter than us, petite with a curvaceous figure à la Marilyn Monroe. 'I'd always imagined that authors of the racy books I read weren't in fact sex Goddesses who typed away in stockings and suspenders, sexy basques and fluffy pink marabou feather slippers, but were middle-aged women in food-stained pyjamas with matted bed hair and unbrushed teeth.'

'Does anyone even buy marabou slippers anymore?'

'I bet Daphne has a pair. I'm seriously disturbed after hearing all of that this afternoon.'

'Me too,' giggled Georgie. 'Oh my God, have you just farted?'

'No!' I exclaimed, shooting her a look.

'Has Sumo followed us out here?' she mumbled, as she hauled her jumper up to cover her nose.

'Jesus,' I groaned, doing the same. 'Georgie! Even Sumo's eyes would water with that.'

'It's not me, thank you very much!' she huffed, raising her voice over the roar of the approaching tractor.

'Well, I doubt it's our new neighbour. Look at her, with her perfect figure. She looks too angelic to fart. All she's missing is a halo on top of those ridiculously gorgeous blonde curls.'

'Everyone farts,' she scoffed, 'even little Miss Perfect there. And I bet even if she doesn't bottom burp, with the amount of sex she has to have to come up with the material to write those stories, she probably fanny farts all the time.'

'Fanny farts,' I giggled, for the first time in weeks. 'I love you, Georgie, you can always pull me out of my pit of gloom.'

'Abbie, seriously, what have you eaten?' she yelled as Richard the farmer drew level with us over the hedge to our left.

'It's not me! Trust me, I've never farted something that toxic before,' I yelled back.

'Can we go home now that we've seen her?' Georgie shouted. 'It's raining now as well, we're going to get all muddy.'

'Fine,' I agreed with a sigh, then a cough and a choke as the God-awful smell became unbearable. My eyes widened in horror as I saw the light "rain" splatter on Georgie's cream jumper. 'Shit!' I exclaimed.

'I know, I should have put my wellies on,' she grumbled as she struggled up onto all fours and her jumper slipped down from her mouth.

'No, shit! It's raining shit,' I shrieked, as a large dollop smacked her in the side of the face and the brown liquid mess started sliding down her cheek. She looked at me wide-eyed and screamed as we both got pelted with forceful jets of wet cow manure coming over the hedge from Richard's muck-spreading machine. I scrunched up my eyes and protected them with my hands as I just lay there, waiting for it to pass, while Georgie tried to get up to make a run for it. Plop after plop of poo fell onto my back, the warm mess weaving itself into my hair as my eyes watered from the smell. Great, just … great!

'Abbie!' Georgie screamed. I slowly pushed myself up to sit back on my feet and used my hands to smear the poop-soaked wet hair back from my face, shuddering to feel the hot, thick sludge coating me. I looked around to see Georgie had tripped and was lying face down in the ploughed field, so much poo on her back she almost blended into her surroundings. I started giggling. The giggle became a laugh. Then the laugh became a full-on roar as my shoulders shook. 'It's *not* funny. First salty scones, then I found out my pensioner neighbours were having more exciting sex than me, then I get covered in cow poo, now mud. I've had a seriously shitty day,' she howled as she struggled up, then turned to face me, a combination of poo and mud coating her front as well.

'A *shitty* day! That's the understatement of the year,' I laughed as I scuttled on my hands and knees away from our neighbour's back hedge, though I was sure she'd have heard the noise we were making.

'How can you laugh at this?' Georgie moaned, globs of cow manure dropping from her as she stood there, unrecognisable.

'Because it could only happen to us, and if I don't laugh right now, I'll probably cry,' I stated, as I scrambled up once I'd reached the boundary of Georgie's garden. 'Come on, let's go hose off.'

'I'm never forgiving you for this,' Georgie huffed, as we headed through her back gate and trudged up her garden. 'I feel sick from the smell.'

'Of course you'll forgive me. I'm your best friend, and if you're going to get showered in manure, who better to do it with than me?'

'My jumper's ruined.' She shot me a glare as we came to a halt outside her grooming cabin.

'I'll get you a new one. Honestly, it could have been worse.'

'How?' she grumbled as we both took a deep breath and sealed our mouths and eyes shut as we hauled our soaked jumpers over our heads.

'We could have been spotted like this by Miss Perfect next door.' I tossed my jumper onto the floor and pulled my t-shirt off as well.

'I guess,' Georgie agreed, doing the same as I kicked off my trainers. 'How humiliating would that have been?'

'Hmmm,' I agreed.

We both stripped down to our underwear, not convinced the poo hadn't soaked through our clothing. Some had definitely run down inside Georgie's jumper. She unravelled the hose she used to clean off some of the bigger dogs that didn't fit in the specially designed sinks for the dog baths inside. I braced myself and shrieked as the cold water hit me, and Georgie did a circuit, making sure to clean my hands, then letting me cover my nose, mouth, and eyes before she did my hair. It was going to take more than a cold hose down to get this smell off us both.

'Ok, do me,' she ordered as I stood there shivering. Of all the days to need a freezing cold outdoor shower, we had to pick a crisp winter afternoon. She screamed like she was being murdered as I turned up the pressure to blast her clean. 'I hate you, Abbie Carter!'

'Oh, shut up,' I laughed.

'Hello?' came a soft and sultry voice. 'Is everything ok?' We turned to face the paved drive that led down the side of Georgie's house to her dog-grooming cabin. Our new neighbour was leaning on the wide wooden gate, watching us with an amused smile on her face.

'Are you kidding me?' muttered Georgie under her breath as she flashed me a glare.

'Sorry to interrupt your … whatever it is you're doing in your wet underwear, but from the screams, I thought you might need some help.'

'We're awesome, thanks,' I replied, crossing my arms over my chest. I wished I could cover more of my non-bikini-season body and seriously hoped I'd shaved my legs recently. Even without make-up, all fresh faced, this girl was a knockout.

'Just hosing off cow manure,' Georgie added, putting her hands on her hips as she tossed her wet hair back over her shoulder and tried to strike a sexy pose as she pulled in her stomach.

'We were walking the dog in the field,' I lied, 'when the muck spreader went past.'

'Really, and I thought it was that you were lying like army commandos, spying on me through my hedge,' she grinned.

'I *really* hate you right now, Abbie,' Georgie glared in my direction again as I felt my cheeks flame. 'It was her idea,' she added, flicking an accusing thumb at me.

'Don't worry, my reputation precedes me. I'm used to people wanting to see the "hussy" next door. I'm Charlotte, by the way, but most people call me Charlie.' She flashed a warm smile as she held out her hand.

'Georgie Basset. So sorry, it was my stupid best friend's idea. I wanted to come and knock on your door like normal people would,' Georgie advised as she went to shake Charlie's hand.

'I wasn't feeling glamorous and I didn't want you to see me looking a mess, but now you've ended up seeing us in our wet underwear, stinking of cow shit,' I added as I shook her hand too. 'Abbie Carter, and I really am sorry.'

'Don't be. You've just inspired a whole "hot lesbians in the country" novel.'

'*Not* lesbians,' we both stated firmly.

'Why don't you go and change and come over for a drink? I've no idea where the kettle is, but I've got my shot glasses and some alcohol out.'

'A girl with my own priorities,' Georgie laughed.

'We're actually supposed to be heading back to Daphne's next door,' I reminded Georgie, before turning back to Charlie. 'Her husband just died and we were having afternoon tea with her. Why don't you give us ten minutes and head over there instead? She has whisky, as well as hot drinks,' I suggested.

'I won't be intruding?' Charlie asked, her dark brown eyes reminding me of Miller's.

'Trust me, she's eager to meet you too. And from what we learned this afternoon, she'll be grilling you for sex tips when she's ready to get back on the horse. She's not as innocent as she looks. Plus, as the village gossip, your book sales in Dilbury will soon go through the roof.'

'Excellent! Ok, I'll go rummage out a bottle of wine for her. See you in a while.'

'Bye,' we both called as we watched her walk back up Georgie's front drive and head left to her house, her perfectly rounded bottom swaying sexily as she went.

'Owww,' I moaned as Georgie punched me in the arm.

'Great way to impress the sexy new neighbour, dripping wet in my unmatching underwear and stinking of shit. I'm so going to get you back for this.'

'Sing a new tune,' I replied, gathering up my wet clothes after first making sure they were inside out to avoid getting any more poo on me. 'I'm taking the back route home before I'm seen by anyone else. Knowing my luck, Heath will be bush trimming as I walk up the front path in my underwear.'

'At least he could help you out, you're overdue a trim. A wax isn't just seasonal, you know,' Georgie laughed.

I scowled at her, then spun around and squelched my way down her garden path. I headed out through her back gate to the ploughed field and turned left to head along the hedge to my gate. I'd had enough humiliation for one day. At least this way, I'd avoid being seen.

'Hello, Abbie,' came a chorus of amused voices. I stood there mortified, dressed in just my wet underwear, clutching my bundle of clothes in front of me, as a large group of elderly village ramblers walked past me, some of the men eyeing me up and down.

'Ermmm, hel … hello,' I stuttered. 'Was a lovely afternoon for a dip in the river, absolutely lovely.'

'In your see-through underwear in the middle of winter?' chuckled Mr. Greggs, the village hall caretaker.

I felt my cheeks burn as I scurried through my gate and ran back to my house before anyone else saw me. Life at the moment just sucked.

Saturday

'What's wrong? You've not been yourself since I arrived yesterday,' Miller asked as he massaged my shoulders. He was sitting on the sofa and I was on the floor leaning back between his legs, as Sumo slept next to him while we watched a film in front of the fire. I drew in a deep breath, trying to pluck up the courage to start the conversation I'd been wanting to have with him since we'd had a disagreement about it. The day Miller had disappeared to clear his head. The day David had died.

'Where are we going, Miller?'

'Back up to bed when the film finishes?' he replied, sounding confused. I shuffled forwards and spun around to sit cross-legged on the floor as I looked up at him.

'I meant us. We've been dating for thirteen months and I'm not sure how much longer I can do this long-distance thing, snatching time with each other here and there.'

'I know,' he sighed, scrubbing his hands up over his handsome face, then running his hands through his ruffled hair. 'I've been thinking about it too, especially since our discussion on Christmas Day. You really won't consider trying out New York with me?'

'How can I? We've already discussed this. There's my job, and I don't want to think about retraining yet in case I hate living over there. Then there's Sumo, who can't fly, and Daphne, who needs me, and … and …' I hesitated and looked down at my fingers intertwined in my lap. 'I'm just not ready to leave here, Miller. It's my family home. It's the last connection I have to my parents.'

'Well, I can't move here, Abbie.'

'Can't, or won't?' I asked, lifting my head to look at him. I felt the air get sucked out of my lungs, like it did every time our eyes locked.

'Both, I guess,' he offered with an apologetic shrug.

'Why not? I know Dilbury isn't exactly cosmopolitan, but we have high-speed broadband for you to work from here, and you have the private airfield down the road so you can keep chartering your own plane when you need to go back to New York for business. Your best friend lives in Shrewsbury now and you have no family over there. It makes more sense for you to live here than for me to live there.'

'It's not that simple, Abbie,' he stated, his voice laced with frustration. 'To start with, I need an office.'

'Then we can get Dad's station kitted out for you. It's large, I could have all of his kit and tools put in a new shed and you could get it done up with all your hi-tech gadgetry.'

'Abbie,' he sighed. 'Even if that worked, I …' He stalled and threw himself back on the sofa with a shake of his head.

'I can't carry on like this, Miller,' I said reluctantly. 'It kills me each time you leave and it's making me miserable. Daphne and Georgie have noticed, and even I'm starting to hate myself for being such a whinger and mope. Being happy when you're here is being overridden by being miserable the large proportion of the time that you're not. What else is holding you back? Is it me, do you not feel strongly enough about me to want to try us living together?'

'Abbie, I love you, I just …' He broke off and stared at me, confusion written all over his face, which matched my own feelings right now. I just didn't understand his objections.

'So you love me enough to suggest that I uproot my life, but not enough for you to do the same?' I snapped as I scrambled to my feet, feeling hurt and angry with him.

'Don't be like that,' he protested, as I went to stand by the fire with my back to him. I wrapped my arms around myself as I stared at the orange flames. It felt like they were burning me from the inside out. The thought that this might be it, that we were finally acknowledging that this relationship could never continue with an ocean between us, that we were realising we could never work unless something changed, was painful. Then I thought of Daphne, about how much more painful it must be to lose someone you'd loved with all of your heart for sixty years. I swallowed the ball of emotion that filled my throat and reached up to wipe some tears from my cheeks. I just couldn't imagine it. I didn't want to imagine it, let alone experience it. Maybe that was why I'd never let a relationship get this far before, I was scared of losing someone I cared about all over again. I was better off on my own than facing the heartache of losing Miller further down the line.

'Don't be like what?' I whispered. I didn't want to lose him, but if he wasn't prepared to fight for me, why should I fight for him?

'You're my first girlfriend, Abbie. I'm still getting used to *being* in a relationship, which is a huge deal for a guy with a history like mine. Why can't we carry on as we are?'

'Because I'm unhappy, Miller. I don't want to be this person anymore, the girl whose mood is dictated by her boyfriend's visits, who spends the rest of her life in a slump when he's overseas. And I think I'm more invested in this than you.'

'How can you say that?' he demanded angrily behind me. His raised voice woke Sumo up, who let out a series of whines and grunts.

'Because you want me to give up everything to try things your way, despite me having valid reasons for not being able to right now, but you're not ready to do the same for me. You can't even come up with a reason to explain why you can't try a few months over here, can you? It's not like I'm proposing or demanding we have a baby. I'm just suggesting you try living here for a while, and you're saying no. So it's me. You're not sure about me.'

'I've never been more sure of anything in my life, Abbie, other than my job,' he said softly as he pressed up behind me, clutching my shoulders as he kissed the side of my temple. I closed my eyes and sighed as I breathed him in. 'I told you that I felt a connection to you the first time I saw you. I've given you more of me than anyone I've ever met.'

'But it's still not enough, is it?' I whispered, the reality of acknowledging that we were in completely different places in our relationship hitting me full force, like a sledgehammer to my heart, sending it scattering. I forced back my tears, not wanting him to see how devastated I was feeling.

'Even if you won't try New York, what we have is enough for me,' he replied as he wrapped his arms tightly around my waist, his hands smothering mine.

'Then we have our answer, don't we?' I replied. I pulled my hands from under his and prised myself out of his arms. I quickly walked towards the lounge door, feeling an ache in my chest.

'Where are you going?' he demanded.

'To make up the spare room for you,' I answered as I gripped the doorframe, not looking back at him. 'I think it's best you organise your plane to take you home tomorrow.'

'You're breaking up with me?' he gasped, an unusually cold tone to his voice.

'We're in different places, Miller. Physically and metaphorically.'

I held my breath, waiting for him to argue, for him to prove that he was more invested in us than I gave him credit for, but I was met with silence. I headed up the stairs with heavy feet, and an even heavier heart, and shut myself in the guest room. Before I had a chance to think about making the bed, I found myself climbing onto it and curling into a tight ball, clutching one of the pillows to me as my bottom lip quivered and I stared at the wall, willing myself not to cry.

The front door slamming made me bolt upright, feeling dizzy and disorientated, surrounded by darkness. It took me a while to remember I'd come to the guest room to make up the bed and had then laid down. I fumbled about and found the lamp switch on the bedside table, realising that I must have fallen asleep. I rubbed my eyes and stood on shaky legs, then staggered to the window. I was just in time to see Miller load his case into the boot of his car. My jaw dropped. Was he seriously leaving without even saying goodbye? I banged on the window, my heart suddenly beating so fast I thought it might explode, but he didn't look up. God damn it, this damn treble glazing was too efficient. I grabbed the window handle and tried to open it, but it was locked and the key wasn't in the keyhole. I found myself flying to the door, then throwing myself down the stairs as I raced to the front door. I threw it open and ran out into the snow barefoot, charging up the path as I saw the red tail lights of his car pulling away.

'Miller!' I screamed. I cursed as I yanked the gate open, misjudging it in my haste and smacking myself in the knee and ribs. By the time I'd made it out onto the lane, he was turning the corner. I started running up the lane, chasing him as I yelled, but I slipped over and fell face first into the cold snow. Just like I had the first night Miller and I had kissed. I hammered the snow with my fists as I started sobbing. Big, fat, ugly tears that I'd bottled up ever since David had died at Christmas.

I cried for my mum. The woman I'd never known.

I cried for my dad. The best man I'd ever known.

I cried for David. And for Daphne.

Then I cried for me. For Sumo, and for Miller.

I was sick and tired of losing people in my life, and I wasn't sure how much more I could take.

I didn't stop crying until my clothes soaked up the snow underneath me and my body went numb. I suddenly felt empty. I rolled onto my back, staring up at the overcast night sky and dulled moon, wiping away the snot and tears from my face with a damp sleeve.

'Get up, Abbie Carter,' I ordered myself. 'You've had your pity party. You always knew it was too good to be true, that a man like Miller would fall for a girl like you.'

I pushed myself up and trudged back to the house, shivering, my feet and hands like blocks of ice. I was surprised to see Sumo framed by the light of the hall, sitting by the open front door and panting as he looked out, wondering what was going on.

'It's ok, Chubbers, I'm still here,' I told him, giving him a quick head rub. 'Though I'm sure you'd much rather it was Miller, wouldn't you, boy?'

He looked up at me with his sad brown eyes, reaffirming my thoughts as I shut and locked the door behind me. I couldn't face climbing the stairs, I couldn't even be bothered to go and get these wet clothes off. I plonked myself in front of the fire, as close as I could get without getting in it, and gritted my teeth as my hands and feet started to prickle painfully back to life. I felt something nudging my arm and looked down to see Sumo trying to push his head under it, so I lifted it up with a frown.

'What are you doing?' I asked. He never came near me voluntarily. But almost as if he knew I needed some comfort, he snorted and snuffled his way to scramble up onto my lap, then plopped down on it with a huff and started licking my hand.

It made me start crying all over again. He'd never done that before.

Chapter Ten
Planting New Seeds
February

IT WAS ONE MONTH post-Miller. One month of radio silence. He hadn't even rung to see if I was ok. Then again, I hadn't rung him either. I was stubborn like that. I wasn't sure I could forgive him for leaving without even a note, let alone a goodbye. And it still stung that he'd obviously never felt about me the way I had about him. But I'd pulled on my big girl pants and was making the best of things, refusing to mope. Which was extra tough, being a single loser on Valentine's Day.

'Stop grumbling, I'm doing all the heavy lifting,' I warned Sumo as he grizzled loudly in his pull-along. I giggled to myself. He was looking super cute in a seasonal white knitted jumper with red hearts all over it, even if his face said he didn't feel quite as enthused about it as I did. Daphne had made him enough for a different one each day of the week, and much as he hated me dressing him in them, he needed the extra warmth. He'd started losing weight and I worried about him in the cold. I tied his lead to the drainpipe of the village shop. 'Don't go anywhere. Not that you can remember what your legs were even invented for, unless it involves food,' I reminded him. He cocked his head, his ears lifting slightly at the word. I rolled my eyes, scratched him behind the ears, and headed into the shop.

'Morning, Abbie,' called Sheila Vickers, the shop owner.

'Morning, Sheila. How are you?'

'Can't complain,' she replied, then proceeded to do just that. I smiled politely as I wandered around the cramped little store while she chuntered on in the background, and filled my basket with goodies for a special spinsters' Valentine's meal tonight, which I was hosting for Daphne, Georgie, and Charlie. We'd commiserate with good food, good wine, and good company. 'So, the cream wasn't doing anything for his haemorrhoids, and there's some things not even a wife wants to know about, let alone push back in, if you know what I mean,' Sheila rambled.

'Or a neighbour,' I grimaced, quickly setting down the bunch of red grapes I'd just picked up with a shudder. Now every time I saw a bunch of grapes, I was going to think of her husband's haemorrhoids.

'Well, everyone said Bonjela would really help, but it hasn't.'

'Bonjela?' I uttered, giving her a horrified look. 'That's for mouth ulcers, not ... bottom problems.'

'Is it? Well, he does have mouth ulcers, too. Oh dear, I wonder if I've switched the creams by mistake. You don't use Anusol on your ulcers then?'

'Ermmm, I'd say not. Maybe the "Anus" part of the name should have given you a clue that you were using it on the wrong orifice,' I chuckled. 'I think you'd better get him to see a doctor as soon as possible. I'm pretty sure putting Anusol in your mouth, or Bonjela on your bottom, can't be good for you.'

'Well, sometimes people have excellent tips, don't they? No point rushing to the doctor or hospital each time you have a problem. You know Mr. Benson up Ivy Lane?'

'Hmmm,' I confirmed as I grabbed some garlic. He was a sweet old chap. Ex-military, very chivalrous, distinguished and well spoken.

'Suffering from terrible erectile dysfunction he was, until Barbara Henderson suggested he try some Miracle Grow.'

'On his penis?' I uttered, looking at her in astonishment over my shoulder.

'Oh no, silly me,' she chuckled. 'That was for Mr. Bentley's petunias.'

'Thank God,' I replied as I put some potatoes in my basket. Miracle Grow really would live up to its name if it made todgers stand to attention after one dose.

'What are you cooking?' she asked.

'Steak with potato au gratin. I've got the meat, garlic, and potatoes, what else did I need?' I pondered as my eyes roamed the shop.

'Viagra?'

'Ermmm, no, I don't think that's in the recipe,' I giggled, marvelling at the total randomness that spewed out of Sheila's mouth.

'No, for Mr. Bentley. Viagra, is it? For a floppy penis?'

'Oh, right, yes, but Mr. Bentley had floppy petunias. Mr. Benson had a floppy ... you know.'

'You heard that too?' she gasped, then let out a series of tuts as she shook her head. 'Well, nothing in this village stays secret for long, does it?'

'Well no, it doesn't,' I agreed. 'But you just told me that.'

'No, I didn't.'

'Yes, you did. You said Mr. Benson from Ivy Lane was suffering from erectile dysfunction.'

'Did I? Oh dear, it was supposed to be a secret.'

'Trust me, I won't be discussing it with anyone,' I said firmly. 'Cream!' I announced proudly, remembering my missing ingredient.

'No, little pills. Mabel Benson said they worked so well, he had to go to the hospital as they couldn't get it to go down.'

'I meant cream for my potato dish.'

'What potato dish?' she asked as she pushed her glasses back up her nose. I sighed inwardly. I swear the conversations in here got more bizarre each time I came in.

'What do you mean you're not coming?' I uttered after I rang Georgie to remind her to bring her homemade sloe gin to pour on the forest fruits meringue I'd made for pudding.

'I sort of agreed to a date,' she said apologetically.

'How do you *sort of* agree to a date?'

'Because I really don't want to go out with him, but couldn't think of another excuse to get out of it,' she groaned.

'Ah, Wayne Davies, the farmer's son,' I giggled. He'd been chasing Georgie ever since she'd kicked her fiancé out, but he so wasn't Georgie's type.

'I figured best to just go, then let him down gently at the end of the night.'

'You've been trying to let him down gently for months. I don't think subtlety is a language he understands, Georgie. Just tell him straight, thanks but no thanks.'

'Too late,' she replied with a heavy sigh. 'He's picking me up to take me to dinner at The Fox.'

'In his combine harvester?' I teased. 'Well, make sure he washes his hands well before dinner. He spends his days with his hands up cow, sheep, and pig bottoms.'

'He does? Whatever for?' she gasped in horror.

'I've no idea, but that's what farmer types do in pigging season, isn't it? Help the babies come out?'

'Pigging season,' she giggled. 'You live in the country, Abbie, you should really get with the correct terminology.'

'Ok, Miss "Know it all". What's pigging season called then?' I challenged, and waited as there was silence on the other end of the phone. 'Ha, you have no idea either, do you?'

'Ok, maybe not,' she admitted sheepishly.

'Maybe it's oinking season, as if you had to shoot that many piglets out, you'd be oinking non-stop.'

'Well, I call it bacon and sausage season.'

'Oh yes, marry him, Georgie. There's an upside to everything. Free bacon for life!'

'Steady on,' she warned. 'One step at a time. Are you going to be ok?'

'I'll be fine, I've got Daphne and Charlie. I know who my real friends are. Go get ready for your hot date and ring me in the morning. I want to hear all about his sausage.'

'Shut up, Abbie,' she laughed. 'Have fun.'

'You too,' I sang, and grinned as she put the phone down. I was so glad she was getting out there again, even if it was Wayne. I shuddered as I thought of his short, stubby fingers. They looked like little chipolata sausages that had been sewn onto his huge spade-like hands. Urgh! Damn it, I still had no sloe gin. I dialled Daphne and let it ring for a while, knowing she was a bit slow getting to the phone. 'Hello,' I trilled chirpily as she answered. I was fed up of everyone worrying about me, so was making a real effort to assure them all I was ok.

'Abbie, dear, is that you?'

'It is. Just wondering if you have any of Georgie's sloe gin? I've run out and I want some for our pudding tonight. Could you bring it with you when Charlie calls for you on her way over later?'

'Oh no! I forgot all about dinner, Abbie. I'm so sorry, but Mr. Bentley asked me if I wanted to go to a tea dance in Shrewsbury for the over sixties.'

'Ah, you watch yourself with Mr. Bentley, he has floppy petunias.'

'I know, Sheila from the shop told me. Said he took Viagra for them, which I thought was for erectile dysfunction, but she swore it straightened them right out.'

'Ermmm, no. As usual, Sheila got confused. Mr. Bentley used Miracle Grow,' I giggled. 'Someone else took Viagra for something else that was floppy.'

'Ah, Mr. Wentnor. Been having terrible problems with his waterworks, I heard.'

'No, I don't think Viagra would help that. He had a urine infection, I picked up some antibiotics for him at the doctors last week and some cranberry juice from the shop. He was ever so grateful.'

'So who's had Viagra? No!' she gasped after a momentary pause. 'Not Mr. Benson?'

'I never said a word.'

'You didn't need to. It must be, it's been years since I've seen Mabel looking as happy as she has the last few weeks at our bridge games.'

'Can we possibly get back to the whole "you on a date" news?' I asked, really not needing to hear that the OAPs in the village were more sexually active than I was.

'Oh, it's not a date, dear. There's a whole busload going from the village. It's a singles' night.'

'Ah, single and ready to mingle.'

'There'll be no mingling of any kind,' she scoffed. 'I just … please don't take this the wrong way, dear. You know how fond I am of you and Georgie, you're like the daughters I never had. But sometimes it does me good to be with people my own age. And you don't want a doddery old codger like me cramping your style on Valentine's night. You should be out with a nice young man. You aren't offended, are you?'

'Of course I'm not. I'm glad you're getting out of the house for once. It will do you good, I worry about you.'

'And I worry about you, too. Georgie has a date, I hear, why don't you?'

'I'm not ready yet. It takes time, you know?'

'I do, dear, I do,' she sighed wistfully. 'Right, I'd better go and take my rollers out. Just because there'll be no mingling doesn't mean I can't still show them the old broad has got it.'

'You'll always have it, Daphne,' I said sincerely. I hoped I'd have half of her spunk at her age. We said our goodbyes and I put the phone down, then slapped my forehead. 'Sloe gin! Damn it.'

I started to dial Charlie, but was halted by a knock at the door. I opened the top half, part of me hoping to see Miller's face on the other side, as I always did when I heard a knock. The disappointment to find it wasn't him was slightly offset by the fact that it was Heath. We'd become quite good friends since he'd started doing my gardening. We had this whole easy banter and harmless flirting thing going on.

'Hey, Heath. You're late, I was expecting you over this morning to plant the new seeds in my flower beds.'

'Hey, Abbie. Sorry, something came up this morning.' He flashed me an apologetic smile.

'It seems Viagra really is working its magic in this village,' I stated with a wink.

'Oh God, you heard about that, too?' he laughed. 'Poor Mr. Spalding, the whole village seems to know.'

'He has erectile dysfunction, too? Wow, it's seriously doing the rounds.'

'Too? Who else has it?'

'Not my place to say. Sheila Vickers let it slip this morning.'

'Well, she just told me about Mr. Spalding needing it. She's such a gossip. I called in for a sausage roll for dinner, but she was all out, but while I was there she also told me that Mr. Vickers has wilted petunias, Mr. Bentley has piles, and Mr. Benson has ulcers.'

'Oh my God, that's so not what she told me earlier. Do you think she's getting dementia? She's been rubbing Anusol in Mr. Vickers' mouth and Bonjela on his piles. She's a health hazard, as well as an unwitting malicious gossip.'

123

'Ouch! That mix up sounds painful. So, if Mr. Vickers has piles and ulcers, that means Mr. Benson or Mr. Bentley have wilted petunias or are in need of Viagra. Hmmm,' he pondered as he crossed his arms and put one hand over his mouth as he rubbed his chin.

'Steady on, Inspector Clouseau. This is turning into a Dilbury's answer to Cluedo,' I laughed. 'Anyway, my borders can wait. Why aren't you home getting ready for a date? It's Valentine's night.'

'Why aren't you getting ready?' he shot back.

'As if I'd go on a date so soon after breaking up with Miller. As it happens, I was cooking a lovely early steak dinner for Georgie, Daphne, and Charlie. But Georgie has a date of her own with the ever persistent Wayne, and Daphne is being taken to a tea dance in town by Mr. Bentley, whom I will neither confirm nor deny has floppy anything. So I'm left with too much food for just Charlie and me.' I bit my lower lip as a light bulb went off in my head. Amazingly, Charlie was single at the moment too. I could set her and Heath up, they'd make quite the handsome couple. 'If you don't have a date, why don't you join us? You'd be doing me a favour. Otherwise, I'll probably end up in my pyjamas all day tomorrow scoffing all the leftovers in a fit of depression, and my arse doesn't need the extra calories right now.'

'You've got a great arse, Abbie. I hate skin and bone. I say feed it some extra calories.' He gave me a grin that flashed off his nice teeth. Damn it. Why couldn't I be over Miller already. Heath was super cute. But much as we got on, there just wasn't any spark there for me.

'Thank you, but any bigger and they'll be shipping me off to the farmers' market to be auctioned off as prize rump. So, join us?'

'I can't gate crash a girlie night,' he protested.

'I insist on it. In fact, she's due over in an hour and a half, we were eating early because of Daphne not wanting to disrupt her own bedtime ritual. Why don't you do what you've got to do in the garden while I cook, and you can come straight in when you're done.'

'Are you sure?'

'Absolutely positive,' I said firmly. 'I'll make you a cup of coffee while I get on.'

'Thanks, Abbie. It would have sucked being alone tonight. Second year in a row.'

I gave him a smile that told him I knew the feeling, even though this would only be my first one without Miller. I left Heath to it and shut the door, then busied myself in the kitchen. Anything to take my mind off what Miller might be getting up to with his newfound freedom. Or who he might be getting up to. I gritted my teeth as I thought of how gleeful Fi-Fi would be to hear we'd split up. If I knew her at all, she'd probably make a move on him again.

From what I'd heard, she was out for my blood. She'd called an ambulance the night of Annabelle's wedding and had had to be admitted. Apparently she'd been put in a gynaecology bed, her ankles in foot stirrups, so they could place bags of ice on her hoo-hah to relieve the burning from my Vaporub in her orgasm cream pot. It had been three nights and two days before it had stopped burning and she'd been allowed home. I giggled to myself as I remembered the glee of hearing that news the first time around. She so deserved it. Though she had no proof it was me, she'd told everyone that it was and she was going to get me back. I reassured myself with the knowledge that even if Miller didn't want me, he definitely wouldn't want her.

I dashed back downstairs, wearing my ripped grey skinny jeans and an off-the-shoulder black jumper, having dressed in record time. I'd only put on a touch of mascara, eyeliner, and lip-gloss, just to make a bit of an effort. Tonight was all about Heath and Charlie.

'Are you done, Heath?' I called, as I looked out to find him just finishing up in the dark, using a head torch to see what he was doing.

'Two more minutes, but I'll have to go home and change. I stupidly didn't do the buttons up on the top of my coveralls and I've got mud all over my shirt.'

'I've … I've got one of Miller's shirts in the wardrobe. You can borrow that to save the trip,' I offered, my stomach churning at the thought of someone else wearing it. It was the black one he'd loaned to me the first night we met, but he'd said to keep it when I'd offered to give it back to him when we were dating. It was all I had left of him.

'Will it fit? I've got big guns,' Heath grinned, flexing his muscles to prove it. Wow, I had a feeling that Charlie was going to be one happy girl tonight.

'Trust me, so does Miller. I'll fetch it down, just come in when you're ready.'

'Ok, thanks,' he replied.

I ran back up and grabbed it, giving it one last sniff, even though it smelled nothing like Miller anymore. I could have sworn my memory kicked in and I got the aroma of cinnamon on it, though. I draped it over the end of the stair post in the hall and went to check on the potatoes.

'Damn it, sloe gin!' I uttered, slapping my forehead. I quickly dialled Charlie, hoping she hadn't already left.

'Bugger, bugger, bugger,' she answered.

'Well, that's a new way to answer the phone. Is that how you used to do it down in the Cotswolds?' I laughed.

'Sorry, Abbie, I'm in pain. I stupidly decided to try and ski down the stairs and I'm waiting for an ambulance, my wrist is killing me.'

'You skied down the stairs? My God. In salopettes, goggles, and everything? Eddie the Eagle style?'

'No,' she laughed, then winced. 'I was being sarcastic. I was rushing, as usual, and slid down them rather ungracefully, with language that Daphne would probably have given me one of her stern headmistress stares for.'

'And you rang an ambulance? You could have just called me.'

'You're busy cooking for Daphne and Georgie, I didn't want to bother you. I was going to call you before the ambulance got here.'

'Actually, neither of them are coming for dinner now, they had better offers, but Heath's here.'

'Oooh, the sexy gardener I've yet to meet?'

'The one and only, and I was thinking it would be a great night to set the two of you up.'

'I thought he liked you?'

'Once maybe, but that was ages ago. Are you really ok? I can come and wait with you.'

'I'll be fine, trust me. I've yet to fill you in on my list of medical disasters. This is nothing,' she replied, just as I spotted blue flashing lights creeping down the lane.

'The ambulance has just gone past. I'll come to the hospital to sit with you.'

'Abbie, honestly, I'll be fine. Enjoy your night with Heath. Don't ruin his evening just because I'm a klutz.'

'Will you message me later, let me know how you're getting on then?'

'As soon as I can, I'll send you an update. Sorry to let you down.'

'Take care, Charlie.'

'You too, have fun with Heath!' she called before the line went dead.

'Damn, there goes that plan,' I sighed. 'Oh pants, and the sodding sloe gin!'

'Come on, don't make me drink alone,' I moaned, as I picked up the nearly empty bottle of wine I'd opened to go with our steak dinner.

'I'm more a shorts man,' Heath laughed, covering his water glass as I tried to pour the last of the wine into it.

'You've definitely got the legs for it,' I nodded.

'And when have you been ogling my legs, Abbie Carter?'

'I wasn't really on woodworm watch when you caught me at the window, Heath … cliff.' I burst into a fit of the giggles, and he laughed and shook his head.

'It's Heath Jones, not Heath Cliff. My God, woman, are you always this easy to get drunk?'

126

'*This* doesn't even qualify as tipsy!' I announced, putting the bottle to my lips and guzzling the last few dregs. 'I'm going to crack open the whisky and you're going to join me.'

'Abbie,' he warned, shooting out a hand to steady me as I wobbled when I stood up too fast.

'Don't be a spoilsport. It's Valentine's night and we both have broken hearts, alcohol numbs the pain.'

'Jesus, I think you'd better stick to accounting,' he laughed as I staggered over to my drinks cupboard, singing Jason Donovan's *Too Many Broken Hearts*, probably out of key.

'Damn it, the cupboard's empty,' I whined, wondering how that had happened. Then again, I'd been drowning my sorrows most nights since Miller had left. 'Come on, get your coat. We're going to The Cock & Bull.'

'They'll talk, the two of us in there together on Valentine's night,' he warned.

'Let 'em,' I stated firmly. 'Besides, Sheila Vickers will get it wrong and tell everyone you need Miracle Grow, I need Anusol, and Mr. Bentley and Mr. Benson went on a Valentine's date at The Cock.'

'Don't forget the petunias and waterworks problems,' he reminded me, making me giggle. 'Ok, come on then. I guess a few drinks doesn't sound like a bad idea.'

The pub went silent as we walked in, especially as I was hanging onto Heath's arm in an effort to stay upright. I'd never been able to hold my drink.

'Evening all,' I called, giving them a salute. 'Eyes off me, one of the actual single girls in the village, I'll have you know. You want to be looking at and gossiping about that … *slut* behind the bar. The finance stealer! No, no, not finance, that's what I do. What's it called, fiancé, ha, yes, slutty fiancé stealer,' I announced proudly, pointing at her and wishing I'd had the guts to come in and do that for Georgie months ago.

'Ermmm, that's Tony's wife, Joyce, not Rowena the barmaid,' Heath whispered, as a collective gasp went around the pub.

'Crap, really?' I squinted as I looked closer and saw Joyce fold her arms across her chest and give me a glare. 'Sorry, sorry, my bad. I was talking about Rowena, not Mrs. Dawson. I'm sure she's not a slut, no, no, no. Unless of course Mr. Dawson likes that kind of thing in the bedroom. Do you–' Heath clamped his hand over my mouth as I continued to drunkenly mumble.

'Sorry, she's had a few drinks,' he confirmed loudly as he escorted me the short distance to the bar.

'I'll say,' chuckled Tony, while his wife continued to glare at me. 'What can I get you, Heath?'

127

'Whisky for me, please. Abbie?' he asked as he took his hand off my mouth.

'I think she's had enough,' Mrs. Dawson stated firmly before I had a chance to place an order. 'Serve her, Tony, and you'll be celebrating Valentine's night alone,' she warned her husband as she headed up to the other end of the long bar to serve someone else.

'Oh, come on!' I moaned, pulling my best bottom-lipped pout.

'Sorry, Abbie, you heard the missus.'

'Spoilsport,' I huffed, plopping myself on a high stool.

'Tell you what, Tony. How about I buy a bottle of whisky to take away?' Heath suggested, peeling some notes out of his wallet.

'Now that I can do,' Tony nodded, as I beamed gratefully at him.

'You really can't hold your drink, Abbie,' Heath laughed as I tripped over a flagstone outside the pub entrance and nearly went flying until he caught me.

'Easy for the man who's had none to say.'

'True. Come on, I don't trust you wobbling down the gravel track, you'll do yourself an injury. Let's take the shortcut,' he suggested, steering me around the side of the pub into the beer garden at the back.

'There's a shortcut? How did I not know this?' I demanded.

'Because it's over two stiles and across a field, where you can't go with Sumo.'

'Why are you called Heath?' I asked as he escorted me to the bottom of the beer garden, towards the rickety wooden structure that went over the fence into the field.

'Because it's my name,' he replied dryly.

'Well I know that, silly. But is it short for something?'

'Yes, you said it earlier,' he advised as he helped me up onto the wooden step.

'Heath Jones?'

'No,' he laughed. 'That's my surname. Swing your leg over and put that foot on the other step.'

'You're called Heath Heath Jones? What kind of name is that?'

'It's just Heath Jones. Heath, Christian name. Jones, surname.'

'Ahhh,' I nodded. 'But what's Heath short for? It is short for something, right?'

'Promise not to laugh?' he sighed, releasing my hand as I straddled the wooden fence and gripped it tightly.

'Promise,' I nodded solemnly. 'Wow, I really am tipsy, I can see two of you. Hmmm, two Heaths. You really are Heath Heath Jones. Or would that be Heath Jones Heath Jones, or Heath Heath Jones Jones?'

'Christ almighty. It's Heathcliff,' he muttered.

'He … Heathcliff?' I repeated, grimacing as I tried to hold in my laughter.

'Yes, Heathcliff. I told you that you'd said it earlier. Everyone calls me Heath, thank God.'

'Damn, I'm going to change my name to Catherine.'

'Why Catherine?' he asked, tucking the whisky bottle under his right arm as he stepped up to straddle the fence, facing me. I giggled and threw my arms wide as I looked up at the sky and sang at the top of my voice, giving him my best rendition of Kate Bush's *Wuthering Heights*.

'Great, I'm never going to hear the end of it,' he sighed. 'Please don't sing anymore, it's definitely not one of your talents.'

'Oh, Heathcliff. It gets so very, very dark and lonely without you,' I chortled, desperately trying to remember the lyrics to tease him. He muttered something, right as there was a loud crack and I slid forwards down the fence at the same time as he did, our foreheads smacking together as we met somewhere in the middle. 'Ow!' I groaned and reached up to rub my head, Heath doing the same.

'Jesus, Abbie. Are you ok?'

I screamed as there was another loud crack and we both dropped rapidly, Heath cursing as we landed astride the second rung of the fence and the whole thing started tipping to the right.

'Heathcliff!' I yelled as I clung tightly to the thin bit of wood between my thighs. Seconds later, I was on my side in the cold, wet grass, the piece of wood still in my grasp between my thighs. Heath was lying facing me with a grimace of pain on his face. 'Owww,' I groaned again, 'something's attacking my bottom and neck.'

'Sting ... ing ... net ... tles,' he mumbled, his face still contorted. 'We've landed in ... stinging nettles.' He let out a pained sound as I winced, the vicious plants attacking my skin through the rips in my jeans and where my jumper had exposed one shoulder. I scratched my neck hard, feeling a welt rising already.

'Are you ok?' I asked.

'Crushed manhood,' he moaned, his eyes screwed tightly shut. 'Give me ... a minute.'

'Oh dear. Is the whisky ok?'

'Great, the whisky's more important than me having the ability to father children in the future?' he grunted, slowly opening his eyes.

'Right now, I'm thinking yes. Valentine's blows.' I reached out and grabbed the bottle from under his arm, then twisted the cap off and swigged some as I lay there before offering it to him. 'Cheers, Heathcliff.'

'Cheers, Abigail,' he replied, knocking some back as I scowled. I hated my full name. Maybe I should just stick to his preferred one and him mine.

I woke up with a start, bolting upright with a groan as I heard someone knocking on the front door. Damn it. My head was banging, I had crusty drool down the side of my face, and my hair was all matted. I tried to comb my fingers through it and pulled out some twigs and leaves. What the hell? The door was banged again, and I swung my legs off the bed as I fumbled for the lamp switch.

I squinted when it came on, and my alarm clock told me it was six a.m. Who was knocking on my door at six a.m.? And why was I dressed in Miller's black shirt, with itchy welts on my legs and neck? I lifted one of my butt cheeks and gave it a scratch, feeling some lumps and bumps on there too. I staggered to check my appearance in the mirror and groaned. I'd scratched my neck so much, it had bruised and looked like I had a huge hickey.

'Ok, ok, I'm coming,' I muttered as the impatient person outside continued to knock. I staggered out to the top of the stairs and focussed my eyes on going down them carefully, grateful to make the halfway landing in one piece. I was already aching all over and I had no idea why. I turned and headed down the last set of stairs, and gasped as I made it down just in time to see Heath, dressed only in a pair of black boxer shorts, falling backwards to land on the hall floor with a thud. Framed in the top section of the open stable door was a furious-looking Miller, who was shaking his fist.

'So, I guess it didn't take long to get over me, huh?' Miller said angrily as he glowered at me, his dark brown eyes mesmerising me like they always did.

'What? Huh? What?' I stuttered, reaching up to rub my eyes, not entirely sure what was going on. No matter that my heart had leaped and started skipping joyfully just to have him back here in Dilbury again, whatever mood he was in. I'd missed him so much, but nothing right now made sense. 'Am I dreaming? Why are you here and what the hell is a half-naked Heath doing on my hall floor?'

'No, you're not dreaming, Abbie, but I sure as hell wish I was right now. How could you do this?'

'Do what? I've no idea what's going on,' I cried, my eyes darting between the two men. Heath was just lying on the floor, completely stunned, while the anger in Miller's eyes seemed to be mixed with confusion and hurt.

'I waited, Abbie. I waited for you to contact me to say you'd made a mistake the day you broke up with me, but nothing. So here I am, chasing you, again, something I never do. Well, I guess I was a fool for thinking you'd be sitting here missing me. I hope you and … your new guy will be very happy.'

'My new guy? I don't have a new guy.'

'Next you'll be saying that that isn't a hickey on your neck. Don't make things worse by lying, Abbie. I've spent the last month regretting how things ended with us, missing you, and it looks like you just went out and got yourself someone else without a second glance in the rearview mirror.'

'I didn't!' I protested, as I looked down at Heath. He let out a groan and reached up to rub his cheek, which had a big red mark on it. Oh God. Flashes of the night started coming back to me. The meal, the pub, the fence breaking, drinking in the lounge, me falling over, then Heath helping me upstairs, taking off Miller's shirt, and dressing me in it for bed. He must have gone to sleep on the sofa and answered the door when Miller knocked. 'Oh God, Heath, are you ok?'

'Hmmm,' he groaned, blinking his eyes as he started to come out of his daze.

'Did you punch him?' I gasped, dropping to my knees to check Heath's face and make sure he didn't have a concussion. Sumo waddled in and started grumbling in the background, as confused as I was at all the commotion this early in the morning. 'Miller, did you punch him?' I demanded as I looked back up at the door, only to find there was no one there.

'I'm fine, go after him,' Heath mumbled, trying to sit himself up.

'Miller!' I shouted as I bolted out of the front door. He was getting into his car, which was parked on the drive right next to Heath's van, which was hardly incognito as it had his name and number all over the side. Damn it! No wonder Miller was angry. It really wasn't looking good at all, despite nothing having happened. 'Wait! It's not what it looks like,' I cried as I shot through the side gate and he started to reverse.

He gave me a sad look, a look that told me that he still loved me every bit as much as I did him, which only confused me more. Why hadn't he fought for us last month if he felt that way about me? He shook his head as he reversed into the lane and turned to head up it, so I ran out and slammed my hands on the bonnet. Ha, he wasn't going anywhere unless he wanted to run me over.

Oh God, what if he was so angry he ploughed me down in a fit of jealous lover's rage? I held his gaze as I tried to make up my mind about whether to stand my ground or let him go. I was standing in the lane in just a shirt, with the largest looking love bite on my neck, blocking my furious ex from leaving, while Heath was hanging over the bottom half of the stable door looking like he was naked, and Sumo was uncharacteristically barking his head off. Those damn ramblers better not be having a dawn walk, or I really was going to be village gossip this morning.

'Move, Abbie,' Miller growled out of the window.

'No! You came back, you came back for a reason, and I don't want you to go. I'm seriously confused and hungover right now, but please stay and we can talk.'

'I'm too angry to talk, Abbie, and I might say something I'll regret, something we can't come back from. And I can't come back while he's there or I'm likely to kill him.'

'Nothing happened, I promise. He looked after me while I was drunk, I fell in stinging nettles, which is why I've been scratching my neck, and he put me to bed. He must have slept on the sofa as I woke up alone when you started banging on the door. Please, Miller. I'm hungover, tired, and tearful. Don't make me worse by leaving me again.'

'Abbie,' he sighed, rubbing a hand over his eyes. I felt myself quiver to hear my name in his accent. He still affected me so badly. 'I was impulsive turning up like this. I want to believe you, but I didn't think this through. I think I should leave and get my head on straight before I come back to see you.'

'You promise to come back?' I asked, with a heavy sigh of resignation. Much as I wanted him to stay, it was rude to kick Heath out through no fault of his own. I didn't want to risk another testosterone display, and I was feeling too ill to have, potentially, one of the most important discussions of my life.

'If you promise to give me time, yes,' he nodded, his fingers flexing around the steering wheel. The fact that he'd kept his car, and obviously the hanger he'd purchased in Welshpool, gave me hope that he really hadn't walked away with the intention of us being over for good.

'Ok,' I said quietly. I straightened up and moved out of his way, cursing as I remembered I was barefoot on the gravel, the little stones biting at my bare soles. I hopped over to the safety of my block-paved drive. 'Don't make me wait too long.'

He gave me a pained, tight-lipped smile and slowly edged forwards as I stood and watched him disappear around the corner of the lane. The only consolation compared to the last time he left was that he looked back. That had to be a good sign.

'It all happens in Dilbury,' Heath stated as he opened the lower half of the door for me while holding an irate Sumo back by his collar. 'Are you ok?'

'No. You?'

'I'll live. I'm so sorry, I shouldn't have answered the door, not dressed, or undressed, like this anyway.'

'It's not your fault. We couldn't have known he was coming back. Right, I need caffeine and something to soak up the alcohol, and I'll get one of those unused steaks for your cheek or it's going to bruise.'

'I'll go pull my jeans on. I don't suppose you have a t-shirt I could borrow?'

'Sure, I'll root one out. It will be a snug fit, mind,' I warned him.

'Oh my God. What the hell's going on?' came Georgie's shocked voice.

'Georgie?' I spun around to see her coming up the path, still dressed in her fleecy Dalmatian onesie she wore to bed sometimes, complete with hood and tiny ears, which made me giggle.

'Morning, Heath. Wow, someone doesn't need to use the gym, do they?' she purred, as she stepped into the open doorway and looked him up and down. His cheeks flamed and he hurried into the lounge, taking Sumo with him and shutting the door.

'What are you doing here?' I demanded. 'And dressed like that?'

'Please, a lover's quarrel and you think I was going to miss all of the action? Daphne woke me up by ringing me to say all hell had broken loose over here. Miller woke her up hammering on your door, so she was watching through the window and rang me to get here as soon as possible. I already knew Heath was here, with that van parked on your drive when I came home last night. Talk about village drama. What on earth's going on?'

'Long story. I'm putting the kettle on and making bacon sandwiches, you in?'

'Hell yes,' she agreed. 'And I have the worst date ever to fill you in on as well.'

'Room for one more?' came Daphne's voice as she hobbled up the path.

'Don't tell me, you want the gossip and to fill us in on your date, too?' I laughed, then winced and clutched my sore head.

'Well, of course. If I wasn't so slow getting down the stairs, I'd have beaten Georgie here. Oh look, an ambulance is coming down the lane. Is Heath badly hurt?'

'No,' I reassured her. 'He's fine, just a bruised cheek and jaw. That must be Charlie coming home. She fell down the stairs last night and had to go to the hospital. Go and stop them, Georgie, she can join us for breakfast, too.'

'I'm dressed in a Dalmatian suit!' she protested.

'Well, I'm only in a shirt, with a suspicious-looking hickey on my neck.'

'I wasn't going to comment,' Daphne stated with a disapproving look at me. 'And don't look at me, the ambulance will be back in Shrewsbury by the time I make it back up the garden path.'

'Fine, I'll go, but you so owe me,' Georgie grumbled. She raced up the path and out through the gate, jumping into the lane with her pink padded paws in the air, which made Daphne and me laugh.

'She'll give the paramedics a heart attack,' I giggled.

'And he'll give me one. Heath Jones, put some clothes on, for goodness sake!' Daphne scolded her nephew as he appeared buttoning up his jeans.

'Sorry, Auntie Daphne, it's not what it looks like, honestly,' he mumbled, his cheeks flushing as Sumo scuttled past him to go and put his nose out of the door to see what was going on.

'I should hope not!' she stated with a disapproving glare.

'Come on up, Heath, we'll find a t-shirt for you before your aunt passes out from seeing what a six-pack looks like. Then again, she did go on a date with Mr. Bentley last night, maybe she already got an eyeful,' I teased.

'Be gone with you,' she scoffed with a flick of her wrist. 'I'm going to put the kettle on. I've got a feeling it's going to be a long morning with all of these stories to share.'

Heath came up to my room and I pulled out a selection of my largest t-shirts for him to try, then I grabbed myself some headache tablets from the bathroom before rushing back down. The front door was shut and I could hear excited voices in the kitchen. I needed coffee. This was all too much at this hour in the morning.

'Charlie, are you ok?' I gasped. She was sitting at the dining table with Daphne and Georgie, her hand in a plaster cast and a purple bruise on her face.

'You should see the other guy!' she teased, then flashed me a wink.

'Is it broken?'

'It was too swollen to be sure if it was fractured, so I'll have to wear this for a while, but enough of the injury talk. I think I'm in love,' she stated with a wide grin. 'I met *the* hottest doctor ever at Accident and Emergency.'

'Tyler Jackson,' Georgie and I sighed at once, thinking of the gorgeous blue-eyed stud of the town who had treated Georgie when she got a dog bite after trying to extract her leg from the clutches of an over-amorous Yorkshire Terrier last year.

'Who's Tyler Jackson?' Charlie said, looking confused. 'This was Dr. Fitton, and my *God*, he really was a fit one. If I hadn't got my hand in this damn cast, I'd be tapping out a whole new "sexy ER doctor" novel about him on my MacBook right now!'

'Damn it,' I moaned, as I gathered five mugs from the shelf and set them on the kitchen island. 'I was going to set you up with Heath, the gardener, Daphne's nephew.'

'Oh, Charlie, he's looking super hot today, all buff and toned,' Georgie nodded, her little ears flapping with the motion. 'Sorry, Daphne, is this grossing you out?'

'No, but *that* is,' she retorted, pointing towards the kitchen door. We all looked over and our mouths dropped. Poor Heath was standing there with a defeated look on his face, my black t-shirt straining around his toned biceps, his midriff completely exposed, and the words "Textually Active" in silver stretched across his broad chest.

'I swear, if you breathe a word of this, I'll make up gossip about you all and feed it to Sheila Vickers,' he warned with a pointed finger as we all burst out laughing.

I made the coffees, humming to myself. Life wasn't so bad. I had my friends, and Miller was going to come back to talk about where we went from here. And I still had Sumo, who'd been far more loving towards me since Miller had left last month.

'Ok, boy, you're next,' I told him as he looked from me to his food bowl and back again. He wiggled his butt and shook his head, making me scream as he covered me in globs of slobber that went flying from his slack jowls, then everyone groaned and covered their mouths as his bottom let rip.

'Sumo!' came a chorus of voices.

Chapter Eleven
A Dog Named Mr. Sumo
March

I STOOD SHIVERING IN the back garden and watched him ride the train around a few times as he sniffed the air, letting out the odd bark when he saw any movement of birds in the bushes. I was so glad he'd asked to come out. He'd been lethargic again the last few days and completely off his food. I'd been on the verge of taking him to the vet, which I was dreading doing in case they told me it was time to let him go, but it was like he'd got a second wind under him today. He'd eaten four helpings of food already and had been out here for much longer than normal.

'Ok, Chubbers, I think that's enough now,' I warned as he chugged past me towards the train stop by the utility door.

He'd lost so much weight that Daphne had had to knit him some new smaller jumpers, but even with the thick red one he was wearing today, I was worried he'd be cold, as it was quite fresh and nippy. I giggled as I looked at him. He looked like some kind of canine bank robber. His jumper came complete with its own form of balaclava that only left his muzzle and eyes uncovered, along with holes for his ears to stick out of.

'You monkey,' I gasped as he firmly patted the go button and started another circuit. He let his pink tongue flop out as he looked back at me smugly, almost as if he was sticking it out at me in a "screw you" gesture. 'Damn it,' I muttered as I heard the phone ring.

My eyes darted from the back door to where he was enjoying his ride, then down the lawn to the locked back gate. It wasn't like he could go anywhere. I bolted for the door and swiped the phone off the kitchen island.

'Has he called?' Georgie asked, full of anticipation.

'No,' I sighed, flopping down on a stool. It had been three weeks since that disaster of a Valentine's night, when Miller had left the morning after and promised to come back. I'd done as he'd asked and given him some space, but I was beginning to wonder if he'd really meant it or if it was just an excuse to get away.

'I'm going to throttle him when I next see him,' Georgie growled. 'Right, put the kettle on. I'm coming over to cheer you up.'

'There's no need,' I said feebly, hoping she'd see through my pathetic attempts to pretend I was ok.

'There is, for you and for me. Arsehole just messaged to say he's on his way as "he wants to talk." Unless he's planning on talking to my fist, I have nothing more to say to him.'

'Greg's coming over?' I uttered, full of surprise. She hadn't heard from him since she'd kicked him out well over a year ago.

'Mmmm-hmmm,' she confirmed. 'So I'm coming to you via the back gate, along with his suitcase of precious first edition comic books, which he left behind in his rush to be with the Dilbury hussy. I'm going to open it, take them all out of their plastic wrappers, then hold Sumo over them so he can drop his stinky load all over his treasured possessions.'

'Sumo doesn't poo on demand, Georgie,' I reminded her. 'His bowels seem to have a life of their own, but he has wolfed down about four days' worth of breakfast this morning, so I'm sure there's going to be a mega-blast anytime soon. Speaking of, I can feel my breakfast rumbling. See you in a minute.'

I looked through the glass of the French doors to see he was still happily circling the large back garden, and dashed to the utility toilet.

'Hello,' called Georgie about five minutes later.

'Put the kettle on,' I yelled from my perch on the toilet. Nothing was happening, but each time I thought I was done and stood up, I had to sit back down again. 'I'm not feeling so great. We have a slight upset tummy situation going on, cramps and everything.'

'I told you that reheating rice was a dangerous pastime,' she called back.

'Yeah, yeah, yeah. Is my boy ok?'

'I don't know. Do you want me to go and check on him in the lounge?'

'He's not there. He's riding the Sumo Express around the garden, refusing to come in.'

'Not when I came in, it was parked at your dad's station.'

'Really? Not up at the house?'

'No, I thought it was odd, too. Not like him to walk anywhere unless he has to. He must have got confused and got off a stop early. I'll go and check the lounge for you. Kettle's on, don't be long.'

'I can't poo any faster,' I hollered with a roll of my eyes. Damn rice. I'd been reheating meals for years without a problem, why today? I sighed with relief as I felt and heard some movement.

'Abbie, he's not in the lounge,' Georgie called. 'I can't see him anywhere downstairs. Is he in there with you?'

'It's a tiny downstairs loo, Georgie, I think I'd know if he was in here with me,' I retorted, but quickly looked behind me, then down between my legs into the toilet bowl, just in case. Crikey, this was going to be a full flush, half a bottle of bleach and brush scrub job.

'Can you check the garden again? He might have gone for a tinkle behind a bush. You shouldn't miss him, he's got a bright red jumper on today.'

'Oh no, the balaclava one?' she giggled.

'That's the one!'

'Poor thing,' she tutted.

I nodded in agreement. He did look pretty funny in it, but it was for his own good. And it wasn't like he was the doggie lothario of Dilbury, needing to make himself presentable for the ladies. I'd just sorted myself out, bleached and cleaned the toilet and scrubbed my hands, when I heard Georgie screeching in the back garden.

'Abbie, Abbie, oh my God!'

'What is it?' I yelled, quickly drying my hands and trying to ignore the fact that my tummy was still cramping.

'Come quickly! He must have shot out of the gate when I came in. He's running up the field!'

'Sumo?!' I exclaimed. 'He doesn't walk, let alone run.'

'I know, but I swear it's him. I can see a red blur heading towards Lord Kirkland's estate.'

'Oh no,' I cried, flinging open the cloakroom door in a panic. He'd been obsessed with the ornamental pond on the front lawn of the stately home when he was a puppy and managed to escape the garden when I used to visit. He'd been caught a number of times pulling out the expensive koi carp and laying them on the grass as trophies. 'It's been about six years since he went there, why now?'

'I don't know, but we need to stop him,' Georgie urged. I nodded and grabbed the lead hanging up by the utility door, then slammed it shut behind me and started to run with Georgie down the garden. We dashed out of the gate, turned left, and chased him up the grass verge of the field. This wasn't doing my stomach pains any good at all. 'Jesus, I'm so unfit,' Georgie panted as we passed behind the village church.

'Don't slow down. If he makes it there before we do, it will be carnage,' I gasped, trying to suck in gulps of air. I couldn't believe how fast he was moving.

'I … so … sorry,' Georgie huffed as we hooked left and vaulted over the metal gate into the narrow track to the right of the Church. It led up past the walled garden where the staff tended to the Lord Kirkland's produce.

I just nodded, too breathless to say a word. Damn it, had Sumo suddenly grown bionic legs? He was still nowhere in sight. I was beginning to wonder if Georgie's imagination had run away with her. We reached the ornate side gate with the Kirkland family crest displayed proudly above it, set into the wall on our right. As they owned the church, they had direct access to it.

'Jesus,' I rasped. My throat was burning, I was hot and sweaty, and my stomach was roiling. I had visions of a whole Sumo shart situation if I bent over too quickly.

'Tell me … about it,' Georgie wheezed as we stepped through the gate onto the gravel path, flanked to the left by perfectly manicured lush deep emerald grass. The manor house was set below us, to our right, backing onto the same field our cottages did. Directly in front of us, running alongside the opposite garden wall, was the long drive that exited the garden, hooked left, and headed out through an avenue of large lime trees up to the main road. But right in the centre of the lawn was the circular pond, complete with carp, and I groaned as we tried to jog over. Georgie hadn't been wrong. The streak of red had been Sumo, and he was currently being wrestled out of the shallow water by none other than Lord Kirkland himself. 'Wow, talk about a stereotypical country gentleman,' Georgie observed as we approached.

He was dressed in tight black jeans, which showcased quite a peachy derrière, a fact that I noticed wasn't lost on Georgie. He had on long brown leather riding boots and a brown tweed jacket and flat cap. From what I remembered, he was quite a looker, only in his mid-thirties, and recently divorced. He managed to lift a soaking Sumo out of the water, cradling him against his chest as he turned around and spotted us approaching.

'Wow, dreamboat,' I murmured.

'Uh-huh,' Georgie nodded vehemently in agreement. He was so dashing, with a square cleft chin, strong jawline, and grey eyes that looked almost violet as the sun bounced off them. Dark hair, peppered with some grey streaks, was just visible under his cap as he tapped his fingers off the brim and gave us a movie star smile.

'Miss Carter, Miss Basset, it's been a while,' he greeted. 'I barely recognised this little chap, it's been so long. Mr. Hulk, was it?'

'Mr. Sumo,' I replied with a gulp, praying Sumo wasn't about to shit all over a real life Baron and ruin his obviously expensive attire. He was just staring up at Lord Kirkland while he panted, his wet tongue lolling from the side of his jaw. I grimaced as I saw him start to move his head from side to side, knowing exactly what was coming. 'Cover your face!' I cried.

'I beg your pardon?' Lord Kirkland enquired, far too politely, wasting valuable seconds as Georgie and I shielded ours instinctively just as Sumo ramped the head roll into a furious shake. I winced as I heard the gasp of surprise and could barely bring myself to look at how much slobber Sumo had just flicked all over him. I peeked out between my fingers, as mortified as he looked right now. He had doggie saliva all over his chiselled cheek, not to mention the cravat, waistcoat, and jacket he was sporting.

'Sumo,' I groaned. 'My God, I'm so, *so* sorry, Lord Kirkland. I don't know what's got into him. He's been on death's door for days, then suddenly today it was like he was a puppy all over again. He barely walks, let alone runs, and before we knew it, he was on his way here.'

'He's ill?' Lord Kirkland asked, as he whipped a cotton handkerchief from his top pocket and carefully wiped his face before dabbing his clothes.

'Terminal cancer,' Georgie confirmed. 'We don't think he has long.'

'Poor little chap. He must have wanted to revisit his youth one last time.'

'I'm so sorry. Please send me the dry cleaning bill and the cost for any replacement fish.' I reached my arms out to take Sumo off him, but he gave me a smile and shook his head.

'I spotted him squeezing through the gate as I was having a walk, so I was able to catch him before he did any damage. Well, to my fish anyway. The poor mite is soaked and shivering. Why don't we take him inside? I can ask Henderson, the groundsman who looks after my beagles, to come and take him for a shampoo and blow-dry while we get his … ermmm, outfit dried off.'

'I can't put you to all of that trouble. I only live on Church Lane, Georgie too, and she runs a dog-grooming business.'

'I insist,' Lord Kirkland said firmly. 'Let's make his last visit memorable. Please, join me, we can have some tea and biscuits in the orangery while you fill me in on the latest village gossip. For some reason, Mrs. Vickers always clams up when I enter the shop.'

Georgie and I giggled like pathetic schoolgirls when he winked at us, then swept out his free arm towards the path that led down to his huge old oak front door. She elbowed me and I elbowed her back.

'That's very kind of you, Lord Kirkland, as long as you don't mind. I'm sorry, I'm not sure if we're supposed to curtsey?' I said.

'No,' he guffawed. 'It's the modern age, Miss Carter. I'm simply lucky enough to have inherited a family title and very lovely estate. And please, call me Maxwell. In fact, I prefer Max, if you don't mind.'

'Then thank you, Max, and please call me Abbie, and this is Georgie, and there's no need for you to curtsey for us, either,' I beamed as we headed down the path.

'Well, I have to say that's a relief,' he chuckled. 'Though a gentleman would bow rather than curtsey.'

'Idiot,' whispered Georgie with a roll of her eyes at me. Max did a shrill wolf-whistle as we spotted another chap in similar attire coming from the stable block, over on the left of the house.

'Henderson, perfect timing. We have a cold and wet guest. Could you take him for grooming and return him to the orangery when you're done? He's a VIP, needs extra special care and handling, please.'

'Certainly, my lord. May I ask his name?'

'Mr. Sumo, or just Sumo, and he also answers to Chubbers,' I nodded as he was passed over, seeming very nonplussed at all the manhandling by strangers.

'And Mr. Su or Chubbalicious,' added Georgie, making the poker-faced groundsman give us a strange look.

'Mr. Sumo will do nicely. He'll be back with you in no time. My lord, ladies,' he nodded as he turned on his heels and disappeared across the gravel in the direction opposite to where he'd come from.

The door to the huge sandstone manor was opened by a butler dressed in formal tails. He nodded at us as we all stepped inside the most enormous galleried hall, with a sweeping stone staircase that rose in front of us. Wow, I felt like an underdressed extra on Downton Abbey right now. I wished I was wearing something a little more glamorous than my Converse trainers, ripped white jeggings, and my black ballet-wrap cardigan. Georgie looked as glamorous as ever, and quite the country Lord's beau, in a pair of black skin-tight jeans, black riding boots, a white shirt, and black blazer.

'Could you ask Mrs. Saunders to serve morning tea for three in the orangery, Braithwaite?' Max asked.

'Certainly, my lord. I'll arrange to have your boots and the ladies' footwear cleaned while you do,' he nodded, subtly pointing out that our muddy shoes, and his master's wet boots, had no place on the polished oak floors. We all removed them, and Braithwaite picked them up and disappeared down the long corridor to the right.

'Poor chap, he'll be having nightmares about guests coming into the house shoeless,' Max chuckled. 'He's already mortified at my efforts to modernise the place since my father passed away. Please, follow me.'

We did, both of us craning our necks to see row after row of ancient oil paintings that obviously depicted his family, who had been living here since the 14th century. While the annual village fête and show was held on the front lawn, the manor house itself had never been opened to the public, so this was a real treat and Georgie and I were taking every advantage to soak it all up. He took us to the left, then gestured for us to take the first door on the right, and we stepped into a very large oak-panelled room that was obviously his lounge. No wonder poor, old-fashioned Braithwaite was having a funny turn. Instead of being old and stuffy, it was full of lovely, bright, modern furniture and artwork. Max led us out of a set of double doors, made of panes of leaded glass, and we stepped into a glass orangery that appeared to run the entire length of the house. In front of us was a fancy white-painted metal oval table with eight chairs around it. Max headed over to the far side of it and held out a seat first for me, then Georgie, then went to sit opposite us so he was facing the garden. I bit my lower lip as I felt my tummy churning. Oh crap, not here. It wasn't like I could ask for a toilet brush and half a bottle of bleach when I went to use the facilities.

'I'm very sorry to hear of Mr. Sumo's cancer,' Max said in a serious tone. 'I know how devastated I am when I lose one of my dogs.'

'Thank you,' I nodded, clenching my bottom cheeks and hoping that I wouldn't end up with a permanent holding-in-a-fart facial expression, but I was taking no chances. I'd seen *Sex and the City 2* and *Bridesmaids*. I was not going to embarrass myself today. Well, no more than I already had. 'And I'm very sorry to hear about your divorce. Owww,' I added as Georgie kicked me under the table. Max just smiled, and I tried to kick her back without him noticing.

'I imagine I've been the talk of the village, for a short time at least.'

'You were,' admitted Georgie.

'Hmmm, then please tell me what scandal hit to displace me from pole position.'

'Floppy penises,' I blurted out, as Georgie said, 'Floppy petunias.'

'Then I sincerely hope it wasn't me that either rumour referred to. I can assure you, and the good villagers of Dilbury, that both my petunias and other areas are looking, and working, exactly as they should.'

We both giggled again, Georgie blushing as she put a hand to her mouth and I shifted in my seat, the pains in my tummy really griping now. Damn it, I really needed the loo.

'Where are you, darling?' came a distant voice, even posher than Rachel's. 'Where's Mummy's little boy?'

'Oh Jesus,' Max groaned, a flush of embarrassment colouring up his cheeks. 'I'm so sorry, it's my mother.'

'We can go,' I stated quickly, shooting up from my seat. The sooner I got my bottom and Sumo's out of here, before we made a spectacle of ourselves, the better. I'd had one run-in with Lady Kirkland at the last fête, when she'd been most perturbed her scones had taken second place. Well, her cook's anyway. I doubted that uptight, toffee-nosed busybody had ever even seen a kitchen.

'Please stay,' Max urged, giving us a pleading look as he reached behind him to ring a bell on the sandstone wall behind him. 'You'd be doing me a huge favour.'

'We'll stay,' Georgie confirmed, trying to tug me down.

'I'm sorry, but I need the toil … the ladies' room.'

'One moment, Abbie,' he nodded as Lady Kirkland swept into the orangery from the lounge. 'Mother, this is a surprise, I wasn't expecting you.'

'Clearly,' she observed, sneering down her nose at me before she air-kissed her son's cheeks, then flashed a scornful look at Georgie. 'I see standards are still slipping. Tea is taken in the drawing room, with one's shoes firmly on.'

'Not now that I'm in charge, Mother. Please try and be on your best behaviour, as you can see I have guests. This is Abbie Carter and Georgie Basset, both live on Church Lane. We were just waiting for tea while Miss Carter's dog is dried off after a dip in the pond.'

'Ah yes, the accountant who fancies herself a connoisseur of scones, jam, and cookies, and the dog groomer. Your reputations precede you both,' Lady Kirkland advised haughtily as she waited for Max to pull out a chair for her. He flashed us an apologetic look.

'Excuse me a moment, Miss Carter needs the ladies' room. Can I trust you to behave with Miss Basset?'

'I would think it would be the other way around, darling. I never trust someone who prefers animals to humans.'

'My God, is she always so frightful?' I whispered as Max escorted me out through his lounge.

'If I could disown her, I would. I dread to think what insults she'll manage to throw at your friend in the few minutes she's left alone.'

'Don't worry about Georgie, she's very quick-witted and not afraid to stand up for herself. I'd be more worried about your mother.'

'Then I sincerely hope your friend doesn't rein it in and ensures my mother's stay isn't an extended one. I got in the habit of allowing her to get away with this kind of behaviour while my father was alive, not wanting to upset him, but now my patience is wearing thin. I'll take you to one of the upstairs bathrooms, as I'm having the ground floor cloakrooms upgraded at the moment.'

'Upstairs?' I gulped as we approached the staircase in front of us, which might as well have been a scale up Everest for the panic that just rose in me. I needed a poo so badly, I was worried that lifting even one foot onto the first step was going to launch a turd missile. At least I had knickers and jeans on to hold it in, but what if I farted at the same time? I couldn't fart in front of a Baron who had the title Lord, no matter if I was calling him Max, like we were old friends. And what if it was diarrhoea? It was going to soak through my white jeggings.

'Inconvenient, I know, please accept my apologies. Right, follow me,' he ordered as he casually jogged up them.

'Crap,' I muttered quietly, then quickly warned myself not to as I sucked in every bottom muscle known to man, and then some. I did an embarrassingly slow walk upwards, knees together, swinging my hips from side to side to avoid lifting my feet too high. I made it up the first set to a landing where the stairs branched off to the left and right, and saw he was standing at the top of the stairs to my left. If he thought my progress was strange as he waited, he was a perfect gentleman and didn't let on. 'Sorry, bad back,' I offered, rubbing it as if to prove my point. He swept open the door on the right and gestured me through.

'It's a little old-fashioned and the water pressure up here isn't great. Would you like me to wait, or can you find your way back down?'

'Oh no, no, no,' I replied, shaking my head vigorously. There was no way I wanted him listening to the likely cacophony of sound as I deposited my load. 'I mean, no need to wait, I can find my way down. *Lady problems*, I might be a while.'

'Ah, say no more,' he nodded with a sympathetic smile. I slapped my forehead as he shut the door. I'm sure if he wasn't so polite and charming, he'd have ordered me to say no more. Could I have shared any more inappropriate personal information? Waddling like a penguin, I made it to the toilet, turned around, and braced myself to whip everything down at speed so I could sit down as fast as humanly possible before anything exploded out.

'On the count of three, Carter. Three ... drumroll ... two ... drumroll ... one, go, go, go!' I landed with a triumphant 'Ha!' to have avoided any mishaps. However, instead of the expected sound of escaping wind and the splatter of pebble-dashing, I heard nothing. I gingerly looked down through my thighs, wondering what was going, and my jaw dropped. 'Jesus Christ. I just gave birth to a chocolate python without even noticing!'

My God. I'd never done a poo so big before, with absolutely no effort at all. It had curled back on itself and the water level in the toilet seemed to be a few inches higher from the dead weight.

'Wow, I've probably lost a whole stone laying that bad boy,' I proudly observed as I wiped, then gingerly stood up, expecting to need to sit down quickly again. Nothing happened, however, and my tummy pains had miraculously gone, just like that. Crisis had been averted. I happily pulled up my clothes, then tugged on the chain that dangled down from the old-fashioned, wall-mounted cistern and went to wash my hands, which took a while with the slow trickling water. Deciding it was better to be safe than sorry, I peeked back in the toilet bowl to make sure I'd not left any remnants and gasped. My poo was still sitting exactly where it had been, intact, but the water in the bowl had risen dangerously high. 'Crap! I've blocked the damn toilet,' I moaned, completely mortified.

I quickly looked around for a toilet brush. I was going to have to break this beast's back and hope that enough water drained so I could try and flush again, but wouldn't you know it, posh people don't have toilet brushes. I wondered if they had special staff who came and wiped their bottoms and cleaned the toilet for them after as I started to panic. I couldn't risk flushing again while it was still in there or I'd flood the bathroom. Equally, I couldn't leave a one-foot turd as a surprise gift for my host either.

I searched the room, desperately trying to find something that would help me, even a sanitary bag that I could try and scoop the poop into to put in the bin, but I was shit outta luck, pun certainly not intended. I gulped and wished I'd grabbed a handbag before I dashed out, I could have shoved it in there. As it was, I had nothing, and it wasn't like I could fish it out and take it down to join us for afternoon tea. Not that it wouldn't take up an entire seat on its own, it was that humongous.

I looked back in the toilet, hoping it might have slithered away, but it was still there.

Brown.

Immobile.

Taunting me.

I sighed as I looked around the room, wondering if I could hide it somewhere, then scuttled out to look up and down the corridor, hoping to see a pot plant I could bury it in. No such luck. I returned to the toilet and stood staring down at it, running out of options.

'Window, Abbie, toss it out of the window,' I exclaimed as inspiration struck. Hopefully the groundsman would just assume it was one of the beagles who'd been backed up for a while. I threw the leaded window open and groaned as I turned to face the toilet and rolled up my jumper sleeve. I tried to make myself a toilet paper glove, then took a deep breath as I reached into the toilet and grasped the stubborn monstrosity. Turned out, surprisingly, that a toilet paper glove wasn't much use at all, and I whimpered as it fell apart and I was left clutching the offending item, praying it was going to hold its shape as I hoisted it out of the water. 'Of all the lows in your life, Abbie Carter, you just sank to a whole new level, literally,' I scolded myself, as I quickly tossed it out and slammed the window shut.

I pulled the chain, relieved to see the water level go down this time, then grabbed the toilet roll off the hook, feeling physically sick as I desperately wiped my wet hand and arm, then ran to the sink to scrub myself as hard as I could. Georgie's text tone of *Who Let The Dogs Out* started ringing in my back pocket, but I didn't have time to answer it. I'd been up here way too long, so I dried myself and hurried back downstairs to rejoin them.

As I walked through the lounge and into the orangery, it was completely silent, so quiet you could almost hear a pin drip. My God, what had happened while I'd been gone? Georgie had a horrified look on her face as she stared at me, her blue eyes as wide as a Frisbee.

'What?' I exclaimed, following her line of sight as she slowly pointed upwards and dragged her eyes up to where she was gesturing.

I gasped and felt my cheeks turn deep scarlet to be faced with my large poo, which was slowly making its way down the glass roof of the orangery, leaving a sticky brown trail behind it. Max was staring up at it as well, his mouth opening and closing as if he was trying to think of some appropriate posh-person words to say. No wonder nothing was coming out of his mouth. I mean, what did one say when a guest's turd was doing the slalom down your conservatory roof? Lady Kirkland had just frozen, mid-bite of an unfortunately timed chocolate-dipped Viennese biscuit, as she stared up at it, looking as if she was about to pass out from the shock. My chance of an invite to this year's summer fête was well and truly screwed. 'Crap!' I muttered.

'It's not funny,' I moaned, dropping my forehead to my freshly scrubbed arms as I sat at my kitchen island. Sumo was safely curled up on his armchair, exhausted from his unusual exercise, as Georgie cackled in front of me.

'I can't believe you had the balls to try and pass off the blame on an oversized *pigeon*,' she howled.

'Well, what was I supposed to do? Turn around and run out of the front door and leave you holding Sumo and my trainers while you tried to cover for me?!'

'Well, if you'd answered your phone, I did send a text saying not to come back in!'

'I was seriously flustered, Georgie. Do you think they believed me?'

'Abbie, seriously, no human being has ever laid anything that big, let alone a pigeon. No wonder you had tummy ache. They knew it was you and were too polite, or shocked, to say anything. It's not every day a turd lands on your glass roof as you're sipping Earl Grey from fine chintz cups, with the butler on standby. And you didn't help matters by trying to back up your totally unbelievable story by rambling on about the fascinating facts of the different-sized animal droppings in comparison to their size. I thought Lady Kirkland was going to have a heart attack, and the look on the poor butler's face was priceless!'

'I was stressed, I ramble when I'm stressed. I can't believe I didn't look first to see there was a glass roof below when I threw it out of the window. I mean, what were the chances?' I groaned.

'Well, next time you're about to try another round of turd tossing, which I think should be introduced as a new event at the fête this year, check what's below first. I nearly died when it splatted above us and I looked up.'

'You nearly died? How do you think I felt when I walked in to find you all staring at it?'

'On the plus side, other than being a bit gooey around the edges, it looked pretty healthy, thick and firm in the centre, conker brown, no random undigested sweet corn or mushrooms in it,' she giggled.

'Not helping, Georgie! Promise me you won't tell anyone about this, *please*,' I pleaded.

'Ok, from this moment, I promise my lips are sealed,' she nodded, miming a zip across her lips.

'What do you mean, *this moment*?' I exclaimed, sitting up to face her. Surely she hadn't told anyone.

'Ermmm, I may have already texted Daphne.'

'No!' I groaned, as if my humiliation couldn't reach new depths. I went to cover my face with my hands, then changed my mind and reached for the antibacterial hand gel bottle instead. I was going through it like water, unable to forget the horror of having touched that poo and having my hand in the toilet.

'Sorry, but it was too funny not to share.'

'Great,' I sighed, shuddering at the sound of the gel as it squirted out of the bottle, sounding like a fart. I'd had as much toilet humour, or non-humour, as I could take for one day.

'And Charlie,' Georgie added with a grimace.

'Georgie!' I scolded, shooting her a glare as I slathered the gel on my hands.

'I'd maybe pretend to be out next time Heath's due to call around, too.' Her grimace soon disappeared as she roared with laughter when my jaw dropped. Heath? She'd told Heath?!

'I hate you, Georgie Basset!'

'Are you ok, Chubbers?' I asked, after he whined when I started turning out the lounge lights. It was like someone had pulled his plug out. All of that youthful puppy energy he'd had earlier was gone. He hadn't eaten any dinner and he looked weak and exhausted. I'd had to carry him home from Lord Kirkland's house as he'd been so tired after his adventure. 'Here, let me put the blanket on you so you're nice and warm. If you're no better in the morning, we'll call Bradley, ok?'

He rested his chin on the seat cushion as I wrapped him up in his blue and white checked fleece blanket, then bent down to kiss his head. He lifted his sad, big brown eyes up to meet mine, making me blink a few times to get rid of some tears. I kissed him again and headed upstairs to brush my teeth. When I pulled the bathroom door behind me and walked across the landing towards my bedroom door, I heard a loud whine, then a pitiful bark, followed by a load of scrabbling and panting. I turned on the light and jogged down the first set of stairs, then turned the corner, and was stunned to find Sumo had made it partway up. He'd given up and was snuffling as he lay uncomfortably with his belly on the edge of one step, his back legs holding him up on the step below and his front paws stretched out in front of him on the one above, as he looked up at me.

'What are you doing? Are you trying to come up?' I queried, as I gently lifted him up and went to take him back down, but he whined again and gave me a pleading look that was normally only reserved for his dinner. 'You want to come to bed with me?' I asked, and was answered with a stinky wet tongue lashing over my cheek.

I took a shaky breath, fighting back my tears. He'd never slept with me, he'd never wanted to, and right now I wasn't seeing it as a good thing. Amidst much protests on his behalf, I carried him back down and grabbed a few of his nappies from the utility room, and a stainless steel bowl, then took him up and settled him down on top of my duvet. His eyes roamed around, taking in the new surroundings as I got him dressed in his doggie liners and went to fill up his bowl with some water, which I set on the floor next to the bed. He'd have to wake me up if he wanted some, as it was too high for him to get down. I climbed in and turned off the light and lay on my side, reaching out to give him a head rub. He snuffled and shuffled his way over to lie against me, then licked my hand and let out a heavy sigh at the same time I did.

I waited by the open front door, pacing back and forth as I breathed in the cold darkness, waiting for Bradley. I'd barely slept. Sumo always snored when he slept, but instead he was wheezing badly. When I turned on the light, worried to death about him, he looked so scared as he caught my concerned gaze. I'd rung the vet immediately, even though it was 3 a.m., then I'd rung Georgie in tears. Ever an amazing best friend, she'd arrived in minutes, her normally perfectly coifed hair tangled, still wearing her red pyjamas covered in black Scottie dogs. She was upstairs with Sumo now, giving him a belly and chest massage, hoping it would calm him down. I took a deep breath and dialled Miller's cell, not sure if I was disappointed or relieved to hear it go to voicemail.

'Miller, it's me, Abbie. I'm sorry to ring, I know I said I'd give you space, but ... but it's Sumo. He's ... I don't think he has long,' I choked, a fresh batch of tears rolling over my lower lashes and stinging my cheeks. 'I just thought you'd ... you'd want to know.' I hung up and sobbed as I wrapped my arms around myself. I wanted him here right now. He had a better bond with Sumo than any of us had. I hated the thought of him never having the chance to say goodbye.

I sniffed and dragged my arm across my eyes as Bradley pulled up in his small van and grabbed a bag out of the boot before hurrying over.

'I don't understand,' I sobbed, when he told us that it was time to let Sumo go after he'd examined him. 'He was eating and running earlier, running so fast we couldn't catch him. He even made it into Lord Kirkland's koi pond.'

'I can't explain it, Abbie,' Bradley said gently as he took one of my hands and smothered it in his. 'Sometimes this happens with humans, too. They take a massive turn for the better, almost finding a new lease of life in their last few hours, then suddenly it leaves them as their body shuts down.'

'Oh, Abbie, I know it's heart breaking, but think about what an amazing last day he's had,' Georgie gently reminded me. 'He ate until he was nearly sick, he rode the Sumo Express, and he ran, he actually ran and went back somewhere he remembered loving as a puppy. He had a bath, a blow-dry, then best of all he got to sleep in bed with his mum, someone he's always loved even if he never showed it until recently. And he's just had one of his favourite massages, too,' she added, trying to comfort me.

I nodded as I sniffed and went to sit on the edge of the bed next to him. What she said made sense, but it was so hard to say goodbye. I took a deep, shaky breath as I lifted him up and put him on my lap, gently stroking him. His paw nudged my hand as he licked it. I'd had thirteen months with him that I shouldn't have had since he was diagnosed. And I'd done my best to make them a happy thirteen months for him. It just sucked that now we'd finally got close, he was leaving me.

'What do I do?' I whimpered, looking at Georgie when Bradley asked if I wanted it to happen now and at home. I wanted to wait for Miller, but what if he couldn't come right away? I didn't want my boy to suffer any more than he already was.

'It has to be the right decision for you and Sumo, Abbie. I know you're thinking that you want to wait for Miller, but he's not here, and if you make the decision to deal with this now, he's going to have to accept that you made a tough choice under difficult circumstances.'

We all looked towards the stairs as we heard a knock on the front door, and I held my breath as Georgie ran down to see who it was, praying for a miracle, but released it to hear Daphne's concerned voice.

'Abbie?' Bradley gently prodded. I looked back down at Sumo, who was wheezing badly in my arms, and I could tell from his eyes that he'd had enough, that he was in pain. I nodded, knowing however hard this was, I was doing what he wanted.

'Let's do it here,' I choked. 'But downstairs, in his favourite armchair. I want to give Daphne a chance to say goodbye, too.' I reached up to wipe away some tears of resignation that I had to let him go.

'You're doing the right thing for him,' Bradley nodded in a reassuring voice. I really hoped that he wasn't lying to make me feel better.

Thursday

I woke up as I heard a car door slam. I was curled up on the sofa, my head on Georgie's lap as she stroked my hair. My eyes were swollen from sobbing, my head was banging, and I was feeling pretty emotionally wiped out. Seeing Bradley finally drive away, with my boy's body wrapped in his favourite blanket, had finished me off. Georgie had cleared away all traces of Sumo at my request, as I thought it would help. I'd only kept my favourite photo of him, riding his train in the garden. Daphne had brought a bottle of whisky over, realising what was happening when she'd seen Bradley's van parked outside, but eventually tiredness had overcome her and she'd had to leave us to go home to her bed. Georgie and I had sat here until the sun was high in the sky, crying, then laughing, as we'd told our favourite stories of a dog named Mr. Sumo that pretty much all involved his gassiness, then we'd started crying again.

'Hey, there's some water and headache tablets here. Can you sit up to take them?' she coaxed. I nodded and did as I was told, gulping them down.

'Shouldn't you be working?' I sniffed when I saw that it was already midday.

'I rearranged today's appointments. You were more important and I didn't want you to be alone right now.'

'Love you,' I murmured as I leaned over to give her a kiss.

'And you know I love you back, sweetie, but now it is actually time for me to leave,' she smiled, giving my hand a quick squeeze before she stood up.

'What about not leaving me alone?' I moaned as I looked up at her confused, feeling exceptionally needy right now.

'I'm not, but you know where I am when you are,' she said mysteriously as she headed to the lounge door. I gasped in surprise as I looked up to see a tired-looking Miller, who was leaning against the lounge doorframe watching us. He gave her a hug, then stepped into the lounge as she left, with a quick smile over her shoulder at me. He didn't have to say a word, his face said it all, as I was sure mine did. I ran to him and threw myself at him as I started sobbing again, wrapping my arms and legs around him like a vine as he held me tightly to him and kissed my hair, his cinnamon scent soothing me.

'You came,' I whimpered.

'Of course I did. I'm so sorry, Abbie. I wish I could have been here for you, I know how much you loved him. We can talk later. Let me take you to bed for a few hours, you look exhausted.'

'So do you,' I snuffled as he turned and started up the stairs.

'So we'll both sleep for a while, and I'll hold you as long as you need me to, ok?' he murmured, kissing the top of my head again.

'How does forever sound?' I whispered, hoping that he wasn't going to leave me, too.

We lay in front of the fire on the sheepskin rug, a thick fur blanket on top of us, my head on Miller's bare chest as he traced a pattern on my shoulder with his fingertips. I kept opening my mouth to ask what I wanted to know, but kept changing my mind and closing it again.

'I'll never lie to you, Abbie,' he said quietly, lifting my hand to his lips and softly kissing the pads of my fingers. 'The answer's no. If it hadn't been for Sumo, I wouldn't have come back yet.'

'Yet,' I repeated, wondering how he knew what I'd been thinking from the moment I first saw him.

'Yet,' he said firmly. 'We're still in different places. You won't move to New York and I'm still not ready to move here. Unless you'll change your mind and agree for us to carry on as we were?' he asked hopefully.

'I can't, Miller,' I replied, more pain fuelling my words, pain I thought I'd released with all the tears I'd shed overnight and this morning.

'I know,' he sighed. 'Deep down I knew that, which is why I wouldn't have come yet.'

'But you did, you came for Valentine's Day. Well, it would have been if I was on New York time,' I reminded him.

'Because I realized that on the most romantic day of the year, there was only one person I wanted to be with. You have no idea how much it hurt me when he opened that door.'

151

'Nothing happened, I promise.' I propped myself up on one elbow as I looked down at him, searching his deep brown eyes to see if he believed me.

'I believe you, and I had Georgie and Daphne call me to tell me the same thing, to try and get me to come back.'

'They did? Oh, they're just the sweetest,' I sighed, my heart warming at the thought of my amazing friends and neighbours.

'They love you, and despite this mess we're in, so do I, Abbie.'

'So we're back at square one, aren't we? What do we do?'

'We don't call this goodbye, and even though we won't see each other, we'll act as if we're in a relationship, even if we're not.' He held my gaze as I frowned, confused at what he was suggesting. He flipped onto his side, mirroring my pose, and reached up to grip my chin as he ran his thumb back and forth over my lower lip, making my breath hitch. 'I think I've found the person I want to spend the rest of my life with, Abbie, and I hope you feel the same, but … it's obviously just not our time right now.'

'So you're saying we stay faithful to each other, even though we won't be seeing each other, and hope that at some stage we're both in the same place?'

'Yes,' he nodded. I closed my eyes and sighed, then shook my head as I felt my heart shatter all over again.

'I hate saying this, but that doesn't work for me either. I could be waiting for years, possibly forever. I can understand your reluctance, I hurt you when I ended it, like your parents hurt you by abandoning you, but I'm tired of being alone, Miller. I'm ready to give you all of me, and I want the same in return, not a "maybe someday in the future". It might be a great offer for most girls, but it's not enough for me. It's like being told I've got the most delicious box of gourmet chocolate truffles, but I'm only allowed a tiny sliver every day and the box has to last me for years. I'd rather have no truffles at all than be tortured.'

'I'm a box of chocolate truffles?' he grinned, his cute dimples coming out full force, though his eyes showed his disappointment in my decision.

'Gourmet truffles. The best I ever had,' I added in a whisper.

'Likewise,' he nodded. 'And that means a lot, Abbie.'

'Will you stay, just for a few days? I'm feeling pretty vulnerable at the moment and I'd really like for you to be here to help scatter Sumo's ashes in the garden.' I felt myself tear up at the reminder that I'd just lost an important male in my life and was about to lose another.

'I'll stay, I want to be by your side when you do,' he agreed, then pulled me back down against him. 'Who'd have thought a generally miserable mutt called Mr. Sumo could make an ocean between us evaporate, even if it is only for a few days.'

'Being miserable was his thing, and I'm going to miss it, terribly. But I sure as hell won't miss his vapour.'

Miller chuckled and tightened his arms around me, and I closed my eyes and reminded myself that this was just another relationship on borrowed time, and I had to make the most of it while I still had him.

Chapter Twelve

Dress Twelve
April

'OH MY GOD! QUICK, hide,' I urged, grabbing Georgie's hand as I dragged her to the large bushy hedge that separated the village shop we'd just left from the main road.

'What, what is it?' she protested as we crouched behind the overgrown green mass.

'Max Kirkland coming this way, looking all handsome and debonair. I can't face him again, not after turdgate.' I scowled at Georgie as she started giggling. 'Don't. I mean, Sumo slobbers on him, and then I ruin morning tea, as well as his conservatory roof. I just can't look him in the eye. I felt so bad I sent him a letter confessing and apologising, and deeply regretted it the moment I put it in the post box.'

'That's how you bruised your hand last week,' she gasped. 'You were trying to haul it out.'

'Yes well, I seem to have a habit of sticking my hand where it shouldn't go, don't I?'

'Why did you post it? With the exception of the church between you, you're actual neighbours, you could have hand delivered it.'

'I might have been seen. It was embarrassing enough facing them on the day, I wasn't about to return to relive the humiliation. I mean, it's not just him or his mother. The butler knew, as well as the groundsman who probably had to rescue it, and I bet it went around the rest of the staff, most of whom live in the village.'

'Imagine how I felt sitting there, especially when they both looked at me for answers before you came down. You really dropped me in it, Abbie, it was a real strain. That's one funny disaster you won't be flushing any time soon,' she winked.

'Enough with the toilet puns,' I groaned. I'd had them non-stop from her since it had happened.

'Oh, don't be a spoilsport, just brush it off,' she teased.

'Sssshhhh,' I warned, as we heard the distinctive sound of the steel taps on his handmade leather shoes striking off the pavement as he strode towards the shop.

'Why's he single?' Georgie whispered as she peered through a gap in the foliage. 'He's very hot for an older guy.'

'He's only about eight years older than us. I bet the fête will be packed this year, now that everyone knows he's on the market again.'

'Hmmm, I'll be there for sure,' Georgie agreed, then both of us went silent and put our heads down as he approached.

'Ladies, wonderful morning for … what exactly is it you're doing down there?' came Max's distinctly well-to-do voice. Damn it, he was so tall he'd seen us over the hedge. I grimaced, not wanting to look up and relive my humiliation.

'You know how fascinated Abbie is with animal poo, we're on a foraging session for specimens,' Georgie announced far too gleefully as she stood up.

'You're welcome to come and collect some from my stables, Miss Carter. Now if you could time depositing it somewhere visible during my mother's next visit, you'd be doing me a huge favour.'

'I'm *so* sorry, again,' I mumbled as I stood up and avoided looking at his face.

'After seeing the look of horror on Mother's face, I may resort to begging you to repeat the incident. I've actually had a blissful month of peace as she's been too mortified to return. I'm terribly sorry to hear about Mr. Sumo, my sincere condolences,' he added, his voice full of warmth and sympathy. I swallowed hard and looked up, knowing it would be rude to avoid eye contact after that.

'Thank you. On *all* counts,' I stressed. He smiled, his grey eyes sparkling with amusement as he leaned in, as if he was about to share a very important secret. Hmmm, he wasn't just a pretty face, buff body, and title. He smelled really good, too.

'Contrary to village perception, I'm actually a little more down to earth than my predecessor, and I do have a sense of humour.'

'You need one around Abbie,' Georgie scoffed, then flashed me an apologetic look.

'Well, I shall leave you to your … foraging. Enjoy your afternoon.' His smile turned into a dazzling grin as he touched his fingers to his cap again and headed towards the shop entrance.

'Wow, swoonworthy,' Georgie sighed as she followed him with her eyes.

'Ask him out,' I suggested as I looped my arm through hers. 'I could see you as Lady Kirkland, mistress of the manor.'

'Me too,' she nodded as we struck out for home. 'But he's not into me, I can tell.'

'Well, he's definitely not into me, turd-flinging woman,' I giggled.

'I think turd tosser has a better ring.'

'I'd prefer neither title, thank you. Either way, I'm not wearing a turd-related fancy dress to the fête if I've not been barred for life.

Could you imagine the look on his mother's face if he announced our engagement?'

'She looks like she's sucking lemons as it is, I dread to imagine,' Georgie laughed, casting one last look back at the shop as we walked away. 'Anyway, I think he's got his eye on Mrs. Smith.'

'No,' I gasped, shooting her a horrified look. 'She's in her late seventies, for goodness sake.'

'Not *that* Mrs. Smith, the Mrs. Smith who lives a few doors down from shop on the hill. You know, Isla, the pretty one who was widowed a couple of years ago.'

'Oh, *her*. Yes, she's very attractive,' I agreed. 'Poor thing, she's only a bit older than us, with a little boy, too.'

'It's so sad,' Georgie nodded. The widow in question's husband had been killed when his army convoy drove over some land mines in Afghanistan. The whole village had attended his funeral at the church, not just out of respect, but because he'd been a lovely guy, always helping out the elderly in the village. He'd even made a fuss over Sumo whenever he'd seen him.

'She deserves to be happy, and to be spoiled by a rich, handsome man, after what she's been through. I think we need to meddle, help speed things along.'

'Wouldn't a big high-society wedding in the village be amazing?' Georgie exclaimed, her eyes lighting up at the thought as we turned right onto Church Lane.

'Don't remind me about weddings,' I sighed. I was still feeling so guilty for saying yes when Tracey Tramwell, another girl from the stupid pact of fourteen, had asked if I was still ok to be one of the bridesmaids for her wedding which, much to my dismay, was later today. It wasn't until I'd accepted that I'd realised it would take my bridesmaid dress collection to number twelve. One away from the dreaded number that would seal my fate as a spinster forever. And it meant that if Georgie wanted to get married, she'd be the one to put the final nail in the coffin. I'd recently found out that the final wedding I would have had to wear dress number thirteen for, my friend Pippa, wasn't likely to happen. She had turned to religion and was considering a vow of abstinence and becoming a nun. Though no amount of penance was going to wash away the amount of sins she'd incurred as class slut for four years in a row, not to mention the introduction of alcohol and drugs to the midnight feasts.

'I'm not getting married anytime soon, Abbie,' Georgie reassured me. 'You'll be married before I ask you to wear the thirteenth bridesmaid dress, and the curse will be broken.'

'You never know what's around the corner,' I reminded her, both of us waving as we passed the row of terraced workers' cottages where some of our neighbours were gossiping on the Chormondley's doorstep. 'Love could hit you when you least expect it.'

'Very true, but I still don't think I'm ready. One day maybe. And speaking of one day, any news from Miller?'

'No.' I sighed at the reminder, having tried so hard to focus on other thoughts so I wouldn't dwell on it and get sucked into a pit of misery again. 'He's messaged me a few times, but I haven't replied. It just makes it harder to be in contact, knowing nothing's going to come of it.'

'I'm so frustrated for you. He loves you, I know he loves you, Abbie. I don't understand why he's holding back.'

'Well, he is and there's nothing I can do about it, so let's focus on getting this damn service for Tracey out of the way this afternoon. What are you going to do with that lovely mane of yours?' I asked, as we branched off Church Lane to head down the bumpy gravel and grass lane that led to our cottages.

'I feel awful,' I moaned as I smoothed the tight emerald green dress over my hips.

'It's a great colour on you,' Georgie advised as she zipped it up.

'I know, it's up there in my top three of dresses, which isn't hard as I hated the other nine. I mean because I shouldn't be wearing it.'

'You'd prefer to streak up the aisle? That's one way to get yourself noticed, I guess,' she teased as she stepped back to give me the once over.

'I wonder if naturists do nude weddings or other important services,' I mused. 'Wouldn't that go against a vicar's religion to just let it all hang out?'

'It goes against mine to think of Reverend Potter doing that,' Georgie shuddered. 'There's no way I'd accept a mince pie from him after the annual carol service, not even if he washed his hands thoroughly in the font first.'

'Change topic,' I urged as I covered my eyes. 'I'm getting a visual of the villagers naked singing "Little Donkey" and it's seriously disturbing.'

'Oh, all of them? How do Max and Heath look?'

'A hell of a lot better than Mr. Benson,' I giggled as I peeked out at her. 'I heard he's in a permanent state of flop, being too afraid to try Viagra again.'

'Well, it was his fault for getting greedy after a few success stories and taking six of them in one go,' Georgie scoffed as she handed me my diamond drop earrings. 'Honestly, what did he expect?'

'I don't think he expected Mabel to try her luck with Mr. Arthur and leave him.'

'When did Dilbury become a hotspot for randy, sexually active pensioners? Have you seen there's now a condom stand in the shop? I think Mrs. Vickers sells more of those than tea bags. It's not right. It's supposed to be us youngsters that are having all of the fun.'

'Maybe as my plus-one today, you'll meet some hot usher and hit it off,' I suggested as I secured the last earring in place.

'Here's hoping,' she beamed. 'Just try and stay out of trouble today.'

'With Fi-Fi there, hell bent on revenge? I seriously doubt that's going to happen,' I responded, a feeling of foreboding washing over me. I was dreading it.

I took a deep breath as Georgie kissed me goodbye, got out of the taxi, and hurried into Shrewsbury Cathedral to take her place. I paid Andy and slowly got out, trying to stall the moment I had to join the group of excited bridesmaids standing outside on the pavement as they waited for Tracey to arrive. I spotted Fi-Fi immediately, her daggered glare towards me slowly turning into a smug smile. She made no move to approach me, so I avoided her and went to talk to some of the other girls, trying to keep her in my line of sight at all times. I was relieved when Tracey arrived and we were hustled into position, but soon groaned as Fi-Fi was directed to stand in front of me. I became progressively more nervous as she remained uncharacteristically silent as one by one, the girls started to filter in to the sounds of the organ announcing our arrival.

I resisted the urge to shove her as I followed her up the aisle, hoping that our tit-for-tat spat was actually over and had been laid to rest. She'd messed with me, I'd returned the favour, it was time to let it go. The cathedral was packed to the rafters. Tracey had gone all out with this wedding and had booked The Shrewsbury Domville for the reception. From what I'd heard, the bill for that six-star venue, and ultimate wedding package for maximum capacity, made many a father's eye water, and not in a good way. Thankfully, despite a feeling that something terrible was going to happen, the service went without incident. Everyone clapped politely as the newly married couple kissed, signed the register, and headed back down the aisle.

'I have to say you're taking it incredibly well,' came Fi-Fi's squeaky voice.

'Just because I'm one of the last two that are unmarried doesn't mean I can't be happy for Tracey,' I replied, not turning to face her.

'Oh, I wasn't talking about Tracey. I was talking about Miller. As if it's not hard enough that you weren't woman enough to hold onto him, it must sting to see him with a date so soon after you broke up,' she announced gleefully. I shot her a shocked look. Miller was *here*? With someone else? 'Oh dear, you didn't know? Hmmm, seems he didn't let the sheets get cold before he went back to his old ways. Maybe there's hope for me yet.'

I swallowed the words of anger I wanted to say back and gripped my white tulip bouquet tightly, determined not to let my right hand do what it was itching to do. Slap her. Or pull her hair. Or maybe even punch her. I'd quite happily do all three if I didn't have all of the congregation's eyes on me, as it was my turn to head back down the aisle. I kept my eyes focussed on the back of her head as I followed her, trying to work out if she was lying to try and get a rise out of me or if he really was here. I didn't dare look for him, just in case. Thankfully, for once, the cathedral had no grounds for wedding pictures to be taken in, so the bridal party were all whisked by limousines the short distance along the old town walls to where The Domville stood at the top of the town park, overlooking the river. I needed the extra time to try and pull myself together. Everything seemed to happen at warp speed, and before I knew it, I was standing in the ballroom as canapés and champagne were being served to all of the guests who'd arrived. I felt claustrophobic and like I was going to hyperventilate.

'Oh God, Abbie,' huffed Georgie as she pushed her way through, looking like she'd run all of the way here. 'Oh no,' she sighed, her shoulders slumping. 'You know, don't you?'

'You've seen him?' I asked, my stomach churning at a rate of knots.

'You haven't?' she replied, giving me a confused look as I shook my head. 'Your expression, you look so devastated that I assumed you had.'

'Fi-Fi told me, but I thought maybe she was just being spiteful. I look devastated? Really? Oh God, I thought I was hiding it well. If I look like that now, how am I going to look when I see him? Is it true? He's here with someone?'

'I'm so sorry,' Georgie confirmed with a grimace. I knocked back the whole glass of champagne I'd snagged a moment ago, trying to dilute the hurt and anger that was bubbling inside of me, but it didn't help. 'I'm livid, Abbie. Absolutely livid! How could he? After what he said to you? I tried to go and have a word with him, to ask him to leave, but it was like he was avoiding me and disappeared every time I got close.'

'What does she ... no, I don't want to know if she's pretty. Of course she will be, it's Miller,' I said quietly as I looked down at my feet. 'I can't believe he'd do that, just turn up with someone else without even telling me.'

159

'I don't agree with what he's done, Abbie, but he did try and stay in contact and you rebuffed him. Maybe he figured you'd moved on.'

'I wish I had. I wish I could, Georgie, but he was the one. He'll always be the one. I just … I really believed I was his too, that he'd realise that and come back to me to try living here, you know?'

'Ok, unless you want to see them, don't turn around. They just walked in. What do you want to do? We can call Andy and get out of here right now, and you never have to see him again.'

'Part of me wants to, so badly,' I told my friend. 'But I don't want to let Tracey down, or give Fi-Fi, Miller, or his new … strumpet, the chance to see that they've got to me.'

'So how are you going to handle this?' she asked with a worried expression.

'With plenty of glasses of champagne,' I stated firmly. I swiped two off the tray as a timely waiter passed. I handed her one and knocked the other back immediately.

'I've got a feeling I'm going to regret encouraging this plan, but here, have mine as well, you look like you need it,' Georgie said, as she swapped my empty glass for her full one. 'Just promise me if I manage to corner him, I can slap him and give him a piece of my mind.'

'As long as I'm not embarrassing myself for the third wedding in a row, I have no objections to you doing whatever you like,' I replied. I gulped back a third glass of champagne and pulled a face as the bubbles tickled my nose and made my head feel slightly tingly already. 'Do I …'

'You look gorgeous, and from the looks he's trying to sneakily cast your way, he still thinks the same, too,' she said softly. I smiled at her, she always knew what I was thinking. I was completely torn. Part of me was curious and wanted to turn around and see him, to check out my replacement, while part of me was devastated and wasn't sure I'd survive it. 'Right, if we're doing this, I'm going to need some liquid courage to handle you drunk. Let's do it in style, two at a time,' she announced.

She grabbed another two glasses of champagne off a second waiter for herself as I set the three empty glasses on his tray, then reached for two more full ones for me. Who needed a floral bouquet? A glass in each hand was a much better accessory.

Quite how I managed to avoid seeing Miller or his strumpet, as that was what I was going to call her because I already hated her with a passion, I wasn't sure. But we were called to take our places and I still hadn't seen them. I was on the far right of the top table, and when I saw Fi-Fi had taken her place at the chair next to mine, I stalled, admiring the five-tier wedding cake that my friend Jess of *Yummy*

Cakes by Jess had made. It was incredible. Some of the lace effect detailing, which seemed to flow down the sides, was so intricate. I took my place and swallowed hard as I finally did a scan of the room. He wasn't hard to spot, even sitting down didn't take away from how tall he was or that mop of dirty-blond hair that I knew so well. My fingers flexed, wanting to run through it and pull the strands on the nape of his neck. His focus was on strumpet as they talked, and it took all of my courage to drag my eyes from his side profile to look at her.

'Stunning, isn't she?' Fi-Fi announced gleefully. I reluctantly nodded as I studied her, wondering why I had the feeling that I knew her, that I recognised her face from somewhere. She wasn't the glamorous type I'd been imagining, cut from the Fi-Fi style of trying too hard. Instead she was cool and edgy. She had one of those haircuts that only certain girls could get away with, shaved on one side with jagged long layers on the other, and it had been dyed such a light blonde, it was almost white, with various bright shades of turquoise, green, purple, and pink dip-dyed tips. Her face was classically beautiful, in perfect symmetry, and she had a pair of rich hazel eyes that suddenly met mine. I gritted my teeth as she had the audacity to smile at me, then she said something to Miller. He looked up at me, holding my gaze for a fraction of a second before he turned back to her and nodded. 'Seems like they're talking about you, Abbie. Not like she has to be scared of the competition, is it?' Fi gloated.

'Oh shut up, Fi-Fi!' I bit, turning to give her a glare. 'Do you know how pathetic it is that you're so miserable in your own life, you have to try and bring everyone else down?'

'You shut up!' she shot back.

'No, you shut up, or I might be forced to do something else that I won't regret,' I warned.

'It *was* you! I knew it,' she said, her tone full of venom.

'Owww, what the hell was that?' I exclaimed, as she pinched my thigh really hard under the tablecloth. She smirked, so I pinched her back and made her squeak, then she replied with a hard punch to my leg. I glared at her and grabbed my side fork off the table, then jabbed her in the side with it, and all hell broke loose.

'Bitch!' she yelped as she shot out of her seat, clutching her newly pronged ribs. She grabbed her glass of champagne off the table and before I had a chance to react, the cold liquid was flying across the air between us and splattering all over my face as a collective 'Oh' rose up from the guests. Without thinking, I stood up and slapped her across the face as hard as I could, her returning slap resonating in the now virtually silent ballroom.

'Harpie,' I bit back as I shoved her, my cheek and palm smarting. She stumbled, and Julia grabbed her before she landed on her lap and pushed her back upright.

'I hate you, Abbie Carter,' she shrieked, shoving me so hard, I staggered and fell backwards onto the corner of the cake table. I heard the gasp of horror from everyone in the room right as I saw the top tier of the cake flying through the air, smacking straight into a gloating Fi-Fi's stunned face.

'Crap,' I moaned as the table collapsed, taking me down to the floor with it, and the remaining four tiers of cake smashed down on top of me to the chorus of shocked 'Ahhhs' and the distraught scream of poor Tracey. I didn't have time to recover from the shock of the fall, or being smothered in icing, marzipan, sponge, and lemon ganache filling, before Fi-Fi was launching herself at me like some kind of WWF wrestling champion. She landed on me with a thud, her eyes barely visible through her cake facial, and started screaming at me while she pulled my hair. Well, that did it, I was not going down without a fight, so I grabbed hers and pulled it back, and all of a sudden we were rolling around on the floor, lashing out with our hands and feet, not to mention a few obscenities that flew from her mouth.

I gasped for air as someone hauled her off me, and I wiped some of the cake away from my eyes to see her struggling in Miller's arms. He'd got her around the waist, and her legs were kicking and her arms flailing as she screamed at him to let her go.

'Are you ok, Abbie?' he demanded, flashing me a concerned look. How dare he! How dare he ask if I was alright when he knew I wouldn't be, with him flaunting his new girlfriend in my face, publicly humiliating me. What he'd done was worse than what psychotic Fi-Fi had. Georgie ran over and stretched out her hand to me, helping me up as I shot him a cold look. I straightened my shoulders, the eyes of three hundred guests on me in my green taffeta, white icing, and lemon cream outfit, then flicked my hair over my shoulders, dollops of cake shooting off.

'I'm just peachy, thank you, Miller. So I guess it didn't take long to get over me either, huh?' I enquired, throwing back the words he'd used on me when Heath had answered my door.

'Get over you?' he replied, a look of panic crossing his face while Fi-Fi continued to writhe in his arms, trying to get back to her cat fight with me. 'Wait, Abbie, it's not what you think. Quinn's—'

'I don't want to know,' I responded firmly, putting one of my sticky palms up in front of me. 'Fi-Fi, you ever do anything like this to me again, and ruin someone else's wedding, I *will* call Dave and let him know what a money-digging, cheating, lying, despicable little … cow, you really are. Tracey, I don't know how to apologise for what we've just done. Please bill me for the cost of the cake, which is absolutely delicious by the way,' I nodded as I licked a smear of cream from the corner of my mouth. 'But I think it's best I leave now, with what's left of my dignity.'

'Mess with my best friend again, and I mess with you,' Georgie growled, pointing a finger at both Fi-Fi and a shocked Miller. She grabbed my hand and pushed her way through the people who'd crowded around to see what was happening as I blinked back some tears, not least from the citrus cream that was smearing my vision and stinging like hell. 'Come on, let's get you cleaned up first, then we're going home.'

I couldn't say anything. It was taking everything I had to try and hold it together right now. All of the pain and humiliation had built up inside of me, and that had been the final straw. I felt like I was about to break and I wasn't sure any amount of glue was ever going to put me back together again. Georgie hurried me down the marble corridor as other hotel guests gasped and pointed at me, just making me feel even worse. She swung open the heavy door to the ladies' room as I heard Miller's distinctive accent calling my name. She looked at me and raised her eyebrows, but I shook my head. I couldn't. I just couldn't face him right now. So she led me inside, letting the door swing shut behind me, cutting him off as he pleaded with me to talk to him.

'Oh, Abbie,' she sighed as she sat me down and turned to the marble countertop to grab some rolled-up facecloths and fill a sink with hot water. I just stared at the floor-to-ceiling mirror opposite me as she gently started to wipe my face, cleaning all evidence of the cake and my make-up away, then tried to get as much as she could off my hair and dress, followed by my neck, chest, shoulders, arms, and hands. 'Walk away,' I heard her warn as the noise of heels on the floor echoed when someone entered the ladies' room.

My eyes drifted over, expecting to see Fi-Fi coming to finish what she started, or maybe even a distraught Tracey to haul me over the coals. Who I didn't expect to see, or want to see, was the strumpet, whose name I didn't even remember. Especially not when she was dressed in some fancy hip designer outfit, looking amazing and smelling like a Parisian parfumerie, and I was in a cake-stained dress, make-up free, with damp lemon-scented hair.

'I came to see if Abbie's alright, and I need to explain,' came her heavy American accent.

'Funnily enough, no, she's not ok, and whatever you have to say, she doesn't want to hear it. Isn't it enough you're with the man she loves, the man who said he'd be faithful until he was ready to give her more? Georgie said, in full protective mode, as she moved between us and folded her arms across her chest.

163

'But that's just it, I'm not with him. I'm not Miller's girlfriend, I'm his twin sister, Quinn,' she stated earnestly. I heard a small gasp from Georgie as I just blinked a few times, not sure if I'd heard her correctly.

'Miller doesn't have a sister, he doesn't have any family, he's an orphan. He was abandoned as a baby, so try pulling the other one,' Georgie shot back.

'He thought he had no family until he tracked me down last month, just like I thought I had none, too. He's been searching for our parents for years. Turns out they're both dead, but he found me. That's part of the reason he didn't want to leave New York, because he was hoping to find someone who could give him answers to his past. We're still not sure how or why we got separated as infants, but we're trying to make up for lost time now.'

'Say I believe you, and I'm not saying I do,' Georgie said firmly, 'why couldn't he tell Abbie that himself?'

'That's not for me to say, I'm only just getting to know him. I'm sure you probably know him a hell of a lot better than I do. But I know what it's like to be raised in the foster system. Kids like us, well, we're not big on trust. We find it hard to let people in and sometimes, if we think we're getting too close to someone, we like to test them by pushing them away.'

'Yeah well, Miller's not a kid anymore. I'm sorry he got a rough deal in life, you too as you seem ok, but that's not Abbie's fault and she's the one who's hurting right now. So thanks for your concern, but right now I'm taking my friend home. Come on, Abbie, let's get out of here,' Georgie urged, turning to offer her hand to me again.

I nodded and took it, keeping my eyes on the floor as we walked towards the door. Quinn was still talking in the background, and as soon as Georgie opened the door, I heard Miller's voice urging me to stop and talk to him, but I kept walking with my head down. He'd wanted time and space, but now I needed it. Right now, I felt like I was drowning and I just wanted some time and space to come up for air, breathe, and regroup.

Chapter Thirteen
The Great Escape
April

'OH GOD, I *SOOOO* needed this break,' sighed Georgie contentedly as she sipped a Mojito on the sun lounger next to me. I trailed my hand through the powdery fine white sand below me, drinking in the view down the beach and out to the stunningly clear blue ocean.

'Tell me about it,' I confirmed, shaking the sand off my hand and grabbing my Mai Tai. I took a decent guzzle through my straw and stretched out my legs, admiring my freshly pedicured feet, complete with appropriately tropical, bright coral nail polish.

I'd left the nightmare of the last few months behind me in England. I'd convinced Georgie to pack up the day after Tracey's wedding and come with me on a last-minute two-week trip, refusing to allow all of that baggage to board the plane with me. I'd factored out my year-end accounts to a freelancer, on the proviso that I'd work my butt off when I got home to check everything was to my satisfaction, and I'd booked this exclusive, luxury spa resort on the Riviera Maya in Mexico, with the second largest coral reef in the world. The fact that I was willing to run away at the busiest time of year for an accountant, a time when I normally thrived, thrilled to be doing the job I loved at such a pivotal time, only proved to me how close I was to breaking and how much I needed to recharge.

We'd arrived a few days ago and were so tired that we'd decided to laze around the infinity pool for the first week, snoozing between cocktails, snacks, and some saucy reading courtesy of our new best friend, Charlie. We'd asked her to come with us, but she had a few author-type commitments that she couldn't get out of. I was kind of relieved in a way. Much as I loved her, I was glad it would just be Georgie and me. She knew me well enough to know when to leave things alone and when it was the time to push me to talk. And that time hadn't arrived yet.

'Hello again,' I purred, dropping my sunglasses down my nose to peer over them at the dishy and very fit specimen of male jogging past. He was wearing a pair of seriously tight trunks, and as he ran by, he flashed a smile Georgie's way. I'd spotted him the first day we'd sat here, then multiple times since, and each time he couldn't help looking at my best friend. I gave Georgie a surprised look when she made no comment and put her nose back into her e-Reader. 'Cat got your tongue?' I enquired.

'What?' she replied, not looking up. I frowned, sure she had a hint of a blush on her porcelain cheeks, which was unusual for her.

'Hot totty alert. He just jogged right in front of us, looking like some kind of bronzed Olympian, then smiled at you, again, and you didn't bat an eyelid. Again. He's gorgeous, so your type. Didn't you see him just now? Or all the other times he's jogged past in the last few days?'

'Hmmm,' she nodded, her eyes still scanning her screen. 'He's ok, I guess.'

'You guess?' I set my cocktail down and swung my legs off the bed as I turned to face her. 'Ok, what's the deal?'

'No deal,' she shrugged, avoiding eye contact by picking up her cocktail and chasing the straw around the glass with her lips before catching it and slowly sucking a load down, trying to stall a reply.

'You little liar, Georgie Basset! I know you too well, what gives?'

'Ok, I saw him. Every. Single. Damn. Time. He's gorgeous. So hot I had to check my bikini hadn't burst into flames from where my body heated up. Happy now?'

'No. Why were you trying to hide the fact that you fancy him?'

'Because ... oh, you wouldn't understand.' She dismissed me with a flick of the wrist, set her cocktail back down, and picked up her e-Reader again. I leaned over and snatched it out of her hand.

'Uh-uh, sweetie. This is one discussion you're not wheedling your way out of. Come on, talk.'

'Fine,' she sighed. 'You know me really well, Abbie.'

'Well, I should hope so, best friend and all.'

'And you are, you so are, but you've only known me with Greg, or the Georgie who's single and totally uninterested in men.'

'Your point being?' I finished my cocktail and raised my hand to one of the waiters who was hovering nearby.

'You don't know Georgina, the girl who's super shy when she sees a guy she likes. Who gets so flustered that she can't speak, let alone look him in the eye. That's why I haven't smiled back, because I think he's gorgeous. I got butterflies in my tummy the first time I saw him.'

'Ok, colour me confused here. When you like a guy, you make out that you don't, thereby ensuring he won't approach you and saving you the embarrassment of admitting you fancy him? Hold that response,' I suggested when she opened her mouth to reply. I ordered two more cocktails and some slices of watermelon, then gestured for her to continue.

'Seriously, Abbie. I'm totally bashful when a guy I like comes to talk to me. I say stupid things and make myself look like a fool and they can't back away fast enough. Best to just save myself the humiliation and not let them know I like them.'

'How the hell did you get engaged to Greg then, or lose your virginity?' I uttered, not following her crazy, twisted logic at all.

'Because I liked them, I didn't *like* them, like them.'

'There's a double-like system in place? When did that come into play?'

'Oh, you know what I mean. Look at you and Heath. You like him, I think in time you could even go on to date him, but you don't *like* him enough for him to be "the one." You'd be settling for Mr. "Ok for now", instead of waiting for Mr. Perfect. And that's what I did, though I didn't realise it at the time. Subconsciously I think I did know, as I didn't feel any stress or tension around Greg or the other guys I dated. Like it didn't matter if they got to know the real me and decided they didn't like me, it wouldn't be any great loss. But with Mr. Perfect ...' She trailed off, a dreamy look in her eyes, until I snapped my fingers and broke her out of her daze. 'With a guy that I feel an attraction that strong to, there's a risk. *It matters*, you know?'

'So you're saying a few looks at a hot face and body jogging past for the last few days and you think you've found Mr. Perfect?'

'You make me sound really shallow,' she protested before slurping up the remains of her drink. 'But I just took one look at him and felt like I'd been winded. Then he caught my eye and smiled, and it was like someone had sucked all of the air out of my lungs. It was like I felt this connection to him, a total stranger. It scared me, so every time I see him coming up the beach now, I make myself not look.' She bit her lower lip anxiously as she studied my face for my reaction.

'Ok, I sort of get that. I felt the same way the first time I saw Miller at Rachel's wedding. But what I don't get is you closing yourself off to the possibility of meeting someone who might be your happy ever after. By letting him think you're not interested, you probably lose any chance of finding out if there's something there. By letting him know, by maybe having a few drinks with him, the worst that can happen is you don't get on and he walks away. No harm, no foul. You're no worse off.'

'But—'

'No buts, because there's a chance that he could really like you too, Georgie. A chance that you could have a relationship, a chance that I might have to put on bridesmaid dress number thirteen for you. Isn't that worth the risk?'

'Of you being a spinster for the rest of your life? Hell no!' she retorted.

'Take me out of the equation. There's no way Pippa's going to last a week in a convent, she'll change her mind and be getting married

167

before we know it, and she'll put the curse on me. You said on the plane ride over here that you'd do anything to see a smile on my face again, didn't you?'

'Yes,' she replied cautiously.

'Well, I'm calling in that promise. I want you to smile back at him next time he jogs past, and to keep smiling every time he looks at you, and to say yes when he asks you to drinks or dinner, which I guarantee he's going to do. No,' I warned as she went to interrupt me. 'You promised, Georgie. This is what I want.'

'You're so mean to me, Abbie Carter,' she pouted. 'I'll only promise if you promise to open up to me before we get on that plane home. Deal?'

Bugger, she had me there, but I wanted to see her moving on from the disaster of Greg, to realise her self-worth again. Slicing open some fresh wounds was a small price to pay for my friend's happiness.

'Deal,' I confirmed.

Tuesday

'I can't do it,' I stated firmly, shaking my head as I stepped back from the cliff edge for about the fourth time.

'Oh come on, Abbie, it's not that high, and it's not like there isn't a beautiful lagoon to catch you at the bottom,' Georgie urged. 'Look, look, are you going to let a precocious twelve-year-old show you up?' She pointed at the young boy who'd been taunting me as he'd queued behind. He gave me a smug look as he jumped over the edge with a whoop of joy.

'Cocky little bugger,' I muttered, craning my head to see if he'd made it safely, but secretly hoping he'd landed on the rocks and broken his leg. I sighed as I saw him swimming away on his back, then gasped as he stuck his thumb and index finger up to his forehead in a "Loser" gesture as he grinned up at me. 'Right, that's it, I'm jumping!' I announced as I pushed Georgie out of the way, needing to do it before I lost my nerve. I took a deep breath and told myself not to look down as I did a standing jump off the cliff.

'Don't forget to ....' Georgie's voice was obliterated by my scream as my stomach remained up there with her, and I looked down to see the lagoon below racing towards me. Out of instinct, I started flailing my arms and legs, like that was going to suspend me in the air, *Roadrunner* style, and stop me from reaching my destination. I tipped forwards and could have sworn I heard a chorus of people hissing through their teeth as I slapped onto the water's surface, my chest, stomach and thighs taking the brunt of the impact, then rapidly sank below the surface. I came up spluttering and choking, my body stinging like I'd just been paddled to death with ping-pong bats. 'You ok?' yelled Georgie.

'Great,' I yelled back, trying to make myself look casually nonchalant about the whole thing, while that damn kid roared with laughter somewhere in the distance.

'You looked like you hit the water hard,' she called. 'You were supposed to tombstone, cross your arms in front of you and go feet first.'

'Never one for tradition, this way was far more exhilarating,' I called back. Bugger, my body was on fire. I managed to swim away from the landing zone and made it to a shallow part of the lagoon where I could stand up and try and catch my breath as I watched Georgie jump. Instead of my bloodcurdling scream of fear, she let out a 'Yippee' as she did exactly as we'd been instructed to do and disappeared into the water like a knife slicing through butter. She surfaced and swam over, then walked up towards me, looking annoyingly like a sexy Ursula Andress or Halle Berry, straight out of a Bond film.

'Wow, wasn't it amazing? I want to do it again,' she grinned.

'Feel free. I'm fancying a tour on the lazy river,' I shrugged. There was no way I was going up there again.

'I'll come back later, I'd rather be with you,' she smiled, grabbing my hand. 'Come on then, let's go and float around the resort. I'm so glad we came, it's amazing here.'

She was right. Although my body currently felt broken, this water park was just amazing. Calling it a water park made it sound like some kind of man-made theme park. It wasn't. This part of it was made up of natural coral reefs and saltwater lagoons, where fish swam alongside you, sea turtles flapped past, and brightly coloured parrots flew overhead. After lunch, we were heading to the section where there were some water slides, and we'd booked an intimate swim with the dolphins. Other than my water slap just now, I was feeling a lot less tense. Daily massages out in a private cabana above the ocean had helped to ease out a few kinks as well, as had the decision to leave my phone behind. I needed a complete break from Miller to think about what I really wanted, as this constant up and down with him wasn't working for me.

With the exception of that damn obnoxious kid taunting me with 'Hey look, it's the chicken,' as he hung over each of the wooden bridges we passed under in our giant inflated rings, the lazy river was

169

gorgeous and relaxing. After lunch, we spent an hour sunbathing as people snorkelled past, then Georgie begged me to climb up the steps to the tallest water slide, which undulated in a straight line all the way down into another lagoon below. I gritted my teeth as we worked our way up. I was really aching from that cliff jump earlier, but wasn't going to moan about it all day. The member of staff at the top grinned widely as Georgie and I stepped up to the slides, checking us both out.

'You, chute one, sit and hold the rails until I tell you to let go,' he instructed Georgie, who did as she was told. She looked striking in a turquoise crochet bikini, which matched her eyes and the blue water that surrounded us.

'You, chute two, lie face down and hold the rails until I tell you to let go,' he ordered me.

'Face down? Are you sure?' I asked, not overly enthused at the prospect of putting my already tender front in the firing line.

'Face down,' he nodded, gesturing for the next couple to step forwards for chutes three and four. I groaned and rolled my eyes as my tormentor swaggered over and looked me up and down.

'Oi, you can knock that off for a start. You look about twelve, I'm old enough to be your mother,' I warned him as he cocked his head to check out my bottom. 'I'm going to sit down, like my friend,' I called over to the member of staff as he ordered another boy to sit for chute three, then told the irritating lad to lie down in the fourth chute.

'What's the matter, too chicken to go head first?' the little tyke called as he got into position. 'Too scared I'm gonna beat you?'

'What did I do to get him riding my arse today?' I asked Georgie, astounded, as I flicked my thumb over my shoulder at him. She giggled and shrugged.

'Didn't you know boys always pick on girls they fancy, Abbie? Go on, do it, wipe that smug smile off his face by beating him.'

'Fine,' I grated, shooting him a glare as I got into position, the glare turning to a fierce scowl as he winked at me.

I took a deep breath as they counted us down, my arms at full stretch as I gripped the rail tightly. The second the word "Go" was called, I propelled myself forwards and shot out of the flat starting area like a canon.

'Ha, take that!' I yelled as I went over the brow and tipped forwards. I gulped as I saw how much of a drop there was to the water out below and ahead of us, but there was no turning back now. I plummeted, then levelled off, then went over the edge again, picking up speed. By the third drop, I was going so fast I could hear the wind whistling past my ears and I lifted slightly, landing back down on the hard, wet surface below with a slight "Oomph." The slight "Oomph" became a loud one, then a forcefully ejected swear word. By the time I

170

was approaching the last few undulations of the slide, I wasn't just lifting in the air, I was freakin' *Superwoman*, taking off and flying through the air before smacking back down and having the stuffing knocked out of me. I could hear Georgie whooping with glee somewhere behind me as I was launched again like a missile. 'Brace for impact,' I screamed as I landed with a heavy thud and took off again from the final hump, slicing through the air.

Instead of just slapping the water for the second time today, like that wouldn't be enough torture, I skimmed across it a number of times like a bouncing bomb. I gasped for air just as I went under, swallowing a load of the salty water as well as something solid. I came up choking and struggling to breathe, with the horrible feeling of something wedged in the back of my throat. One of the lifeguards at the edge waded over to help me and escorted me to the side, encouraging me to spit it all out.

'Oh my God, Abbie, are you ok?' Georgie uttered as she came up beside me. She screamed and covered her face with her hands as I coughed up a load of water, and something light brown in colour spewed out with it as well.

'Is that ... is that ... a friggin' *corn plaster*?' I shrieked, then choked, hardly able to believe what I was seeing.

'I'm going to be sick,' Georgie moaned, her tanned and freckled face turning a light shade of green.

'Not in the water,' the lifeguard quickly replied.

'Oh no, we don't want puke in the water, do we? I mean, that would just up the gross factor even more than me swallowing someone's manky toe covering,' I coughed, fighting the urge to be sick myself. My stomach started roiling as I continued to gag, so I quickly turned around, not wanting to look at the offending item. Instead I was confronted by the kid, whose eyes ejected on stalks as his mouth gaped.

'Abbie, your top's missing,' Georgie giggled, pointing to my chest. I quickly covered my bare breasts with my hands, my cheeks turning the same colour as my slide-slapped chest, stomach, and thighs. The lifeguard looked around, spotted it floating in the water not far away, and raced off to retrieve it.

'Great tits!' muttered the boy, still staring.

'Don't think I won't slap you just because you're a kid,' I hissed at him.

'Go on then, it'd be worth it when you have to let them go to do it. I wouldn't mind another look.'

'Yeah, me neither, Todd,' nodded his friend, who'd sidled up beside him. I just stood there, speechless, still trying to catch my breath

171

from the shock of my journey and impromptu meal, the thought of which made me cough again.

'That was so cool, the way you were flying through the air,' Todd grinned, looking suitably impressed.

Cool? With bad boys my size? Cool was the opposite of how my chest and stomach were feeling right now. They were on fire from the succession of beatings they'd taken as I'd bounced my way down. Never had I wished for a flat chest more than I had during that descent. In fact, I was amazed my boobs were still facing forwards and not as flat as pancakes or poking out of my back. 'You need the kiss of life?' he asked, looking hopeful.

'No!' I retorted. 'Look, don't you have girls your own age to go and flirt with?'

'Yeah, but you're like … a Playboy model. You're hot.'

'Your friend is super fit, too,' Todd's friend added. 'I'll have her and you can have *Supergirl*.'

'Jesus,' I sighed, looking at Georgie for help, but she was too busy laughing and no use at all. 'Just tell me I beat him, that I beat you all, and that all the humiliation and the disgusting snack was worth it.'

'Win? You set a new record, lady. Instead of just a free picture of you coming down the slide, my manager's confirmed you'll get a free video of it as well,' nodded the lifeguard as he handed Georgie my white bikini top.

'Oh wonderful, my pain and shame immortalised, I'm thrilled,' I replied with more than a hint of sarcasm, which seemed to go completely over his head. But despite being in some serious pain, I was secretly chuffed I'd beaten Todd. And being seen as hot by a twelve-year-old, while incredibly wrong on so many levels, was also kind of a morale boost. 'You and you, beat it,' I ordered, flicking my head to them both as they just stood there, transfixed on my hands and hoping for another glimpse. I sighed when they made no move to disappear and turned my back on them as Georgie quickly helped me to dress.

'Quite the fan club you have going on,' she observed with another giggle.

'I can just see the headlines back home if we don't shake them off soon. *Abbie Carter, the flying water slide flashing speedster, jailed in Mexico for grooming young boys.* Seriously, where are their parents?' I shook my head as I started having a coughing fit, the thought of that gross plaster making me want to throw up.

'Kids now get so much more freedom than we ever did,' she agreed. 'Come on, let's go and get you some water. You need to sit down for a while and rest after that. Didn't it hurt?'

'Like you wouldn't believe. I'm in so much pain right now,' I groaned.

'I'm good at massage,' came an adolescent voice behind me.

'And I'm good at spanking, so you'd better scuttle off unless you want to be hauled over my knee,' I warned, shooting him a look over my shoulder, then coughing again.

'Can you report a teenage stalker?' I asked as I zipped up my wet suit. I'd just spotted Todd and his friend watching us from the benches that were dotted around the lagoon the dolphins were in.

'It is starting to get a bit creepy,' Georgie agreed. 'I'm just hoping we don't roll over on our sun loungers at the hotel tomorrow and find them both there, staring at us.'

'I think your new beau will have something to say about that,' I grinned, elbowing her in her ribs. She blushed and giggled.

'He's not my new beau.'

'I have a feeling he will be soon. We've moved from him smiling at you, to you smiling back, to him waving, to you waving back, then the exchange of the word "Hi" to each other as he jogs past every half an hour. You'll be on a date pretty soon.'

'Shut up, he's just being polite,' she grinned as we padded along the floating deck platform to where the trainers were waiting with the other couple doing the swim with us. Four dolphins were zipping back and forth in the water, occasionally sticking their heads up, looking as excited as we were.

'He doesn't direct his smiles and sexy, deep-voiced "Hi" at me, Georgie. And seriously, with a body like that, he doesn't exactly need to jog the amount he does. It's just an excuse to see you. You wait until we're home and I feed the data I've been collating into my spreadsheet. You'll see it's gone from one jog a day to ten in just over a week, increasing exponentially.'

'We're not going on a date. I'm not after a quick, hot holiday romance, and he could live anywhere in the world. I may never see him again.'

'He's got a very British "Hi,"' I observed. 'I'd lay bets on him being an army officer or something.'

'Look at you, Miss "FBI profiler" from one word.'

'Ask him out then and prove me wrong,' I challenged.

'Damn it, fell right into that one, didn't I?'

I laughed and we shut up as we joined the group and listened to our brief. One by one, we were each asked to sit on the edge of the platform, with a bucket of fish behind us, and our dolphins were called over for an introduction, for which they'd be rewarded. Georgie and I gave each other a watery-eyed, emotional, and excited smile as the first

173

dolphin squeaked excitedly and rose up to offer the lady a kiss. They were such adorable creatures. It swam backwards and did a somersault, then came back for its reward.

Georgie giggled her head off as her dolphin rested its head on her thigh and smiled up at her, allowing her to stroke the underside of its snout, then it shot off to do some acrobatics and came back for its fish.

'Ok, Abbie, you're next. Sit down, legs apart, so Mahi can get up close. No fish until he's performed for you.'

'Ok,' I grinned, quickly taking my place and dangling my legs in the water. Mahi came zooming over, chattering his jaw as he rose up, flippers on my thighs, and gave me a kiss. 'Ahhh, he's so sweet,' I cried.

'Stroke him, Abbie,' Georgie coaxed as she did the same with hers. I did, and giggled as he dropped back into the water and stuck his snout into my crotch.

'Hey, down boy,' I laughed. He pulled away when the trainer tapped him and ordered him to go and perform. 'He's friendly,' I grinned over at Georgie.

'I need to know what perfume you're wearing today, as you've got it going on,' she winked. I looked up as Mahi dipped and dived and zoomed back towards me, rising up to stick his flippers on my thighs as he came for another kiss.

'Steady on,' I warned him, rubbing under his snout again as he started bobbing back and forth, his tail thrashing in the water.

'Abbie, I need you to slide backwards now,' one of the trainers ordered.

'What?' I asked as I continued to stroke him.

'Slide back, slide back away from Mahi *now*,' he repeated, the urgency in his voice making me look up at him in surprise.

'Why–' I began to ask, but was cut off in my prime as Mahi launched himself up and knocked me backwards, my head hitting the bucket of fish as I did, and I screamed as it all slithered out, smothering my face. *First corn plasters, now a bucket load of stinky fish. What had I done to deserve this,* I wondered. I struggled to push myself up while I held my breath, again at serious risk of throwing up from the smell and gross texture on my skin. I was pressed back down onto the platform as Mahi landed on my stomach, making me gasp for air. His excited cries filled my ears as I felt him bouncing up and down on me, the sound of his tail smacking the water mingling with my panicked gasps. 'He's going to eat me alive,' I shrieked, as various hands quickly tried to move the gutted fish away from my face and chest.

'Oh, Abbie, he's not hungry, he's horny!' Georgie roared. 'He's trying to mate with you!'

I kept my eyes firmly closed and felt myself vomit a little in my mouth as the smell of the small fish, as well as the large one currently trying to impregnate me, got too much. As soon as they managed to slide him off me into the water and helped me up, I turned around and threw up in the bucket they'd thrown his fish back into. When I finally stood up, with my hands on my hips, feeling and smelling pretty grotty, my three companions were trying to hold in their laughter, while the male trainer had gone to try and calm the amorous dolphin down. I gagged again, the smell of fish radiating from me horrendous.

'Come with me, Abbie,' Juana, the lady trainer, suggested. 'We'll get you showered and changed. You can't go in the water smelling like this or they might bite you.'

'As opposed to mating with me?' I mumbled, covering my mouth and nose with my hand.

'Are you ok?' Georgie called as I started to walk away. I put up one hand in a warning. 'I'm sorry, but it was pretty funny,' she yelled to my retreating back.

'Ok, we've moved Mahi over to Stephen, and we're giving you Tiki,' Juana advised as she walked me back to the group, all of whom were in the water with the dolphins now.

'Will he try and hump me, too?' I asked, feeling a little nervous, especially as three sets of shampoo under the open showers hadn't got rid of the scent of mackerel. The last thing I needed to add to my battered body and stinky aroma were dolphin bites as they tried to eat me.

'Tiki's a girl, with a very sweet disposition. She's smaller than Mahi, too. We called another trainer in so that I can stay by your side,' she smiled. 'There's no need to worry.'

'After the day I'm having, forgive me if that doesn't reassure me,' I replied, as she made me sit on the platform to try again. This time she put the bucket of fish behind her as she sat next to me.

Georgie flashed me a smile and a thumbs up before turning around to enjoy her experience. I swallowed a ball of nerves as Tiki came over. She wasn't going to try and mate with me and there were no fish for me to fall back into, so as long as Mahi stayed with Stephen, I'd be fine. My nerves soon left me as the pretty little dolphin came to say hello. I swore she had the biggest smile I'd ever seen on anyone, human or mammal, as she came back for a second kiss and gratefully accepted the fish I offered her.

I squealed with excitement as I was lifted up by Tiki and Georgie's dolphin, Luna, and flew through the air, held up by the tips of their noses. The excitement was slightly muted when I dropped back down into the water, my body groaning its protest.

'How amazing was that?' Georgie laughed, clapping as I held onto them and they zoomed me back over to where she was treading water. 'Best day ever!'

'It may have offset the rest of the day,' I agreed, my enthusiasm suddenly dampening as I heard Mahi's name being yelled and spotted a curved *Jaws*-like fin speeding through the water towards us. 'Oh God, he's coming back for me!' I cried.

'"Run, Forrest, run!"' laughed Georgie as I quickly started swimming for the platform, Tiki and Luna flanking me as if they knew I was in trouble. That or they were after some kinky dolphin shenanigans with Mahi themselves. Maybe they saw me as competition for the alpha and were about to tag team and take me out. I felt something shove me from behind, which stalled my escape, and I flipped over to try and see what was happening, only to find Mahi was nosing his way into my crotch again.

'Help!' I yelled, not sure if trying to push him away would anger him. Juana and one of the other trainers were swimming towards me at speed, but Tiki and Luna did a spectacular backwards somersault to dive under water as they tackled him. Not wanting to be an unwanted extra in a potential fishy ménage a trois, I made a break for it and struck out for the platform, which wasn't too far away. There was a combination of laughter and yells behind me as I started to hyperventilate. I was going to be drowned by a highly-sexed male dolphin, or worse. Did dolphins have penises? This one was so determined to get at me, I wasn't convinced my wet suit would give me any form of protection. I reached up with shaky hands and hauled myself up out of the water, but either I was too slow or that damn bionic horny dolphin was too fast. He pounced on my back, flattening my upper half to the deck, my legs dangling in the water as he started to thrash against my backside, his flippers whacking my arms as he emitted a load of high-pitched squeals.

'Please don't tell me this is being filmed as well?' I moaned, as the trainers struggled to remove him from his doggie, or rather, dolphin position behind me.

'If it is, that's one video I'm definitely buying,' Georgie laughed as she hauled herself up next to me.

Monday

'You know, in spite of everything, I kind of don't want to go home,' I sighed, as I did up my seatbelt buckle on the plane.

'I know what you mean,' Georgie agreed. 'How are you feeling?'

'Tender. Still,' I confirmed. I'd been so unbelievably stiff the night we'd returned to our hotel after the waterpark adventures. By the time I'd woken up the next day, I'd had the most horrendous black bruises on my thighs, arms, back, and chest. I'd had to stay in the villa for two days as it was too painful to move. Then I'd only been able to sunbathe in a black kaftan, as I'd looked like some kind of domestic abuse victim.

'And have you made a decision regarding Miller?' she asked. We'd talked about it at length, but I was still torn over whether to walk away for good or try again to make it work.

'No, what about you? Are you going to ring Weston?'

She gave me a look and scoffed, then rolled her eyes. He'd finally plucked up the courage to come over and talk to her, and I'd witnessed the painful encounter. She'd been hardly able to talk, which had made him go the same way, so I'd suggested they have drinks and dinner that night. When she returned, with me sneakily watching their embarrassing goodbye, she'd told me categorically that much as she fancied him and still felt a connection that she hadn't with anyone else, it had been the worst date she'd ever been on. Including her date with Wayne Davies, the farmer's son in Dilbury. I'd winced, knowing how bad that had been. But Weston had returned unexpectedly the next morning to offer her his phone number.

'So that's it? You're not going to give him a second chance? He lives the other side of Shrewsbury, less than half an hour from Dilbury, which is an amazing stroke of luck.'

'I'm not the kind of girl who rings a guy. I like them to do the chasing, just like you do. If he rings, we'll see, but I got the impression he really wasn't that into me.'

'Wow. Apart from guessing correctly that he was ex-forces, I really got that one wrong. I swore I saw hearts in his eyes as he said goodbye to us yesterday.'

'Well, Mahi and Todd had hearts in their eyes when they spied you, it doesn't mean you'd have had a great relationship with either of them,' she retorted as the plane engines started up.

'Don't remind me,' I shuddered. 'Does my hair still smell fishy?'

'It's gone now, thank God. Right, I'd better get some snacks out to keep us going until they serve the food.'

'Lovely, I'm already feeling a bit peckish despite nearly eating the entire all-you-can-eat breakfast. What did you get?' I had a craving for chocolate, proper creamy British milk chocolate. This foreign stuff was awful.

'Something to help you get plastered,' she giggled, as she slapped a packet of the donut-shaped corn plasters on my lap.

'Next time I'm coming with Charlie and you're staying at home,' I warned her with a shoulder bump.

'Please. After the last two holiday accidents she had, no one would ever want to go away with her. She's a walking disaster, more accident prone than you are. And that's saying something. Ok, you're not in a corn mood, how about some fish?' she suggested, pulling out a tin of chocolate sardines, which made me give her a warning scowl. 'No? Maybe you're in need of some tender loving instead,' she suggested, a small stuffed grey dolphin magically appearing from her bag.

I giggled and shook my head, wondering what other mickey-taking tricks she had in there. Disaster day aside, this holiday had done me a world of good. I felt like I was back on top form, ready to tackle anything.

The question was whether Miller was at the top of my priority list.

Chapter Fourteen
Words Of Wisdom

I LOOKED AROUND IN shock as I heard the thunder of feet pounding up the wooden stairs to my office. I had no clients due. I'd rearranged them to keep the last two weeks clear so I could catch up on my year-end work after our impromptu trip. The oak door swung open to reveal a panting Georgie. She put her hands on her hips and bent over to try and catch her breath.

'Ok?' I asked, swivelling around in my leather office chair. She nodded and held up one finger as she gulped down some air.

'Da … Da … Daph … Daph …'

'Daphne?' I suggested, trying to hurry her to her point. When she nodded, my stomach dropped and I shot up out of my seat. No! What had happened to her? I was not losing Daphne as well. Georgie must have seen the panicked look on my face and gestured with both palms to calm down.

'Jesus, I really need … to get to … a gym,' she uttered.

'No arguments here, but what's wrong with Daphne? You're scaring me, Georgie.'

'Did you know … she was moving?' She gave me her poignant stare, the one that said she was going to have a go at me if the answer I gave wasn't to her liking. I blinked at her a few times as I tried to process the question. Daphne was moving? The thought of it made my chest hurt.

'No, where did you hear that? She told you and she didn't tell me too?' I asked, feeling somewhat slighted. That waste-of-space son of hers had obviously finally stepped up, but he lived down south. Was he taking her back there? I couldn't imagine not seeing her every day, getting my daily updates on the village gossip from her or receiving well-meaning, and often very sage, advice.

'I had no idea, until I just … crikey, do you have some water or something, I'm dying here,' she huffed, as she leaned back against the doorframe and wiped her brow.

'*I'm* dying here,' I retorted. 'And you've hardly done a marathon. You've run up a lane past two houses.'

'A long lane and a very bumpy one at that. I could have twisted an ankle. I'm really not feeling the appreciation for dropping everything to come and tell you the news.'

'I don't *know* the news, you haven't spat it out yet!' I reminded her.

179

'Oh right, sorry.' She levered herself off the door and walked over to me as I stood with my mouth slightly ajar, wondering when she was going to get to the point. My eyebrows raised as she lifted up my cold, half-drunk cup of coffee and gulped it down.

'Please, make yourself at home,' I suggested. 'Would you like some lunch brought in while you finish my accounts? I can just wait until this evening to hear what's happening with one of the most important women in my life.'

'I can't do my own accounts, that's why I pay you. No way I want to touch this lot,' she retorted as she gestured to the open account books I was surrounded by, and the large Mac screen I'd been studying my formulas on. 'Jesus, this is my worst nightmare. I hate maths.'

'Georgie! For the love of God, get to the point!' I demanded. 'Where's she moving to?'

'I've no idea, that's why I came here to see if she'd told you and not me. I was going to be really annoyed if you said yes.'

'Then how do you know she's moving? If Sheila Vickers told you, I wouldn't believe a word. I've heard she's just been diagnosed with dementia, and not a moment too soon, bless her.'

'No one told me. I was just waving Portia the poodle goodbye after her pre-show cut and blow-dry, and there was a man putting up a "For Sale" sign by her front gate.'

'No,' I announced firmly. 'She is *not* moving down south to be with that waster who doesn't even want her. If she needs more help, then we'll take extra shifts. This is her home, she's lived in Dilbury all of her life. Forget it, not on my watch.' I grabbed my keys, then Georgie's wrist, and dragged her out onto the landing.

'I know we see her as family, Abbie, but we're not. What can we do to stop this? Especially if she wants to go?'

'I'll never believe she wants to go voluntarily, Georgie, never. She loves this village and … and …' I stopped and huffed out a breath as I blinked back some tears.

'You're scared she's going to leave you too, aren't you?' Georgie said softly as we stood at the top of the stairs. 'That her going means she doesn't love you, love us, enough.'

'Am I selfish for thinking that? I know I'm not her daughter, but I can't help but think we've been closer to her than her son ever has. She's really leaving us?'

'I've no idea, which is why I'm here. Come on, let's stop torturing ourselves and go and find out.' She made me lock up, then took my hand and pulled me along behind her as she trotted down the stairs, having found a renewed sense of energy. We walked with determination up my drive and were halted in our tracks by a 'Cooee!'

We turned to see Daphne standing on my doorstep, about to knock on the door.

'I'm so sorry, I had no idea he was putting up the board today. I wanted to tell you first, but you were so busy with work and I was trying to find a good time,' she called, looking as upset as I was feeling.

'You're leaving us? Leaving Dilbury?' I asked, the hurt in my voice I'd hoped to disguise shining through, as we headed through the side gate to approach her.

'You really think I could leave you girls and the village that I love? I should scold you both for thinking how little you mean to me,' she advised with a wagging figure and stern look.

'You actually *are* scolding us both,' Georgie observed.

'Well, I'm cross,' Daphne retorted as she reached out to hold onto one of the oak-beam canopy supports. 'How could you think you mean so little to me?'

'But you're selling your house!' I reminded her. 'Where are you going?'

'Flat on my arse if you don't get me inside and into a comfortable seat soon,' she warned. 'These legs are over eighty years old, they've held me up for far too long. Now get the kettle on and I'll tell you the news.'

I sighed and kissed her cheek, then opened up. Georgie helped her inside and we all headed to the kitchen. I busied myself getting down some mugs and putting the kettle on, while Georgie settled Daphne in her favourite chair at my table and asked her what was going on, but she refused to answer until we were all sitting down. I took over some steaming hot coffees, then put some of my homemade white chocolate chip cookies on a plate in the middle of the table. Both of them eyed them suspiciously, then looked up at me.

'They have sugar in them, I ate one for breakfast,' I assured them with a roll of my eyes, then a giggle as their hands shot forwards to grab one each and they started chewing. I sighed as I looked at them. They were Miller's favourite, which made me sad, but I was relieved that Daphne wasn't leaving the village. These two women meant the world to me. 'Come on then, the suspense is killing me.'

Daphne finally filled us in, saying that she was finding it harder and harder to get up and down the stairs, and that as much as she loved her cottage and living next to us, it was too painful being surrounded by so many memories of her husband. She said she needed to be somewhere that was easier to navigate and that didn't upset her every time she looked around and remembered happier times with him. I understood her logic. For some people, they'd never want to leave, but I'd had to remove all of the things in the house that reminded me of Sumo, including replacing his favourite armchair. It hurt too much to have them around.

'So where are you going?'

'Well, it all came about during a game of bridge while you were away,' she advised, leaning in as if she was sharing an important secret, so Georgie and I did too. 'There's a few of us widowed pensioners in the village, all of us living in houses that are too big and don't suit us anymore. None of us want to leave the village, so Albert came up with a very clever plan.'

'Which is?' I prompted as she sat back to drink her coffee and nibble on another cookie. I was very impatient today, everyone was taking far too long to get to the point.

'You know he had a large win on the lottery a few months ago?'

'Hmmm,' I nodded, remembering the excitement of the winning ticket having been purchased in the post office. We'd had the press here, and even a news crew. It was quite the publicity for our little village.

'Well, he's invested it in the old school house, that big Victorian place down Ivy Lane. He's having it converted into ten self-contained, one-bedroom apartments, with lift access to the first floor, a communal lounge, games room, and kitchen diner. I've paid a deposit to secure one, and so have some other OAPs from the village. Mr. Bentley, Mr. and Mrs Vickers too, so the shop is going on the market. We'll all chip in to pay for a team of carers to do shifts.'

'So it's like an old people's home, but you get to keep your independence if you want, and still live in Dilbury with your friends?' I asked, my heart warming at the thought that she'd only be a five-minute walk away.

'And I still get to be near you girls,' she beamed, leaning over to put her old, arthritic hands on top of mine and Georgie's. 'What do you think?'

'I think it's bloody brilliant,' I enthused, feeling very emotional.

'Me too, Daphne. Oh, I'm so happy to hear we aren't losing you for good.'

'You can come and visit whenever you want, and I might even get one of those zippy motorised scooters so I can nip to the shop, assuming there will still be a shop, and come and visit you both here, too. They won't be ready for another couple of months, but I thought I ought to set the wheels in motion.'

'Well, if you get an offer and need to move out before your apartment is ready, you can come and live here,' I offered, smothering her hand on mine with my other one. 'I'm so glad you're doing this. Those stairs of yours were worrying me, and it's lovely to think you'll be surrounded by friends. And who knows, maybe romance will blossom with Mr. Bentley,' I teased. She blushed and smacked my hand with a girlish giggle. I knew how fond she was of him.

'Well, enough about me putting my life in order. It's time to talk about the two of you.'

'What about us?' Georgie asked as I went to fill up the kettle again. I was going to have to work through the night to catch up on my books, but I knew from Daphne's tone we were both in for a lecture, and Daphne wouldn't leave until she'd said her piece.

'You're going to be thirty this year, Abbie, and you're not that far behind her, Georgie, and neither of you are married. It's about time we sorted that out.'

'Daphne,' we both whined in unison.

'No,' she said firmly. 'I'm supposed to be the stubborn old goat in this little friendship of ours, too set in my ways to change, but I'm embracing it while you both sit here refusing to do the same. Georgie, Abbie told me this nice young man you met on holiday has rung you and you haven't rung him back!' she scolded.

'The date was a disaster, Daphne,' she groaned.

'It wasn't all peaches and cream on my first date with David either, you know,' she reminded her, making me smile. We knew the story, I'd never tired of hearing her tell us. 'But when you get that connection with someone, when you feel those butterflies, there's something there and it's worth persevering. Love isn't easy, you know. It's not all a bed of thornless roses, you have to take the rough with the smooth. Mr. Perfect doesn't exist, and you're both too intelligent to let yourselves believe that he does. That's where love comes into a partnership. If you both love each other, that love bridges the faults and anchors you together through any storm. He doesn't have to be perfect, and neither do you, but together you are perfect for each other. So, you are going to ring this Veston back–'

'Weston,' Georgie giggled as I carried the coffees back over, along with more cookies.

'Veston, Heston, Weston, whatever,' Daphne scoffed with a dismissive, and frankly impatient, flick of her wrist. 'You're going to ring him back. Even if you don't want to go on another date with him quite yet, you can start by talking on the phone, or texting, or sexting, whatever it is you youngsters do first. I know it's not hip or cool to actually physically see a man nowadays until you've had a virtual relationship, but you have to start somewhere. It's time to put that Greg behind you.'

'Hear, hear,' I confirmed with a nod. 'Been telling you that for ages, Georgie. Listen to the wise one, she speaks perfect sense.'

'And don't think you're getting off scot-free, young lady,' Daphne warned me with a firm stare, making me grimace and wince.

'You tell her, Daphne, as she's not listening to me!' nodded Georgie triumphantly as she sat back in her chair and folded her arms over her chest. 'I've told her that she's letting an ocean ruin what was a perfectly good relationship, that if she really loves him, and I know she does, even *two* oceans shouldn't keep her from him. True love knows no bounds,' she added with a poignant look at me, reminding me of our discussion on holiday.

'Of course I love him, and despite everything, I truly believe he loves me, but he's holding back and I don't understand why. I don't want to be the needy girl who chases him. I want a man who goes for what he wants, who puts himself out for me. I want a man to chase me, not the other way around, and it seems he won't.'

'For an intelligent woman, Abbie Carter, you really can be stupid sometimes,' Daphne sighed.

'Owww,' I protested as she finger-flicked my forehead. 'What was that for?'

'For not opening your eyes and seeing the truth,' Daphne replied, making me give her a puzzled look.

'He's already chased you, Abbie,' Georgie reminded me. 'This is the man who didn't do relationships, who never followed up on a woman, and he did that for you. He flew all the way here on Valentine's Day. Ok, he was a day late with the time difference, but he came.'

'And he left,' I reminded her in return.

'And he came back when Sumo died,' she added.

'And he left again. Then he didn't tell me about his sister, and upset me by turning up at the wedding with her, letting me think that he'd moved on. We've already discussed this, *at length*. Nothing's changed,' I muttered stubbornly.

'But you're missing the point, Abbie,' Daphne sighed, shaking her head at me. 'We're talking about a man who has never known any love in his life, until he met you. His own family abandoned him. Women have only ever wanted him for his looks or his money. Then he met you. He broke out of his mould and took a risk and gave you his heart.'

'And I gave him mine,' I reminded them both, tears prickling at my eyes. 'But it wasn't enough.'

'Says who?' Daphne retorted. 'You girls are so obsessed with finding Mr. Perfect, and I told you he doesn't exist. Miller has baggage, Abbie. He may be a confident alpha-male when it comes to his business affairs, but when it comes to matters of the heart, he's a scared young boy, terrified of being abandoned again. He's testing you. He's let you in, but he's keeping himself at a distance to see if you'll pursue him, if you really love him enough to go and claim him the way his parents never did. And you haven't.'

'But my life is here,' I objected.

'You're using that as an excuse, because you're not perfect either. You've had loss in your life and you're clinging onto remnants of the past instead of letting go and grabbing your future. He's a billionaire, Abbie. So what if he wants you to live in New York. You can afford to keep the cottage here and he'll fly you back and forth whenever you want. You won't have to work if you don't want to. And no matter where in the world you are, Georgie and I will still be your friends.'

'You're saying I should go and tell him I'll move out there with him?' I gulped as I looked at them both, and they both nodded. Daphne grabbed my hand again and held my gaze.

'He came looking for you after the wedding, but you'd already run away. We had a long talk and you know what he said?' she asked.

'No,' I said as I shook my head, as obviously I didn't.

'He said "I've made a fool of myself, chasing ghosts of people that obviously never really wanted me in their lives, and now Abbie. For once, I just want someone to make a fool of *themselves*, to go out of *their* way and put *their* heart on the line to show me how much they love me."'

'He said that? He thinks he's made a fool of himself chasing me?' I asked quietly, a solitary tear rolling down my cheek as I realised his parents had hurt him so badly, he wasn't really convinced that I'd ever loved him. I'd been sitting here thinking he didn't love me enough, and he'd been doing the same. We were two scared, and scarred, people. But I'd been lucky enough to have love in my life, from my dad, my friends, and even my gassy pooch. Who had Miller had? All along I'd been waiting for him to come and sweep me off my feet and prove himself to me, and he was sitting in New York doing the same.

I suddenly realised that he'd never break first. He'd not been shown enough love to make him believe it was worth the risk. So I needed to show him that he *was* loved enough for someone to make a fool of themselves. Because he *was* worth it. He wasn't Mr. Perfect, and I sure wasn't Miss Perfect, but Daphne was right. As two halves, we were imperfect, but together we could be stronger. Together we could fill each other's flaws and become a perfect whole.

'Are we booking you a flight?' Georgie asked, a hopeful look on her face.

'We're booking me a flight,' I nodded, then giggled as they both let out a screech of delight and gave each other a high five. 'But for this plan to work, I need some time to put some wheels into motion,' I added, not to mention working through the next few nights to complete my accounts.

185

Chapter Fifteen

Woman On A Mission
June

'MOVE IT, LADY. YOU already paid, so I switched off the meter and now I'm losing money,' the increasingly irate driver grumbled, as I struggled to get out of his yellow cab.

'I'm sorry, does it look like I'm not trying to move?' I retorted, flashing him a glare, which was pointless, as he wouldn't be able to see it anyway. 'How about instead of bitching at me, you help me?'

'I'm not running a charity here, I'm on the clock.'

'Andy would have helped me,' I muttered as I tried to sit up again and failed miserably. Plus Andy wouldn't have cussed, blasphemed, or hollered and gesticulated out of his window the entire journey from the hotel either.

'Who the hell is Andy?'

'Someone who could teach you a thing or two about manners. Are you going to help me or not?'

'All you have to do is sit up and get your fat ass out of my damn cab,' he grated.

'Oh, I'm so terribly sorry, my bad. If only you'd told me earlier that all I had to do was sit up. Why didn't I think of that? Oh, wait, I did. What do you think I've been doing floundering in here for the last five minutes? It's hardly conducive attire for one to bend at the waist. And for your information, my "ass" isn't fat! It's this outfit,' I bit back, then gasped as he muttered some nasty words about me under my breath. 'I can't believe I gave you a tip!'

'I'll give you one. Get the Hell. Out. Of. My. Damn. Cab. Or I'm driving away with you still hanging out of it,' he yelled, then he started muttering in a foreign language as he gestured with his arms wildly, showing his exasperation. When I heard a cough from outside, I angled my head to try and look through the open cab door, where my feet and legs were sticking out.

'Is everything ok in here?' came a male voice. He was immediately assaulted with a barrage of raised voices from myself and my uncharitable driver, telling him exactly what wasn't ok in here. 'Easy, easy, let's all calm down a minute,' he suggested.

'It's him, he's the problem,' I announced, whacking the back of the driver's head as I attempted to gesture in his direction.

'You see … you see what I'm having to put up with? Crazy British women, they're all the same,' he yelled.

'Ok, miss, give me your, errr, hand and I'll help you out,' came the friendly voice.

'Thank you! See, chivalry goes a long way,' I told the taxi driver as my knight in shining armour grabbed me around the wrists and gently tugged me into a seated position, then somehow yanked me out of the cab and steadied me on the pavement as I wobbled. 'Thank you so much. I don't suppose you could grab my basket from the floor, could you? These hands aren't much use.'

'None of you is,' Mr. Foreign huffed.

'Right, that's it, I've had enough of your attitude. Get out of that cab and come and face me like a man to apologise,' I ordered as I waddled to his window. I gasped again as he stuck up his middle finger and sped away from the kerb the second he heard his back door shut. 'How rude! Is everyone in New York so rude?' I asked my helper, turning around to try and find him.

'It's a busy city, everyone has places to go and things to do. You British are more polite. Here's your basket,' he advised as he hooked it over my arm. 'Where are you going dressed like this, a kid's birthday party?'

'No, I'm going to see my boyfriend, or rather my ex-boyfriend. Actually, I've no idea what we are anymore, but I wanted to surprise him,' I nodded, squinting as I tried to see what this man looked like. I could just make out he was in some kind of security uniform.

'I'd say you'll accomplish your mission,' he chuckled. 'Where are you meeting him? I can turn you around to face the right direction to go.'

'He's here. This is the entrance to AMD, isn't it?'

'It is. I work here, so take my arm and I'll escort you to the reception area. You'll need to sign in, if you can, and let them know who you're here to see.'

He helped loop one of my arms through his as we did a slow walk across the pavement, or "sidewalk" as Miller liked to call it, and I heard the whoosh of some electric doors opening in front of us. I remembered the lobby from when Miller had given me a tour. It was a huge space, well-lit from the glass façade, with shiny black marble floors and a long reception desk that had AMD in big chrome letters above it on the wall. To the left of reception were some security turnstiles, manned by armed security guards who vetted you before allowing you access to the lifts. I really hadn't thought this through properly.

'Are we there yet?' I asked, trying to angle my head to see while struggling to breathe. I was so hot.

187

'You're here, miss. Good luck with the surprise,' he confirmed.

'I would shake your hand, but I'm not really in a position to. Thank you so much, Mr. ...?'

'Thomas, just Thomas,' he chuckled.

'Then I'll let Miller know how kind you've been to me.'

'Miller?' he questioned. 'You're here to see Mr. Davis?'

'I am,' I confirmed.

'Are you Abbie Carter?'

'How did you know that?' I exclaimed. I'd thought my disguise was foolproof.

'Mr. Davis has only ever had one girlfriend, Miss Carter. We met briefly when he showed you around last year, though I'd never have recognised you in this.'

'No, I guess not,' I giggled.

'Well, let me sign you in and I'll escort you up to his office myself.'

'That's really good of you. Phew, is it always so hot in New York in June?' I asked, feeling perspiration gathering on my forehead while some trickled down the back of my neck.

'Yes, but dressing like that doesn't help,' he laughed. 'Mr. Davis really will be surprised, you're drawing quite a crowd down here.'

'Excellent,' I confirmed. That was the point. I was here to prove how much I loved him by making a total fool of myself, and so far it seemed to be going to plan.

'Ok, I'm not sure the lanyard will fit around your neck, so I'll just carry it for you,' he offered as he helped me to shuffle off again. I could just make out the turnstiles as we approached them and he advised me to walk forward. I did, but bounced straight back. I tried again, and the same thing happened. I could hear lots of chuckling around me.

'What's happening?' I asked Thomas.

'I think your hips are too big to go through. How about you turn sideways?' he suggested, taking my basket off me. I nodded and did as I was told and started to edge to my left. 'You need to suck in your stomach,' he advised when I seemed to get stuck.

'Ok,' I called, whacking my hands against it and straining to move to the left. 'Ha, I can feel the bar on my left thigh.'

'Great, keep going, it will spin and let you through.'

I kept shuffling, panting, and squeezing my way through the gap, then squealed as I felt my right leg being lifted up into the air. I froze, in some kind of arabesque ballet position, as a wave of laughter surrounded me.

'What's happening now?' I called, totally aware that I was currently reliant on this poor guy.

'You're too big to get through,' Thomas called from behind me.

'So what do we do? I'm pretty uncomfortable like this.'

'I can imagine. We either reverse the mechanism and pull you back out, or I get some of the guys to help me lift you up and carry you over. But they'll all need to come upstairs with me, because there's turnstiles to enter each floor as you exit the elevators.'

'Damn it,' I groaned. 'If you pull me back out, can you get Miller to come down to the lobby instead?' In fact, that would probably be even better than me seeing him in his office. This way he'd witness my public humiliation, he'd see how much of a fool I was prepared to make of myself in front of lots of his staff.

'I'm pretty sure I can,' he confirmed, then I heard the crackle of his walkie-talkie. 'Hey, Luciano, it's Thomas down in the lobby. We've got a lady stuck in turnstile four, can you back it up for me? … Yes … No, you aren't seeing things,' he chuckled. 'Yes, it is a pretty brightly colored outfit .... No, she's a VIP, here to see Mr. Davis. Great, thanks. Ok, Miss Carter, steady yourself,' he called.

'Steadying,' I called back. Jesus, I was going to pass out in a minute. This was hotter than lying on the beach in Mexico. I breathed a sigh of relief as I heard a clunk and my right leg dropped to the floor, then I had to make another concerted effort to work my way back out of the narrow channel to return to the lobby.

'Right, I'll let him know you're here,' Thomas advised, putting my basket back over my arm.

'Can you … I know I'm asking a lot, but is there any way you can get him down here without him knowing it's me?'

'If he tries to fire me when he gets down, you'd better put in a good word for me,' Thomas warned.

'I promise, I'll tell him I made you do it,' I nodded.

'Please don't. I'm highly trained to deal with unwanted visitors, admitting that you forced me to do this would make me come off in a much worse light.'

'Thank you,' I stated sincerely as I heard him walk away. I turned to squint and saw him at the reception desk making a call. Then he returned a short while later. 'Ok?'

'He'll be down in a minute, but he didn't sound very happy that we weren't able to sort out the crisis I faked ourselves. Come on, let's move you back a bit, give people space to get in and out through security, ok?'

'Will you tell me when he's here? I'm having a lot of trouble seeing clearly. I'm so hot I'm sweating, and I think my mascara has run in my eyes too,' I huffed. What had I been thinking? All of a sudden I felt nervous and panicky. What if I really did come off as a complete fool, too big a fool for Miller to take me seriously? What if this made him

189

walk away for good? I swallowed hard and tried to compose myself. We weren't together now. After this, we either would be or we'd be over for good. At least one way or the other I'd know and could stop torturing myself.

'He's here,' whispered Thomas, spinning me slightly.

'What's going on, Thomas?' came Miller's annoyed voice. 'I had to interrupt an important call for a … a … what the *hell* am I looking at?' he demanded, confusion saturating his tone.

Hardly surprising, really. I'd imagine that it wasn't every day that a CEO of a company was summoned down to his lobby, only to be faced with a giant yellow Winnie the Pooh bear, complete with a red "Pooh Bear" t-shirt, pudgy hands and feet, rotund stuffed stomach and bottom, and a life-like head with a pot of "Hunny" balanced on top of it. I could barely see anything through the mesh eyeholes and film of disintegrating mascara in my eyes, but I took a deep breath of hot recycled air and prepared myself to sing Elvis's *Teddy Bear*.

I grimaced as I heard how out of key I was, and heard the laughter and chatter rising around me. Then I remembered some dance moves I'd practiced with Georgie, Daphne in tears of laughter as we'd come up with something not too taxing for someone in a costume like this. I got into my groove, tapping my large feet as I swayed, then doing a one-hundred-and-eighty-degree spin and shaking my plump stuffed backside at him. People starting cheering, egging me on as I screeched away, Elvis probably turning over in his grave as I slaughtered his short, sweet love song. I had no idea what Miller's reaction was, if he knew it was me inside this yellow suit, or if he was even still there as I finished and panted.

'I want to be your teddy bear, Miller. Will you be mine?' I called, then wobbled as someone turned me around, presumably Thomas, to make sure I was facing him.

'Abbie? Is that you?' Miller exclaimed, surprise and wonder in his voice. I nodded, then gasped in some fresh air as the head of my Pooh suit was lifted off me and another round of cheers came up from the crowd that was circling us.

'Hey,' I smiled as I saw Miller standing in front of me, his face a picture as he shoved the head into Thomas's arms.

'Hey,' he said warily, holding my gaze, his brown chocolate pools setting my tummy on a washing cycle of emotional spins. I couldn't believe how much I'd missed him. 'What are you doing here?'

'You said you wanted someone to make a fool out of themselves for you, so here I am, doing just that,' I announced, throwing my padded arms out to the side.

'I thought … I'm confused, Abbie. You made your feelings for me pretty clear when you walked away from me at Tracey's wedding, then left the country and ignored my calls,' he added quietly.

'I was shocked, hurt, and upset, so I ran, without my phone. I didn't get any of your messages until I came home. But I've had time to think, to decide what I want, and it's *you*, Miller. I want you. So badly that I'm even prepared to give up everything to move here to be with you.'

'You are?' His eyebrows raised in surprise as he put his hands on his hips, making me lick my lips. He looked so dashing in his three-piece tailored business suit. We must look like such an odd couple right now. The hardcore businessman and a sweaty, make-up-streaked padded bear.

'I am,' I said firmly, slowly dropping down to one knee on the floor and setting my basket to the side of me as people started to whisper in the background. I tried to throw back the red and white checked cloth covering the contents of the basket, but with my fake hands I couldn't, so I looked up to Thomas and gestured with my head to the cloth, which he quickly bent down to whisk away. I heard Miller take in a sharp breath through his teeth as he saw the contents. I'd baked six white chocolate chip cookies, his favourite, in the shape of hearts, then I'd written on them in red icing and carefully laid them in the basket in order. I felt myself tear up as I looked up and read to him out loud the words I'd written on them. *I Love You, Marry Me Miller.*

A collective gasp went up around us, but I didn't look away. I kept my eyes firmly on his, trying to read his expression as he stared down at me, his gorgeous eyes moist with emotion. I just wasn't sure what that emotion was right now. I probably looked a state, with sweaty Pooh helmet hair, running mascara, and a big fat yellow tummy. Was he embarrassed, was he mortified, was he touched, what?

'Miller?' I whispered, my bottom lip starting to wobble as his mouth repeatedly opened, then closed, no words coming out. How stupid was I going to feel if he said no now, and I had to pick up my basket and my Pooh head and shuffle out of here, then get another load of abuse from the next rude cab driver?

'Abbie, I …' He shook his head and ran his hands up over his face and into his hair, leaving it in that ruffled mess I'd always loved so much. 'You're really willing to leave Dilbury, to leave England, *for me*?' he asked, astonished.

'Yes,' I breathed, with no millisecond of hesitation. I wanted him to be sure of my feelings for him. He swallowed a lump in his throat and nodded.

'And you want to *marry* me? You're asking me to marry you?'

'Yes,' I said firmly. He nodded again, and I could see the cogs in that brain of his whirring, then he chewed his lower lip for a moment as he studied me.

'Then no. My answer's no,' he replied with a firm shake of his head.

'What?' I cried, my heart exploding into a thousand pieces as everyone around us gasped, and I heard a few murmurs of sympathy. I choked back some tears, wishing I was in a position to get up and run from here as fast as possible, but Miller dropped to his knees in front of me and clasped my face. 'Don't, please don't touch me,' I whispered, a few tears breaching my defences and rolling down my cheeks. He'd just rejected me. Feeling him touching me, seeing his handsome face so close, smelling his cinnamon-bun aroma, it was all too much right now.

'I'm saying no, not because I don't love you, Abbie, but because I *do* and because I've been an idiot,' he stated earnestly as he held my gaze. 'I've been too scared to take the next step with you, letting my fears come between us. But I'll be damned if I'm going to let you be the man in this relationship. If anyone's going to propose, it's going to be me, and I'm going to do it properly. So no, right here, right now, my answer is no. But you'd better say yes the moment I ask you, ok?'

'You're … you're saying you'll ask me?' I whimpered, more tears cascading down my face. I was on the emotional rollercoaster of my life this year, most of it having happened in the last ten minutes.

'I am,' he confirmed, and a loud cheer almost lifted the roof of the lobby off, then people started applauding as I sniffed and laughed, then whacked him with one of my huge paws.

'You just nearly gave me a heart attack,' I moaned. 'And I'd better be clear, I want to get married soon. I wasn't proposing to have some ridiculously long engagement if you're thinking you can string this out. And I want a baby. Again, soon.'

'A baby Davis?' he queried, his eyes going wide. I swallowed and nodded, wondering if I was pushing him too hard. We'd never really had a proper discussion about children, about how he felt about them, or if he even wanted them.

'Soon, to it all,' he agreed, a soft smile breaking out on his face. 'No stringing, though I am having a hard time taking you seriously right now. Do you have *any* idea how ridiculous you look in that outfit?'

'Well, duh!' I scoffed with a roll of my eyes. 'That was the whole point.'

'Thank you, thank you for making a fool of yourself and proving to me that I wasn't alone in this.'

He dipped his head and lay a passionate kiss on me, still clutching my face, our lips merging in a heated and fiery, and long overdue, reunion. I melted, sagging against him as everyone's clapping intensified and the cheering got louder. I flung my arms around his neck, never wanting to let him go, but we had to break the kiss, both of us laughing, when I realised I'd just nearly knocked him out with my paws. 'God I love you, Abbie Carter,' he murmured. 'But after this little public display, where you've totally emasculated me, I'm never going to be able to pull out the tough and hardened boss card or command the respect of my employees ever again.'

'You could go all caveman and dominant, toss me over your shoulder, spank me, then carry me up to your office,' I suggested. He guffawed with laughter and had to let go of me as he clutched his sides.

'You're the size of a small house! How the hell did you get here? Please tell me you didn't fly over in that?'

'No,' I giggled, 'though I got some funny looks at customs when they opened my case, and they sent a load of drug-sniffer dogs to check it out. I was worried they were going to call me into a private room for a rectal examination. I arrived last night and stayed at The Domville, then created quite a scene in their lobby as I waddled out dressed like this and dived head first into a cab. Thomas was an angel pulling me out when I arrived, you owe him a big thank you.'

'An angel. I've heard you called many things, Thomas, but never an angel,' Miller winked up at him.

'There's a first time for everything, sir,' he nodded, still dutifully holding Winnie's head.

'Can you call my driver for me? I'd like him to escort Miss Carter back to The Domville.'

Thomas nodded and headed over to reception to make the call.

'I'm not staying with you?' I pouted. I'd missed him so much, and now that we were seriously doing this, I wanted nothing more than to fall asleep in his arms tonight.

'Unfortunately I have a few urgent calls to make that I can't put off. Why don't you go and get out of this,' he gesticulated at my sweltering suit, 'and change into something a little sexier. I'll pick you up later to take you out to dinner. Pack to stay with me and we can talk then, ok?' He planted a tender kiss on my forehead, lingering for a moment, and then helped me up. I blushed as I saw everyone watching us, some of the women with soft looks on their faces, others looking distraught that he was taking himself permanently off the market. 'It really means a lot that you did this for me, Abbie,' he repeated as he held my gaze.

I smiled shyly at him, feeling a cocktail of emotions as we just stared at each other. We were doing this, really doing this. I wanted to do my *Teddy Bear* dance again, I was so happy. Mixed up in my joy was a tiny sliver of sadness as it sank in that I'd be leaving Dilbury behind, only returning from time to time. New York was going to be my home now.

'Sorry to interrupt, Sir. Guido has just left the parking garage, he'll be pulling up outside any moment,' Thomas advised as he sidled up beside us.

'Then I'd better walk Miss Carter out,' Miller stated.

'Thank you, Thomas, so much. Would you like a cookie?' I offered as I managed to hook my paw through the basket handle and lift it up.

'I couldn't possibly, they're very special and very personal cookies,' he replied.

'Then I'm going to bake you some special "Thank You" ones, as I couldn't have done this without you.'

'Well, if you insist,' he grinned. 'I'm rather partial to peanut butter ones.'

'Consider it done,' I confirmed.

'Many congratulations on the upcoming engagement.'

'Thank you,' I smiled, managing to get close enough to give him a peck on the cheek, which made him blush. I took Miller's arm and he roared with laughter as I shuffled along, polishing his marble floor with my big padded feet as I swayed, my stuffing-enhanced hips bouncing off his firm ones.

'I've missed this, us,' he admitted.

'Me too. And I have so many questions for you, including all about Quinn. You have a twin sister!'

'I do,' he nodded with a proud smile on his face. 'I think you're going to get along really well, she's a really sweet girl, despite the crazy haircut and piercings. I'm so sorry about the wedding. I was going to come and talk to you at some point, but I saw how jealous you looked to see me with Quinn and I saw the chance to get back at you, which was very immature of me. I just wanted to make you feel like I did when I found Heath at your house. I didn't expect the whole cat fight, cake wrecking, fleeing from the country scenario to go down.'

'Apology accepted, but in the future, let's talk to each other, no more running,' I suggested, as we stepped out of the air-conditioned building and the heat of the New York summer slammed into me, taking my breath away. I was going to need some serious hydrating as soon as I got back to the hotel, and it was going to take some adjusting to a new climate.

If Guido the driver was bemused by the appearance of his boss with a headless Winnie the Pooh and Thomas carrying the oversized stuffed head behind us, he didn't show it. He just tipped his cap and opened the back door of the black town car. I assured them all that after getting

194

in on my front, then struggling to roll over and sit up to get out, I was best going in bottom first to lie on my back. After a few minutes of me trying to force my backside in the car, and them pushing me from the front, it was clear it wasn't working.

'Why are we messing around? Let's just unzip the suit,' Miller suggested, reaching behind me to tug on it.

'No,' I cried, batting him with my paws. 'I'm only wearing underwear. I can't walk into The Domville in my bra and knickers with Winnie the Pooh's head under my arm and a basket of cookies in the other.'

'Only bra and panties? Really?' he purred with a twinkle in his eye. 'Are they sexy ones?' he whispered in my ear.

'No, but they will be by the time I see you later,' I whispered back.

'Excellent,' he grinned, his tone making me giggle and my cheeks flush.

'Ok, new plan. I'll go in sideways, head first, but you'll have to lift me up and feed me in,' I suggested as I looked at all three of them, and they reluctantly nodded. My basket and the head were put on the pavement and I squealed with laughter as they lifted me up and managed to slide me horizontally into the back of the car. Guido set the head on the passenger seat and went to get into the driver's side as Thomas waved goodbye to me.

'Here's your cookies.' Miller wedged the basket between my stomach and the centre console. 'I stole one,' he added with a grin as he took a bite of one in his hand. I peered into the basket to see that he'd nabbed the "Miller" one.

'Why not the "Love" cookie?'

'Because now, other than about fifty of my employees witnessing it first hand, there's no record of my girlfriend proposing to me. It just says, "I love you, marry me."' He grinned as he bit off another section of it.

'Was that *your* proposal, as it wasn't exactly heartfelt!'

'No,' he laughed. 'You'll know when I do.'

'And by choosing the "Miller" cookie, you're eating yourself,' I added.

'Don't worry, I'll let you eat me later,' he winked, a devilishly playful look on his face that made my stomach warm. 'See you in a while, baby.'

'See you in a while.'

He shut the door and waited for us to pull away, and I grinned and clapped my paws together. I was his girlfriend and his baby again. And I loved it!

I twirled in the mirror, checking out my appearance. After having a huge yellow tummy and hips for most of the day, I was pretty happy looking at my figure right now. To show off my lovely Mexican tan, I'd put on a white, thin-strap maxi dress that skimmed my feet, with the pair of bright multi-coloured heels that I'd been wearing at Rachel's wedding, the first time we'd met. A bright turquoise clutch bag and some silver jewellery completed my summery, and not overtly sexy, look. I was still Abbie Carter, country girl at heart. I'd pinned my hair back on one side and swept it over my other shoulder, then made an effort with my eye make-up.

I wasn't sure why I was nervous, but it kind of felt like a first date, like we were starting over. I guessed we were in a way. We'd both acknowledged our flaws and were prepared to try this regardless. I quickly pulled my mobile out of my clutch when it started ringing Elvis's *Teddy Bear*, my new ringtone for Miller, and I felt those butterflies in my tummy starting to stir.

I answered, feeling giddy with excitement, and he told me a hotel porter was on his way up to collect my bags, and Guido, who was already waiting outside, would be taking me straight to him. I hoped I was dressed up enough. Last time I'd stayed, he'd taken me to some quite fancy restaurants, the kind you had to book months in advance, but he'd been able to snag a table at short notice. There were bonuses to having money and a recognisable name. He'd found it highly amusing, though, when I'd admitted to him that gorgeous as the gourmet food had been, I much preferred the slices of pizza and New York cheesecake we'd had from a walk-in place in Little Italy.

Guido was waiting with the AMD luxury limo and helped me into the back with a smile as the hotel porters loaded my two cases into the boot. Then I sat back and gazed out of the privacy windows, drinking in the vistas of my soon-to-be new home. I wasn't sure I'd ever get used to living in a city, but being with Miller was more important.

I was surprised when instead of pulling up at his building on the Upper East Side, Guido parked at the head of Central Park. As I stepped out of the car, my breath was stolen from me. Miller was waiting, never looking more handsome, in a bespoke custom-fit tuxedo, standing by a horse and carriage. The two horses and fairy-tale, Cinderella-style carriage were white, and everything had been adorned with red roses.

'I thought it would be a nice night to have a ride around the park, to end a memorable day in a memorable way,' he confirmed, as I stared up at him in awe. He kissed me, then helped me up into the carriage and jumped in himself, draping his arm around my shoulder as our driver and an assistant called the horses to walk on.

'This is amazing,' I cooed as I snuggled against him, my eyes wide with excitement as we trotted through the park, a number of other carriages following us. The sun was just setting as we pulled up at the Bethesda Terrace, with a magical fountain set below it.

'Come on, let's go for a walk,' Miller suggested as he hopped out and held out his hand to assist me.

'What's going on? Is tonight a special horse and carriage night for gay couples and we've gate crashed?' I asked, as I noticed sets of men alighting from each of the four carriages that had followed us.

'No,' Miller laughed. 'It can be kind of dangerous in the park at night. They're some of my security team, to make sure we're safe and to give us some privacy.'

'Privacy for what? I've got to tell you that after an over-amorous dolphin called Mahi tried to mate with me in broad daylight in Mexico, I'm over the whole public-sex thing.'

'We have a lot of catching up to do,' he said with an incredulous look, then wove his fingers through mine as he led me down the steps at the side of the terrace and across to the imposing fountain. I gasped as the warm white lights that had lit up the fountain and terrace changed to hues of red, pink, and purple.

'It's so beautiful, Miller,' I exclaimed, gazing up at it in wonder.

'I thought you'd like it,' he confirmed, letting go of my hand as I stepped a little closer. 'And I figured as our relationship started with water, it would be as good a place as any to take it to the next level.'

'You want to climb in the fountain?' I giggled, as I leaned over the side of it and dipped my hand into the cold water. 'Miller?' I looked around, wondering why he wasn't answering me, and inhaled sharply, my hands flying to my mouth to see him on one knee, holding out an exclusive Havershams' leather ring box.

'I promised soon, Abbie, and I like to keep my word. These last few months without you have been the most miserable of my life. I've missed your crazy sense of humor, your laugh, your smile, your cuddles, and your kisses, especially your kisses,' he grinned with a twinkle in his eye. 'Marry me, Abbie Carter. Marry me and start a family with me, so we can give our children a life filled with all of the love that we missed from some of ours. Marry me and–'

I cut him off in his prime by throwing myself at him, thudding against his chest as I dropped to my knees and threw my arms around his neck.

'Yes, yes, yes, yes, yes, YES!' I cried. He laughed and wrapped his arms around me tightly as he kissed my neck.

'I wasn't done, I had a whole heartfelt speech prepared.'

'It doesn't matter, you had me at the first "Marry me," Miller.'

197

Chapter Sixteen
June

♂ HE PUT A RING ON IT ♀

'WE'RE DOING THIS? WE'RE really doing this?' I asked, yet more tears appearing for the umpteenth time today as we hugged each other, the soothing noise of the fountain behind us gurgling away.

'We're doing this,' he confirmed, gently prising me away from his body, then sliding one of his hands across my cheek to palm it as we exchanged an emotionally charged look. He leaned forwards and kissed me softly. It wasn't a kiss of passion, the kind of kiss that ignited my body, but a loving kiss, the kind that ignited my heart and reminded me how in love I was with this man. 'You realise you said yes without even seeing the ring?' he whispered as our lips parted, but our foreheads remained touching.

'I'm not marrying the ring, I'm marrying you,' I reminded him.

'Which is why I should have asked you sooner, Abbie. You have no idea what it means to me that you're not bothered that I'm August Miller Davis, that you'd marry plain old Miller Davis, the kid that came out of the foster system without a penny to his name.'

'You should be so proud of yourself, Miller, for what you've achieved. I know I am. How did you sort ... I only left you a few hours ago, how did you organise all of this and a ring so fast?'

'The flowers, the carriage ride, and the colored fountain were easy, money talks,' he chuckled. 'But the ring, well, that was harder. I spent weeks searching for the perfect one, the one that you wouldn't feel embarrassed or uncomfortable wearing because it was too ostentatious for you. But I also wanted one that told everyone how much you meant to me, that warned other guys to take a hike, that you were already taken. But most of all, I wanted it to mean something to us both. I wanted it to remind us of the first moment we met, that split-second that took both of our breaths' away because we knew we'd just looked at our soul mate.'

'Weeks? But ... I only proposed today, I don't understand,' I replied, my eyes flitting across his face in confusion.

'I came to England with Quinn with the intention of proposing to you, Abbie, wanting to have my only family, my new sister, with me when I did. But I royally screwed up my chances of that when I was tempted to make you jealous first, to make you realize how much you wanted me, and you ran away instead. I already had the ring, I just needed the girl.'

'You've got her,' I nodded vehemently, overwhelmed to know that even though I thought I'd chased him, he'd been chasing me first without me knowing it. I knew how hard that must have been for him. I swallowed a lump of emotion as he slowly opened up the leather box, and I inhaled sharply, stunned. Traditional it wasn't, massive it wasn't, but it was the most beautiful ring I'd ever seen, and the second I saw it, I understood the significance, which made it even more special. It was a slim platinum band with a modern design that had a square white diamond at its centre, then brightly coloured square and rectangular diamonds of varying sizes surrounding it. I saw purple, pink, yellow, orange, green, turquoise, and fuchsia. 'My dress, it's my technicolour bridesmaid dress,' I exclaimed in wonder.

'I got it to remind me of the first moment I saw you, but if you hate it as much as you did that dress, I can get you another. I can get you anything you want, Abbie,' he stated earnestly.

'No, the dress I hated, the ring though … *My God*, the ring … I *love* it, almost as much as I love you,' I uttered, tears of happiness streaming down my face as he slid it onto my ring finger, then clasped my face and kissed me, full of passion this time. We finally broke for air and he wiped the tears off my cheeks, then kissed the tip of my nose.

'When's your flight home?' he asked as he helped me to my feet.

'Sunday lunch time,' I stated apologetically. 'In case you said no, I didn't want to be here any longer than I needed to be.'

'I'm sorry I made you doubt what you mean to me, Abbie, I never meant to hurt you.'

'Nor me you,' I said sincerely, accepting his hand. Our fingers laced together tightly as we walked back towards the steps, his entourage following at a discreet distance. We stayed silent on the journey out of the park, just soaking up the atmosphere, smiling at each other, letting everything sink in. I kept looking down at my ring in amazement. I was engaged. I was really engaged. Maybe the curse of "never the bride" was really going to be broken. I couldn't wait to ring Georgie, Daphne, and Charlie to tell them the news.

I couldn't stop laughing when I discovered that our exclusive restaurant booking was none other than the pizza and cheesecake shop in Little Italy. He'd reserved a window countertop seat, and we sat on high stools feeding each other gooey slices as people stared at him, overdressed in his tuxedo, and we toasted our engagement with a cheap bottle of their best sparkling wine. Despite all of his money, Miller was realising it was the simple things that made him happiest. And he'd made me so happy by coming here and not going crazy with an expensive celebration.

'Seriously, how much more cheesecake are you going to eat?' he groaned, as I started forking his leftovers. 'I haven't seen you in forever, I want to get you home so I can check out the sexy underwear you promised me.'

'We have all the time in the world now for you to check me out in sexy underwear,' I reminded him. I really needed to go on a shopping spree while I was in one of the shopping capitals of the world. Shrewsbury was great and all, but New York was going to take some beating when it came to kitting myself out to make sure I kept my man satisfied. 'Oh, Miller, I'm so happy,' I exclaimed as I looked down at my ring again.

'Me too, baby. So, it looks like instead of attending weddings, we have one of our own to plan.'

'So it seems. Are you the rare species of male who wants to be involved in the planning?'

'Afraid so. I already know where, and I won't take no for an answer because it's important to me. But I'll leave the when and the reception to you.'

'Oh, ok,' I replied, somewhat subdued. I already knew where I wanted to have it, but it wasn't like I could have everything my way. We were a couple, it was a joint decision.

'I want us to get married at home.'

'A service in your penthouse?' I asked, slightly confused, as I swallowed the last delicious crumb of his cheesecake and dabbed my lips with the napkin.

'No,' he replied, shaking his head. 'Home is Dilbury, where your heart and your friends are. And wherever you are, Abbie, from now on I'll follow.'

'I'm not sure I understand what you're trying to say.' My heart was beating fast at the implication. I loved him, I'd accepted that I needed to be in New York to be with him, but deep down I'd always miss Dilbury, I'd always have an element of sadness that we couldn't make it work there as our permanent home.

'A man's job is to make his woman happy, Abbie. And the fact that you were prepared to leave behind all of those memories, and your friends, to be here with me means more than you'll ever know. But I've had time to think too while we were separated, and I planned to tell you this when I came to England last time, before you crumpled my heart and left. New York isn't my home, it's just a convenient base. I've never really had somewhere I could call home. I moved from town to town, family to family, until I talked my way into a job as a sales assistant at a gaming shop and worked my way up to manager, where I was able to earn the money I needed to set up my own firm from my apartment. I settled in New York when my company went global because it fit my needs at the time, and I felt bound to it as I searched for my family. But the truth is, the times I've felt most at home have been the times in Holly Cottage, with you, in Dilbury.'

'You're saying … you're saying you want to move to England, to live with me in Dilbury?' I whispered, hardly daring to hope that was where he was going with this.

'I am,' he confirmed as I stared at him, totally elated. 'I'd obviously need office space there, and I'd still need to come to New York on a regular basis for meetings, but I can oversee things from pretty much anywhere in the world. It's time I took a step back and let my directors do the job I pay them so well for, running my company, while I focus on the designing and testing, which is what I really love.'

'So what you really want is an excuse for a cushy gaming room so you can sit and play all day,' I laughed, wondering if anything could possibly make this day better.

'Pretty much,' he chuckled in response. 'But your cottage isn't big enough if we want children, which I think we've already agreed we do. How would you feel about us extending it, adding on a few more bedrooms and some space for me to work?'

'To make it into our home, while still having memories of my childhood, my dad, and Sumo? I'd feel amazing about it,' I confirmed excitedly.

'Then forget your flight on Sunday. Stay with me for a while, give me a few days to arrange for some time away in England, and we'll head back together next Friday and start making plans for the house and the wedding, ok?'

'Ok,' I confirmed, as I leaned forward to plant an ecstatic kiss on his face and promptly slipped off my stool and landed on the floor with a thud and a cackle of laughter.

Miller made some calls as we headed back through the city to his, and I checked the time before FaceTiming Georgie first, propping my iPhone up on my knees. I had to force myself to stop bouncing them, I was so excited to share my news with her. She answered in an instant, her sparkling azure eyes wide with anticipation as she spoke in an excited rush.

'Oh my God, I've been on tenterhooks all morning, Daphne too. She's here waiting for the news with me. Let me angle the screen so you can see us both,' she suggested, everything moving in and out of focus until I finally saw them both sitting next to each other at her kitchen table.

'Oh, Abbie, *please* tell us it's good news?' Daphne's nervous voice asked.

'He put a ring on it!' I squealed, holding up my hand to the camera for them to see. I laughed as their screams of excitement filled the limo, and Miller shook his head, an amused smile on his lips as he tried to carry on with his business call. I filled them in on the day's happenings and suggested they remain sitting down before I told them that we were coming home, that I wasn't leaving Dilbury and it would be our main base. 'Georgie,' I moaned, tearing up again as she started sobbing.

'I'm sorry. I know I said I was fine with you moving away, but I lied through my teeth. I was just trying to be the supportive best friend. I never wanted you to go, and I was so upset that you were going to leave us, and now I'm just so happy that you're not,' she sniffed, disappearing off screen for a second and returning with a box of tissues. She pulled one out to wipe her eyes and honk her nose.

'When and where will you get married, Abbie?' Daphne asked.

'Miller said he wants to get married in Dilbury church, which has made me so happy, but we haven't discussed the rest, other than we both want it to be soon. But I need to ask you both something important first. I don't have my dad to give me away, and I can only think of one person who could ever stand in his place, who would make it truly special for me, and that's you, Daphne. You've been like a mother to me ever since I was little. I'd really love it if you'd walk me up the aisle and give me away?' I waited with bated breath as her eyes filled with tears and she snatched the box of tissues that Georgie was hogging out of her hands.

'Oh, Abbie. You know I think of you and Georgie as the daughters I never had. I'd be honoured to,' she nodded, blowing her nose as Georgie did hers again. 'But I'm so slow on my feet. We're going to have to have a serious think about your entrance music, or they'll be playing *Here Comes The Bride* about fifty times on repeat by the time I escort you from the door to the altar,' she sniffed, wiping away her tears.

'How about we get you one of those fancy zippy scooters you mentioned then, and you can drive me up the aisle?' I suggested, making them both laugh.

'I think Reverend Potter will have something to say about that!' she scoffed.

'We'll work it out, Daphne. I don't care how slowly we make our way to Miller, as long as I reach him. And Georgie, my dear, *dear,* friend, Georgie. You know that there's no one else I could ever consider for the position of chief bridesmaid, don't you?'

'Well, I should think not!' she retorted sternly, before breaking into a wide smile and eagerly nodding her acceptance.

'I'll ask Charlie to be a bridesmaid too, and maybe Quinn, Miller's sister. I'm going to spend the day with her tomorrow, getting to know her. I really just want a nice, quiet, simple wedding with friends from the village and Miller's friends.'

'It sounds wonderful, Abbie, but aren't you forgetting something?' Georgie added, pulling a face at me.

'What?' I asked, giving her a puzzled look. It wasn't like it was going to be a huge wedding. Neither of us really had any family to speak of and our circle of close friends was pretty small.

'The pact,' she reminded me with a tut. 'The thirteen bridesmaids from school, including that horror, Fi-Fi?'

'Oh no,' I groaned, my shoulders slumping in defeat. I didn't want a ridiculous big wedding, I didn't want sixteen bridesmaids, and I certainly didn't want that vicious tramp turning up and ruining my big day, the way she'd ruined the last two weddings. How the hell was I going to get out of this?

'What's wrong, baby?' Miller asked, tucking his phone away as he put his arm around me. After congratulations and hellos had been exchanged between him and the girls, I filled him in on my dilemma. 'I don't know what the problem is,' he shrugged. 'It's your day, you do what you want. Invite who you want, leave out the people you don't want, and if they don't like it or take offence, tough.'

'My thoughts exactly, Miller,' nodded Daphne, and I looked at Georgie in despair.

'Guys, you just don't get it,' she added, backing me up. 'All of these women have spent a lot of money on Abbie's dresses, no matter how hideous some of them were. It's a real slap in the face to not return the favour and leave them out of pocket.'

'Then it's simple. We're honest about only wanting a small affair,' Miller stated, 'and I'll pay for you all to have a luxury bachelorette party weekend somewhere abroad, and buy them all a designer dress for a night out. How does that sound?'

'Expensive,' I retorted, still worried about how they'd react.

'Not to me it's not. I'm sorry to be harsh, Abbie, but most of these girls aren't your real friends, Fi especially. I don't mind you inviting the ones you do like to the wedding as normal guests, but getting married is about us exchanging our vows in front of the people who are important to us, not some show-off, one-up-manship spectacle to outdo each other. Deal?'

'Well said,' called Daphne.

'Got to admit he has a point, Abbie. If they're going to take offence after an offer like that, it's no great loss if they cut you out of their lives, is it?' Georgie added.

'I guess not,' I conceded. 'Ok, we have a deal.'

'So, when are we doing this?' Daphne asked.

'Baby, you wanted soon. You tell me where and when and I'll make it happen,' Miller confirmed, kissing my temple. I bit my lower lip as I gazed up at him.

'Well, we're already agreed on Dilbury church, but Dad always dreamed of me having an evening reception at Severn Manor at Christmas time. I'd love to do it, for him as well as for us,' I advised, my heart fluttering at the thought that after years of imagining, it might finally come true.

'The place I walked you home from in the snow, right? The night we had our first kiss?'

'Yes,' I nodded, touched that he remembered that important moment in our relationship.

'Then consider it done,' he nodded, kissing me again.

'You can't plan a wedding at Severn Manor just like that,' Georgie scoffed. 'It's one of the premier wedding venues in the UK. They're booked *years* in advance.'

'Then it's a good thing Abbie's marrying a man of means who can be very persuasive when he wants,' Miller grinned as he looked down at me. 'Money talks, and I don't care how much it costs, I'm giving my girl the wedding of her dreams *this* Christmas.'

'Miller,' I whispered, my eyes filling with tears.

'I want me a Miller,' Georgie sighed, sniffing loudly before blowing her nose as she started crying again.

'Well, if you'd just ring Veston back, maybe you would,' scolded Daphne as she dabbed her watery eyes.

'Weston,' Georgie and I chorused.

'Who's Weston?' Miller asked.

'We have a lot to catch up on,' I reminded him.

'We do,' he agreed. 'And lovely as it is to see you, ladies, I'd like to spend some time with my gorgeous fiancée, so if you'll excuse us, we can discuss plans when we come home this weekend.'

'Fiancée,' I repeated, giving him a dreamy look. I loved the sound of that word rolling off his tongue. He smiled and clutched my chin, then started to kiss me, softly at first, then with more urgency. My hands found their way up into his soft hair, tugging at it as my body ignited into a primal need to reconnect with him, and I let out a low moan of pleasure as he groaned.

'Ermmm, hello, still here, creepily watching and gagging,' called Georgie with a giggle.

'Good night, you two, see you soon,' murmured Miller as he reached over to terminate the call, then pulled me back into his arms.

Chapter Seventeen

The Dress
December

I WAS HAVING A flashback to the nightmare of Rachel's final dress-fitting day as I headed from the same changing room in *Bridezilla* down to the private viewing room, where Daphne, Georgie, Charlie, and Quinn were waiting patiently to see me in my dress. My stomach felt like a stormy sea, churning and wild. I was getting married next Saturday, and I was having serious regrets. Not about Miller, about this damn dress!

I'd tried on so many over the last few months, despairing of ever finding one that I loved, so I'd settled. And right now I felt like crying. Like most little girls, I'd dreamed of finding a handsome prince and wearing the perfect dress on the day I exchanged my vows with him. Well, I'd struck gold with Miller, but the dress … *my God*, the dress. What had I been thinking?

I stopped just short of the double doors to the room and looked down at myself. Maybe I was just getting overly anxious. After all, it was the biggest day of my life. It was an expensive designer creation, it couldn't be that bad, could it? I covered my face with my hands and tried to take some deep breaths. Georgie and Daphne had come on the first two dress shopping events, when I'd come away empty handed. Only Georgie had seen this one so far, as Daphne had had another viewing on her cottage and couldn't make it.

Georgie hadn't been overly enthused when I'd showed it to her a few weeks ago, but her head had been all over the place at the time dealing with something else, so I'd just taken her lack of enthusiasm with a pinch of salt. But now I was wondering if I should have paid heed to her muted response. There was no way I'd get another dress altered in time, and with my curves, it wasn't like an off-the-rack one would fit perfectly. I took a deep breath, gathered up the skirt, and walked into the room. All four women looked up at once.

Quinn choked mid-sip of her champagne, spraying a fine mist of it in front of her as she coughed and shook her head.

Daphne's hand flew to her chest as her jaw dropped, and she looked over the top of her glasses with an 'Oh my.'

Charlie dropped the canapé she was eating, her empty fingers remaining frozen by her parted lips.

And Georgie, well Georgie threw herself back on the horseshoe-shaped sofa as she roared with laughter and clutched her stomach.

'So, it's a big thumbs up for the dress, huh?' I stated sarcastically, as Maggie, the shop owner, helped me up onto the podium.

'Abbie, please tell me this is some sort of a joke?' Daphne exclaimed.

'It's even funnier that it's not,' Georgie howled, reaching up to wipe some tears from her cheeks.

'And I thought I was the one with the racy mind. Wow, Abbie, I … I … I … You know what, I actually have no words,' Charlie added, throwing her hands in the air.

'Wow, you Brits have a totally different style when it comes to wedding dresses,' observed Quinn in her strong American accent, looking from me to my friends, then back to me again. 'You look like you're going to that fancy dress thing you have, what do you call it? With the preacher in his collar?'

'Vicars and tarts,' I sighed, looking down at my overly enhanced cleavage and the plunging neckline. 'I'm going to be getting married looking like a tart.'

'Abbie, really, what were you thinking?' Daphne added with a shake of her head. 'That's not a tart's wedding dress, we need to upgrade it to a slapper's. I think I can see nipple through the sheer fabric!'

Charlie looked at Daphne wide-eyed as Georgie started snorting and hyperventilating in the corner, and I sank like a high-rise block of flats that had just been demolished, crumpling down into a heap on the podium.

'What's a slapper?' asked Quinn, looking bemused.

'Someone who wears a dress like that on a night out, let alone at a wedding. My God, Reverend Potter will have a heart attack, never mind the rest of the male guests,' Daphne stated, fanning herself with her hand as she shook her head. 'Abbie, please tell me this is a joke, that you have the real dress in the changing room.'

'This is a highly expensive piece of couture,' Maggie stated, with more than a touch of offence in her tone as I put my head in my hands.

'Cowture more like, as it looks like a heap of crap,' Georgie howled. 'Oh, Abbie, did it seriously look *this* bad when I saw it last time?'

'You approved this?' Daphne gasped. 'Georgie Basset, what were you thinking? She'd have looked classier going up the aisle in a see-through bikini!'

'Is it really that awful?' I moaned, lifting my head. With only a week to go, I needed reassurance right now, not all of this negativity.

'I may not know what a slapper is, but I'm pretty sure that if the guests can see you need a wax on your hoo-hah, it's not a good thing,' Quinn shrugged.

'I'm leaving it until the last minute, in time for the honeymoon,' I protested.

'What beautician do you go to?' giggled Charlie. 'It doesn't have to be long enough to plait between waxes.'

'Stop, stop,' gasped Georgie. 'My sides are hurting, I can't take any more!'

'*You* can't?!' I cried, feeling on the verge of tears of utter despair. 'I'm getting married in a week and this *is* the dress! There are no alternatives, I've tried on everything in the shop and hated them all, and this has been altered to fit me already.'

'Abbie Carter, that has *not* been altered to fit,' Daphne stated as she rested her linked hands on her tummy and gave me a prudish look. 'If it had been, your breasts wouldn't be heaving out of the top like two giant watermelons, and the only man who should be able to see the bride's knickers on the day is the groom.'

I looked down at it again and groaned. Seriously, what had I been thinking? It was a thin-strapped affair, with a see-through lace bodice that had a sweetheart neckline which plunged at the front down to my belly button. At the hips were rows and rows of shiny white satin ruffles that cascaded into a long train at the back, but it scooped up at the front, showing the top of my thighs, and apparently my vagina, while showcasing my legs. They were right. It was hideous, crass, and … slutty!

'I wanted to look sexy for Miller, to make sure he remembered how I looked on our special day,' I moaned, my shoulders slumping in defeat at my epic fail.

'I think everyone's going to remember how you looked,' Charlie chortled. 'Intimately. They'll need to have paramedics on standby.'

'Miller loves you for being you, Abbie. I haven't known you as long as these other ladies, but this isn't you, and honestly, I think he'd be horrified if you turned up on Saturday in this.'

'I'm horrified. Even that hussy barmaid Rowena would have more class than to wear this monstrosity on her wedding day,' Daphne added.

'So what do I do?' I begged. 'I'm all out of options. Georgie, for God's sake, stop laughing! You saw it, you saw it and you said it was unique and unforgettable.'

'Well, it is,' she agreed, sitting up and grabbing a tissue from the box, which were meant for everyone to wipe away tears of pride and happiness, not hysterical laughter. 'Just not in a good way.'

'And you let me buy it? As best friend and chief bridesmaid, it was your duty to be honest with me, to stop me from making a fool of myself. Some best friend you are!' I grated, my stress levels rising.

'She has a valid point, Georgie,' agreed Charlie. 'If you were my best friend, I'd sack you from the position.'

'Very valid,' added Daphne, flashing her a glare. 'And I'd never speak to you again.'

'Poor Abbie, what are we going to do? She can't wear this and the wedding's on Saturday,' Quinn reminded us all.

'Ok, ok, enough with the Georgie bashing,' she replied, wiping her eyes and sitting up straight. 'I was distracted on the day we saw it, then woke up in a cold sweat the week after, realising it was awful and that it wasn't the right one for Abbie, so I rang Maggie. But she told me it was too late, that the alterations to fit Abbie had already been started.'

'Still not winning any "best friend of the year" trophies, Georgie,' Daphne scolded.

'Well, I should,' Georgie said firmly, 'as I didn't just accept that. I'm sorry, ok, I thought it would be a good giggle to let you all see this dress, as there was nothing we could do about it anyway. I didn't mean to upset you, Abbie, I thought you'd see the funny side.'

'Not funny, Georgie, I'm close to tears! And what do you mean, "this dress?" There is no other dress. I'm totally screwed.'

'I think the title of "bestest and most awesome friend" will be bestowed back on me in about five minutes,' she said with a gentle smile at me. 'Maggie, is it ready?'

'It is,' Maggie nodded.

'Well, don't just stand there, go and get it to show Abbie!'

'What's going on?' I demanded, forcing myself to stand up as Maggie trotted out of the room.

'Wait a minute and you'll find out,' Georgie told me. 'But if I know you at all, and I think I do, no matter what these naysayers may say after I made *one* mistake on an off day,' she added with a scathing look at the other three, 'I think you're going to love what I've had done. At least I hope so. I hope you're not going to be mad with me for not getting your approval first.'

'Approval for what, Georgie?' Daphne demanded, taking the words right out of my mouth. 'Stop talking in riddles and put us, and poor Abbie, out of our misery.'

'Look,' Georgie smiled, flicking her head behind me to the door. There was a gasp as everyone did as they were told. Charlie and Quinn both raised their hands to their mouths, and Daphne snatched a tissue out of the box as her eyes filled with tears.

I slowly turned around, my heart stopping for a second, as I saw Maggie standing there with the most stunning white vintage lace wedding gown I'd ever seen. It had a Bardot neckline, off the shoulder, with three-quarter sleeves. The bodice and skirt had a soft white satin lining, so unlike this current dress, no hint of nipple or vagina was going to be seen. It nipped in at the waist, where there was a thin white satin belt adorned with a gorgeous crystal embellishment, then the lace skirt fell to the floor at the front and flowed out into a small train at the back. I swallowed a lump of emotion in my throat. It was perfect. If I could have sketched my perfect dress, I was looking at it right now. Something about it seemed so familiar, but I just couldn't put my finger on what it was as I stared at it.

'Do you like it, Abbie? I had it altered to fit you, based on your measurements for your current dress. I wanted it to be a surprise,' Georgie said behind me.

'I … I … I *love* it, it's stunning,' I whimpered, realising that I had tears of sheer relief and happiness rolling down my cheeks. 'Why does it seem so familiar? There's no way I would have overlooked this when I tried on all the dresses in the shop.'

'You don't recognise it?' Georgie asked in a surprised tone.

'I … feel like I know it, but I just can't place it,' I replied as I turned to face her. She grabbed a tissue from the box Daphne was hogging and walked over to me.

'The picture in your lounge, on your bookcase. The one next to the picture of where you and Miller first met, when you fell into his arms at The Abbey,' she said with a smile as she dabbed away my tears with a tissue. I gasped, my hands flying to cover my heart as I twigged immediately.

'It's my mum's wedding dress,' I whispered, a slew of positive emotions warming me up from the inside out and making a fresh batch of tears start to flow.

'I remembered seeing it up in your attic months ago when I helped put away hideous bridesmaid dress nine after Miller returned it to you, so I snuck in while you were busy with clients the other week, got it down, had it dry cleaned, and asked Maggie if she could do a quick turnaround on adjusting it. I hope you're not mad with me?'

'I'm mad you put me through this torture this morning,' I told her in a mock scold. I flung my arms around her neck, hugging her tightly to let her know she was forgiven. 'Of course I'm not mad. I'm over the moon. It's the perfect idea, I can't believe I didn't think of it myself. My mum and dad may not be here, but it's like I'll have a little bit of them with me on my special day.' I sobbed as Georgie started crying too and hugged me back.

'Careful, you're going to get mascara on this dress,' she warned.

'So? I already paid for it, or rather Miller did.'

'Please tell me we can have a burning party for it,' Daphne called. 'I've never seen anything so hideous in my life.'

'No,' I said firmly, straightening up and wiping my cheeks. 'As it happens, I know just the person to send it to.'

'No, you wouldn't,' gasped Georgie. Fi-Fi had turned down the offer to come on my hen weekend in Malta, so she'd missed out on Miller's offer to get her a designer dress as compensation for not being a bridesmaid at our wedding. Turns out Dave had come home and caught her cheating on him, so he'd thrown her out and cut off her monthly financial allowance. Last I heard, she was hanging out in all the hot spots in Cheshire, trying to snag herself a Premier League footballer.

'Please, a slutty dress for a slut, it's perfect for her,' I beamed. 'This way she gets an expensive dress and I don't have to hear her moan how she got me one and I didn't return the favour.'

'I have no idea who you're talking about,' called Quinn, 'but can we please see you in the new dress, Abbie?'

'Yes, please go and change,' agreed Daphne.

'Quickly,' Charlie giggled, holding up her champagne glass for a refill as Maggie's assistant brought in another bottle.

'Go,' Georgie nodded, taking both of my hands in hers. 'I can't wait to see what it looks like on you. Am I forgiven?'

'I'll tell you in five minutes,' I teased, kissing her on the cheek.

After I'd put on the dress I stood outside the door again, but this time there was no need for a deep breath. This was the one. The fact that it had been Mum's made it even more special. I hadn't realised that Mum's figure had been just like mine. Somehow the dress minimised my bust and hips, but left me with a sexy hourglass shape without being exaggerated to the point of looking like a cartoon character. I just knew Miller was going to love it. I walked in, my smile virtually lighting up the room as I lifted the skirt and climbed up onto the podium. This time I was met with the sound of gasps, then the sound of multiple tissues being ripped from the box, as all four of them starting nodding and crying in unison.

'Gorgeous,' sighed Charlie.

'Stunning,' whispered Quinn.

'Beautiful, so beautiful,' sniffed Daphne.

'Perfect,' smiled Georgie. 'Oh, Abbie. Your mum and dad would have been so proud to see you looking so amazing. Are you happy with it?'

'It's the one, Georgie,' I confirmed, my voice breaking with emotion as I started crying again and Maggie clapped with tears in her eyes too. This time I wasn't settling. This was *the dress*.

'Ok, I'm coming down,' I called as I stood at the top of the stairs, my hair and make-up having just been finished. I had my royal purple suede peep-toe shoes firmly in place, matching the luscious deep colour of my bridesmaids' dresses. I was getting married three days before Christmas, so I'd wanted a rich and festive feel to my theme. My only disappointment was waking up this morning to find that the snow I so desperately wanted hadn't arrived.

Instead it had been a cold, crisp day. It was already dark outside as we were having a late afternoon wedding at the church, followed by an evening reception up at Severn Manor. I dreaded to think what it had cost Miller to book them at such short notice, and at a time when they normally refused to do weddings, as they were focused on catering for people who liked to eat out at Christmas.

I was met with a chorus of gasps and exclamations as I came down to find my four friends waiting for me at the bottom of the stairs. The three girls were all in purple satin dresses, with white belts to match my dress, and matching small round posies of white calla lilies and white and deep purple roses. How Sarah at *Rosie Posie* had managed to find ones that perfectly matched their dresses, I'd no idea. She was amazing, and I'd been thrilled when I'd gone to check the floral arrangements in the church last night. Quinn had even had her hair tips redone for the occasion, from multi-coloured to just purple, and Daphne was wearing an off-white dress with a purple jacket, with a purple and white buttonhole pinned to it. We'd finally convinced her to use a walking stick, as she was getting too wobbly on her feet to manage without, but she was doing amazingly well for her age.

She was moving into her new apartment soon, and I'd been over the moon last night when Quinn shared her news with us. Miller had purchased Daphne's cottage for her, and she was moving to England, too. She had no family in the US, other than Miller, and as he was going to be living here most of the time, she wanted to be close to him. Plus, she'd fit in so well with Georgie, Charlie, and me, we had a really tightly knit circle now. We all stood together holding hands, smiling at each other with tears in our eyes as our photographer James continued to take the relaxed, casual shots I'd asked for.

'I'm getting married!' I whispered.

'The curse is well and truly lifted,' Georgie nodded, with a proud and happy smile on her face. 'You look just ... wow, Abbie.'

'I've never seen you looking more radiant or beautiful, Abbie Carter,' Daphne agreed.

'Stunning,' added Charlie.

'I really don't want to imagine how my brother's going to react when he sees you, as it will scar me for life, but I've got a feeling he's going to be dragging you up to the hotel suite the second you arrive,' Quinn laughed, making me blush. 'I'm so happy, Abbie. I've been alone for so long, and now I have an amazing brother and a new sister too!'

'Hey, how about me, Daphne, and Charlie? Are you saying we're not much cop?' scolded Georgie.

'I have no idea what that means. You really need to give me a British expressions prep course,' Quinn stated, looking suitably confused.

'She's saying she sees herself as your sister as well. You've become part of this little family here too, Quinn,' I clarified.

'You are, you're a lovely girl, Quinn,' added Charlie.

'Even with that hair and the ring in your nose,' nodded Daphne, giving it another disapproving look that made us all laugh. She wasn't afraid about voicing her distaste for it. 'You need to watch Wayne Davies, the farmer's son. He'll be putting a rope through it and leading you to the farmers' market.'

'She'll be off the market soon if I have anything to do with it,' I added. 'I couldn't fix up poor Heath with Georgie or Charlie, so I've got high hopes of setting him up with Quinn.'

'Who is this guy that no one wants? Do I really want you trying to dump him on me?' she retorted. 'Does he look like a slapped ass?'

'Arse,' we all corrected with a laugh. She was trying so hard with our language and expressions.

'Hell no,' Georgie uttered. 'He's super hot, both Abbie and I quite fancied him at one point, but the timing was off and we're parked firmly in the friend zone now.'

'I'd already fallen for McFitty, Dr. Fitton, by the time I met him, but if my crush ever fades, Heath's one stallion I'll be attempting to ride,' Charlie giggled.

'Then let's get to the church and meet this stud, it's been a while since I had a ride,' grinned Quinn.

'Girls, this is my nephew we're talking about,' groaned Daphne with a despairing shake of her head. The small smile on her lips gave away how much she loved being a part of our group and banter though. She was the most amazing octogenarian I'd ever met. 'Come on, before poor Miller thinks Abbie has changed her mind. The curse isn't lifted until she says the words "I do,"' she reminded us.

We all headed out into the star-filled night, Quinn taking Daphne's arm as she balanced herself with her cane and Georgie carrying my train, as Charlie locked up and put the key back under the plant pot. As we headed out of the gate onto the lane, I nearly cried again as I saw that it had been lined with lit candles in special bags with perforated snowflakes on them. They cast pretty shadows up the hedges, the flickering light guiding us all the way up to the church's front door. The carved beams of the outer porch had twinkling fairy lights wrapped around them, and there were more candle bags on the stone mullion window ledges outside. It all looked magical. Reverend Potter was waiting, Bible held firmly in his hands with a warm smile on his face.

'You look beautiful, Abbie. So like your mum on her wedding day in this very church. Did I ever tell you that your parents were the first couple I ever married?'

'No!' I exclaimed. 'Really?' My God, what were the chances, and how much more perfect could today get for reminding me that they were still here with me?

'She walked from that very cottage up the lane in that dress, just like you,' he confirmed, making me choke up as Daphne looped her arm through mine and squeezed my hand. 'Right, we have a very impatient groom waiting inside. Shall we get this show on the road?' he asked.

'Yes, please,' I nodded, full of excitement. I hadn't seen him for two nights, the girls had insisted on it. So he'd been staying up at Severn Manor with his best man Dean, Rachel's husband. I was still in that madly-in-love phase, so even two nights apart had me missing him like crazy. Reverend Potter opened the heavy old oak church door and disappeared inside. A few minutes later, after making sure my veil was in place and my train was suitably draped, Georgie blew me a kiss, wished me good luck, and stepped inside, followed by Charlie, then Quinn. The organ started up immediately, and the butterflies in my tummy went wild with anticipation.

'Now you're sure about this, Abbie?' Daphne asked seriously. 'You youngsters don't seem to see marriage as the serious commitment that it is, giving up at the first hurdle. David and I had plenty of hurdles in our time, but we worked at it, and each one we overcame only made our love stronger.'

'I'm sure,' I nodded, squeezing her hand in return. 'I've never been more sure of anything, even my love for maths, and you know how much I love a good spreadsheet,' I stated earnestly, making her nod her head and laugh. 'I'd rather jump hurdles with him than run a flat race with anyone else, Daphne.'

'Then what are we waiting for? Let's get you married, my darling girl,' she beamed, then coughed and wheezed slightly as we took our first steps towards the open church door. 'Crap!' she exclaimed, making me giggle. She was spending too much time around us, picking up our bad habits. 'My pelvic floor isn't what it used to be, and I'm really wishing I'd taken you up on that electric scooter suggestion right about now. That walk up the lane has damn near killed me!'

'Miller and I got you one for Christmas, it's wrapped up in our garage. Let me run and get it,' I suggested, giving her a concerned look.

'Over my dead body,' she scoffed. 'I promised to walk you up the aisle and I will, however slowly. Though if he wants to get it out after the service, I wouldn't say no. You're too good to me, Abbie. I do love you, you and Miller. I really think you've found a good one there.'

'Don't start me crying already, Daphne,' I warned. 'We have plenty of time for all that afterwards.'

'Just saying, don't let him go. If I've got an electric scooter, I'll be able to chase him down if you do. He's quite the dish.'

'He certainly is,' I laughed, and held her arm steady as we entered the church.

We did a very slow walk up the aisle, passing the small congregation who were all cooing as they watched me pass, making me blush.

I'd been accustomed to being the centre of attention at the last few weddings, for all of the wrong reasons, and I was just praying nothing would go wrong this time. I tried to use our slow pace as a chance to take it all in. I'd told the villagers they were all welcome to come in after the guests had taken their seats, and the small church was crammed to the rafters. Even Lord Kirkland was there, flashing me a dazzling smile and dipping his head in greeting. I really did need to meddle. He still hadn't asked out Isla Smith, and seeing how lovely he was, never once reminding me or making me feel embarrassed about the whole turdgate incident, I wanted to do something nice by way of an apology.

I breathed in the aroma of the lovely Christmas cookie-scented candles that Georgie had chosen and placed along the aisle. Sarah's softly pungent purple and white flowers that adorned the ends of each pew looked gorgeous. I was already fighting tears, imagining my mum feeling as excited as I did as she walked up to meet my dad, without seeing the back of Miller's blond hair peeking out from under his top hat as he stood facing the altar. His broad back was rocking the fitted morning suit he was wearing, complete with tails and highly polished shoes, and that delectable muscular backside of his. He'd completely embraced the English traditional wedding attire, and I was so happy. I was a traditional girl at heart, a traditional country girl. I breathed a sigh of relief as I made it to stand next to him without incident. I looked up at him as he turned to face me, his eyes filling with tears as he drank me in while I did the same. Georgie had made sure that Miller, Dean, and the ushers all had purple cravats to match the girls' dresses. He was the epitome of my Prince Charming.

'Wow,' he breathed, shaking his head and looking stunned. I wanted to high-five Georgie for my dress and the way she'd done my hair, swept in cascading curls over one shoulder, the way Miller always found so sexy.

'Back at you,' I whispered before turning back to face Daphne, who was already crying. Georgie hurried forwards to help steady her as she lifted my veil back and kissed me on both cheeks.

'One of the happiest days of my life. Thank you for allowing me to be such a special part of it,' she said, her old eyes glistening.

'No, thank you. I'm so proud to have you be here for me,' I said sincerely, kissing her back. Georgie helped her to her seat on the front row, then came and took my bouquet from me and adjusted my veil again, tears in her eyes too. 'Don't,' I warned. 'I promised I wouldn't cry until the vows.'

'I'm just so happy for you, for both of you,' Georgie smiled.

'It will be you next,' I teased, making her blush and roll her eyes.

'He's fidgeting. Turn around and let him see you properly.'

I did as I was told, and Miller immediately clasped my face to give me a gentle kiss, which turned into a slightly longer and more passionate one that had the congregation laughing. Someone yelled in an American accent, 'Talk about jumping the gun. He hasn't said kiss the bride yet, Miller.'

'I haven't seen her for over two days,' he called back with a loving smile at me as he let me go and laced his fingers through my right hand, squeezing tightly.

'Trust me, after just one year of marriage, you'll be begging for two days away from her,' called someone else, causing another wave of laughter to ripple through the church.

'Hey!' I warned with a laugh myself. 'Don't put him off before I've even got the wedding ring on my finger.'

'You're stuck with me for life, ring or no ring, Abbie Carter,' Miller warned. 'Too late to back out now.'

'Never,' I confirmed, giving him an adoring smile. We were going to face all of those hurdles together, as one.

We exited the church, where the villagers were waiting to shower us with purple and white confetti, and James snapped away, getting lots of pictures. Miller led me under the arched gateway that took us onto the lane and I burst out laughing to find a pink scooter, the kind you'd see zipping around the streets of Italy, complete with a "Just Married" sign and pink and red cans tied to the back, matching coloured balloons tied to the handle bars, and two hot pink helmets on the seat.

'What the hell is that?' I giggled.

'I know I should have booked a Rolls Royce or something, but you made a fool of yourself for me in the Pooh bear costume, so I figured it was time I returned the favour,' he chuckled, exchanging his top hat for a very feminine helmet as his mates whooped in the background. 'Everyone told me brides normally go with pink bridesmaid dresses, so I organised this, and then I received a parcel this morning from Georgie with the purple cravats and it was too late to change it all.'

'You're crazy,' I laughed as he hopped on, James snapping away with his camera.

'I am, and it's too late for you to trade me in for a new model, Mrs. Davis, so hop on,' he ordered with a wink.

'Mrs. Davis!' I beamed at him. Abbie Davis. I felt so happy. And so relieved. I'd half expected Fi-Fi to barge in and shout an objection or start another cat fight, but it had gone without a hitch. I carefully put on the helmet he offered me, trying not to ruin my lovely hair, and Georgie helped scoop up my train and dress as I straddled the back behind Miller. It raised more whoops from the guys as I flashed off my blue garter and a large proportion of leg. Georgie giggled as she gently tucked the dress around me while I gripped hold of Miller's waist.

'And yet you're still showing less flesh than the other dress,' she winked.

'What other dress?' Miller called.

'It's a long story. Let's just say this isn't the dress that you actually paid for, thank God.'

After asking Georgie to make sure that someone accessed the garage to get Daphne's electric scooter, we set off up Church Lane at a slow pace, amidst much cheering from the guests and hooting of the scooter horn by Miller. Most of the villagers had now lined the lane, waving us off, and I even spotted Paige Taylor in the crowd, our very own world-famous supermodel.

I rested my head on Miller's back, never feeling happier. Getting married in New York just wouldn't have been the same. The moped was so slow that virtually everyone had overtaken us by the time we made it to the private tree-lined drive that led to Severn Manor. I was half expecting to see Daphne whizzing past us on her new chair, too.

'Close your eyes,' yelled Miller. 'I don't want you to see the surprise yet.'

'What surprise?' I called, doing as I was told.

'You do know the meaning of the word, right? Or is it an American word you Brits don't use?'

'You've moved here, Miller Davis, and married one, you're as good as a Brit now,' I reminded him as I tickled his ribs, making him squirm and laugh, and I clung tighter as the scooter wobbled. 'And when were you going to tell me about Quinn moving next door?'

'Remind me that she's useless at keeping secrets, if ever I decide to share one with her again,' he huffed as he pulled to a stop and cut the engine. 'You don't mind?'

'Of course I don't!' I exclaimed, reaching blindly behind me to clutch the seat as Miller kicked down the stand and started to get off the scooter. 'I was dreading having a neighbour we didn't like moving next door. Daphne even turned down two offers from people we didn't think would fit in. I'm thrilled, it will be so nice for you to have your sister, your family, next door.' Not to mention three of my four best friends living next door to me. At least Daphne was only across the village.

'You're my family now too, Abbie Davis,' he reminded me. 'And seeing you in this sexy dress makes me want to forget the evening reception and drag you up to one of the suites to carry on trying to make a family of our own.'

'I'm sure no one would notice if we snuck away to your suite for an hour,' I suggested as he lifted me up into his arms. I quickly clung to him, feeling disorientated with my eyes shut.

'Much as I'd love to, I think they would, star attractions of this whole event and all,' he laughed. 'Besides, I don't have the suite any more. We're leaving for our honeymoon later tonight, the jet's fuelled and ready to go.'

'We are?' Well, that was a surprise that Quinn hadn't ruined, I had no idea. And worse, I had no idea where we were even going. I'd had to pack for arctic conditions, as well as tropical climates, before Dean came down this morning to whisk my cases away.

'Mmmm-hmmm,' he confirmed. 'Damn, have I told you how beautiful you look, wife?' he asked, planting a kiss on my forehead.

'Yes, but I won't tire of hearing it, husband,' I grinned. I was stunned at what greeted me when he set me down and told me that I could open my eyes. The entire front of Severn Manor looked like a scene from Narnia. There was snow everywhere. On the roof, the windowsills, on the twinkling Christmas tree outside, all over the grass. In fact, I was even standing in it, but it wasn't cold. I looked up at Miller, completely confused. Delighted, but confused. 'I don't understand, there's so much and it wasn't snowing.'

'You wanted a snowy Christmas wedding, so I made it happen with a few industrial fake snow machines, and when the guests walk out of the patio doors onto the back terrace, they'll find an ice skating rink, too.'

'I think I'll keep you,' I squealed, throwing my arms around him as I gave him a grateful kiss. It was just how I'd pictured my perfect reception.

Even Miller gasped as we finally entered the reception hall. I'd gone for an icy silver and warm purple theme. Large pillar candles with a garland of fairy lights circling them stood on frosted-glass stands in the centre of each of the guests' tables. We had silver-sprayed twigs and fir cones, the same coloured lighting scheme and draped panes of material forming a canopy above us, and there was a roaring fire in the gorgeous inglenook fireplace. The scent of the hot mulled wine the guests were drinking permeated the air. It was everything I'd hoped it would be and more.

They all stood to applaud us as we entered and took our seats at the top table, passing the cake table that I'd asked the staff to make doubly sure was secure after the disaster at poor Tracey's wedding. Jess had outdone herself with purple, white, and silver macaron croquembouches on silver stands, resembling Christmas trees, the largest of which had edible silver-leaf snowflakes hanging from its base. Dad would have just loved this, he'd have been so happy for me. And me? I was just ecstatic.

After we'd eaten the most sumptuous five-course meal and drank copious amounts of champagne, making the laughter and chatter in the room completely infectious, it was time for the speeches, and Miller helped a very tipsy Daphne to her feet.

'For those that don't know me, I'm Daphne Jones and I've known Abbie Carter, no, no, Abbie Davis now, since she was this high,' she began, bending over to indicate how high off the floor and almost knocking herself out as she smacked her forehead on the table. I heard Georgie snort with laughter as the table shook and Miller quickly helped Daphne back up and checked she was ok. 'Crikey, who put that there? I just put my back out,' she giggled. 'The last time was when Mr. Jones and I tried the rowing boat position from the Karma Sutra!'

'Oh no,' I groaned, covering my eyes as I giggled and the rest of the guests joined in. She was hammered. This was about to get even more entertaining.

'Don't try the Catherine wheel one then,' someone called.

'Or the bridge. How do you think I got that double hernia last year?' came another voice that sounded just like Mr. Benson's.

'Must have been all that Viagra you took by mistake,' Daphne teased. 'Had you imagining you were fifty years younger. Now, where was I?' she asked, squinting at her speech cards. 'Ah yes, since she was this high.' She bent over again, and Miller caught her just before she head-butted the table for the second time.

'We get it, she was very young,' he said, straightening her up.

'Pretty as a picture and look at her now, the most beautiful bride I've ever seen. I tell you, I couldn't be more proud if it was my own son in that dress. Not that he's a cross dresser, I hasten to add, no, no, no,' she confirmed with a serious face and wagging finger, as other people startled chuckling. 'Just making the point that friendship, and good whisky, is thicker than blood. I love this girl as if she were my own. She's treated me like she was my own, been there for me when my son hasn't, or wouldn't. And there's nothing I wouldn't do for her,' she stated, with a so-there nod.

'Likewise, Daphne,' I replied, blotting my eyes with my napkin. Miller put a comforting hand on my shoulder as he remained standing, supporting Daphne with his other hand in the small of her back.

'If you ever hurt her, Miller Davis, I still have a shotgun licence and a twelve-bore hidden under the cushions of my sofa,' she warned.

'Oh my God,' Georgie exclaimed. 'I kept saying there was something hard in the sofa and no one believed me. It could have gone off, I could have ended up with bottom shrapnel!'

'I think we'll put that into safe keeping,' Miller advised, 'and as for using it on me, you'll never have to. It's that nephew of yours you need to worry about after I found him half-naked with my girl last year.' He shot a wink at Heath, who shook his head, an embarrassed pink hue settling on his cheeks at the reminder.

They'd actually become really good friends, which was excellent, as I'd be able to have him over for dinner at the same time as Quinn. I'd already spotted them eyeing each other up across the room, both quickly looking away if their gazes crossed. I was going to have to trade in balancing accounts and turn my skills to matching up pairs in the village if no one ever made the first move.

'So I want you all to raise your bottoms to Miller and Abbie, glasses up,' Daphne called, everyone laughing out loud as she got her words muddled up.

'Steady on,' I exclaimed as she downed her champagne, while the rest of us took a polite sip.

'Oh dear,' she giggled, settling her fingers on the table as she swayed. 'I do believe I'm a little tipsy.'

'Make that a lot tipsy. I think you ought to sit down,' I warned her, worried she was about to keel over.

'Oh no,' she moaned, closing her eyes as one hand clutched at her stomach. 'Oh, Abbie, I'm so … oh dear … I'm so … so sorry.'

'What, what's wrong?' I cried, shooting to my feet in a panic. I'd lost David on Christmas Day, surely I wasn't about to lose Daphne on my wedding day?

'Aunt Daphne?' Heath called as he leaped up from his seat nearby and started racing over. He was a few feet away when the most God-awful belch, the kind that rumbles up from deep in your stomach after guzzling a bottle of fizzy pop, came gurgling out of Daphne's mouth. Seconds later, her top set of dentures flew across the room and landed with a plop in Rachel's glass of champagne.

'Oh, I'm so verwy sorrwy, how wude,' Daphne giggled, her lack of teeth affecting her normally eloquent voice. Quinn burst out laughing as Daphne burped again, while Rachel just stared at the set of teeth floating in her glass with an unreadable expression. 'How wude,' Daphne repeated. 'Thank goodness it wasn't a bottom burp. At my age, you've got no chance of keeping in a five-course meal. We could have had a whole Mr. Sumo shart situation if the wrong end had blown.'

'Oh my God, she's completely wasted,' I laughed.

'I've never seen her this bad,' Georgie agreed as she struggled to compose herself. The rest of the guests either sniggered or looked completely mortified to see an eighty-year-old acting like a teenager. But that's part of what I loved about her. She could be sage and wise old Daphne, or one of the girls that had us all in fits of hysteria. I'd never met anyone like her.

'Heath, grab her teeth back off Rachel, who looks about to pass out, and help Miller carry Daphne up to her bedroom,' I ordered. We'd treated her to a night at the hotel so she could enjoy herself, I just didn't know how much she already had enjoyed herself. I'd never seen her so drunk. 'She needs to sleep this off for a while.'

'So, Mrs. Davis, was your day everything you'd hoped it would be?' Miller asked as he undid his jacket buttons after laying me down on the bed in his private plane.

'Everything and more,' I nodded, propping myself up on my elbows to watch him strip off his jacket. 'And if August, lead stripper of AMD, is about to make an appearance, it would just make the perfect day even better.'

'Then sit back and enjoy the show, August aims to please,' he advised with a waggle of his eyebrows. I giggled and sat up, reaching behind me to undo my dress. 'What are you doing, baby?'

'Taking off my dress.'

'Oh no you don't,' he warned. 'You're keeping it on. You look amazing in it. Don't worry, I'll work around it,' he winked.

'Dress on, got it,' I nodded, palming the mattress below me instead as he kicked off his shoes, and one flew into one of the wall lights and smashed it. 'Hmmm, I think you might need a bit more practice at this.'

'Practice makes perfect, and I'm planning on doing a lot of practicing. That dress might not be coming off the entire honeymoon, you look so damn sexy in it.'

'Fine with me,' I confirmed with a smile and a blossoming of my heart. I'd done it, I'd finally done it. I'd broken the curse and found the man, and the dress. This was the best day ever!

Chapter Eighteen
Mr. Barker
February

'WHERE ARE WE GOING?' I asked Miller as he shot down some country lanes in Oxfordshire, enjoying testing out his new Mercedes GLE. We'd just had a romantic Valentine's weekend at Le Manoir aux Quat'Saisons, Raymond Blanc's famous hotel and gourmet restaurant, and I'd assumed we were heading home.

'To get your Valentine's present,' he replied, flashing me a smile.

'I've just had my Valentine's present, and a very lovely one at that,' I reminded him.

'That was just a getaway, for both of us, not your actual present.'

'You don't need to spoil me so much, Miller. We're married, you've already got me.'

'I know, but I really wanted to get you this. Plus it will make me feel better to know you have this when I'm not at home. You know I worry when I'm in New York.'

'Is this about the whole "key under the plant pot" thing again?' I asked with a roll of my eyes. He just didn't get how safe Dilbury was compared to New York. 'Are you taking me to get one of those rocks for the garden that's really a secret key hideaway? As that's as much use as a chocolate teapot, all the burglars know they exist. I bet they look at all the rock gardens first now, rather than under the plant pots or front door mats.'

'Actually no, it's not, but I have asked Heath to install a wall-mounted combination key safe while we're on the topic,' he advised, as the Sat Nav told him to turn left and we pulled into a large private gravelled drive. 'It's more important to be security conscious, especially now that the work on the rear extension is about to begin.'

'Honestly,' I muttered under my breath as he got out and came around to open my door. I'd never felt safer than I did in the cottage. He was blowing it all out of proportion. I'd half expected him to suggest we have a team of his security guards patrolling the lane at night.

I shrugged it off, as I knew he was just being protective. It was quite endearing most of the time, but lately I was finding it annoying. In fact, I was incredibly irritable this week. I wasn't sure what had me so grumpy. I was really tired at the moment and was having to make a concerted effort not to snap at people, which wasn't like me.

'Come on,' he said, helping me out and pulling me against him for a quick kiss. I winced as he crushed my chest against his, my breasts feeling really tender. Of course, I was due on, that's why I was tired and moody. What with the wedding, the honeymoon, and catching up with everyone when we got back, it was no wonder I'd lost track and forgotten.

'What's here?' I asked as he led me to the front door of a large old stone house, set substantial and beautifully kept grounds.

'You'll find out in a minute,' he replied mysteriously as he rang the bell. The door opened revealing a ruddy-faced man in his fifties.

'You must be Mr. and Mrs. Davis. I'm Rupert Bonneville,' he greeted with an outstretched hand, which Miller shook. 'So glad you found us. Come on in, they're just finishing up their lunch.'

'We can come back if we're interrupting at a bad time,' Miller offered.

'No, not at all. Honestly, they're almost done, so it's perfect timing,' he replied, gesturing for us to step inside.

Miller gave my hand a gentle tug as I wondered what was going on. Rupert shut the door and led us down a soft grey painted hall, with large old flagstones on the floor, and took us into a huge kitchen diner with a glass wall that faced out onto the garden at the rear. There was no sign of anyone eating, so I was feeling rather confused as he led us to a side door which he threw open. All of a sudden, my ears were assaulted by the sound of tiny excited barks and the pitter-patter of of claws on the old stone floor as we followed Rupert into a huge conservatory. 'Here they are.'

'Oh my God,' I cried, my heart fluttering to see five tiny white fluffy puppies scampering around inside a large four-sided pen, while a larger dog, who I presumed was their mum, lay on a plump rectangular dog cushion watching them.

'Aren't they adorable?' Miller asked, squeezing my hand.

'They look like little teddy bears,' I laughed, letting go of Miller's hand to crouch down as one of them came scampering over and barked at me. 'Can I touch it?' I asked, looking up at Rupert for confirmation first. He smiled and nodded.

'I'll let you into the pen so you can sit down and interact with them all, see which is your favourite.'

'I don't understand, what's going on?' I replied with a frown, glancing across to Miller.

'We're here to chose one for us. They're pedigree bichon frises,' he confirmed, leaning on the wooden rail. 'I know you prefer smaller dogs, and while I thought about a bulldog again, I wanted a dog that can come on a plane, so it can fly with us whenever we travel to New

223

York. We've got first choice for you to pick the one you want and it's coming home with us now.'

'Are you serious?' I exclaimed as my heart leapt with excitement. I'd really missed not having a dog, but to be honest, I'd felt disloyal to the memory of Sumo to even think about going to look for another. I'd never have suggested it, or done it on my own, but somehow Miller making the choice that we were having one took that weight off my shoulders.

'Is that ok?' he asked gently. 'I know no dog will ever replace Sumo, and I didn't want to surprise you with one I'd picked, since I knew how much it broke your heart that he wasn't as loving with you as he was with other people. I thought it was best to let you choose a puppy that you bonded with.'

'Is that ok?!' I scoffed, then laughed as I felt a little wet nose nudging my hand through the bars of the pen and looked down to see the bravest of the pups lick me. 'It's wonderful!'

'Come on then, let's get you both inside. Best to sit on the floor and let them come to you, though it looks like you've already got a fan,' Rupert chuckled.

I nodded eagerly and pulled my hand away as I stood up. The pup let out a bark and bounced back and forth, like it had springs attached to its feet, its tiny tail wagging ten to the dozen. Rupert opened up the pen in the one corner, to give us room to squeeze in, and caught the pup as it tried to zip out. When we sat down, the mum just lay there, relatively unperturbed by our arrival. Three of her pups had gone to cuddle up to her, their eyes full of fear, and another was sitting closer to us, appraising us apprehensively. As soon as Rupert set the original bundle of fluff back down inside the pen, it trotted over and tried to climb up onto my lap.

'Miller, look,' I cooed as I gently stroked it.

'I think you've already bonded with him,' Rupert said as he watched me pick the pup up and hold him gently against my chest, then receive a sloppy lick as a reward. 'He's never been that friendly with me or my wife.'

'Oh, he's adorable,' I breathed, smiling at Miller as I got a neck wash from the little guy. Miller laughed and held out one of his hands, which he slowly offered to the pup, and was rewarded with a lick and a nuzzle himself, then an excited bark. 'I don't know much about bichons, what are they like as pets?' I asked, hardly able to tear my eyes off the fluffy ball of gorgeousness in my arms.

'Very sociable and easy to train, but they don't like being left alone. They need regular grooming, as they shed a lot and their coats are quite thick and fluffy.'

'Not a problem. My best friend is a dog groomer and lives virtually next door,' I confirmed, reluctantly passing the pup over to Miller when he asked for a turn.

'They're not normally known for their barking, but this one's extra vocal today,' Rupert stated, as the pup continued to vocalise his enthusiasm at our petting between excited licks of Miller.

'Oh, hello, little one,' I said quietly as as the bravest of the other puppies came a bit closer to see what was going on. I offered it my hand and it leaned in and sniffed, but as soon as I tried to stroke it, it scampered back to the safety of its mother. I turned back around to find the original pup was struggling to get off Miller's lap to come back to me. 'Oh, Miller, can we have this one? He's so friendly.'

'Of course we can. Anything to see that amazing smile of yours,' he confirmed, offering me a kiss as he let the little mite come back to settle down on my lap for more cuddles. 'Is that ok, Mr. Bonneville?'

'Of course it is, and please call me Rupert. I have all of the paperwork in my office, and we can leave your wife to play while we go and set up your car with the cage, bedding, and accessories as discussed. Would you like a drink, Mrs. Davis? I can hear my wife back in the kitchen.'

'No, I'm fine, but thank you for the offer.' I gave him a grateful smile as I tore my gaze from my adorable new little boy.

'See you in a minute,' Miller said, leaning over to give me a quick kiss. 'Now you have your own teddy bear.'

'I do,' I nodded, giving him a grateful smile. 'Thank you, this was such a thoughtful gift.' Miller climbed over the edge of the pen to save opening it again, and I focused my attention on my new puppy. I wondered what Sumo would have made of him. 'What are we going to call you?' I asked him. He barked again and I laughed. 'Noisy little fellow, aren't you? How about Mr. Barker, Teddy for short?' I suggested, laughing again as he licked my hand.

There, it was settled. Mr. Teddy Barker. I picked him up and held the squirming bundle of fur in front of me, unable to break the smile on my face.

'Awww, you're just so cute! Who's the cutest?' I said in a baby voice. 'Who's the–' I let out a startled cry as cute Teddy decided now would be an appropriate time to relieve himself. A jet of warm pee splattered my face, some entering my open mouth, and ran down onto my cream jumper.

'Oh dear, didn't Rupert warn you? He's been a bit slower with the toilet training than the others, especially when he's excited,' came a laughing female voice behind me. I put Teddy down, stuck my tongue out, desperately trying to wipe it clean on my sleeve. 'I'll go and get you a cloth.'

'Unbelievable,' I grimaced, wiping the pee from my face as Teddy darted back and forth, his tail wagging incessantly as he yapped and tried to encourage his siblings to play. 'First I get the gassy dog that hates me, now I've got the dog that loves me so much, he engages in non-consensual water sports.'

'What was that, dear?' Mrs. Bonneville asked as she reappeared with a damp cloth, some kitchen towels, and a glass of water for me to rinse out my mouth with.

'Nothing, just muttering to myself,' I answered as I stood up and accepted the damp cloth first. I closed my eyes and gave my face a good scrub, then moved down to rub my jumper, but it was so damp, I had to carefully peel it off, grateful I had a shirt on underneath.

'Come on out of the pen for a minute. You can go and rinse your mouth over the kitchen sink and I'll get you something stronger to take away the taste,' she said as I stuck out my tongue and shuddered.

'Thank you.' I did as I was told, then swilled the brandy she returned with around my mouth before swallowing it down.

'First time dog owner?' she asked when I gave her the empty glass back.

'No, but it's been a while since I've had a puppy, I forgot what they're like. Will his mum and brothers and sisters be ok? I feel awful taking him away from them.'

'She'll pine for a while, but she'll soon get over it, they always do. I hope you don't mind dogs in the bedroom, as they don't like being alone, and he'll probably find it extra hard being away from them for the next few nights.'

'As long as he doesn't pee on me in my sleep, I have no problem him joining us in the bedroom,' I confirmed, looking over to watch him tumbling around with his siblings.

Miller couldn't stop laughing about the whole pee incident as we drove away, with Teddy in his new travel cage in the back of the car. We had to pull over shortly after we left, though, as he was whining and sounded so upset that it broke my heart. We got him out and I cradled him on my lap, but not before putting a puppy training pad on it. I'd learned my lesson, that was for sure. He was just so different to Sumo. He adored being stroked, having his tummy tickled, and was a real nuzzler and licker. He soon fell asleep, curled up against me, and I caught Miller's soft smile as he looked over at me.

'I love him, despite the whole peeing in my mouth incident,' I told him.

'Good. I was worried I might have done the wrong thing.'

'Best surprise ever,' I nodded, stifling a yawn.

'Tired again?' Miller asked, flashing me a look of concern.

'Hmmm,' I confirmed as I reclined my seat a little and laid one cheek on it so I could watch him driving. I'd never tire of looking at him. 'Everything's caught up with me and we've got to help Daphne pack up and move, then move Quinn in, and before you know it, I'll be doing year-end work for my clients.'

'I'll hire a firm to do all the packing and moving, so all you have to worry about is settling in Teddy and your work, ok?' He reached over to run his knuckles gently down my cheek, and I managed to kiss them before he gave Teddy a gentle head ruffle.

After a quick pit stop at the supermarket, Miller running in while I stayed with our boy in the car, we made it home. Teddy was wide awake and spent the next hour sniffing around the ground floor of his new home, as we did our best to puppy proof it and set out his new beds and food bowls. I made sure Sumo's dog flap was locked, not wanting Teddy to escape.

It wasn't long before there was a knock at the front door, so I opened the top half to find Georgie waiting, hopping impatiently from one foot to another.

'Well? Is it here?' she asked, angling her head to look back and forth.

'You knew about the puppy?'

'Well, duh, of course. We had to have a discussion about whether you were ready, what breed to get, etc. So? Are you happy? Boy or girl? What did you call it?'

'Hey, hey, slow down,' I laughed as she excitedly fired off the questions. 'Come on in, quickly, as he's a fast little bugger.'

She did as she was told and I quickly shut the door behind her. 'You got a boy again?'

'We did. Mr. Barker, Teddy Barker, he's quite the conversationalist. Let's grab a coffee first, then you can come and see him. Miller made a fire, and he's curled up in front of it fast asleep. He's just so adorable, despite peeing in my mouth and all over me.'

'How in the hell did he pee in your mouth?' she laughed. She laughed even harder when I told her my story as I made us some hot drinks.

'So, here he is,' I said as I led her to him in the lounge.

'Oh my God, so much cuter in the flesh than in the pictures Miller showed me,' she cooed as she sat in the armchair by the fire and leaned over to study him. He was fast asleep, totally out for the count. So far we'd had no snoring, grunting, wheezing, or farting. 'I can't wait to start grooming him for you. His hair is so long, I can experiment with different trims and shapes.'

'Oh God,' Miller groaned as he put his arm around me. 'I'm not taking him for a walk with some girlie pom-pom hairstyle, thanks, Georgie.'

'Hello, this is me! With the exception of prancing Portia, who I have to do like that under duress, dogs should look dog-like.'

'He'll look cute no matter what,' I yawned, as there was another knock on the front door.

'I'll get it,' Miller said, kissing my temple before he strode out.

'Is it here?' came Daphne's voice.

'Did everyone know about the pup but me?' I asked. Georgie just grinned and nodded.

'Where is it?' Daphne asked as Miller helped her inside.

I just sat back and smiled as Teddy woke up and regaled them all with some excited woofs and started bounding back and forth between us all for cuddles. His little legs were so small, and he was doing so much running, that he was going to wear himself out again in no time at all.

'He's gorgeous, but it doesn't look like you'll be needing my knitting skills for Teddy, not like you did for Sumo,' Daphne sighed as he cuddled up in her lap for some love.

'No, but … oh God, sorry, I don't know what's wrong with me, I'm so tired at the moment,' I mumbled as I yawned again. 'What?' I asked, as Daphne and Georgie exchanged a look and Miller chuckled. 'What?'

'You have no idea why you're so tired?' Daphne asked with a smile.

'I've overdone things.'

'Hmmm, and that's really all?' Georgie said in a sarcastic tone, quirking an eyebrow at me.

'Ok, we've been a bit active lately, wedding, honeymoon, and all.' I blushed and Miller started laughing.

'Yes, we have, but that's not what they're implying, Abbie. Do you really have no idea?' he asked.

'I don't know what's going on,' I complained, looking at each of them in turn and trying to get a clue as to what they were thinking.

'When was your last period, Abbie?' Daphne asked.

'I'm due any time, which doesn't help.'

'Gosh, have you always been so slow?' Georgie laughed, shaking her head. 'You're not due any time, Abbie. You were due a few weeks ago. You're pregnant.'

'No!' I exclaimed. 'No way, we only started trying just before the wedding and I'm not due until now.'

'No, baby, you're late,' Miller confirmed, kissing me as he gave me a loving smile. 'You're regular as clockwork, but you've probably lost track since we've been so busy. You're constantly tired, you've started getting a bit irritable, you–'

'I'm *not* irritable,' I bit back, feeling panic rising. I'd wanted a baby for so long, but I'd prepared myself for a long period of trying and failing. Not everyone was lucky enough to get caught right away, if at all.

'Yeah, right,' Georgie scoffed. 'Irritable example right there,' she pointed as she swirled her finger at me. I swallowed hard and looked over at Daphne, who nodded, then I glanced up at Miller.

'I'm really overdue?' I whispered. 'I could be pregnant?'

'There's only one way to find out,' he confirmed, planting a kiss on my forehead. 'I picked up a couple of tests when I did the grocery shopping. Come on, let's do it now.'

He led me to the cloakroom, where he'd already set the packets out on the sink, then told me to come out when I was ready. I shut the door and picked up one of the boxes, reading the instructions in a daze. How could Miller and my best friends have picked up on the signs before me? Surely I'd know first, they had to be mistaken. I was just late from all of the stress of the dress and the wedding. That was what it was. It was just stress.

I walked back into the lounge ten minutes later in a daze. Georgie and Daphne were sitting down, Teddy still sleeping on Daphne's lap, but Miller was anxiously pacing in front of the fire. All three of them turned their heads in my direction, with expectant looks on their faces. I took a deep breath and nodded, still in shock.

'I'm pregnant.'

Daphne and Georgie immediately cheered, with exclamations of "I knew it!" Teddy woke up and started barking, and Miller ... I'd never forget the look of pride and happiness on Miller's face. He strode over to me, hauled me against him, lifted me up, and kissed me as he spun me around in a circle.

'We're having a baby,' he beamed, as I clutched his face and bit my lower lip, feeling anxious.

'We just got a new puppy. I don't even know if I can be a good mum to Teddy yet, what if I'm rubbish with a baby?' I moaned, needing some reassurance right now. I was thrilled and terrified all at once. It was a very strange feeling.

'Don't be ridiculous,' he laughed. 'Besides, we have months before it will be here. You'll have had plenty of practice with Teddy by then and he'll be completely house trained.'

'He's a dog, Miller. This is a baby, a real life baby! I'm not sure I'm ready. I'm Abbie Carter, disaster Carter, I'm not responsible mother material. What if I screw this up?' I uttered in a panic as he set me down.

229

'Sssshhhh,' he coaxed, cupping my face in his hands as he kissed me again. 'For a start, you're not Abbie Carter anymore, you're Abbie Davis, and it will be a first for me too, but we'll make it work.'

'No mother's ever ready, Abbie, no matter how much she may want a baby. Finding out you're having one is a life-altering event. I know there's going to be times that you wish you had your mum here to tell you what to do, to be a shoulder to cry on, to help out as you find your feet, but you have me,' Daphne said in a calm and reassuring voice, nodding gently at me as I looked over, trying to pull myself together.

'And me. I've got no knowledge or mother skills, but I can be the supportive best friend. Bring you cups of calming tea, cuddle you when you need some love or want to cry, slap you when you turn into a raging hormonal bitch,' Georgie offered, making me shake my head as I laughed. 'And you've got Charlie, too.'

'And Quinn, and *me*, Abbie. I'm going to be here for you every step of the way, and you know that after what I went through, this kid is never going to want for anything, emotionally or financially.' Miller ran his thumb over my lower lip as his eyes sparkled with happiness. He gave me a reassuring smile as well, one that calmed me down immediately. He was right. Together we could do this, with the support of Daphne and my friends. It was time to put the old Abbie Carter behind me. I was now Abbie Davis, wife and mother of a white fur ball and soon-to-be baby.

'I'm so happy for you, Abbie, congratulations,' Georgie uttered, as she came over with tears in her eyes to hug me. I let a few out as I returned the embrace. I was pregnant. I was having a baby. I had to keep repeating it to myself to make it sink in.

'Hey, am I not much cop?' Miller said, throwing one of her favourite British phrases back at her in his best English accent, which made us all laugh. She turned to hug him as I looked over at Daphne and bit my lip again. She stayed seated but held out her arms, and I ran over and kneeled beside her. We managed to embrace even with the arm of the chair in our way.

'You'll do fine, Abbie,' she said quietly, laying her wrinkled old cheek on top of my head. 'You have the biggest and most loving heart of anyone I've ever known. Look how you are with me, how you were with Mr. Sumo, who rarely showed you any affection in return. This baby is going to be the most loved and happiest baby ever. And I'm going to be so proud to be able to help you.'

'What would I do without you, Daphne?' I sniffed, sitting back on my heels and wiping my eyes.

'I hope we have a few more years together before you have to find that out,' she replied, as she wiped her own. 'But on the bright side, I'd better start knitting again. We have a baby Davis to keep warm.'

I brushed off her scary reminder that our time together was limited and focused on the happier thought of all of the planning we had to do before a baby arrived. I looked down as Teddy seemed to sense something momentous was happening and woke up with a bark.

'You may have lost your real brothers and sisters, Mr. Barker,' I told him as I lifted him up, 'but you're going to get one who, one day, is going to love you so much. You'll have a little friend to play with soon. What do you think of that?'

I was rewarded with another stream of pee in the face, and everyone else burst into fits of laughter as I spluttered and Teddy barked. This motherhood lark was going to take some serious getting used to.

Epilogue
All's Well That Ends Well
June
Five Years Later

'ABBIE, ARE YOU COMING down? Everyone's here,' Miller called up the stairs.

'I'll be there in a minute,' I confirmed as I washed my hands and stared at myself in the mirror. A very different Abbie was looking back at me compared to the one pre-Miller. A much happier Abbie, one whose life seemed pretty damn perfect.

I left the en-suite of our master bedroom, which was in the new extension of the house, or not so new now, and headed down our own set of stairs that came out next to the utility room. Beside that was what had been my new ground floor office, as Miller had taken over my larger one up above the garage. But I didn't need an office now that I was no longer working, so Miller had converted it into his gaming room. The extra extension had also given us a new guest room that was accessed from the upstairs landing of the original part of the house. Downstairs, in addition to the games room, it had provided one long room that ran along the back of the house, from the kitchen diner to the lounge, so you could do a complete circle of the ground floor rooms and main staircase. It meant we had a nice family room as part of the kitchen, and extra space for Jackson's toys.

I smiled as I stepped out of the bi-fold glass doors that spanned the back of the house. My nearly five-year old son was riding around the garden on the Sumo Express, with his blue train driver's cap on and chubby Teddy in Sumo's old carriage behind. While Teddy was most definitely a Mummy's boy, Jackson was all about Miller. That is, unless he fell over and hurt himself, or was hungry, then it was me he wanted. He was a gorgeous little boy, having all of Miller's features, cheeky smile, dimples, dark brown eyes, and dirty-blond hair. He was going to be a heartbreaker when he was older.

'There you are. What were you doing?' Miller asked as he headed over in his chef's apron, a pair of tongs in his hand. We'd invited our loved ones around for a barbeque for my birthday and they were all on the terrace, seated around the huge patio table, Daphne in her comfortable electric wheelchair. The sound of their laughter and chatter warmed my heart. My life was everything that I'd dreamed it would be, and then some.

'This and that,' I replied, accepting a kiss, then returning it as I put my arms around his neck and made sure it lasted.

'Hmmm,' he groaned. 'What was that for? Is this chef's apron doing it for you, baby? I can always wear it to bed later.'

'No,' I laughed, smiling up at him. 'You do it for me, you're all I need in bed.'

'If only,' he replied with a roll of his eyes. 'I miss the days when it was just the two of us in our bed.'

'God, me too,' I agreed. Teddy loved nothing better than climbing the stairs we'd had to have made for him, as the bed was too high for him to jump up, then snuggling down against us at night. Then, more often than not, we woke up to find Jackson had crawled in between us sometime during the morning. We'd had to upgrade to a super king-sized bed to accommodate our family. But waking up and seeing all three of my boys sleeping there with me was one of the best feelings in the world.

'Hey, stop hogging her, Miller,' Georgie called. 'We have important girl stuff to discuss.'

'Whose wife is she?' Miller replied.

'I'll make it up to you later,' I whispered, brushing his lips with mine again. 'Why don't you grab the boys to help you cook while us girls chat?'

'They're a hindrance. Heath wants more coals on the fire, Dean wants less, and the others are arguing over whether sausages should sit in the grooves of the grill or across them.'

'No one wants a gritty sausage that's dropped.' I winked, making him laugh and smack my backside playfully. 'Can you find a few minutes to–'

'Mummy!' yelled Jackson, interrupting as he chugged behind us, and Teddy barked a greeting at me.

'What, sweetie?' I asked, my stomach still fluttering to hear myself being called that.

'I'm *hungry*,' he moaned as he pressed the button to stop the train by the house.

'Already? You only had breakfast a while ago, and don't think I didn't spot you eating one of Teddy's biscuits either. I've told you they're no good for you,' I warned him with a wagging finger. He giggled and bit his lower lip. He was completely fearless with anything he considered to be edible, as well as playing and climbing, which terrified me.

'They're yummy though,' he nodded with a serious expression.

'Yummier than Mummy's cookies?' Miller asked with a mock gasp. Jackson grinned and shook his head as he jumped off the train.

'No, silly billy. Those are the absolute best,' he exclaimed, giving his dad an *honestly* look. He ran over to put his arms around my knees and looked up at me through his dark lashes. 'But I can't reach the cookie jar.' He pulled a sad, pleading face, which made us both laugh.

'Which is a very good thing,' I replied, hoisting him up as I made a mental note to move all of Teddy's biscuits and cans of dog food up out of reach as well. I'd even caught Jackson with a spoon in Teddy's food bowl one day when he was younger, eating the gravy-smothered chunks.

'Not when I'm hungry,' Jackson pouted.

'You're always hungry, son.' Miller ruffled his hair and planted a kiss on his head. 'One cookie, that's all. Lunch will be ready soon.'

'Not if you don't cook it,' I reminded him as Jackson snuggled up against me.

'What were you going to ask me, baby?'

'It can wait, go cook. Be with you in a minute,' I called over to my friends at the table.

'If you're getting the cookies out, I'll have one,' Daphne responded.

'Oh, me too,' chorused Charlie, Quinn, and Georgie.

'Rachel?' I asked. We'd become closer, more because of Miller and Dean being best friends. She'd never be in my closest circle of Daphne and the three girls, but we got on well. She'd been to Fi-Fi's wedding to a footballer last year, which I thankfully hadn't been invited to, and had been mortified to find out that the "slutty dress" Fi wore had once been mine. We'd had a good giggle about that.

'I'd love one too please, darling,' she nodded.

'Oh no, now *everyone* wants one of my cookies,' Jackson sighed. 'Will there be enough left for me?'

'Yes,' I laughed as I carried him inside. 'Besides, they're not *your* cookies, they're for everyone. You know I always bake enough for you and Daddy, plus spares. But we can make some more together tomorrow, how does that sound?'

'Can we make doggie-shaped ones, like Teddy?' he asked, his face lighting up. Teddy was his best friend. He just adored him and Teddy was so protective of him.

'We can make any shape you want,' I confirmed, smiling as he squealed and clapped, then pursed his lips for a kiss.

'Ok, now that all of the wedding talk is out of the way, how are you, Daphne? What's the news from the school house?' I asked. She was so happy in her new flat. We visited her often and still had her over for Sunday lunch. She was able to come all the way on her electric scooter if the weather was nice, like today. She'd even got herself a boyfriend, none other than Mr. Bentley. They'd sit holding hands as they watched the spectacular Shropshire sunsets from the communal lounge, which looked out to the Welsh hills in the distance. He'd never replace David, but I was so happy that they had each other. He'd zoned out and fallen asleep when we all started talking excitedly about the upcoming wedding and last-minute arrangements. Dilbury was going to be a hive of activity this summer.

'Well, you heard about poor Joyce Weathers?'

'The one whose husband died this week?' Quinn asked. It was strange to hear her and Miller now talk with a slight British inflection to their American accents.

'Well, it was Charlie's fault,' Daphne nodded, with a tongue in the side of her cheek as she gave Charlie a look.

'What did I do?' Charlie exclaimed indignantly. 'I only met him at the village fête this year.'

'Joyce had been reading one of your saucy books, got a bit excited, and convinced Frank to try out a position you'd written in one of your stories.'

'Which one?' Charlie asked, leaning in with a curious expression as the rest of us groaned and shook our heads, really not wanting to know.

'The wheelbarrow,' Daphne confirmed. 'He only had a heart attack from all of the exertion and effort of trying to keep her legs in the air and fell on her. She was found pinned under him the next morning, as she hadn't been able to get up to ring the emergency alarm.'

'No!' we all gasped, Georgie covering her mouth as she tried not to giggle at the thought of it.

'And that's not the worst of it,' Daphne advised.

'I'm already pretty grossed out, do we really need to hear more?' groaned Quinn.

'They had to call the fire service out, as rigor mortis had set in and, well, let's just say I think it took a crow bar to separate them.'

'Oh my God,' I winced, covering my eyes as everyone else chuckled. 'Charlie, you've made Dilbury a hot house of old age pensioner iniquity.'

'I think I'd better start putting a disclaimer in my books,' she laughed.

Miller opened some champagne and set more bottles of beer on the table as we all gathered around to tuck into our feast, laughing and joking, especially with Dean telling us some new stories from Miller's youth.

'Mummy,' Jackson yelled from the bottom of the garden, 'I got Teddy poo all over me.'

'Great,' I sighed. 'Why does he want me for the messy jobs and Miller for the fun ones?'

'I'll sort him out,' Miller smiled, grabbing the box of wet wipes off the table.

'Don't eat it please, Jackson!' I called back, making everyone laugh. I didn't dare admit to them that I was being serious, it had happened before.

'Ewww, it's stinky. Bad Teddy,' Jackson scolded, as my boy bounced around him, yapping.

I had half an ear on the conversation at the table as I watched Miller trying to clean Jackson up. Teddy stole a fresh wipe from the box and raced around with it clutched in his jaws, shaking his head as he growled. There they were, my boys. My family. My heart and my home.

'Excuse me a minute,' I said to no one in particular as I got up and left the table and made my way down the garden.

'I still don't understand how you got it all over your hands, Jackson,' Miller was saying as he wiped his own.

'I was moving it, Daddy.'

'Why? You know to tell me or Mummy to come with a poop bag to scoop it up.'

'Teddy was sniffing it. I thought he was going to eat it. Mummy said it's naughty to eat poo, that it makes you poorly, and I didn't want Teddy to be poorly. He's my bestest friend in the whole wide world.'

'He is, isn't he?' I agreed as I joined them and put my arms around Miller's waist. 'Maybe we ought to find you both another best friend to play with. Would you like that, someone you and Teddy could have fun with?'

'Who?' Jackson asked, his eyes curious as he looked up at me. I looked up at Miller with a smile, holding his gaze.

'Well, Mummy's going to be having another baby in about seven months' time, so you'll have a little brother or sister to play with.'

'Yay,' Jackson squealed as he clapped his hands. Miller gawped at me, blinking a few times. We'd got pregnant with Jackson so fast, we'd assumed it would happen that way again when Jackson was two and we decided to try for another. But it hadn't. We'd been devastated that after two years, nothing had happened. All the tests we had recently had showed nothing was wrong, so we couldn't understand it. We'd pretty much assumed it wasn't going to happen again, until Georgie and Daphne had spotted the signs before me, just like last time. Miller had been busy with a new game release and hadn't noticed.

'Seriously? We're pregnant again?' he asked, searching my eyes, as if he was fearful that I was pulling his leg.

'Seriously,' I confirmed. 'I'm seven weeks according to the test I took earlier in the bathroom.'

'God, Abbie! Best. News. Ever,' he exclaimed. His smile lit up his face as he lifted me up onto his hips and we kissed. My stomach did a somersault just like it always did when he kissed me. It was a feeling I never wanted to lose. 'I hope it's a girl this time,' he whispered against my lips.

'Me too,' I confirmed, linking my arms behind his neck as we smiled contentedly at each other. 'How about you, Jackson? What would you like, a boy or a girl?'

'Dunno,' he huffed. 'Will it be fluffy like Teddy?'

'No,' laughed Miller as I giggled and buried my face in his neck. 'It will be like a tiny version of you.'

'Oh,' Jackson responded, not sounding overly enthused at that bit of news. 'I'm not sure I want one then. I love Teddy's fur.'

'Well, we can't send it back!' I teased, lifting my head to roll my eyes at Miller.

'I'm gonna have no cookies soon, not with all these new people who are gonna want to eat them,' Jackson moaned.

'You and your cookies,' Miller chuckled. He smiled adoringly at me, making my stomach flutter, then kissed me again. The sound of his watch alarm forced us to break our embrace. 'Sprinklers,' he confirmed. 'You cancelled the timer, right?'

'No, that was your job,' I reminded him.

'No, I said, "We can't forget to cancel the sprinklers today," when we were having breakfast.'

'Well, that's not asking me to cancel them, Miller. That's a statement.'

'So you haven't?' he asked, a panicked look crossing his face as his eyes darted up to our friends who were all sitting at the edge of the lawn.

'No,' I replied quietly. 'I take it that means you didn't ei-' I screamed as the lawn came to life, jets of cold water showering us both. I also heard the yells and screams of our guests as they tried to move out of range. Jackson chortled with delight, loving nothing better, other than his cookies, Teddy, and train rides, than playing in the water spray in the summer heat. Teddy yapped and jumped up and down, biting at the jets that were attacking him. 'Damn it,' I wailed, the water saturating my clothes as Miller started laughing.

'What is it with you and me and getting wet, Abbie Davis?'

'I've no idea,' I laughed, using one hand to push my wet hair out of my face and thinking back to the first day I'd met him when we'd both got soaked. 'But if the offer's still on to take a hot shower with you, I'm all over that action.'

'We have to kick out our guests first,' he reminded me as we started squelching our way back up to the house.

'They're wet too, they'll all want to get home.'

'And we have a four-year-old who we can't leave alone.'

'We can ask Auntie Quinn to watch him,' I suggested.

'Someone's desperate,' he observed with a wide smile.

'Make the most of this phase, before the super-tired and extra-irritable one kicks in again,' I warned him, feeling my heart racing as I drank him in. Was it normal to still be so madly in love after nearly eight years?

'I'll take you any way I can get you, baby,' he murmured, kissing the tip of my nose. 'I love you. You, Jackson, Teddy, Quinn, and now my new little bump. I've finally got the family I'd always dreamt of. You've made me so happy today.'

'You make me happy every day, Miller,' I said, never more sincere. 'I'm so exceptionally happy you chased me through the sprinklers all that time ago.'

'Even when I'm grey and old and zipping around in an electric scooter like Daphne, I'll still chase you through the sprinklers, Abbie.'

I put my head on his shoulder as he carried me over to where our guests were trying to shake off the water, while Jackson and Teddy raced around, trying to get more on them.

I'd truly believed I was cursed the day I'd stood there in that rainbow dress, but it turns out it had led me to my own pot of gold. Miller. I had everything I could ever wish for, and then some.

The End

Did you enjoy *Never The Bride*?

If so, I'd be really grateful if you'd take a moment of your time to leave a review on Goodreads and Amazon, even if it's only a sentence or two. They are so important to authors in helping other readers find our work.

Thank you!

If you enjoyed this, then try my other romantic comedy, *Until We Collide.*

http://mybook.to/UntilWeCollide

Availbe to kindleunlimited subscribers

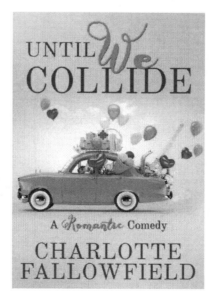

The first 10% of Until We Collide is available for you to sample for free on Wattpad:

www.wattpad.com/user/charlottefallowfield

Next Release

I'll be staying in Dilbury for a while, bringing you more romantic comedy tales from the villagers, including Quinn, Charlie, Heath Jones, and Lord Kirkland, as well as a newcomer to the quaint English village, Fleur Dubois.

Georgie will be back this August in her romantic comedy story, *The Great Escape – Dilbury Village #2.*

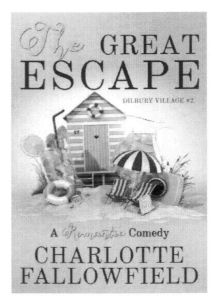

A tropical beach paradise in Mexico was the last place Georgie Basset expected her decimated heart to be jump-started again, not after she'd been jilted the year before by her fiancé, leading to said breakage. But when she spotted Weston Argent jogging along the beach, all bronzed with ripped muscles like some Greek God out of a modern day Baywatch scene, she nearly choked on her cocktail. She knew immediately she was in trouble, she'd never reacted so strongly to a man on first glance.

However, after a disastrous first date with him, she headed back home to Dilbury, resigned to never seeing him again. That is, until Weston turned up unexpectedly at her dog grooming parlour with Bertie the French bulldog, a species she had a real weakness for. She couldn't help but wonder if fate was playing a helping hand. But each time she saw him, their encounters never went smoothly, resulting in some mortifying and hilarious escapades. Despite their undeniable attraction, there was something about Weston that she couldn't quite put her finger on, something that concerned her.

When the truth finally came to light, Georgie was convinced that all men were dogs, except she knew that was an insult to dogkind. Ever the meddler, her best friend, Abbie, intervened, knowing in her heart that despite what had happened, Weston was full of good intentions, and was undoubtedly Georgie's Prince Charming.

The question remained, could he convince Georgie of that, or would he forever remain in the dog house?

Newsletter

To receive my quarterly newsletter, which includes release updates, giveaway information, and teasers, simply sign up here:

http://eepurl.com/bvwKoD

My website holds the most comprehensive information about me, as well as my current and up-and-coming releases, but you can also follow me via my other social media links or join my Facebook fan group, "The Fallowettes."

www.charlottefallowfield.co.uk

C.J. Fallowfield

If you enjoyed my humour and don't mind some steamy scenes, angst, drama, and suspense, then check out my humorous erotic romance novels, written under the pen name C.J. Fallowfield. These are strictly for the over 18's.
All are available to Kindleunlimited subscribers
http://author.to/CJFallowfield

Shrewsbury

While the village of Dilbury, Severn Manor, and Lord Kirkland and his estate are all fictitious, the gorgeous medieval town of Shrewsbury, set in the heart of the Shropshire countryside, does exist. I was lucky enough to grow up there, and I still live nearby. Shrewsbury is famous for being the birthplace of Charles Darwin, for hosting the renowned annual Shrewsbury Flower Show, and for being crowned Britain in Bloom's Champion of Champions in 2014. Full of historic architecture and quaint boutique shops, it's well worth a visit.

Some of the businesses mentioned are also real, tried and tested. Here are some links for you to find out more about them, and Shrewsbury itself:

Shrewsbury
http://www.shrewsburyguide.info

JOL Photography – James & Caroline Bloor
http://www.jolphotography.co.uk

Rosie Posie Wedding Flowers – Sarah
http://www.rosieposieweddingflowers.co.uk

The Peach Tree
http://www.thepeachtree.co.uk

Yummy Cakes by Jess
https://www.facebook.com/Yummy-Cakes-by-Jess-308665832503066/

6919

61867233R00135

Made in the USA
Lexington, KY
22 March 2017